APEX 2

Chris McInally

SEVERED PRESS
HOBART

APEX 2

WWW.SEVEREDPRESS.COM

ISBN: 978-1-925840-01-8

PROLOGUE

As day gave way to night, the Glades came alive with the cheeping of insects and the cawing of birds. Just shy of dusk, the remainder of an orange sun hovered over the quavering line that signified the distant horizon.

Below, the dark, still waters of the far-ranging slough caught rays of amber light cast by the remnants of the lingering, liquid-gold sphere. Despite the receding sun taking some of its heat with it, the air remained hot and heavy. In fact, it would stay that way all through the coming night, as well as into the following morning. Certainly, southern Florida was known for its humid climate. Perhaps more than that however, it was known for its eclectic wildlife which included (among many others), animals such as panthers, bears and alligators.

Concerning the latter, there was one individual that stood out large, and in more ways than one- especially around Florida City. Ask any of the locals and they would tell you 'Big Buck' was fifty years old, if he was a day.

Moving just below the tranquil veneer of the surface, Buck coursed steadily through the jade-tinted waters belonging to the region known as the Southern Glades. At fifteen feet from snout to tail, old Buck was a truly impressive specimen of *Alligator mississippiensis*. In fact, he was one of the largest of his kind. That in itself really said something. After all, the American alligator is the largest native reptile on the North American continent. Even so, Big Buck's position below the murky waterline meant that virtually his entire grey-black frame was obscured from view. Save for the big bull gator's bony nostrils and protuberant, obsidian, marble-like eyes poking through the rippling liquescent surface, his ridged, armoured hide was otherwise totally submerged beneath the green waters. And as one might expect, this really didn't do the big guy any justice.

What's more, the volatile combination of Buck's hulking size and disagreeable temperament (which only seemed to worsen with age) ensured that he was the dominant male alligator in the Southern Glades region. Indeed, both humans and others of his species all knew this fact to be true. Simply put, Big Buck was boss in these here parts. Still, the ancient gator's scaly hide was littered with battle scars. These had been collected during tussles with rival males in days now well-bygone.

Whilst his imposing size endowed him with confidence, Buck was also an experienced brawler, as his disfigured corpus readily attested. In all his years, the gator had yet to be bested by a foe. Not surprisingly, the hulking beast cruised leisurely onward, unconcerned with potential adversaries and threats.

Meanwhile…

Pressed flat against the muddy substrate, with its lobed fins splayed out wide on either side of its brawny mass, the predator waited patiently. Despite its imposing size, the animal's presence was obscured by the dim, olive-coloured water, in addition to the dense collection of debris littering the swamp-bed. Nestled amongst the gnarled limbs of sunken, water-logged tree branches, the cautious creature blended in with its gloomy surroundings nigh on perfectly.

Camouflaged to the point where it was effectively invisible, tiny minnows hunting for *Daphnia* and other similar microscopic prey items darted about in front of the waiting carnivore; the assemblage of tiny fish totally oblivious to its presence. Ignoring the pesky swarm of shimmering, silvery-scaled fish, the larger animal returned to scanning its dim environs for more suitably-sized prey. Cricking its stubby, barrelled neck, the predator arched its broad head back on an angle, altering its perspective of the watery realm surrounding it in hopes of locating a more satisfactory meal.

Of late, prey was becoming scarcer. Indeed, the creature's stomach churned hungrily as it waited, the acids contained within calling out for much-needed nourishment. It knew it needed to feed… and soon. Furthermore, its mate and their new brood (their third together) required sustenance as well.

Suddenly, its attentive garnet-coloured eyes snapped upwards as a serpentine shadow glided smoothly overhead. The winding profile briefly blocked out the little amount of light remaining beyond the surface of the liquid world. Completely unaware of the danger residing below, the meandering figure coursed on by its voyeur, the animal's thick, corrugated tail powering the massive lifeform through the slough. After hours of waiting, the predator's patience had paid off. Allowing its target some space, the hunter waited a few seconds before pushing off from the substrate. The swift and violent action instantly dispersed the hyperactive school of minnows that had converged around it, churning up a cloud of muddy debris in the process.

The curious creature climbed silently through the dim water column, gradually closing the gap between it and its oblivious quarry. Shadowing the snaking form from below, the killer moved parallel to its target at first, gauging the tortuous shape with its bulging, scarlet eyes. It had encountered a number of others like it before; several of them quite recently, in fact. Although, none of them were as big as the individual it was now stalking. Nor had it attempted to take the others down. Something in its DNA seemed to ward if off from engaging with this particular species… *usually*. Not in this instance, however. The animal's hunger overrode its inherent fear of the brutish creature. No longer could it afford to pass up such nourishing meals. The famished beast knew it would have to be careful if there was any hope of it being successful.

With a mighty thrust of its rounded caudal fin and adjoining keel, the hunter increased its speed. The ravenous stalker proceeded to cut left and then quickly right. Continuing to zig-zag in this fashion, the creature searched for an opening, hoping to exploit some opportune angle or the like which might make its deadly mission that bit easier to accomplish.

Next, the beast descended a few feet. Levelling out, it weaved in between sunken pieces of driftwood as it skimmed the slough's uneven bottom, preparing to strike at its prey's soft, crème-coloured underbelly. The killer's rounded jaws parted into a menacing smirk, exposing its three inch-long, rapier-like teeth. Employing another vigorous flick of its paddle-shaped tail fin, the animal surged eagerly towards its target. Then, hyper-extending its jaws in shark-like fashion, the creature's ugly and ravenous visage morphed into a silent scream.

Within a matter of seconds, the killer collided with its prey, catching the big reptile totally off-guard. Driving its blunted muzzle into the alligator's bloated torso like a battering ram, the beast's bowed fangs pierced its target's tough flesh briefly thereafter. Sinking them deep into the meaty tissue beneath, the hungry beast secured a firm and painful hold of its startled quarry. Blood- dark and red- rushed from the injured reptile's body as it roiled about, lost in its agony. Attempting to flee its attacker, the alligator's initial surprise was quickly overtaken by an unfamiliar emotion: *fear*.

Intertwined, the two animals rolled in the water, locked as they were in the visceral heat of mortal combat. The dark waters frothed and bubbled around the two struggling behemoths, almost as if they were boiling over. The gator thrashed manically from side to side as it tried desperately to free itself from the clutches of its mysterious assailant. Still, the reptile's attacker held on stubbornly; the two opposing sections of its vice-like maw clamped down hard. Indeed, each violent twist and turn from the gator resulted in the predator's teeth digging agonisingly deeper into the former's flesh, working to puncture organs and shear through ligaments. Then, for what was only a fraction of a second, the killer relaxed its jaws. For a fleeting moment, the alligator thought it had a chance of escape… only for its attacker to bite down harder the second time.

To its credit, the scaled goliath fought back as best it could, turning and aiming its wedge-shaped jaws at the aggressor, albeit ultimately to no avail. Snapping them savagely, the two portions of its elongated maw slammed shut on nothing but algae-laden water, turning the liquid to a sizzling, whitish foam.

Then, as suddenly as the mysterious attacker had appeared on the scene, it was gone. Fleeing post-haste, the shadowy assailant wrenched free a large section of grisly, pink-red flesh. With its ragged and bloodied prize held firmly between its bowed teeth, the beast disappeared into the liquid maze of the Glades, leaving its unfortunate victim behind to bleed out.

In the end, Big Buck never knew what hit him.

Like its assailant, the gargantuan gator rushed from the scene, a sizeable, gaping wound carved into its barrelled belly. Pain proceeded to diffuse throughout its body, resulting in an odd pulsing sensation akin to an electrical current. Confused, terrified, and mortally injured, the humongous reptile desperately sought safety for itself. Blood, thick and crimson, gushed from the reptile's yawning wound, like oil leaking from the breached hull of a tanker; the unfortunate creature's life-force ebbing away with each second that passed.

For the first time in five decades, Buck was finally able to appreciate how his prey must have felt.

MONDAY

1.

Keeping his sharp, hazel-coloured eyes on the road stretching out before him, Antoine Jackson made to adjust his truck's air-conditioning dial one more time. Focused on the road ahead, Antoine felt about for the familiar dentation that jutted out from his vehicle's dashboard with the tips of his long, nimble fingers. It didn't take him long to find it.

With a flick of his thickset wrist, Antoine twisted the dial up to the maximum setting. To the frustrated man's relief, a wave of chilled air immediately rushed out at him. Unfortunately, this only lasted for a split-second before the stream of air went warm again. It was official, his pick-up's air-con system was now kaput. To be honest, it had been a long time coming. Antoine didn't really look after his truck the way he should. Of course, this now meant Jackson would have to arrange a service through Jenny back at the departmental office ASAP.

"Piece of crap," Antoine mumbled, cursing the faulty machinery.

Jackson was acutely aware of the beads of sweat inching down his temples, the briny liquid irritating his dark, African skin. The disgruntled driver fidgeted in his seat, alternating between slowly rolling his broad shoulders backwards and forwards, and straining his thick neck from side to side; all tell-tale signs as to his current sense of unease. Before long, he knew the pick-up's cabin would be like a sauna, so Antoine decided to wind the driver's side window down in an attempt to relieve his growing discomfort. The resulting gust of humid, Floridian air was better than nothing, Antoine supposed.

Home, sweet home, he thought sardonically.

Heading south out of Florida City, Jackson drew steadily closer to his destination: Southern Glades Golf Club. The course itself was situated on the northern periphery of the Glades, about fifteen minutes from Florida City proper. His office had received a call from the club's owner, Bill Casey, earlier that morning requesting the presence of a game warden *immediately*.

Call-outs to golf courses actually weren't that unusual for Antoine, or others in the employ of Florida's Fish and Wildlife Conservation Commission (known more commonly as the FWC). Critters often wandered out of the Everglades into residential and commercial areas. As a result, they had to be removed and relocated in the interests of public safety. It was a phenomenon that was becoming more and more common with each passing year: a direct and undeniable result of continued human encroachment on what remained of the Everglades ecosystem.

Strangely, of late, rather than the usual lone animals that had somehow got lost, they were having to deal with groups of them. It was as if they were migrating, despite the fact that many of them were non-migratory species. Only last week, Antoine was called out to a home in the city's west to deal with a cane toad infestation. In the end, he and his deputies removed just shy of one-hundred-and-fifty of the ugly bastards from an elderly woman's backyard. This all came about after the toads took it upon themselves to congregate around her pool. As to why the animals did this, it was anyone's guess. Antoine certainly had no idea.

Within the FWC's Florida City branch, Antoine Jackson was the senior-most warden belonging to the Division of Habitat and Species Conservation. So, it was inevitable that he would have to respond to Casey's request. To tell the truth, Antoine wasn't a fan of Mr. Casey. In fact, most (if not all) of those who worked for the local branch of the FWC weren't that enamoured with the man. As such, Antoine wasn't all that looking forward to meeting with Casey that morning. He found Bill to be a rather self-important character, and thus he was more than a little pompous in his dealings with those he deemed inferior to himself. By all accounts, this was a trait he had inherited from his late daddy. As the owner of SGGC (which he had also inherited from his father), Casey saw himself situated at the top of Florida City's social elite. Even so, despite having to deal with clients like Mr. Casey, Jackson still enjoyed his job as a wildlife warden. Certainly, he enjoyed it much more than his time as a police officer back in Daytona Beach, that's for sure.

Turning off the main highway, Antoine slowed his silver-bodied pick-up to little more than a roll as he approached the entrance to the golf course. The complex's familiar, tall, iron-wrought gates- framed on either side by swaying palm trees and elegantly crafted red brickwork- very quickly came into view. Looming large before him, he noted the letters SGGC monographed in gold into the impressive metalwork.

Antoine's eyes were instantly drawn to the figure of a squat, male security guard standing in front of a small, cuboid booth. He was dressed in a light tan, short-sleeved shirt (much like Antoine's own FWC uniform shirt) and a pair of black slacks on top of some pristinely-polished dress shoes. It quickly became apparent that the guard was turning back patrons in their cars, a clipboard held in one hand and a small walkie-talkie in the other. The man appeared to be in his mid-fifties. Balding, pot-bellied and moustached, his eyes were hidden behind a pair of aviator-style shades at the end of a bulbous, purpling nose.

Jackson watched as a black sedan in front of him performed a U-turn, hurriedly leaving the scene. Red-faced and flustered, the grey-haired driver within was noticeably perturbed at his denial of entry. Taking his cue, Jackson moved his pick-up closer to the rather ominous gateway. Slowly, the fat security guard edged towards Antoine's driver-side window, his clipboard and free hand both held high. Leaning forward slightly, the man looked into the cabin at the smiling warden. As he did this, the guard snatched a fleeting glance at his clipboard. Before Jackson even had a chance to explain his business to the individual, the fat security officer spoke over the top of him.

"Mr. Casey has been expecting you," the stubby guard grumbled rudely, stepping away from the truck without another word to Jackson.

A moment later, the guard placed his walkie-talkie to his mouth, the man's bulldoggish jowls shaking as he spoke into the clunky device. Try as he might, Antoine couldn't hear what he was saying however.

The man returned to his little booth, and a moment later the tall set of gates parted in front of Jackson, allowing the warden access to the sprawling golfing complex beyond. Watching the chubby rent-a-cop stand aside, Antoine couldn't help but think the security guard must really hate his job. Then again, maybe he'd just had a bad morning. After all, it certainly couldn't have been easy working for Mr. Casey.

"Great way to start a Monday morning," Antoine murmured as he planted his foot and pumped the gas.

The flat-topped golf buggy skirted the undulating knolls of the pristinely maintained, avocado-coloured course. Jackson rode shotgun whilst one of Casey's employees played the role of chauffeur. Moving at a swift pace, Antoine had a hand clamped firmly against the crown of his head, trying to keep his dark green cap, emblazoned with the FWC logo, from flying off.

The driver- a rather pretty, young female- was dressed immaculately in a white polo shirt, matching knee-length shorts, visor and tennis shoes. The young woman kept her eyes aimed straight ahead as she deftly directed the buggy through the maze of rolling mounds and bunkers. Antoine got the distinct impression she had the lay of the course memorized. Be that as it may, her style of driving still had him feeling more than a little nervous about the remainder of the journey.

If the warden remembered correctly, her name was Kirsty. Or then again maybe it was Kristy. In either event, she couldn't have been more than twenty-one or twenty-two. Pasty-skinned and freckled, the young woman's wiry and wavy, ginger hair fell past her shoulders, cascading down her sprightly back. Her blue eyes appeared to glimmer in the mid-morning sunlight, focused as they were on the jade expanse ahead of them. The girl hadn't said a word to Antoine since they climbed into the golf cart, some ten or so minutes beforehand back at the complex's opulent, marble-floored reception area.

"Big talker, huh?" Antoine tried to break the ice, his hand still firmly on his head.

In response to the warden's flippant comment the redhead shot him a sideways glance and then a quick (and admittedly pathetic), half-hearted and patronizing smile.

Silence it is then, Antoine decided. *Little bitch.*

They were just about to ascend a small hill when the ginger-haired driver unexpectedly slammed on the vehicle's brakes. The buggy jolted to a shuddering halt, shocking Jackson almost out of his skin. With his other hand, the wildlife warden had to grip the frame of the buggy in a concerted effort not to fly out of it.

"Where'd you learn to drive?" Antoine asked bug-eyed, his heart pushing up against his tonsils. "Desert Storm?"

The redhead gave him that ingenuous smile once more, and still couldn't bring herself to say anything. Quick as a flash, the mute female was out of the cart and scaling the hillock with her long, freckle-laden legs, all without bothering to wait for Antoine. The game warden scurried after her, more than a little perturbed with the woman's increasingly aloof attitude. It didn't take the pair long to reach the smoothed top of the hummock.

"Wait a min-" Antoine yelled at the young woman's back.

What Antoine Jackson found on the other side of the rising knoll took his breath away... and not in a good way.

2.

"Big Buck…" Antoine breathed in disbelief. His usually bass-filled voice was barely audible, even to the redhead standing just off to his right.

Going by the size of the savaged, scaly carcass alone, it just had to be Buck, Jackson decided. There was no other gator around in the Southern Glades that even came close to rivalling Buck in terms of sheer size.

He came here to die. Antoine gathered silently as he took in the alligator's gored and prostrate form.

The putrefying remains of the hulking grey-black gator were stretched out in the middle of one of the golf course's pale, sandy-bottomed bunkers: a sight of grim juxtaposition if ever there was one. It was only a second or so later when Antoine noted a nearby white flag drooping limply due to the lack of a breeze, the crumpled pennon signifying that they were on the thirteenth hole.

How fitting, Jackson thought grimly to himself.

Much of the ovoid sandpit's walls and bottom had been dyed a disgusting shade of reddish-brown by the alligator's dried blood, clumping portions of the sand together into a kind of macabre cement mixture. Flies buzzed hyperkinetically, the irritating winged host attracted to the pungent scent of rotting flesh carried by the hot morning air. Jackson's eyes went straight to the semi-circular wound carved into the reptile's right-hand side. It was massive… and in his opinion, quite unnaturally so.

"Jesus…" he gasped.

What could have done this kind of damage to an adult gator, especially one as big as Buck? he asked himself.

The warden's mind raced as he tried to go over the possibilities in his head. Yet, the answer eluded him. What's more, he knew the reason *why* it evaded him. The fact was, there shouldn't have been anything big enough in the Glades to take out Big Buck. Plain and simple. That thought alone seriously unnerved Antoine Jackson.

"Jackson!" came a familiar, albeit unwelcome, voice. "I want this thing gone from my course *ASAP*! I have preparations for the Club's fiftieth anniversary celebrations to finalize! It is *this* weekend you know!"

Antoine momentarily shifted his gaze from the decomposing remnants of Big Buck to the course's owner, William Casey III. The hairs on his arms immediately bristled at the sight of him. Casey quite often had this effect on people.

"Good to see you too, Bill," Antoine said sarcastically, putting his hands on his hips and nestling his thumbs into the beltloops on his blue jeans. Simultaneously, the cagy redhead shuffled in behind the warden, seemingly less-than-enthused about being in the presence of her incensed employer.

From his elevated position atop the knoll, Antoine looked down on the course's owner, who was striding determinedly towards him up the jade incline. Dressed in dark slacks and an unspoiled and well-tailored, white, long-sleeved shirt, Bill Casey was a lanky fellow, with a slick, greasy-looking blonde combover, and a prominent hooked nose, set between a pair of pale green eyes. Antoine often likened him to a vulture-Hitler hybrid cooked up by some mad scientist; something he would obviously never admit to the man's face. After all, only the insane appreciated being compared to Adolf Hitler, at least in this day and age anyway. Then again, maybe Casey wouldn't mind the comparison. Egotistical prick that he was.

The bird-man approached the game warden with another male close in-tow. Caucasian too, the second man was only slightly taller than Casey, but much broader in the chest and shoulders, as well as the arms and legs. What would have been a dark head of hair was shaved close to the scalp, and the man was dressed in a pale-coloured pair of slacks and a tight-fitting, maroon polo shirt. The unidentified male's blue eyes were cold and fierce, much like those of a predator. Added to this, he was possessed of a boxer's flat nose. In Antoine's estimation, the imposing individual had 'bodyguard' written all over him.

Probably ex-military, Antoine thought to himself as he appraised the fellow. Why Casey felt the need for a bodyguard in south Florida, Jackson honestly had no idea. It wasn't exactly Deadwood.

As they joined the waiting wildlife warden at the crest of the hill, Antoine didn't offer his hand to Casey, or his muscular companion for that matter. In any event, neither of them appeared to mind his seeming lack of common courtesy towards them both.

"So?" Bill Casey asked heatedly, expecting Antoine to know what he meant right off-the-bat.

"So, *what*?" Jackson tried to keep his cool with him, rather perturbed by the man's pushy tone.

"*So*," Casey narrowed his olive eyes, "how long before this *thing* is gone from my course?" He gestured towards Big Buck with an open and rigid skeletal hand.

"It's an alligator," Antoine clarified for Casey. Twice now the pompous dick had described Buck merely as a 'thing', as if the gator was of no real consequence.

"I know what the fuck it is," Casey snapped, "I'm not an imbecile!"

"Never said you were," the warden responded calmly, trying to hide a growing smirk.

"How long?" Mr. Casey went on, not willing to be baited any further.

"As long as it takes," Jackson answered, his tone nothing short of dead-pan.

Antoine loved winding up people like Bill Casey. There was nothing better than throwing a spanner in the works for fuckers like him; self-important dickheads who expected everything to be done on their schedule.

Asshole. Jackson narrowed his eyes at the man.

"What do you mean, 'as long as it takes'?" Bill's cheeks flushed bright red with anger.

"I mean precisely that," Antoine gave the man a blank stare, "*as long as it takes*," he emphasized.

Bill Casey's bodyguard glared at the impassive warden, his lips contorting into a kind of snarl. Going into cop-mode, Jackson watched the man carefully, trying to assess how much of a threat the big guy actually posed to him.

"I need this fucker gone from my course!" Casey barked savagely. "Can you do that for me, or not?"

"Certainly, I can," Antoine replied with a toothy, but no less forced smile. "Just need to make some calls first, though. Buck's a big boy, after all. Gonna need some serious help moving the remains. You could always lend a helping hand… if you like."

"I don't care what you have to do," Bill threw up his arms, "just get it done! *Quickly!*"

Antoine didn't respond to Casey this time around. Instead, he turned away from the irate man-child and his goliath-sized minder. Next, he slowly edged his way down the bunker's embankment towards the dead reptile. Digging his boots into the soft carpet of grass, he steadied himself. Behind him, Jackson heard Bill telling the red-haired woman to keep him up-to-date with developments. Gradually, the annoying man's voice faded out as the game warden went about his duties, becoming lost amidst the host of thoughts swirling about in his own head.

Jackson squatted down in front of the battered carcass, his eyes trailing along Buck's ridged, elongated body. Slowly, they wandered up to the alligator's wedge-shaped cranium. Antoine's eyes were drawn to

Buck's prominent conical teeth set into the animal's top jaw. The array of yellowed, conical fangs overlapped the reptile's bottom lip, giving him a kind of predatory smirk that only true killers possessed. Antoine noted that the gator's eyes were closed over; this made Buck look rather peaceful laying there.

An intense feeling of sadness permeated throughout Antoine's being in that moment. Big Buck had been around for a long time, after all. If the stories were true, he had been scaring the shit out of locals and tourists alike for several decades now. The big bastard was a mainstay of the region for God's sake. For a moment, Jackson thought he might shed a tear for the big guy.

Antoine put a palm flat against the reptile's hardened form. Despite the morning heat, Buck's body felt quite cold. The man's fingers glided down the alligator's scaled, uneven remains towards the yawning injury etched into its lower torso. Looking into the gory cavity, Jackson found a ghastly, pink-red mess of congealed blood, mangled muscle and ruined tissue within. What's more, tubular, slime-coated organs spilled out from the gore-edged orifice, whilst flies crawled over the exposed layers of fetid flesh. Not to mention, it stunk to high hell, as one could imagine.

Doing his best not to puke up his breakfast, Antoine decided he should take some pictures for the report he needed to file. Getting to his feet, the warden retrieved a compact digital camera from the back-pocket of his jeans and began taking pictures of Big Buck. Shifting positions with each shot, he made sure to cover all his angles.

"What do you think did it?" a female voice asked from somewhere behind him.

Antoine pivoted on the spot to find the ginger-haired golf course employee looking down expectantly at him from the arched ridge of the bunker. He'd actually forgotten all about her for a moment.

"Honestly," the warden looked up at her, "I have absolutely no idea… and that fact right there scares the shit out of me."

3.

Excitement, peppered with a healthy dose of curiosity, gripped Doctor Alex Scott as he and his eye-catching assistant, Tahlia Mohan, made their way into the Florida City morgue. They were met at the building's reception by a rather tall and awkward-looking young man. Indeed, the lad was possessed of a mop of messy blonde hair, slack jaw, and a pair of large, black-framed spectacles. He also wore a tight-fitting laboratory coat that was clearly several sizes too small for him. Alex instantly got the impression that he was a medical student, most likely volunteering at the morgue to gain practical experience, and thereby augment his on-going studies. Either that or he had somehow managed to escape his handlers.

As for Doctor Scott, dressed in a pair of pale-coloured cargo-shorts, tennis shoes and a faded yellow t-shirt, he didn't look very academic (if indeed it was possible for one to *look* academic at all). Youthful and full of vigour, Alex had recently turned thirty. Still, however much he may not have appeared to be at first glance, the young man *was* a biology lecturer. Furthermore, he was a rising star at Florida City University, well on his way to a full professorship. Tall and athletic with medium-length, wavy, brown hair and tanned, freckled skin, Alex Scott looked more college athlete than science geek.

Appearance aside, he had completed his PhD in herpetology three years prior, and after the publication of two ground-breaking articles in a renowned academic journal (one of which won an award), he came to the attention of FCU's biology programme, the head of which snatched him up quick-smart. The rest was history, as they say.

By his side was Tahlia Mohan. Tahlia was one of the doctor's many undergraduate students, and his unofficial assistant (as he had yet to take on any postgrads in a mentoring role). The young woman volunteered her time, helping him in the lab back at FCU in exchange for extra credit points towards her undergraduate degree (even during the semester break, as they currently were).

From out-of-state, Tahlia had joined FCU last year, and quickly proved herself to be a dedicated and more than capable student, with a rather promising future. Ever attentive, the young woman's chestnut-coloured eyes never missed a thing. Easy on the eyes for that matter, the exotic-looking young woman was twenty-three and petite, with beautifully smooth, caramel skin. Her hair was long and straight, hanging almost to her backside, and coloured a deep shade of onyx that gleamed hypnotically in the light. As they strode towards their destination, Miss Mohan looked like she was ready for a day at the beach, attired in a loose-fitting, floral-patterned turquoise dress that ended just above the knee, a pair of sandals, and a small handbag flung casually over her right shoulder.

Led steadily deeper into the eerie facility by their silent and somewhat gawky guide, it was early in the evening as the pair navigated the hallways of the dimly-lit mortuary. Doing their best to keep pace with their mute, long-legged Sherpa, Alex and Tahlia took in their surroundings. The trio were flanked left and right by uninviting, dull grey walls, marked with the occasional noticeboard or fire extinguisher. Overhead, the lighting was somewhat subdued. It seemed like only one in two lights were turned on. Furthermore, save for themselves, there didn't appear to be anyone else moving about the morgue. The combination of these factors gave the place a somewhat dank atmosphere. In fact, it was the perfect setting for a horror movie.

Without warning, their guide came to an abrupt halt. Spinning sharply on his heel, the bespectacled man signalled to a doorway on their left. "Through there," he told them in a low voice. "At the end of the hall."

Alex and Tahlia exchanged uneasy glances between them, but beyond this they didn't falter as they stepped through the entrance and into the passageway proper. Together the pair entered a corridor slightly narrower, and even more poorly-lit, than the one they had just left behind.

"Straight ahead," the giant told them as he hovered by the doorway. "He's waiting for you in the dissection room."

"There's a sentence you don't hear every day," Miss Mohan quipped nervously, her voice soft and unassuming.

Doctor Scott smiled but didn't say anything to begin with. As for the lanky intern, he just stared blankly at them, his bottom jaw sagging away from the rest of his big head.

"Thank you," Alex told their guide, before coaxing Tahlia somewhat nervously to his side.

Doctor Scott and Miss Mohan quickly turned away from the intern and continued down the claustrophobic passage, towards a waiting set of heavy-looking polished metal double-doors. Cast against the pale walls flanking the pair, their shadows, long and skinny, crept ahead of them like ethereal spectres. Both Tahlia and Alex felt the temperature drop several degrees as they approached the waiting portal at the end of the corridor. Tahlia quickly came to regret her choice of flimsy attire as a wave of goosebumps spread over her body. Likewise, Doctor Scott wished he had worn a pair of pants at least, instead of settling for just shorts.

"Alright," Alex nodded to his assistant, trying to ignore the lingering chill, "let's see what all the fuss is about."

Stopping in front of the heavy-set double-doors, Doctor Scott made to push them open for Tahlia in proper gentlemanly fashion.

"No, you first," she shook her head with a warm smile. "The Commission did request your expertise, after all."

"Well, if you insist," Alex smiled warmly, the man's sense of excitement overruling his chivalry.

Pushing his way into the room beyond, Doctor Scott didn't get more than a few steps before he planted his feet and stopped dead. Behind him, Tahlia slammed into his back, letting out a sharp yelp of surprise as her cheekbone bounced off his rigid and partially flexed shoulder blade.

"Holy shitballs!" Tahlia exclaimed in a shrill voice, her big eyes peeking over Alex's shoulder. "That's one big gator!"

"That's a big gator, indeed." Doctor Scott blinked several times, not quite sure whether to believe his eyes or not.

It was immediately apparent that the dissection room had been cleared of all tables and instruments to make room for the hulking reptile's corpse. Also, spread out across the length and breadth of the wide room's floor were several light-blue tarpaulin sheets, on top of which lay the deceased alligator.

Gathering himself, Alex stepped deeper into the room, making space for Tahlia. The duo stood in silence for a few seconds, surveying the reptile's ravaged carcass. Suddenly, a tall figure appeared from the shadows at the periphery of the doctor's vision, a little over to his right. Snapping his head up, the herpetologist had to force himself to take his eyes away from the sight of the decomposing alligator to look at the mystery person. Subsequently, it was several moments before Alex properly deciphered the profile of the bald-headed, African-American man looking rather expectantly in his general direction.

"Doctor Scott, I presume," said the game warden. "Thank you for coming. My name is Antoine Jackson; we spoke on the phone. The Commission really appreciates having you on board with this one."

"I'm honoured, Mr. Jackson," the biologist shook the wildlife warden's proffered hand. "This is my assistant," the doctor motioned to Tahlia standing behind him. "Miss Tahlia Mohan."

"Pleased to make your acquaintance," Jackson offered his hand to the young lady with a smile.

"Ditto," Tahlia responded with a curt nod, before stepping forward to join the two men and shake the warden's hand.

Once pleasantries had been exchanged, Antoine took a step backwards, his hands coming to rest on his hips. He didn't say anything for a short time after this. Like the others, the man's eyes were inevitably drawn back to the impressive, scaly grey-black mass taking up much of the room's centre.

"Quite a specimen," Alex said, breaking the silence, his eyes trailing all the way from the tip of the behemoth's blunted snout to the end of its thickset, ridged and tapered tail.

"Big Buck," was all Jackson could think to say as the trio admired the dead reptile together.

"Big Buck?" Alex scrunched up his freckled features, before casually wiping a strand of hair out of his eyes and looping it behind his ear.

Peeling his eyes away from the dead creature Alex looked at the warden, his expression one of total confusion. Then he turned to Tahlia, hoping to gain some kind of clarification on the matter from her, but she simply shrugged at him as if to say 'I don't know either'. Alex sometimes forgot she was an out-of-towner just like him.

"The alligator," the wildlife warden replied, clarifying the point. "He's known around these parts as 'Big Buck'. He's kind of a tourist attraction."

"I see," Scott nodded.

Alex found it funny that in almost two years he had never heard of this celebrity alligator. That's what he got for spending so much time in the lab, he supposed.

"How did he get here?" Tahlia asked, her expression one of astonishment. "Inside the morgue, I mean. He's so big!"

"It took a lot of favours, not to mention some good old-fashioned elbow grease," Antoine informed her. "And some serious machinery," he quickly added.

Tahlia just stared wide-eyed at the beast, unable to form anymore words as she tried to imagine the effort that had been put into moving it. There followed a few moments of uncomfortable silence after Tahlia and Jackson's exchange, before the latter restarted the conversation.

"I am gonna cut to the chase, Doctor Scott; I think I am out of my depth on this one. Like, *really* out of my depth. That's why I requested your expertise. Buck here was discovered early this morning not far from Hole Thirteen inside Southern Glades Golfing Complex, in much the same state as you see him in now."

"Look at the size of that bite wound," Tahlia interjected as she suddenly found her voice again; the girl's round, dark eyes still locked onto the scaly cadaver. "What could have done that?"

"That's exactly why I called in the doc here," Antoine motioned to the now silent herpetologist.

Doctor Scott had detached himself from the other two by this point, and thus was only half-listening to their latest exchange. By now he was crouched down at the alligator's corpse, examining the yawning wound gouged into its right-hand side.

"Alligators are the apex predator in the Everglades region," Doctor Scott quickly went into full academic-mode, finding his voice once more. "Therefore, it is hard to think of any other indigenous species that could do this." He continued with his monologue, "Which means, we may have to entertain the possibility of something else. Something *alien*, you could say. Florida has been exposed to a plethora of introduced species in the last six or seven decades, as you are no doubt aware, Mr. Jackson," Alex's mind went over the possibilities as he spoke, "but, once again, I can't really think of any that could do this kind of damage to an alligator of this size. He must be somewhere in the region of one-thousand pounds and fifteen feet long!"

"You can't think of anything?" Antoine probed, eager for answers. "Native or introduced?"

Alex mulled it over for a second, reconsidering the options. What he came up with unnerved him.

"Maybe one. And I have to say, it is a bit of a stretch. Of all the recorded species - native or introduced - resident in the Everglades," Alex replied, "I can think of only one of them that has the potential to inflict this kind of injury on the region's apex predator. And like I said, I am really reaching on this one."

"Which species then?" Jackson continued to push for an answer.

"Please give me a moment," the doctor continued to peer perplexed into the putrefying wound. "I would like to clarify a couple of things before jumping to any conclusions. There's no point getting all worked up over what very well could be nothing."

Antoine made a *humph!* sound and crossed his arms at this. All the same, if it meant getting some answers, then he was happy to indulge the doctor and his methodology.

"Tahlia," Alex ignored the warden's petty vocalizations, "my measuring tape please."

Tahlia obediently approached her mentor, retrieving the requested measuring tape from her handbag.

"Here," she said, handing the instrument over, before pulling out a pen and a notepad from the same bag. She knew the routine. Actually, she had the routine down pat.

"Have you considered some kind of boating accident?" Alex enquired thoughtfully. "A collision with a propeller, for instance? Surely, a propeller would be capable of inflicting this kind of injury."

"No accidents have been reported," Antoine answered brusquely. "I had one of my subordinates check with the sheriff's office this afternoon."

At this, Alex began measuring the wound whilst Jackson and Tahlia looked on in perplexed silence.

"The bite wound is almost two feet in diameter!" Alex gasped. "Fifty-one centimetres to be exact."

Tahlia scribbled down some notes based on this information, fighting to keep her cool and appear professional. Her mind was racing. The whole situation was just unreal. It was all so unusual. When she woke up that morning, the last thing she expected to be doing was investigating an alligator whodunit.

So much for just another boring day in the lab.

"Whatever did this is *big*," Scott informed them, "potentially as big as Buck here. If indeed we can rule out the likes of a boating accident."

"Fuck me…" the wildlife warden leaned back against the wall. He had suspected as much, but hearing the herpetologist confirm it made it that bit more real somehow.

"Obviously," Alex went on, "I only have the bite wound to go on - if that is in fact what we are looking at. Still, it's a pretty good indicator of the animal's size - the predator, I mean. Or rather, *potential* predator."

"Okay then," Antoine crossed his arms, "so what is it?" His patience was wearing thin.

"I think we are dealing with a shark," Alex confessed without much hesitation at all. "Possibly a Bull shark. If so, then it is a large one. They are known to make their way into the Everglades from time to time. It is the only animal I can think of that fits the bill."

"Bullshit, doc!" Jackson blurted out, failing to restrain himself and remain professional. He vocalized his protestation despite the fact that he knew the doc was right about Bulls venturing into the Everglades. "This isn't Lake Minerva!"

"Lake Minerva's locals probably reacted much the same way," Tahlia spoke up. "At least, in the beginning. And we all know how that turned out." She felt a knot tie in her stomach at her own mention of Lake Minerva. It always brought to light uncomfortable memories for her.

It had been almost two years since the 'Lake Minerva incident', as it was now known. Yet, the subject still lingered not only in the public consciousness but the academic realm as well. Human cost aside, the ramifications of that situation had been monumental for the environmental sciences. It was perhaps the greatest example yet of nature gone awry resulting from humanity's folly: an entire ecosystem had been converted from freshwater to saltwater, which in turn opened the floodgates for the lake's colonization by alien species. Things could and would never be the same. Lake Minerva was a warning to the world-at-large, the natural balance of things was in flux. It was as if Mother Nature was trying to find a new equilibrium as it attempted to cope with humanity's increasing interference.

"Obviously, my speciality is reptiles, so I will have to consult a colleague of mine in order to be sure. She is a qualified marine biologist." Alex's thoughts wandered fleetingly to his postgraduate days, and an old female classmate in particular with whom he had stayed in touch. "I will contact her the first chance I get."

Jackson didn't respond to either Doctor Scott or Tahlia, instead he just shook his head in disbelief, silently letting it all sink in. Alex on the other hand went back to inspecting the putrefying reptile. As for Tahlia, while the two men were distracted with their own respective ponderings, she slid away her notepad and pen. Next, the young woman casually retrieved her iPhone from her handbag. In a matter of moments Tahlia's fingers were gliding deftly over the device's touchscreen. The text message she hurriedly composed read:

`We might have another Lake Minerva on our hands.`

`Will keep you updated as things develop on my end.`

4.

Hailey Benson's heart battered forcefully against the inside of her chest cavity. Yet, while every breath was a struggle, she pushed herself onward, determined to finish her evening run. As always, the young woman's left thigh throbbed with pain, the angry sensation dispersing throughout the remainder of her leg. Even so, she tried not to think about it. Instead, Hailey focused on finishing her work-out and making it to the end of the block, back to her parents' house where she knew a refreshing shower awaited her. The mental image of the tiled bathroom, complete with a modern, glass-encased shower unit and pristine white spa bath, beckoned to Hailey, working to tantalize and encourage her.

Her injury - despite being almost two years old and supposedly healed - made working out difficult for the young woman. In a way though, she was used to it, as painful as it was. She wouldn't let it stop her, that's for sure. Thankfully, the black track shorts Hailey wore helped to hide most of the semi-circular pattern of scars etched into her tanned skin. In fact, she rarely chose attire that didn't hide them from the world.

The marine biologist's collection of troublesome mutilations resulted from an encounter with a thirteen-foot-long, female Mako shark almost two years previous, whilst working as a research assistant on a university-funded project. For a time, Hailey had been somewhat of a celebrity as a result of her experience with the predator at Lake Minerva. Subsequently, images of the young woman were splattered across magazine covers and newspapers, not to mention social media and other sections of the internet. However, whilst she had survived the shark's deadly rampage, her friends and colleagues hadn't been as lucky. Hailey had even lost her mentor- and lover- Professor Thomas Willard to the fearsome predator.

Rarely a day went by when Hailey's thoughts didn't return to the horrific events that unfolded on Lake Minerva. In a way, it was inescapable. It was a part of her now. That was all part of the trauma she had incurred, Hailey supposed. Her medication (combined with a militant exercise routine) was supposed to help alleviate some of the symptoms associated with her post-traumatic stress disorder that she now suffered from. With that being said, she still experienced the occasional nightmare filled with teeth and blood… usually her own blood.

In the beginning, the anxiety medication was supposed to be only temporary. Unfortunately, things didn't work out to plan. Hailey soon found she needed it to stay centred. Missing just a single dose could be disastrous for her well-being as her system struggled to cope without its calming influence. After all, what happened to her wasn't exactly run-of-the-mill kind of stuff. In other words, she needed something to take the edge off. Exercise and medication was her solution to this problem. For a time, she had tried therapists, but they didn't help, at least for her anyway.

After running almost five kilometres, the young woman's nimble physique was drenched with sweat, the salt-laden fluid seeping relentlessly from her body's vast array of pores. Indeed, the grey-coloured singlet she wore clung to her skin, soaked through as it was. Still, as disgusting as she might have felt, Hailey turned more than a few heads in her figure-hugging workout clothes. Most of those heads belonged to middle-aged men taking their dogs out for an evening dump; men who quickly checked to see if their wives were watching them.

Hailey's toned and limber legs brought her closer to her destination. The soles of her running shoes pounded hard against the smoothed pavement, beating a steady rhythm. Emerald eyes focused ahead, the young woman's auburn hair was pulled back tight into a ponytail that bounced with each animated stride. Gradually, a familiar white double-storey house crept into view. The sight of its pillared entrance, flanked either side by stretching bay-windows, sent a renewed jolt of adrenaline through the young woman's system, emptying the last of her body's reserves and fuelling the final stretch of her exhausting journey.

"C'mon, you can do it," Hailey spoke to herself under her breath, "Piece of cake, kiddo. You've done it a million times before."

Hailey sprinted up the sidewalk, heading for the paved path that bisected her parent's oh-so-suburban and spotlessly trimmed front lawn.

"Almost there," she coaxed herself further, albeit this time through clenched teeth and shallow breaths.

Reaching the end of the pathway Hailey doubled-over, putting her hands on her knees as she did so. She had done it, and felt all the better for it (even if her body hated her). Ragged breaths proceeded to escape the exhausted woman's pursed lips as she tried to regulate her breathing. After about a minute, Hailey straightened up, beginning to feel better.

Letting out a long, slow breath, the young woman turned the doorknob and stepped through the threshold of her parents' home. To her left was the living room. As usual, her mother and father were seated in their respective leather recliners watching the television intently. Even so, neither of them were engrossed enough to ignore their daughter's arrival. Both of them called out to her as she entered, the pair turning slightly in their seats to face her. Flashing them both a smile, Hailey slipped off her running shoes before heading up the stairs towards her bedroom.

Even after nearly two years, Hailey still found it strange to be back in her parents' home. It was the house Hailey had grown up in as a teenager. As such, she knew it well. Yet, she never felt quite settled (at least these days, anyway). The young woman had her reasons of course. For a while, she had been out in the big, bad world, making her own way, and not to mention doing quite well at it. Sadly, Lake Minerva changed all that.

Hailey was forced to move back in with her parents after the university decided to rescind her fellowship following the Minerva incident. This effectively put her out of a job. Furthermore, as if no longer being able to pay the rent wasn't enough, she had to undergo rehabilitation therapy because of the injury to her leg (and one of her thumbs). Still, at the time, therapy and moving back in with her parents had been the least of her worries. At one point, the university threatened to sue Hailey for negligent use and destruction of university property (used during her attempts to track and tag the errant Mako). Thankfully, this eventually came to nothing when the university realized how bad it would look suing a woman who the media had dubbed a hero. As much as Hailey hated the media attention generated by the incident, in the end it was that same attention that was responsible for saving her ass.

There's always two sides to a coin. As her grandfather used to say.

It was funny how things worked out… sometimes. Still, a nagging voice in the back of her mind told her the university may return for their pound of flesh one day. In either event, Hailey would just have to wait and see. After all, there was nothing else she could do.

Taking the stairs two at a time, Hailey turned right, delving into her bedroom. Quickly shedding her soiled clothes, the young woman stripped down to just her underwear. Next, she undid her ponytail. Shaking her head gently from side to side, Hailey let her brownish-red-coloured hair fall about her shoulders. Moving back out into the hallway, clad in only a black sports-bra and matching panties, Hailey headed straight for the bathroom. Naturally, with no one else in the house, except for her parents seated downstairs, she wasn't too concerned with being modest.

At first, the shower was everything that Hailey knew it would be. Cool and refreshing, the cascade of water washed away the film of sickly-sweet sweat covering her lissom body, working to reinvigorate her. For a while, she became lost in the rushing torrent, simply revelling in the sensation of it all. Unfortunately, Hailey was forced to cut her relaxing cleansing short. The young woman suddenly became aware of her mobile phone screeching to be answered from her room back down the hall.

Hailey stepped gingerly out of the glass cuboid encasement before wrapping a towel around herself. Darting into the hallway a few seconds later, Hailey left a series of wet, yeti-like imprints in the beige carpet. Racing into her room, the young woman snatched the bleating phone from atop her burgundy bedcovers. Hailey smiled when she read the caller-ID. Quickly answering the call, she placed the phone to her ear.

"My favourite Floridian," Hailey greeted her caller cheerfully, a thin smile edging across her lips.

Of all Hailey's 'friends' from her university days, Alex Scott was the only one who had bothered to stay in touch, especially after Lake Minerva and the fallout that accompanied it. To her dismay, Hailey discovered that she had become a social leper almost overnight, at least in academic circles. No tertiary-level institution would go near her after that, despite making a plethora of job applications to colleges and universities all over the country, and not to mention even some overseas. She suspected her former employer had something to do with it. Not Alex though, he was different. In addition to talking on the phone, they stayed in touch via text messages and email, as well as social media. Although, they had yet to see each other in person since reconnecting. In fact, the last time they had shared one another's company was at their graduation ceremony.

"It's good to hear your voice, Benson," Alex's tinny voice came in from the other end.

"Ditto, *Scott,*" Hailey told him, stressing his last name with a laugh. "How are things down there?"

"Pretty intense, actually." Alex saw no reason to ease into the conversation. "That's actually why I'm calling."

"Really?" Hailey's interest was immediately piqued. "Are you okay?"

"Oh, I'm fine," Alex responded, "it's nothing like *that*." Whatever 'that' was. "I need your professional opinion on something," he told her.

"Professional opinion?" Hailey asked, both perplexed and intrigued. "On what exactly?"

Benson had to admit, even if only to herself, it felt strange having someone ask for her professional opinion on a matter. After Lake Minerva and everything that resulted because of it, Hailey didn't really look at herself as a marine biologist anymore, especially since becoming an academic pariah. It was the last thing she expected from people in all honesty.

"It might be better if I just show you," Alex suggested.

"Show me what?" Hailey chewed her bottom lip, confusion written large in her expression.

"I have some pictures I'd like you to take a look at," Alex explained. "Can I email them to you?"

"Yeah," Hailey moved toward her bed. "Just give me a second to boot up my laptop. I'm just gonna put my cell down. Okay?"

"Sure thing," Alex replied, more than happy to wait.

Hailey removed her towel, discarding it onto the floor. Next, the young woman retrieved a fluffy white dressing gown from her bedroom wardrobe and quickly donned it. After that she situated herself on her bed, propping up her laptop in between her thighs and putting her iPhone back to her ear.

"So, what do you have for me?" Hailey asked as she opened up a browser window.

"I have some photos," Alex explained somewhat hesitantly, "of a dead alligator - a big one - and I am not sure exactly what killed it."

"Send them through to my email," Hailey instructed him, a hint of excitement in her voice.

"Sending them now," Alex told her.

Hailey's laptop chimed as the email was delivered to her address about ten or so seconds later. The marine biologist instantly felt her pulse quicken. What's more, butterflies began to bounce about in her belly as she opened the electronic message, not fully sure of what to expect from it.

"Okay," she said, her jade-coloured eyes taking in the array of attachments at the top of the email. "I've got it. Tell me everything that I need to know." With a flick of her index finger Hailey opened the first image, and her jaw dropped.

On the other end, Alex explained the situation as best he could. He tried to recall everything that Jackson the game warden had told him, in addition to all that he had surmised from his own inspection of the alligator's remains. This included giving his friend at the other end of the line the gator's weight and length, and anything else he thought might be relevant, including- most importantly- the dimensions of the massive wound gouged into the reptile's lower abdomen.

As she listened, Hailey's emerald eyes pored over the images of the scaled beast. The email contained a dozen pictures, all taken from different angles and distances. Slowly, she cycled through them, trying to be as thorough as possible with her analysis. To be honest, Hailey was taken aback by what she saw and the brutality of it all. For a while, she didn't say anything. Then a thought occurred to her.

"Why do you need *my* help?" Hailey questioned her old classmate suspiciously. "Surely you know someone down there that could help instead of me."

"I thought… considering your… history…" Alex suddenly seemed reluctant to speak.

The lightbulb went off then inside Hailey's head.

"You think a shark did this?" she asked, her tone a little more heated than she meant it to be. "Don't you?"

"Do you?" Alex probed.

Hailey hesitated for a second, considering it.

"It's possible, I guess." Hailey looked over a grisly close-up of the bite wound for a third time. "The wound pattern is consistent with a shark bite, superficially speaking." Hailey's eyes glided absentmindedly toward the tract of scars etched into her upper leg before quickly flicking back to her computer screen. "Based on location, I would assume a Bull shark or similar species."

"It's just as I feared then," Doctor Scott breathed in dismay.

"Hey look, there are other possibilities," Hailey offered, trying her best to be optimistic.

"I could really do with some help down here, Hailey," the herpetologist told her, trying his best to sound nonchalant. "I could talk to the university or the Wildlife Commission, maybe get you on board as a consultant-"

"Sorry, but that's not gonna happen." Hailey stopped him right there. "Putting aside the fact that FCU wouldn't touch me with a ten-foot bargepole, I'm not interested in hunting monsters. Been there, done that. Once was more than enough- believe me. Just forget about it, please. Thanks for the offer. But, like I said, I think it's best if you forget about it."

"Like you said," Alex interjected, "there are other possibilities. There's no guarantee we are dealing with a shark, at all. And I'm not asking you to get in the water."

"Still not interested," Hailey retorted, flatly. "Whatever it is, the fucker's got big teeth. That's enough to dissuade me."

"Is there anything I can say that would change your mind?" Alex's tone reeked of desperation.

"I'm afraid not," Hailey's tone for that matter was rather sombre.

"Okay then," Alex was unable to mask his disappointment. "Look, thanks for your help. It means a lot. I'll keep you updated, I suppose."

"No problem," Hailey replied. "Oh and one other thing…"

"Yeah?"

"Try not to get yourself killed."

5.

Parched by the inescapable heat, and after a long day's travel over a challenging array of terrain, the slender, tawny-coated feline craved water. Food on the other hand could most certainly wait, at least for the time being anyway.

Crouching close to the moist ground, the big cat dipped its rounded head to the water's edge, parting its froth-laden jaws. Lapping at the cool liquid with its muscular pink tongue, the animal's usually erect ears were pinned back against its skull, the predator on guard and listening intently. Each vigorous flick from the fleshy organ resulted in a cascade of ripples swelling away from the panting feline's position. The cougar was located at the periphery of a dense collection of tropical vegetation, commonly referred to as a 'hardwood hammock', where it merged with the adjacent marshland leading out into an adjoining slough. The subsequent surges of undulating liquid captured the light of the full moon hanging above. Indeed, the silvery, ethereal sheen emanating from the gargantuan sphere endowed the swamplands below with an almost numinous aura.

Native to the Americas, the cougar goes by many names; these include sobriquets like mountain lion, puma, panther and catamount. Scientifically, the species of large feline is known as *Puma concolor*. Extremely adaptable in terms of habitat, the species can be found as far north as Canada's Yukon peninsula and as far south as the Andes mountain range that cuts a trail through seven South American nations.

There is still some debate as to whether or not the variety resident in Florida is a distinct subspecies of cougar. Known colloquially as the Florida panther, or more simply as *the* panther, there are said to be only one-hundred-and-fifty or so left in the state. The Florida Panther National Wildlife Refuge- an area in excess of twenty-six thousand acres- was established in Florida's southwest in 1989, in an effort to preserve the animal's presence in the state. Although, that is not to say their range is restricted to this area alone.

This particular male panther frequented the Southern Glades quite regularly in fact. He was very much a transient, roaming wherever he pleased in search of food, and when the time of year was right, a suitable mate.

At seventy-five kilos, the male was a hefty specimen when compared to others of his kind. Yet, although deemed a 'big cat', cougars are nowhere near the size of an African lion or the like. Still, this male was impressive for what it was. Young and in his prime, he stood three feet tall at the shoulder. What's more, his physique was long and sleek, each muscle toned to perfection. In short, he was the epitome of sinuous.

Chin hovering over the waterline, the male's pupils were dilated and alert, taking up much of his large golden irises, something not that uncommon for the time of night. He watched intently as a slight breeze skirted through the wall of swamp-grass situated across the darkened slough, little more than a stone's throw from the cat's position. The palisade-like collection of reeds bent noticeably with the incoming draught. Furthermore, the gust of wind provided momentary relief for the dehydrated animal, helping to usher away some of the night-time heat. Shortly thereafter the wind changed direction, and with this the resulting draught brought something else with it.

Within seconds, a pungent, musky scent caught the feline's undivided attention. Wrinkling his snout, the offensive odour filled the predator's nostrils, ensnaring him. Immediately, the male's olfactory senses registered that the scent was coming from somewhere off to his rear. Moreover, it was close. Very close, in fact. Fur bristling from a combination of primal aggression and nervous anticipation, the panther spun to meet its approaching adversary as a hefty jolt of adrenaline flooded its system.

***

Commonly referred to as the Burmese python, the species *Python bivittatus* should not be at home in the Florida Everglades. But it is… and it has been for quite some time.

Supposedly resident in the Everglades since the 1980s, it wasn't until 2000 that the existence of a breeding population was officially acknowledged by authorities, as well as the scientific community for that matter. As for the size of said population, estimates vary from thirty-thousand individuals to in excess of a quarter-million. This surprising situation is thought to be the result of unwanted pets released into the wild after they had become too difficult and/or too large for their owners to care for. In effect, a mixture of laziness and lack of foresight and consideration has been responsible for invoking what some conservationists believe to be an environmental catastrophe (or at the very least, the beginnings of such).

Of the approximately five-hundred introduced species documented to be present in Florida, reptiles and amphibians account for around one-hundred-and-fifty of them. Out of all these exotics, the Burmese python is perhaps the most well-known. Indeed, southern Florida's tropical climate has ensured that there exists a hospitable environment capable of sustaining many exotic species, and not just the Burmese python. As concerns *P. bivittatus*, so serious has the situation become in recent years, that some biologists fear the species will eventually eclipse the American alligator as the ecosystem's apex predator. Such a development has the potential to be disastrous, primarily due to the alligator's role as a keystone species in the Everglades; a role which *P. bivittatus* wouldn't necessarily fill should it replace the American alligator.

As constrictors, Burmese pythons are efficient killers who literally squeeze the life out of their quarry. They do this by way of wrapping their bodies around that of their chosen prey item, before slowly proceeding to suffocate it. During the long and painful process, bones will be broken and blood vessels burst as it squeezes tighter and tighter. Once they get their length around something, it is extremely unlikely that it will get away from them.

At that moment, the snake trailing after the panther was an 'albino' variety of *P. bivittatus*. Indeed, such specimens have long been popular in the pet trade because of their distinct appearance, and some of those released into the Everglades have not only survived but managed to pass their unusual genes onto their progeny. At no less than twelve feet, the serpent's meandering corpus was a swirling mixture of lemon-yellow and white markings. On either side of its deceptively small head sat marble-like, lidless red eyes that stood out like a demon's.

The two animals were less than twenty feet apart when their eyes met. The panther sat by the water's edge, its hind paws partially submerged. On the other hand, the snake sat further inland, nestled amongst a mattress of leaflitter and mould-slathered bogwood, trying to obscure its approach.

Coiling its length into a quasi-cone shape, the reptile 'tasted' the air with a series of animated flicks from its sinister-looking forked tongue. The pinkish member vibrated excitedly as it registered the feline's distinctive heat-signature. Sizing up its prey, the snake's head hovered as if suspended from a marionette's string, wavering from side to side.

For its part, the big cat let loose with a savage hiss, flashing a quartet of glistening incisors in an attempt to ward off the encroaching, serpentine killer. This was accompanied by a throaty and powerful roar that stole through the night air, carrying for miles around.

Neither the python nor the panther picked up on the presence of a third party to their primal parley.

***

Cautious and silent, the armoured mass glided forwards. Breaking out of the confines of the sawgrass prairie, the beast cut a gentle, V-shaped wake through the otherwise still sheet of obsidian water. Entering the marsh, the shadowy profile stealthily approached the hardwood hammock beyond, using its lobed appendages to help it manoeuvre over the more difficult knots of vegetation.

In addition to a ridged covering of hard, rocky osteoderms, the dark hide was possessed of a series of tall, needle-like spines connected via a thin, fleshy membrane, running through its centre. The wicked-looking combination of spines and webbing stood out tall like a ship's mast and sails. Zeroing in on its target, the ominous silhouette resembled a living man o' war; what's more the creature was just as deadly.

Poking through the shimmering surface of the slough, the creature's nostrils inhaled the muggy night air eagerly. A heavy, odorous scent immediately caught the hunter's attention. It belonged to a species of legless, slithering reptile it had hunted and killed before. However, its olfactory senses picked up on another, albeit weaker, scent coming from somewhere nearby as well. The predator's brain struggled to understand the information being relayed to it as it attempted to decipher the identity of its potential prey. Confused and wary, the killer slowed its advance, unsure how it was going to proceed.

Unaware of the encroaching danger, the panther arched its slender backside into the air, its tail dancing like a scorpion's stinger as it simultaneously lowered its front half. Preparing to strike, the feline dug its curved claws into the soft soil of the marsh about its hindquarters, the slick carpet of mud sliding between its parted toepads. Muscles tensing, the big cat made to challenge the python.

Yet, it wasn't meant to be.

A frothing, crystalline geyser unexpectedly erupted towards the panther's rear! In a flash, a yawning set of jaws quickly emerged from the glistening, liquid maelstrom. Cavernous and lined by bowed, blade-like fangs, it resembled the orifice of some over-sized Venus flytrap. Then, like an orca deliberately beaching itself to get at a sunbathing seal, the scaly creature launched itself up the muddy embankment adjoining the dark body of water. Sliding on its slime-ridden belly, the ravenous predator closed unforgivingly on the bewildered feline. Taken by surprise, the panther could only shriek in terror, followed by agony. In less than a second, the thing's sabre-like teeth latched onto the cougar's hindquarters; the collection of curled incisors puncturing skin and then flesh in quick succession, before ultimately drawing a cascade of blood from the subsequent wound.

Focused as it was on the malodourous reptilian scent that had first drawn it to the hammock, the killer was briefly confused when it tasted mammalian blood, before remembering the second mysterious smell. Still, it didn't stop to reconsider. Its quarry may not have been what it expected, but it was nourishment nonetheless… and the creature couldn't afford to be picky, not with a new brood to provide for.

A moment later, the cougar was gone from sight. Vanishing completely, it was dragged beneath the sloshing waterline, the terrified animal's ear-piercing screams replaced first by choking gurgles, and then finally silence. Save for the undulating waves left behind, it was as if nothing had happened.

Confused and slightly disorientated, the python didn't wait around. It made for the nearest tree, eager to put as much distance as possible between it and the water- or rather whatever was *in* the water.

If the unnerved python had waited a few seconds longer, the befuddled reptile would have witnessed the cougar's unexpected and dramatic reappearance. Exploding out of the water- *terrified, drenched and bleeding*- the roaring feline fought to escape the murderous fiend's mighty, fanged jaws. Clawing manically, the cougar desperately tried to find some purchase and make it to safety, hoping to drag itself out of the swamp and into the marshland where it might have had a chance.

Its assailant had other ideas however.

With a juddering tug, the fanged horror yanked the shrieking feline backwards, towards the black stretch of glassine water once more. As it was dragged further and further into the slough, the big cat let loose with a mournful chorus of mewling, but it was no use. There would be no pity shown. Not tonight. Then, with one final bone-jarring jerk, the mysterious killer pulled its prey under and the night grew deathly silent once more.

TUESDAY

6.

Moving determinedly through the dense undergrowth of the hardwood hammock, Professor Jennifer DeMarco trudged onward, each step seemingly more difficult than the one which preceded it. The flustered woman's exhaustive morning constitutional wasn't a lonely one, however. Rather, she was accompanied by a fellow academic, Tim Kahana, as she struggled to navigate the awkward stretch of tropical terrain. DeMarco's faithful companion was a PhD candidate under her supervision, whom she brought along to assist her.

All around the twosome there stretched a maze of jade that seemed to extend into eternity. Overhead, long, drooping leaves hung from bowing tree limbs like the green fingers of grasping giants come to snatch them up. As for the shrubbery, the claustrophobic collection of vegetation sprang up from the litter-strewn ground to hover about their waistlines, reeds and leaves clinging to them both.

Leaving the hammock behind some minutes later, Jennifer and Tim descended a short incline, delving into a still section of swampland. With each exaggerated, sloshing step, the pair fought to remain upright, their submerged feet sinking into the saturated soil beneath them. The air was hot and heavy, which certainly didn't make the going any easier on either of them. What's more, swarms of insects buzzed annoyingly about their eyes and ears, the monotonous vibrations threatening to drive them to the brink of insanity… and then throw them right over the edge.

"Just a little further," Jennifer said aloud, looking at the display on the black GPS transponder gripped in her right hand.

Professor DeMarco was an athletic woman, possessed of a slim physique and long, toned legs. Still, even she struggled to traverse the mixture of stagnant pools and thick nests of swampland shrubbery. By now it felt as if every one of her body's muscles ached; hot and on fire. Like the rest of her frame, the woman's freckled cheeks were blanched with a layer of sickly sweat. Raven-haired with sparkling blue-green eyes, the doctor was just shy of forty, but she could easily be mistaken for a thirty-year-old. As always, whenever out conducting fieldwork Jennifer kept her hair in a tight bun, so as not to let it interfere with her vision whilst she hiked. In addition to the plethora of irritating insects, a bad hair day could ruin a perfectly good excursion. At least, that was her experience anyway.

Tim Kahana on the other hand wasn't what you would call athletic. He wasn't obese, but he was certainly overweight. Although strong, he was far from what could be considered fit, at least in the cardiovascular and aerobic departments anyway. As such, the young post-doc was lagging behind his supervisor by several meters.

"Hold up," he pleaded breathlessly, wiping clotted strands of black hair out of his weary, cerulean eyes.

Tim's Hawaiian heritage was evident in his larger build and tanned complexion, not to mention the array of traditional tribal tattoos covering his left shoulder, which at that moment were partially covered by the sleeve of his T-shirt.

Overseen by Professor DeMarco, after four gruelling years Tim was now in the latter stages of his postgraduate studies. Upon being awarded a scholarship to FCU he hadn't wasted any time in requesting Professor DeMarco to be his primary supervisor for his PhD dissertation. Luckily, she agreed to take him on. This was a great honour in itself, as she was the pre-eminent expert in her chosen field of felinology, after all.

Both academics were attired in olive-green waterproof, dungaree-style overalls, and knee-high rubber boots; perfect for tackling the Everglades and its eclectic mixture of terrain. Each of them carried a rucksack containing the necessary equipment for their mini-expedition, which wasn't much more than a few rations that barely sufficed for lunch. They hadn't been on foot for more than an hour, still the heat and difficult topography made it feel like they had been going for half a day. Tim in particular found himself wishing their journey would just hurry up and end already.

"It's just up ahead," Jennifer told her student excitedly in between ragged breaths.

"Thank God," Tim panted breathlessly, his voice frail and raspy from exertion.

Wiping sweat from his brow a few seconds later, Tim looked up ahead of himself. He was surprised to see Jennifer's nimble profile had come to a halt amongst the choking nest of pale reeds encircling them.

"Professor?" Tim asked, somewhat puzzled.

At first, Tim thought the senior academic hadn't responded to him. Then he heard Jennifer's sobs. Muffled as they were, he only just managed to make them out amidst the chorus of rustling undergrowth and cheeping insects.

What's she so upset about? Tim wondered.

The young man approached his mentor cautiously, each one of his steps measured. Tim quickly became aware that his heart was racing; the blood pounding vehemently in his temples. In addition, the lad's breathing had become quick and shallow. Pins and needles suddenly took root in his hands as well, spreading up his forearms all the way to the elbows.

"Professor DeMarco, what is it?" Tim reached for Jennifer's quivering shoulder. "What's wrong?"

Suddenly, she spun to face him. Tears running down her cheeks, the professor threw herself at Tim. Distraught, Jennifer pulled the young man close, wrapping her arms around his neck and burying her head into his broad, spongy chest. After the initial shock wore off, Tim returned the hug, placing his thickset arms ever so gently around the woman's slender physique.

"It's okay," he cooed, trying his best to be supportive. Tim had never seen Jennifer like this before. He was honestly at a loss as to what to do.

Jennifer DeMarco continued to sob, her sorrowful moans growing louder with each breath. Still rather confused, Tim lifted his gaze away from the shuddering professor. It was then that Tim's bright eyes fell upon the grotesque sight responsible for leaving his mentor so upset.

"God… no…" Tim Kahana breathed as a wave of realization inundated him.

Their worst fear was a reality: 'Xavier' was dead. The panther- or more accurately the panther's remains- lay at the periphery of the marshland just shy of the adjoining swamp. The poor feline had been sawn in half it seemed. Or was it bitten in half? In either event, all that remained of Xavier was his front portion, his tawny legs stretched out and rigid, with his rounded head buried into the grimy bed of soil. Everything from the chest down was gone. Ragged chunks of eviscerated flesh and muscle leaked sickeningly from the enormous gaping cavity left behind. Blood seeped into the adjacent section of swamp, tinging the short, sheening spit of water a haunting shade of crimson; a sight that nigh on churned the young man's stomach.

When they set out that morning, following the signal picked up by their GPS transponder, the pair had expected to find a tracking collar which had come loose from its target animal. It wasn't uncommon for the cougars they monitored to lose their collars from time to time. DeMarco's study of the Florida panther population in the Southern Glades was now in its sixth year. Therefore, dead panthers were always a possibility that had to be considered. As such, she had come across deceased cats before, but all of them had been panthers in their later years. It was expected that such specimens would expire eventually. This on the other hand wasn't expected… at all. Xavier was in his prime; young and full of vigour.

Still clinging to one another, the pair grew silent as each of them contemplated the implications of their gruesome discovery. It was several minutes before one of them said something.

"We have to contact the FWC," Jennifer lifted her head away from Tim's shoulder. "Something's wrong here… very wrong."

Alex and Tahlia followed close behind their seasoned guide Antoine, who for his part effortlessly cut a swathe through the near-smothering sea of reeds encircling them. Since leaving behind their truck, the threesome had fallen victim to the myriad ravenous insects that called the Southern Glades home. Each of them itched from head to heel with bothersome bites. This was despite the entire group having donned matching dark green, FWC-issued, waterproof dungarees, and not to mention caking themselves in copious amounts of mosquito repellent.

Slogging through the dense marsh in single-file, rubber boots and all, the trio soon came upon a rather unnerving sight. In fact, the small clearing before them was possessed of the same aura one might associate with a crime scene. The claustrophobic space was crowded with a handful of figures all sporting the same dungaree-style garments as themselves. Most were FWC officials; all of them junior wardens under Jackson. However, Alex noted two other individuals present who- although they were dressed much the same as everyone else- didn't quite seem to fit in. He quickly realized that they wore casual clothes under their overalls, in much the same manner as himself and Tahlia, which the uniformed wardens obviously did not.

Civilians. Alex figured. *Like us.*

But who were they? Jackson had given the doctor and his companion very little information this time around. Antoine seemed more interested in getting to the scene than explaining the particulars of it all. Very much in the dark, all they knew was that another animal had been found dead, this time deep in the Glades.

Focusing his attention on the out-of-place pair, the doctor's eyes were drawn to the female in particular. He wasn't attracted to her in the conventional sense, although he had to admit that she was a good-looking woman. Rather, there was something familiar about her. Alex couldn't help but notice by the woman's side, sitting there with a hand placed affectionately on her shoulder, was a robust young man with caramel-coloured skin several shades lighter than Tahlia's.

With his curiosity piqued, Alex broke away from Antoine. Tahlia shadowed her teacher as he carefully approached the raven-haired woman. Advancing towards the female, Doctor Scott watched her intently. His eyes scoured the woman from head to toe as he tried to place her. The herpetologist was certain he knew the woman from somewhere. The lad (who in truth was only a few years younger than Alex) standing by her side even looked vaguely familiar as well. Then unexpectedly she looked up at Alex; the woman seeming to sense his hesitant approach and curious stare.

Tears gleamed noticeably in the woman's turquoise eyes, the liquid brimming at the reddened edges of her eyelids. In that instant Alex came to a realization: he *did* know the woman. In fact, they were members of the same faculty at FCU.

"Jennifer?" Alex called out. "Jennifer DeMarco?"

"Doctor Scott," Jennifer responded, recognizing Alex immediately. The startled woman clumsily tried to wipe away the tears from her flushed and freckled cheeks. "Please forgive me, I must look a mess," Jennifer blushed, clearly embarrassed by her current state.

"Hardly," Remembering his manners, Alex did his best to be kind to her.

Professor DeMarco smiled gratefully at her colleague's last comment, just as one more tear emerged from the corner of her left eye, and rolled down her reddened cheek.

"You discovered the panther," Alex surmised, his eyes surveying the admittedly odd, but no less gruesome, scene.

"Xavier is his name," Jennifer DeMarco explained, sniffling noticeably. "I tagged him almost five years ago as part of my research project."

"I see," Doctor Scott nodded as he tried to remember the specifics of her study, but came up short.

"I checked his electronic ID, as I always do," Jennifer went on, "and found he hadn't moved in almost twenty-four hours."

"So you came looking," Alex finished for her.

"Yes," Professor DeMarco nodded. "We were hoping it was just something as simple as his e-tag coming loose."

Out the corner of his eye, Alex caught Antoine watching his exchange with the distraught Jennifer. Even though the man didn't say it, the doctor could tell the grim-faced warden was growing impatient. He had that intent 'let's get on with it' look in his eyes. In short, Antoine Jackson wanted to know what was responsible for taking out the big feline. He needed to know if it was at all connected to Big Buck's death. Ultimately, Antoine had to know if there was a marauding predator on the loose in his neck of the woods. As such, the man's impatience was certainly understandable.

"I hate to do this, but I best get down to business," the herpetologist announced as he edged away from his colleague, albeit with some regret. "The Wildlife Commission has asked me here to consult for them," Alex motioned to the looming figure of Antoine Jackson.

DeMarco smiled appreciatively at this. She understood how things were. Alex got the distinct impression that she was fighting back more tears. To be honest, he felt sorry for the woman. It wasn't uncommon for a biologist- in any field- to become attached to the animals they studied. Jennifer DeMarco was obviously one of them. It came with the territory, after all. In the end, there wasn't much you could do about it really.

With Tahlia in tow, Doctor Scott joined Antoine by the decapitated panther's remains. Alex proceeded to pull his mobile phone from the breast pocket of his overalls. Using the device's built-in camera function, he began snapping pictures of the decomposing beast. Dropping down on his haunches a moment later, the herpetologist leaned in to get some close-up shots of the animal's gruesome wound.

"If you don't mind, I think I'll send these pictures to my contact," Doctor Scott told the grimacing game warden, who at this point was virtually standing over him. "For clarification purposes, of course. I'll be sure to let her know that it is strictly confidential."

"Do you think that the same animal is responsible for this?" Antoine queried.

"I think it is possible," Alex responded. "But I will still have to clarify."

"This is some serious shit!" Tahlia exclaimed, her brown, doe-like eyes growing wide with astonishment.

So engrossed in their discussion were they that the herpetologist and his two companions failed to register the appearance of a shadowy, elongated profile stealing through the body of water beside them. Moving just a few inches shy of the glass-like surface, the shape was only a couple dozen feet out from their position. Nor did they pick up on the intruder when it doubled back; cutting a subtle wake through the water as it coursed towards the shoreline. On its return leg, the creature's grooved flanks casually breached the otherwise calm waterline like some primeval submarine. Crystal-like water rolled off its back in small streams, revealing a row of savage, webbed spines lining its gnarled, rocky hide.

"Hanson! Peters!" Jackson suddenly called out. "There's probably no point in you two hanging around here any longer, you've done everything you can. Good job; both of you. Take Professor DeMarco and Mr. Kahana here back into the city."

Alex craned his neck and watched as two of Jackson's green and tan-clad deputies excused themselves, before promptly disappearing into the brush maze with their charges.

"Nicholls! Romero!" Antoine called to the remaining deputies. "We are gonna need to move this mother. Head back to your truck and get us a couple of tarpaulin sheets, will ya?"

"You got it, boss," one of the men replied heartily. Alex wasn't sure if he was the one named Nicholls, or if he was Romero.

Alex returned his gaze to the big cat as the remaining wardens disappeared into the lush, tropical abyss. He remained by the feline's side for a time, contemplating the cougar's final minutes on this earth. Unsurprisingly, the subsequent mental images he managed to conjure up weren't pretty- not in the slightest.

"So do you think our shark attacked as the cougar was exiting the water?" Antoine asked the doctor.

"More than likely," Alex answered, getting to his feet. "Without any additional information, I can't think of any other plausible scenario that would explain this." Doctor Scott motioned to the butchered feline with an open hand.

Next, accompanied by Tahlia, the two men stepped away from the mutilated cat.

"Have you ever heard of anything like this before?" Tahlia asked both of them, the worry evident in her dark eyes. "I mean, a shark attacking a panther? It sounds pretty out there."

Both men stared silently at her and then shook their heads in unison.

"This just gets weirder by the minute," Jackson admitted out loud, taking off his cap and wiping sweat from his creased and darkly brow. "Weirder and weirder," he murmured placing the cap back on his bald head.

Zoning out momentarily, Alex returned his attention to his mobile phone. He brought up the images he had just taken of Xavier and sent them through to Hailey Benson in several messages. Attached to the last image was the text:

`Could whatever killed Buck be responsible for this?`

Alex slid his cell back into his pocket to await a reply-

-and almost jumped out of his skin as his ears registered a sharp *claaap!* followed by a sizzling *hiss!* With his heart racing and pulse pounding, it took Alex a moment to realize both sounds had emanated from somewhere behind him. After which, it took the biologist only a nanosecond to realise it had come from the general vicinity of the dead feline.

As one, Alex, Antoine and Tahlia spun on their heels, their thick, rubber soles squelching in the marshy soil. The panther was gone. Vanished. The water beyond the marsh's edge roiled and rippled, clearly disturbed by something large; although that something was no longer in attendance it now seemed… or at the very least it was residing just out of view. Subsequently, a thinning layer of white froth bubbled along the length of the olive-coloured surface. Gradually it dissipated as the shimmering, liquescent tapestry calmed, returning to its normal state.

"What the hell was that?" Tahlia exclaimed, her deep, hazel eyes glistening with fear.

"It came back for the cougar!" Antoine choked. "It fucking came back for it!"

"I don't like this one bit…" Alex told his companions in a frightened and hushed tone. "We need to leave- *now!*"

Antoine snatched a small two-way radio from his belt and began barking into it, trying to raise his deputies on the other end. Alex on the other hand ushered Tahlia away from the marshland clearing, looking worriedly over his shoulder at the now deceptively serene body of water beyond.

7.

Sheriff Walter Crawford's office was a cramped one. Furthermore, it wasn't properly air-conditioned. Not surprisingly, a musty coalescence of unpleasant smells lingered in the air: a sickly mixture of body odour, hard liquor, cigarettes and aftershave. The latter was an obvious attempt to mask the other three scents. Unfortunately, it didn't work well, if indeed at all.

The office's pallid grey walls were plastered with an assortment of certificates, placed alongside pictures of the sheriff at various stages in his twenty-something-year career. That being said, the Sheriff Crawford on display in the pictures looked much haler than the one sat in front of his three visitors at that very moment. Age, and no doubt the rigours of the job, had gotten the better of Walter Crawford- that much was certain. Even from the most fleeting of glances one may have cast in the man's direction. His once slick, jet-black head of hair had turned grey-white, just like the handlebar moustache framing his bulbous, pink-purple lips. Although Crawford's skin had maintained its tanned complexion, it now sagged from his bones in wrinkled flaps almost like curtains. Furthermore, the man's thick forearms were covered in tattoos, all of which had faded and warped over the years. The only thing of Crawford's that hadn't changed in his near-sixty years were his eyes. They remained a cold, penetrating shade of grey.

The dour-looking man said nothing to begin with as he appraised his guests from the other side of his chipped and scuffed work desk. Walter didn't look happy to see them. This was despite the fact that he had absolutely no reason to be disgruntled with them (at least yet, anyway). After all, the sheriff had no idea why they had requested to meet with him in the first place. The fact was Walter Crawford was just that type of guy: an asshole. An exceptionally grumpy kind of asshole.

"What can I do for you three?" the sheriff finally enquired of them, the man's voice gruff and his tone unapologetically perturbed.

"We need your department's help in shutting down access to the Southern Glades." As per usual, Antoine didn't waste any time getting down to business.

"That's one helluva request, son." If the sheriff was taken aback by the forcefulness of the warden's statement he didn't let on. "Why, might I ask?" the lawman queried a moment later.

Fidgeting with the FWC cap gripped in his sweaty palms, Antoine didn't respond right away. Instead, he turned to Alex Scott seated off to his right.

"This is Doctor Alex Scott," the game warden introduced his colleague to the sheriff. "Alex is a biology lecturer at FCU."

Crawford growled something incomprehensible as he switched his gaze to the academic across the table from him.

"Sheriff Crawford," Alex shifted in his seat as he joined the conversation proper, "we have reason to be believe there is a large predator on the loose in the Southern Glades."

Walter Crawford looked at Alex as if to say; 'Well no shit, Sherlock'.

"You're not from around here, are ya son?" Crawford eyed Alex suspiciously.

Before Alex had a chance to reply, the sheriff went on.

"So far, you haven't told me anything I don't already know," the lawman explained matter-of-factly. "Southern Florida- *the Everglades especially*- is a dangerous place, with a lot of dangerous wildlife in residence. Everybody knows that- whether they are a biologist or not. Yet, you expect me to help you close down access to the Glades because a large predator may be 'on the loose'." He used his fingers to make air-quotes on the last three words, much to his guests' collective disdain.

"*Diiiick…*" Tahlia breathed a little too loudly at this.

The sheriff grimaced at her, his top lip curling. Suddenly, all eyes were on her. The young woman could feel her cheeks burning up almost immediately. Tahlia couldn't help herself, she had to say something, the guy- in fact, his whole demeanour- was utterly infuriating.

Ignoring Tahlia's interruption, Alex went on, trying his hardest to impress the seriousness of the situation on the lawman. Although, he made a mental note to chastise Tahlia later for her behaviour. The academic was fully aware of how flimsy their case was. Still, they had to do something. Even if they were wrong, it was better to be safe than sorry.

"What you said is correct, sheriff," Alex Scott kept Crawford's steely gaze as best he could. "The Glades are home to various species of predatory animal. However, what we are trying to tell you is that there is something unusual going on out there."

"Unusual how?" Crawford sniffed, switching his gaze back in Tahlia's direction momentarily, before settling for watching the young woman out the corner of his eye. He obviously wasn't going to let her previous comment slide that easily.

"There have been two killings in the last two days," Alex explained.

"If people were going missing in the Southern Glades," the sheriff smirked arrogantly, "I think my department would've heard something about it. It's a big part of how we make a living, after all."

"Not people," Antoine interjected. "Not yet, anyway."

"What do you mean, 'not people'?" Walter Crawford probed, the frustration evident in his disgruntled tenor.

"Animals," Alex clarified, a little sheepishly.

"Dead animals?" Crawford gave them an 'are you serious?' look. "This is all about some dead animals?"

"An alligator and a cougar," Alex answered, doing his best to ignore the older man's condescension. "So far, anyway."

"A dead alligator and a dead cougar in the Everglades," Crawford leaned back in his chair, twirling his fat, tubular thumbs. "Now that is strange, isn't it?"

Neither Alex, Antoine nor Tahlia appreciated the lawman's blatant sarcasm. In fact, Alex even began to reconsider his previous decision to reprimand Tahlia for her little outburst.

"Look sheriff-" Antoine edged forward uncomfortably in his seat.

"No, you look warden!" Walter Crawford extended a big, sausage-like index finger toward Jackson before slapping the top of his desk. "You can't seriously expect me to help you shut down access to the Southern Glades on account of two dead critters now, can you? I mean be serious! The number of tourists we get this time of year provides a massive boost to our city's economy. We'd be shooting ourselves in the dicks! And all that for two dead critters?"

"Whatever this thing is, it's large and nasty enough to have killed Big Buck," Antoine told the sheriff, cutting in before the other man had time to say anything else. "Imagine what it could do to a human victim!"

Jackson's statement gave the sheriff reason for pause, however momentary it proved to be. Walter Crawford knew all about Big Buck, he was a Florida City native, after all. Born and bred, just like his father, and his father before him. Recovering his composure, Crawford brushed aside the revelation that Buck had been killed, and continued with his diatribe.

"Once again, I'm gonna need something a bit more concrete than a dead gator and its feline friend," Sheriff Crawford told them flatly, his tone softening… just barely.

A silence descended upon the room after this. Alex and his two companions exchanged looks of disappointment, mingled with hints of confusion. The sheriff on the other hand looked on impassively, unimpressed and impatient for them to leave his office.

Antoine was the first to speak; he knew the jig was up.

"I think it is time we were leaving," Antoine got to his feet, pushing his chair rearwards with the backs of his long legs.

Alex and Tahlia quickly followed suit.

“Sheriff,” Antoine nodded as he placed his FWC cap over his sheening scalp, trying to be polite.

Following on Antoine’s heels, Alex and Tahlia mumbled their goodbyes. Sheriff Crawford simply tilted his square-shaped head ever so slightly in their direction. Trailing behind the other two, Tahlia stopped at the doorway and turned back to face Crawford. Standing in the doorway she looked the sheriff right in the eyes and mouthed the words ‘I don’t like you.’ Crawford didn’t seem to care too much.

Exiting the sheriff’s office a moment later, the dispirited threesome entered a bustling bullpen area complete with computer-laden desks, filing cabinets, office staff, and wandering sheriff’s deputies.

“Well,” Tahlia’s hazel eyes switched between Alex and Antoine, “that was a waste of fucking time.”

Locked away in his office at FCU, it was late in the evening when Alex finally garnered the courage he needed to contact his old friend, Hailey Benson. They had been in touch earlier that day after she responded to his text message. As it turned out, Hailey was in agreement with him; whatever killed the gator could very well have killed the panther as well. Now with that settled, Alex had a different question to ask her, and it was a request he didn’t look forward to asking.

Outside, visible through his office window, the sun continued to lower its blazing mass behind the dark line of the horizon. Shrinking into nothingness, the burning titan cast hypnotic ochre rays over the shadowy world beneath it. Yet, as the world darkened, so too did Alex’s mood; the weight of the question he had to ask bearing down on him.

The doctor knew how the impending conversation with his friend was going to go. In his estimation, the outcome was nothing short of inevitable. What he intended to ask of Hailey was a big request, especially considering her recent history, and all the emotional and psychological baggage that came with it. Even so, Alex had to try all the same. After all, peoples’ lives could very well depend on it. Or so the troubled academic reckoned to himself. Sitting behind his heavyset desk, Alex stared down introspectively at his inanimate cell phone. Battling to maintain his composure, Alex fingered the device nervously, spinning it around on the spot.

Is this for me? Or her? Asked a familiar and doubtful voice. *Or both?*

“To hell with it,” the man snarled, snatching up the phone suddenly.

Tapping away at the touchscreen, Alex dialled Hailey’s cell. Placing the phone hesitantly to his ear, he waited for the young woman to answer his call at the other end. It didn't take long. Alex's heart jumped up into his throat at the sound of Hailey Benson's soft, welcoming voice.

Stretched out on her bed, thousands of miles away, the young woman lay flat on her back, dressed only in a satin nightgown. Staring up at the off-white ceiling, Hailey felt relaxed after her scheduled evening run. Adding to the serene atmosphere was the icy, bluish hue from her television screen saturating the otherwise darkened room. Unbeknownst to her, the young woman's tranquillity wasn't going to last very long.

"How goes the monster hunt?" Hailey chirped heartily without even offering her caller a proper 'hello'.

"Not good," Alex replied sombrely from the other end.

"How so?" Benson asked, somewhat intrigued. Using her thumb and forefinger, the young woman absentmindedly twisted a lock of her fiery hair whilst she spoke.

"Our local sheriff isn't the most helpful of characters," Alex explained flippantly.

At these words, images of the late, dour-looking Michael Ramirez unexpectedly flashed inside Hailey's mind, instantly casting her back in time to the shores of Lake Minerva. A pang of sorrow knotted her stomach together as she recalled his sombre and somewhat haunted features. Shaking off the mental cobwebs after a few moments, the biologist returned to the present conversation.

"Let me guess," Hailey said, "the sheriff isn't buying your theory on the shark."

"Something like that," Alex told her flatly. The doctor didn't even bother to explain that he and Antoine hadn't told the sheriff they suspected a shark may be responsible for the growing collection of dead wildlife piling up in the Southern Glades.

Hailey thought about what to say next during the brief interlude that followed. She wracked her brain for something positive and encouraging to say, but it didn't come to her. In any event, it didn't matter. Doctor Scott beat her to the punch.

"I could really do with your help down here," the herpetologist breathed into the receiver. "I know I've asked before but-"

"No!" Hailey jolted upright in bed, barking back without the slightest hesitation. "I told you already- *no way*."

"But-"

It was no use, Hailey continued to speak over Alex, bawling down the line at her pleading friend all the while.

"No!" Benson's voice was full of force, even as it came out high and shrill. "I can't go through that kind of nightmare again!"

"I get it," he tried to sympathize, lowering his voice.

Big mistake.

"No- that's just it- you *don't* get it!" Hailey blared at her friend. "How could you? It wasn't you who faced down that fucking thing! And it wasn't you who lost your friends and colleagues in the process! I watched them get eaten alive for Christ's sake!"

"You're right, I can't possibly understand what you went through," Alex admitted, quickly backtracking. "But could you live with yourself if it kills someone? Honestly, could you?" He tried his best to reason with her. "Knowing that you might have been able to do something to stop this thing?"

"Fuck you!" Hailey snapped in frustration, unable to muster a more articulate retort. "*How fucking dare you!* I'm not some friggin' superhero! This isn't my responsibility!"

Alex rolled with the punches, shrugging off her venomous comments.

"I've arranged flights and accommodation for you," Alex went on, landing a shot of his own which managed to stall Hailey's verbal assault for the time being.

"Wait…" Hailey's voice instantly lost its sting as she was overcome with a sense of surprise. "What did you say?"

"I've booked a flight," Alex answered. "It leaves tomorrow evening, and I've also organized a motel for you. Your return flight is in two weeks' time."

"How did you get the university to agree to that?" Hailey demanded, totally perplexed by this unexpected revelation.

"It doesn't matter," he said curtly. "It's done now."

"Well, you shouldn't have," Hailey replied point-blank.

"Well, I did." Alex was beginning to get frustrated. "I've emailed you the details. At least think about it. You being here could be the difference between life and death for someone."

Hailey saw red. Then black. Then red again. Anger overcame the flustered woman, crashing over her in what could only be described as an emotional avalanche. Ever since Lake Minerva, Hailey struggled to control her emotions when placed under pressure- her anger especially. She didn't like it. Indeed, Hailey tried very hard to keep herself in check, but sometimes a situation was just too much to handle. This was one such situation.

"You had no right to do that, Alex!" Hailey screamed into the phone, before slamming it down beside her on the bed with a *whump!*

Shaking uncontrollably, Hailey reached for the lamp perched on her bedside table. Wrapping her fingers firmly around its bulbous base, she tossed the light across her room and into the opposite wall. The ornament's ceramic body shattered on impact, exploding into a mixture of jagged shards, accompanied by a fine, mist-like dust.

About thirty seconds later, Hailey's father burst into the bedroom. Flicking the light-switch on, he stood there in the doorway, huffing and puffing from his hurried sprint up the stairs. Bald and wrinkled as always, he hovered cautiously by the opening, refusing to enter the bedroom proper, unsure of how his daughter might react to the intrusion.

"What's wrong?" the man's pale eyes nervously appraised Hailey's quivering outline.

Hailey didn't answer him, the words she attempted to summon catching in her throat. Instead, the young woman moved to the foot of her bed on weak and trembling legs. Next, Hailey fell into her father's arms, tears brimming in her vibrant green eyes. Finally mustering the courage to enter the room, Hailey's father only just managed to catch his distraught child as she crumpled in on herself near the foot of her bed.

Sobbing loudly, Hailey seethed with anger as she buried her face into her father's familiar, bony chest. She just couldn't believe that Alex would actually try to guilt her into going to Florida like that. What's more, the asshole had just gone ahead and booked flights and a motel of his own volition. It was as if Alex just expected her to fall into line. He should have known better than that. After all, Alex knew what she had been through, and the damage it had done to her- inside and out. Hell, the whole world knew.

How could Alex be so inconsiderate?

This wasn't the Alex she knew. Or more accurately, it wasn't the Alex she remembered. Then again, time could do a lot to someone. Ultimately, for better or worse, people change. Hailey was certainly living proof of that fact.

Meanwhile, on the other end of the telephone line, Alex hung up after several long seconds of silence. Defeated and deeply demoralized by the turn of events, the academic was at a total loss as to what to do now. Leaning back in his chair and placing his hands behind his head, the herpetologist let out a long, woeful sigh.

"Shit," he breathed regretfully.

WEDNESDAY

8.

Although the bleeding had stopped, the juvenile's maw continued to throb with pain as a result of the crooked, metallic instrument lodged in its ugly face. Poked clean through the thin membrane of wrinkled skin, the barbed object hung close by the hinge of the animal's jaw. In fact, the presence of the foreign object meant the beast was no longer able to close its mouth properly, forcing its bottom jaw to hang slightly agape. Still, battling through the pain and discomfort, the animal continued on its course up the slough in search of new prey.

Its journey was most likely going to be a lonely one, the creature's smaller sibling having ventured off in a different direction some hours before. Even so, before long they would no doubt reunite and return to their parents' lair together, grateful for the sanctuary it offered them. Hopefully, they wouldn't return empty-handed either. Their parents' latest brood relied on the older siblings almost as much as their progenitors to provide sustenance for them. Working as a unit was the key to their survival, and survival of course was paramount.

René Delacroix, or 'Mumbles' as he was known around those parts of Florida City he frequented, was a simple character. Although, that is not to say René was simple in the sense that the man was slow-minded. Rather, his simplicity stemmed from his desire to lead a minimalist existence, free of the complications modern life brought with it. Unlike the majority of Florida City's affluent natives, he wasn't interested in fancy cars or mobile phones fitted out with all the latest technological trappings. Instead, René preferred just the essentials. Nothing more, nothing less. Life was more tolerable that way.

Born and raised in the meandering bayous of Louisiana, René was a Cajun. His first language therefore was Louisiana Creole. Predominantly French, the remainder of the colourful hybrid language was supplemented with an array of Native American, and even African dialects. Therefore, he was quite literally a breed apart from the English speakers of Florida City. Still, he made do with the little amount of English he managed to muster when the need arose; hence the nickname Mumbles, given to him by those select few in Florida City who were lucky enough to be acquainted with him.

René hadn't been out of Louisiana for long, barely three years in fact. In any event, being detached from his homeland, people and culture hadn't slowed René down much, if at all. Ever-resourceful, René more than managed to make a decent living for himself. Indeed, the man's days back in Louisiana had given him everything he needed to survive on his own. As the old saying goes: you can take the boy out of the bayou, but you can't take the bayou out of the boy.

René had one particular skillset that was the cornerstone of his existence. During his forty-plus years living in the Louisiana backwaters, René- like many other Cajuns- honed his skills as an alligator hunter. In fact, Mr. Delacroix subsisted mainly by hunting gators, even to this day. What gator meat he didn't sell, he ate himself or froze for later consumption.

Leaving behind his spartan, one-bedroom shack perched on the edge of the Glades, René's battered and rust-speckled boat motored noisily through the still slough. It was early morning and the sun was only just peaking over the horizon. The hungry Cajun was heading out to check on several of his alligator snares, all of them set the day before. These devices weren't much more than anchored lines of rope connected to barbed hooks with chicken carcasses attached to the ends of them. They were nasty and simple, but nevertheless effective.

A squat man with a potbelly, Delacroix stood at five-five, with arms and legs like tree trunks. Underneath his dark blue overalls, René wore a tattered and soiled T-shirt which had once been white in colour (much like his underwear). The man's bald head was covered with an equally dishevelled skip-cap, the fabric of which was stained with all manner of fluids, and not to mention frayed around the edges.

On either side of him and his vessel, walls of needle-like sawgrass blades swayed with the breeze. The draught felt good against his bronzed skin as he rushed down the length of the wide channel. Motoring onward, René's speeding boat cut a harsh, foaming wake through the liquid landscape, shattering its calm façade. Watching the horizon with his small, pale blue eyes, René scanned for his lines from the rear of the small boat.

Spotting his first snare a few moments later, René eased back on the throttle, slowing the spritely craft to a gentle crawl. Gripped by a sense of anticipation, the Cajun's heartrate quickened. Hoping to find a big, fat, juicy gator at the end of his line, René's steely eyes flashed in the direction of the bolt-action rifle nestled at the fore of the little vessel. It was one thing to catch a gator, but it was another thing entirely to kill one. Strong, and equally as feisty, they didn't go down easy. Not by a long shot.

As was common, the waters of the slough were murky, tinged green as a result of the cornucopia of free-floating algae species that inhabited the waterway. Inspecting the near-impenetrable liquescent sheet a little closer, Delacroix found that he couldn't see much further than a few inches deep. If he had landed himself a gator, René certainly couldn't see it. The hunter wouldn't know for sure until he was right on top of it. This was a daunting prospect, but a grim reality not only of his chosen lifestyle but his favourite trapping method.

Bringing his boat to a complete stop, René pulled up alongside his partially submerged snare. Quick as a cat, Delacroix grabbed hold of the length of rope and yanked back hard on it. The chicken, barely touched, flew out of the water at his face. Unflinching, René dangled the hunk of dripping-wet white meat in front of him for a second, surveying it closely.

"*Merde!*" the man snapped, tossing the dead piece of poultry back into the water. He would come back tomorrow for that one, René decided.

Within about a minute or so, the Cajun was off again. Flying through the channel's dark waters once more, he headed for his next line, feeling slightly less optimistic than he had been at the outset of his journey. It was another fifteen minutes before René came upon his second line. Since alligators were known to be territorial, he always made sure to give ample space between snares to increase his chances of landing something.

René cut the motor completely this time around. His craft momentarily glided to a halt, the fore of the vessel's hull nudging into the palisade of sawgrass adjoining the broad body of water. Stepping forward vigilantly, Delacroix reached out for the length of rope, which was visible just below the jade waterline. Snatching up the line, René was surprised to find it came away easier than the last. *Much* easier, in fact.

Eyes narrowed, René found there was nothing at the end of it. Indeed, the bait was gone. Something had taken the chicken- *hook and all.* René growled incomprehensibly to himself as he appraised the severed line. It was clear to him that the rope had been chewed right through. Somewhere out there was a pissed off gator with a mouth or gut full of barbed metal.

Crafty little bastard, Delacroix thought irritably.

Perplexed by his discovery, René failed to notice the ominous and somewhat blurred silhouette lingering in the water, a short distance from his boat. Long and wraith-like, the figure cruised just below the surface, about a dozen or so feet off his starboard side. Unseen and sinister, the dark, stretching apparition cruised leisurely on by the rear of his boat. Then, just as Mr. Delacroix was about to push off and head for his third and final line, he suddenly thought he caught what appeared to be movement out the corner of his eye.

"Huh?" he muttered, turning sharply on the spot.

The Cajun cranked his neck to get a better look. But whatever it was- if indeed there had been anything there in the first place- was gone by the time René turned to inspect it. For several minutes, the Cajun scanned the smooth waterline for signs of the spectral, amorphous outline he thought he might have spotted. Silently, the man wondered if it was the alligator responsible for absconding with his line. Perhaps it had come back. Such a thing wasn't outside the realm of possibility. Yet, it seemed there was nothing there. The water was calm, and appeared virtually undisturbed, in fact. Maybe his eyes (combined with the early morning light) were playing tricks on him.

Shrugging to himself, René went back to inspecting the severed line in his hands. Facing the sawgrass prairie once more, Delacroix was oblivious to the mysterious shape's reappearance. All it would have taken to see the ominous outline was for the man to glance over his shoulder, back the way he came. Unfortunately, his attention was focused elsewhere.

In the distance, an unmistakable, spiked and ancient-looking hump breached the surface of the slough with next to no commotion. Emerald-coloured water cascaded off the creature's charcoal back, the liquid running in thin rivulets down its stone-like hide.

At thirty feet and closing, René Delacroix remained oblivious to the encroaching terror. Instead, he set about trying to undo his line. He might have lost his hook, but he could salvage what remained of the rope. Well, that's what the Cajun intended to do anyway.

***

Surging forward, the torpedo-shaped beast picked up speed as it let loose with several solid thrusts from its spike-rimmed caudal fin. Carving through the green body of water, it closed on its quarry with a vengeance, driven by a single primal instinct... *hunger*. Then, at twenty feet from its target, the creature dove out of sight once more, delving into the murky depths of the slough.

Reeling in the last of the loosened line, the Cajun took a seat by his outboard motor. Next, René threw his vessel into reverse. Looking over his shoulder, he manoeuvred away from the sawgrass prairie and back into the slough proper. He didn't get far, however. Unexpectedly, René's outboard went dead, the machine spluttering out like a wet fart.

"*Feet pue tan!*" Delacroix cussed at the faulty engine.

Spinning out of his seated position, René turned to get a better look at the outboard motor. Standing hunched over the engine, he took a closer look at it. Grabbing the choke, the outdoorsman yanked back hard on it, attempting to restart the motor. Yet, try as he might, the engine did little more than cough at him in response.

Meanwhile, beneath the deceptively serene veneer of the slough's jade surface, the would-be killer advanced on its unsuspecting prey. At less than ten feet from its target, the creature pitched upwards on a sharp angle. With the grace of a fighter-jet, the fiend peeled its muscular mass away from the channel's muddy, debris-laden bottom, aiming for the boat's corrugated underbelly.

***

Distracted and exasperated by the engine's refusal to kick over, Delacroix stood back from the device, taking a moment to consider his options. Hands on his hips, René stared uselessly at the faulty contraption, mumbling away in Creole to himself as he tried to decide what in the hell to do next.

The sudden impact that followed a moment later shocked the poor, unsuspecting René to his core. At first, Delacroix didn't understand what was happening. It was like his world was turned upside-down and inside-out. All René could tell was that something had collided with his vessel, possibly striking it from below, causing the boat to list sickeningly to one side. Behind him, René heard the vessel's metallic hull crack open, accompanied by a noise not unlike breaking bones. As the metalwork peeled open, a rush of frothing, greenish swamp water seeped into the craft.

Thus, taken completely by surprise, René's brain barely had time to register the bone-jarring reverberations that wracked his body. Before he knew it, the Cajun was sailing through the air, his stomach rolling over inside him. Next, he plummeted into the cold water below, his skip-cap disappearing amongst a section of wiry sawgrass. Landing flat on his back with a heavy *crack!* René sank beneath the olive-coloured waterline. His grubby clothes quickly became waterlogged, working to weigh him down. Shocked by the confusing sequence of events, the terrified hunter opened his eyes underwater in an attempt to orientate himself. René quickly wished he hadn't. Indeed, the sight that greeted the beleaguered fisherman sent a near-paralysing and glacial chill down his spine.

Eyes, bright like stoked embers, appeared from out of the liquid gloom; fierce, hungry and intent. So vibrant and entrancing were the orange-red spheres confronting René, that the man didn't spot the blunted, gnarled snout, even lined as it was with dagger-like incisors, until a few seconds later. It was several more seconds before he noted the strange metallic glint situated by the hinge of the ghastly set of jaws in front of him. René suddenly thought of his missing hook. This was the thing that had taken his bait- not a gator. Now it had come back for him!

Lungs burning, and not wanting to wait around any longer, the terrified man kicked out hard with both his legs. Breaching the surface quickly thereafter, Delacroix drew in a deep and desperate breath. The man's eyes immediately locked onto his little boat's partially-rusted hull, the remainder of its silvery frame sheening in the early morning light. Next, René hurriedly made for his vessel, the hunter's broad arms animatedly punching into the water around him.

Behind Delacroix, the tips of several snaking, needle-like vertebrae swiftly appeared, poking through the water's surface like cathedral spires emerging from the early morning mist. Subsequently, the fearsome creature they belonged to cut a prominent, foaming wake through the shimmering waterline as it raced toward René. Graceful and determined, the beast moved with the efficiency of a heat-seeker locked onto an enemy aircraft; relentless and unforgiving in its cold, measured ferocity.

Adrenaline dispersed throughout the Cajun's stunned system, sending the man's senses into overdrive. Panicking, René gave it everything he had, kicking and thrusting to get to his wayward vessel, sending up miniature geysers all around him with each determined stroke. He was only a few feet from his boat now. It was *just* out of reach. He could make it.

Or so René hoped.

In between strokes, the Cajun managed several backwards glances at his encroaching stalker. He couldn't believe his eyes. The animal- or rather what René could see of the horrifying creature- pursuing him was like nothing he had encountered before, whether in the Everglades or back in the Louisiana bayous. One word immediately sprang to mind: *primordial.*

The primal nightmare trailed hurriedly after its quarry. Wending its scaled, tubular girth through the water like an anaconda, it closed the distance between them inch by inch with ease.

Deep down in its gut, a now familiar burning sensation drove the creature to the brink of madness. It *had* to feed, and it would stop at nothing to accomplish said task. Drawing closer, the monster cranked its jaws wide in anticipation, eager to taste blood and feast on raw, succulent flesh.

In the meantime, Delacroix reached for his boat, the man's fingertips coming to within centimetres of the lip of its hull. Unexpectedly, something appeared at the periphery of his vision, off to his right. Momentarily distracted by this, the object's sudden appearance worked to stall the man's previously hurried progress.

Snapping his neck around, René hovered in the water for a fleeting moment trying to decipher the other shape. His eyes widened as they trailed over a second, slightly smaller armoured hump, lined with the same distinct webbed vertebral column.

Two of them! Fucking two of them! His mind screamed. *This can't be real! This isn't happening!*

Forcing himself to look away, the Cajun grabbed for the hull of his boat-

-at the same time a searing pain lanced up his left leg! In that single horrifying moment, his limb felt like it was ablaze. No, actually it felt more like his leg had been dipped in lava! Trying to shake himself free, René screamed to the sky above as he felt the first creature's teeth puncture his skin. Muscles and ligaments were shorn in two a millisecond later, before bones were chipped and scraped amidst the chaotic and violent fracas that ultimately ensued.

Gritting his teeth, Delacroix grabbed a hold of his boat, his wet fingers curling around the lip of the vessel's slippery frame. Pulling himself up, the Cajun cried out once more as the predator bit down harder. The beast wasn't about to let go of the gushing limb locked between its cluttered collection of teeth- at least not without one hell of a fight. Blood proceeded to pour freely from the chaotic set of punctures dotting René's wounded leg. As his blood seeped into the water, the slough's olive façade around Delacroix was transformed into a macabre, shimmering, burgundy tapestry.

Still, René wasn't about to give up either.

Determined to survive, he clung to the side of the boat, his grip strong and vice-like, the veins in his tanned arms bulging. Lugging himself up the side of the boat, the drenched Cajun managed to throw both elbows over the lip of the hull, using them to anchor himself there. The pain in his leg was intense, almost as if bolts of lightning were riding up the mangled member. Tears rolled down the terrified man's plump cheeks as the creature's teeth continued to grind excruciatingly against bone.

Delacroix turned to look at the thing latched onto him. Jutting out of the water was the beast's fanged orifice, his bloodied leg, wrapped in shredded denim, secured firmly within. Just beyond the dim liquid surface, those now familiar lava-like eyes still glowed, watching emotionlessly from behind the liquescent curtain. For a moment, their eyes met. René couldn't help but feel that he was looking into the eyes of the Reaper himself.

What the hell are you? The question flashed in René's panicked mind, as the poor fellow struggled to escape the murderous fiend's rapier-toothed clutches.

Determined to feed, the scaly monstrosity flicked its clamped jaws to-and-fro with a remorseless intensity, the violent and painful action fuelled by a deadly mixture of hunger and desperation.

Looking away as he howled in pain, René prepared for what he knew must come next; that is, if he was going to survive. Somehow, he was going to have to pull his leg from the beast's jaws. That is, if he hoped to make it inside his boat and away to safety. The Cajun did his best to prepare himself; beginning by sucking in a deep breath through gritted and yellowed teeth. René knew it was going to be painful- unbearably so. Regardless, he tensed his muscles, intending to launch himself inside the boat-

-as the second monster's jaws wrapped themselves around René's right leg!

"Aaahhh!" René squealed in agony, his back arching violently as he shrieked, the veins protruding from his reddened neck.

Suspended over the ledge of the boat- his body half-in and half-out of the water- René Delacroix screamed as the two monsters played tug-of-war with him, their bloody and sadistic game threatening to tear him apart, right up the middle no less!

God have mercy!

Then, forgetting about the excruciating pain for the briefest of seconds, the struggling Cajun began to fear his little vessel might capsize as he watched its frame listing more and more. With its bowed, shell-like chassis rolling towards him, he realized then that it was his weight (combined with that of the two monsters clinging to him) which was bringing the vessel close to tipping over. Worse still, the man's heart sank a second later as his rifle fell from the boat. With that, his last hope disappeared.

Then suddenly, several things happened all at once.

The boat began to rectify itself and René felt himself falling into it. At the same time, a hideous *craaaaack!* filled the air. This was followed quickly by another similar sound. Both noises resembled the snapping of kindling, albeit magnified a thousand-fold. Still, in reality it was much worse than the mere snapping of a few twigs. Both of René's leg bones finally gave way under the immense bite pressure exerted by the two beasts dangling precariously from his struggling figure. The Cajun thought the pain before had been unbearable, now he knew how wrong he was.

Not wasting any time, the first beast- the larger of the two- veered away from the boat with a savage tug, dragging its meaty and bloodied prize with it, the ravaged limb fastened firmly between its craggy lips.

The second animal followed suit a moment later, a scarlet trail pluming away from it. Together the two hunters vanished into the liquid ether, their darkened hides merging near seamlessly with the algae-choked waters around them.

Shrieking hysterically, René Delacroix was left clutching his mutilated legs; his right limb severed above the knee, and the left below! Blood proceeded to pool around him. The scarlet liquid spewing from his body mixed with the murky swamp water that continued to seep into the boat via its cracked hull. Together they morphed into a sickening, shit-brown-coloured soup.

By this point, René was on the verge of unconsciousness. He was simply in far too much pain for his body to function or cope any longer. Darkness played at the edges of his vision; as if the spectre of Death was reaching out for him. Even so, amidst this mental fog, the Cajun reached out for the choke once more. Mustering every bit of his drastically fading strength, René yanked on the cord… and miraculously the engine kicked over.

9.

Jim McCaffrey and Lou Bonafonté were old war buddies, having served side-by-side in the first Gulf War. Since retiring from the Army, the two ex-servicemen now lived comfortably off their respective military pensions. Indeed, it was during their time in the Service that they hatched a plan to relocate to Florida City, all with the intention of living out their twilight years in the sun.

Adjusting to civilian life certainly came with its challenges though. Especially for individuals like themselves who hailed from a military background. Not long after their dream became reality, McCaffrey and Bonafonté found that whilst the sun was in abundance, there was a wealth of spare time to be had as well. This was made more difficult by the fact that family were few and far between for both men. In the end though, thankfully they had each other to rely on. As such, Jim and Lou spent practically all their time together these days, mostly fishing the maze of criss-crossing waterways that formed the Southern Glades.

In fact, at that very moment, the pair were perched on the periphery of a hardwood hammock jutting out into the Glades at the latter's northerly boundary, not far from where SGGC met the expansive section of wetland. Considering the short distance from the golf course and the traffic that barrelled down the adjoining highway, it was still a fairly peaceful spot from which to do some fishing.

Lounging in a set of cheap collapsible camping chairs, attired in cargo shorts and brightly-coloured polo-shirts, each man had his rod rigged and line already in the water. Despite the earliness of their visit to the waterway, both Lou and Jim clutched a cold beer in their respective off-hand. Fuck it, they were retired after all, they could do what they liked. In between the two men sat a flaming-red-coloured chiller which doubled as a makeshift table containing more beverages within. What's more, atop said chiller sat a tub of nightcrawlers to go at the end of their lines. By all accounts, it had the makings of quite a good day.

"Nice morning for it," Jim McCaffrey told his friend, swigging away at the can gripped firmly in his big hand.

From behind a cheap pair of corner store-bought shades, the ex-serviceman's azure eyes scanned the glimmering liquescent sheet stretched out in front of him. Once upon a time, Jim's slicked back shock of white hair had been a vibrant ginger; a strong reminder of his Irish heritage. Even though he was now in his mid-sixties, Jim McCaffrey had maintained a muscular physique; the physical legacy of years of gruelling training in the employ of Uncle Sam.

Off to Jim's left sat his long-time companion and comrade-in-arms, who did little more than grumble a reply to his pal's innocuous statement. Unlike his friend, Lou's hair had long since receded. Although it had retained its charcoal colour, Lou now had a horseshoe-shaped head of hair, which spent most of its time hidden under a fading, red trucker's cap. He was shorter than Jim, but not by much. Likewise, his soldier's body hadn't deserted him just yet either.

Somewhere off in the distance, a mechanical buzzing could be heard, disturbing the otherwise calm scene. Slowly but surely, the noise grew louder, which gave the impression that whatever it belonged to was drawing nearer. Both men had picked up on it, but neither of them paid it much attention, at least to begin with. However, as the noise grew louder, and thus harder to ignore, the pair couldn't help but prick their ears, trying to locate the source of the somewhat irritating commotion.

"Is that an airboat?" Lou asked quizzically.

"Nah," Jim replied without missing a beat, "not the right sound, and not loud enough either."

"Yeah," Lou responded. "I think you might be right."

Looking to his right, Jim sighted a black, fly-like speck suddenly detach itself from the shimmering line of the horizon, some distance down the channel. He estimated it was about half-a-klick away. With the minutes ticking by, the shape steadily increased in size, as did the pitch of its engine. All in all, this made it much harder to ignore.

"What the hell is that?" Lou leaned forward in his seat, peeking past the figure of Jim.

McCaffrey didn't answer his friend. Instead, he kept one eye trained on the growing dot, grimacing slightly as he squinted at it, trying to get a better look at the strange object.

"It's coming in fast," Lou commented before taking another swig of his beer. "Whatever it is."

"You can say that again," Jim replied as he got to his feet, still clutching his rod.

Lou joined him a moment later, rod in hand also. Together, the puzzled duo watched the spot begin to take form: it was a boat. Watching the spritely vessel intently, Jim came to a sudden realization.

"It doesn't look like anyone is piloting that thing," McCaffrey said aloud. "At least, I can't see anyone in it."

What's more, the boat was too low in the water. On either side of the small, seemingly empty vessel, frothing, full-bodied wakes churned, the roiling liquid almost spilling over into the craft itself. If not for the evident lack of passengers, Jim may have considered the vessel had been overloaded. Instead, it was more likely that the boat was taking on water, he decided.

"The old thing's struggling," Jim told his companion. "I can tell ya that much."

Suddenly the beleaguered vessel veered towards the twosome, kicking up a thick spray which caused both men to jump with fright. Seemingly out of control, and closing rapidly, its motor roared with gusto. Backing up, Jim and Lou discarded their rods quick-smart before blundering into their seats, tangling their legs amongst the chair frames, and worse still, spilling their beers.

"Shit!" the men cursed in unison as they hurriedly attempted to flee.

The boat was almost on top of them at this point, bearing down on them like a charging hippopotamus. Then unexpectedly, the craft's outboard went silent, cutting out completely. Even so, driven by sheer momentum, the boat continued to advance towards them at a swift pace, albeit slowing somewhat with each second that passed.

"C'mon!" Jim waved at his friend to follow him.

More than a little unnerved by developments and taking no chances, Jim and Lou continued to back away from the edge of the hardwood hammock, leaving behind their chiller and chairs, along with their spilt beer cans and downed rods. Neither was quite sure exactly what to expect as they hadn't spotted an occupant yet. Even for two well-travelled Army vets, it was a truly bizarre sight to behold. Despite having lost a significant amount of momentum, the boat continued at a solid pace towards them. Rather worryingly, it wasn't far off making landfall at this point.

"Back up some more!" Jim ordered as the boat came to within feet of the hardwood hammock.

Powering on virtually unperturbed, the vessel floundered to a dramatic and screeching halt, its bowed metallic chassis riding up the edge of the tropical hammock! In the end, the craft ground to a halt less than a dozen feet from the two men, colliding violently with their mangled chairs and abandoned chiller.

"The beer!" Lou cried.

"Forget the beer!" Jim scowled at his friend. "You asshole!"

They stood in stunned silence for a brief spell, gripped by uncertainty. Then slowly mustering some courage, Jim waved for Lou to follow him. Cautiously, the pair crept towards the boat. Each man craned his neck. Nervously inspecting the battered craft, they tried to get a look inside, whilst remaining at what was hopefully a safe distance. Ultimately, what the veterans found inside the vessel drained the colour from their faces.

Jim was right, the boat was- or rather *had* been- taking on water. Swamp water, dark and filthy, leaked from the boat's cracked chassis now, the liquid dribbling out onto the soil of the hammock underneath it. Even so, a decent amount of water remained within. However, the thing responsible for unsettling the two ex-servicemen was the thickset figure lounging amidst the putrescent puddle which had formed inside the craft.

Unmoving, the man lay towards the aft of the boat, his head propped up against the outboard with one hand hanging limply from the throttle. At first Jim thought the man's legs were submerged. That was until McCaffrey noted the two broken and bloodied stumps poking through the murky surface a little further down the length of the boat.

"Jesus H. Christ…" Jim breathed, putting a hand to his mouth.

There followed a few more moments of stunned silence as the men stared at the pair of ruined and bloodied limbs jutting out of the filthy water.

"I'm gonna call an ambulance," Lou spoke first.

Lou Bonafonté reached for the cell in his pocket but stopped short when his friend raised a hand, making to speak.

"I wouldn't worry about an ambulance, bud," Jim McCaffrey told him quietly. "I don't think he's going anywhere."

"What… because he's got no legs?" Lou appeared slightly puzzled.

"No, you retard!" Jim shouted with exasperation. "Because he's fucking *dead*!"

Had it not been for the police scanner application on his cell phone, Antoine Jackson probably would have known nothing about the discovery of René Delacroix's remains (at least for a while anyway). He was just over an hour into his shift when a shrill voice unexpectedly sounded through the device.

Proceeding to dole out the available information, the voice explained that an unidentified male- deceased- had been discovered with severe injuries to both legs on the water, a short distance from SGGC. Within about sixty seconds of overhearing the preliminary details, Jackson was on the phone to Doctor Scott, arranging to meet him at the scene.

A short while later, Jackson rendezvoused with Scott and his ever-faithful assistant, Tahlia. Together the trio left the highway and their vehicles behind. Venturing into the hammock on foot, they marched through the tropical undergrowth, swatting aside inconvenient stalks of vegetation and hordes of insects alike. As had happened on their previous outing, well-acquainted as he was with the topography of the local wetlands, Antoine led the way for them. Although this time, Antoine made sure to appraise them of the available information.

Peering inquisitively into the distance, Antoine could just make out a small clearing, less than fifty feet from his group's position. Drawing nearer, he noted that the hollow was filled with several figures, all but two of whom were dressed in tan-coloured slacks and collared, short-sleeved shirts.

Sheriff's deputies. Jackson felt himself tense at the sight of them.

Antoine slowed his approach, whilst signalling for his companions to do the same. He knew right off the bat that Crawford wasn't going to be happy about him gate-crashing. Closing a little further, Jackson spotted what appeared to be the metal frame of a small recreational fishing boat that had run aground, which several deputies were now crowded around. Beyond this, he caught glimpses of a liquid carpet; the slough's waters sparkling hypnotically as they captured the sunlight emanating from overhead. Then as the small group came to within a few feet of the clearing's edge, one of the deputies finally spotted the trio.

"Hold it right there!" the young man raised a hand, signalling for them to halt.

While Alex and Tahlia obediently stopped dead in their tracks, Antoine continued to approach the stick figure-thin, peach fuzz-faced lad. The game warden clearly wasn't intimidated and as such wouldn't be dissuaded from his task. On the other hand, the deputy- who was in his early to mid-twenties- clearly lacked the confidence that naturally came with experience. This was what separated him from the likes of Jackson. In the end, he didn't stand a chance.

"Florida Wildlife Commission," Antoine told the deputy calmly. "Please stand aside."

Ultimately, it only took these few words for the skinny deputy's resolve to waver. Unsure what to do, he looked at Antoine for a second, then glanced aftward, searching for some kind of support from his loitering colleagues.

"Uh… boss!" the young man called out, his tone clearly nervous.

Watching from further aback, Tahlia and Alex stayed put as a familiar face approached their companion at a hearty pace. It was Sheriff Walter Crawford. As per usual, the man didn't look pleased to see them. More so in particular however, Crawford didn't look happy about seeing Antoine.

"There's no need for you to be here, Mr. Jackson," Crawford growled at the warden. "Everything's taken care of."

"The sloughs are my jurisdiction," Antoine responded quickly, his tone measured. "It is standard protocol that my office be notified. You know that. So, tell me sheriff, why is it that my office wasn't contacted regarding this matter?"

"Because this doesn't involve any flora or fauna," Crawford smirked.

"That seems a little presumptuous," Antoine said coolly. "Have you completed your investigation already?"

"Don't mess with me, boy." Crawford edged closer to Antoine, sticking a rigid, fat finger in the warden's face. What's more, the sheriff's half-a-dozen younger cohorts began closing ranks around their superior.

"Be careful who you're calling 'boy', sheriff," Antoine said flatly, getting right in the man's moustached grill. "The last thing you want is your words getting taken out of context."

Then to his two companions' surprise, Antoine swiftly turned his back on the incensed sheriff and his gang of cronies.

"Don't worry guys," Antoine waved at Alex and Tahlia, smirking devilishly. "Case closed. Nothing to see here. Sheriff Crawford has cracked it." The sarcasm in his statement was nigh on palpable. So much so that Crawford just couldn't bring himself to let it go unchecked.

As Antoine spun back around to face Crawford, the sheriff made to grab him.

"I wouldn't do that if I were you sheriff!" Alex called out apprehensively.

"Why?" the belligerent man's bottom jaw dropped a nanosecond later.

There was Tahlia standing with her cell-phone out, using the camera function to record his angry exchange with the wildlife warden. As her big brown eyes met the lawman's small, dead grey ones, she gave him a playful wink.

"Say 'cheese'!" Tahlia snickered wickedly at him.

There was an awkward moment where the sheriff stood with his arms and hands stretched out away from his body, his fingers splayed out as if trying to grip some imaginary object. It wasn't long however before he snapped out of his trance and withdrew them.

"Bitch," the sheriff grumbled, reluctantly stepping away from Antoine and back towards his subordinates.

The last thing Walter Crawford needed was his office to become embroiled in a social-media shit-storm. He might be a prick, but he wasn't a stupid prick.

"Your cooperation is much appreciated," Jackson told Crawford with a broad and toothy smile.

"Fuck you!" Crawford snapped in a low, anxious voice, silently praying that the girl's mic wouldn't pick up his angry words.

"Sorry," Antoine replied, "you're just not my type. Thanks all the same, though."

Antoine turned to the doctor and Tahlia, proceeding to wave them over to him. Needless-to-say, it was uncomfortable as the threesome navigated their way through the host of tan shirts and glinting, gold badges. Unfortunately, Tahlia endured the worst of it as the younger men in the group subjected her to catcalls and perverted requests. Miss Mohan held her own though; she had quite a venomous tongue on her it turned out. Once they had made it through the gauntlet, the sheriff and his underlings remained at the periphery of the hollow, making sure to keep their distance from Antoine and his cohorts.

"Nothing but a good old-fashioned boating accident," Crawford called out haughtily, placing his arms across his chest as he watched the trio moved towards the battered vessel.

Ignoring the sheriff, the trio immediately converged on the metal craft, eager to see for themselves. Off to their left stood two older men, both silent and dressed in civilian clothing. The taller of the two had a thick head of white hair, whilst the shorter man wore a red cap. Antoine gave them a quick nod of acknowledgement, which they both politely reciprocated.

At least some people still have manners, Antoine thought to himself.

The game warden assumed that it had been they who discovered the body, for the simple reason that the pair would have no other reason to be there. Crawford certainly wouldn't have tolerated their presence if they were just a pair of rubberneckers, that's for sure. Antoine made a mental note to question them later.

Meanwhile, edging towards the boat, Tahlia gasped with shock when her eyes happened across the sight of Delacroix's butchered remains. Stomach rolling over inside her, the young woman turned to her mentor for comfort.

"Oh my God…" the young lady gasped.

Alex dutifully took Tahlia in his arms, pulling the onyx-haired beauty close to him. On the other hand, as a former cop, Antoine wasn't as easily unsettled as his learned friends. Instead, he went right to work, leaning over the side of the beat-up vessel.

"A boating accident!" Antione exclaimed disbelievingly, shouting in Crawford's direction. "C'mon now, sheriff!"

Immediately on the defensive, Sheriff Crawford stepped away from his gang of deputies and back towards Jackson. "That's what I said," Crawford snarled. "Isn't it?"

“So, enlighten me, what’s the scenario here?” The warden asked rhetorically, dropping to a crouched position as he went into full cop-mode. “Our friend here decided to go for a swim in alligator-infested waters, before accidentally cutting off *both* of his legs with the help of the boat’s propeller?”

Crawford halted just as he was about to say ‘Well, yeah.’ Then, failing to come up with a more adequate response, the man instead scowled hard at Antoine, venom welling in his steely gaze.

Ignoring the irate sheriff, Jackson continued to hover by Delacroix’s remains. Pulling a pen from his breast pocket, Antoine leaned in close, inspecting the corpse’s severed limbs. The warden found one leg was cut off above the knee, whilst its counterpart had been excised below the joint.

“I don’t know about you sheriff,” Jackson tapped and prodded the gory stubs one after the other, “but these breaks aren’t exactly what you’d call even. They are jagged; the bones having snapped at different points after being subjected to significant pressure. Even if our victim here had fallen in, or decided to go for a little swim, a propeller should have sheared right through these, in a similar fashion to a buzzsaw, albeit not quite as precise, admittedly.”

“The guy fell in Jackson,” Crawford bawled. “Just let it go!”

Unfortunately, the warden wasn’t about to let it go. Whether the victim fell in or not, the sheriff’s explanation didn’t address the reason for, or condition of, his severed limbs. So, while Antoine and the sheriff engaged in yet another verbal to-and-fro, Alex busied himself with comforting Tahlia.

“Are you alright?” he asked, the concern evident in his tone.

“Yeah,” she smiled, looking up at him. “I’ll be fine. It was just a bit of a shock. I know Antoine told us what to expect… but still… seeing it for yourself is… different.”

“Yeah, I understand.” Alex smiled down at her. “It had me feeling a bit queasy, too.”

“Thanks,” she said, gently pulling away from the doctor’s comforting embrace.

“I have to get some pictures,” Alex explained. “Will you be okay on your own?”

“You’re only going to be six feet away,” Tahlia laughed. “I’m sure I will survive.”

Alex blushed, his freckled cheeks turning a deep scarlet as he realized how dumb his question had been. In that moment, he felt more like a sophomore than a lecturer. Even so, it was obvious Tahlia appreciated his concern. As the academic made his way toward Antoine, the doctor couldn't help but pass by the disgruntled sheriff who was returning to his subordinates, apparently now finished arguing with the belligerent game warden.

"Sheriff?" Alex called to Crawford.

"*What?*" the agitated lawman barked back.

Alex took the man's outburst in his stride, brushing it off there and then. "Do you have an ID on the body?"

"His name is René Delacroix. A local hermit," Crawford answered pointedly. "What's it to you anyway?"

"Um..." Alex's voice trailed off as he struggled to come up with an appropriate answer.

In any event, the sheriff didn't wait around for one. The man simply spun on his heel and marched away, running a large paw over his handlebar moustache, all the while continuing to bitch and moan incomprehensively.

Although he couldn't make out most of what the sheriff said, Alex was certain Crawford called him an 'asshole' as he stormed off. Ignoring the disgruntled lawman, Alex reached inside his short's pocket and retrieved his cell. He quickly began typing a message to Hailey Benson, which simply read:

`R. Delacroix.`

Waiting for a reply, Alex craned his neck to check on Tahlia who was fiddling with her own mobile phone. Before he had a chance to ask her what she was doing, his cell chimed.

Hailey's reply read:

`What's that supposed to mean?`

Alex hadn't even been sure she would respond to him at all, let alone that quickly. He was a little shocked, actually. On balance, he had done a grade-A job of pissing off his old classmate. Yet, there was her reply, plain for him to see.

Standing there staring at his phone, Alex Scott couldn't help but think he had shot himself in the foot. From here on out, things could only go one of two ways in his estimation. Once he replied to Hailey, she would either accept what had to be done, or she'd never talk to him again. Alex dialled her number a second later.

Hailey answered on the first ring. "Yeah?"

"René Delacroix," Alex clarified. "It's the name of the first human victim."

Hailey didn't respond. Instead, Alex was met with a stony silence. In fact, for a moment, Alex thought she had hung up. That was until he heard Hailey breathing into the phone.

"C'mon, Hailey," Alex whined. "Do I really need to say it?"

"Say what?" the young woman's tone was ice-cold.

"Please, I really need your help." Alex's voice was shaky. "Don't forget, I was there for you when you needed me. Everyone turned their backs on you after Lake Minerva- *except me*. Remember?"

Alex didn't like the thought of guilting her into coming, but at this point he saw no other way. He was desperate- and human lives were at stake. Whatever Hailey came back with, he knew it wasn't going to be good. In the end, Alex was right. It most certainly wasn't good. Not even close.

Abruptly, the phone cut out and Alex was left standing there, a repetitive, high-pitched tone blaring in his ear. Feeling utterly defeated, his shoulders quickly sank. Staring at his feet, Alex felt his stomach drop. Next, he turned to walk away and miraculously his cell phone chimed to life, ringing out.

"Hailey?" Alex said looking at the caller-ID on his screen, before placing the device to his ear. "Hello?"

"You piece of shit! I can't believe you just did that," Hailey roared down the line. "You cold, manipulative fuck! You better be waiting at the airport when my flight gets in... asshole."

Abruptly, the line went dead again before Alex even had a chance to say anything.

The subsequent feeling that overcame Doctor Alex Scott was a bittersweet one. He stood there in the clearing unsure what to do next, his emotions see-sawing between relief and guilt.

10.

Struggling to sleep as a result of the argument with Alex the night before, and not to mention a slew of horrifically vivid nightmares, Hailey Benson was already wide awake in her bed when morning finally broke. In fact, she had been in and out of consciousness since around 3am, waking intermittently to find herself drenched in a cold sweat each time. Not surprisingly, it had been a long night for the lass and she was in no mood to tolerate any bullshit.

Sprawled flat on her back with her pupils dilated, the young woman wasn't doing anything other than just staring blankly at the ceiling. She'd been in this state for hours, hovering on the verge of catatonic. It was late morning by this point, the argument playing over in her mind like a spurned lover's favourite song on repeat.

Everything changed however when Alex's text messages started to come through. Hailey hadn't expected to hear from him so soon after their latest conversation over the phone. That white-hot rage Hailey had experienced the night before returned, as if on cue. Hailey felt it well up inside her chest first, before she expelled it in an angry cascade of semi-coherent profanity. Indeed, tears played at the lids of her eyes as she screamed down the phone at him for a second time, such was her emotional torment.

Later, despite struggling to rid herself of her anger, the young woman somehow managed to tear herself out of bed. Hailey Benson had finally cracked: she was going to Florida City in search of a savage killer. Like it or not.

The remainder of Hailey's morning and following afternoon was spent organizing herself for the journey to southern Florida. First, Hailey called her weekend job and told them she wouldn't be available to work her scheduled shifts for the next two weeks (which didn't go down too well with the manager, but frankly Hailey didn't care). Next, following a quick shower, the young woman started packing her things. After that, Hailey informed her parents of her plans in the middle of their lunch. Naturally worried by their daughter's sudden decision to up and leave, Hailey managed to allay their fears after explaining she had been offered a consulting job at FCU. Unsurprisingly, Hailey neglected to mention there was a possible large predator on the loose in the Everglades. By then it was starting to get on and Hailey needed to be on the road, if she intended to make her flight. Thankfully, her parents dropped Hailey at the airport, and several hours later she was cruising at thirty-seven-thousand feet.

Talk about a whirlwind ride, Benson thought to herself as she gazed out over the carpet of clouds unfolding beneath the airplane.

Touching down in Florida some hours later, Hailey felt like she'd been hit by an eighteen-wheeler. This was partly because the young woman had barely eaten anything all day. Admittedly, she snatched an apple on the way out of her parents' house, but beyond that she had eaten nothing else as she refused to touch the airline's version of food.

Hurriedly exiting the baggage claim section of the airport, Hailey strode determinedly into the swell of people, dragging her luggage behind her. Emerald eyes focused firmly ahead, she scanned for some sign of Alex Scott. Hanging loose, the woman's fiery head of hair gleamed in the artificial light, the curled strands bouncing with each animated stride. Even in only a pair of jeans, a lavender-coloured singlet top and a pair of tennis shoes the young woman was striking. Indeed, her natural beauty was augmented by her exuding air of confidence; a confidence literally earned with blood, sweat and tears. That being said, there was also a harshness there; a sternness that hadn't existed until after her experiences at Lake Minerva.

Spotting Alex's freckled cheeks and wavy brown hair amidst the multitude of faces, Hailey instantly zeroed in on him, a fierce intent proceeding to manifest in her glistening eyes. Alex seemingly hadn't noticed her yet.

Good, Hailey thought.

Benson noted that to her friend's right stood a tall and handsome African-American man with a shaved head in a pale tan-coloured uniform. Whereas to his left was a petite, exotic-looking female with round, enthralling hazel eyes. Locking onto the young woman, Hailey was hit with a strange feeling, almost like déjà vu, but not quite. There was something about the young woman that seemed familiar, however equivocal the feeling may have been.

Who is she? Do I even know her? Hailey wondered, unsuccessfully trying to place the girl from memory. *Or is it just my mind playing tricks on me?*

Edging nearer, Alex finally picked his friend out of the crowd. The doctor's eyes twinkled as a warm smile spread across his boyish and deceptively innocent features.

"Hailey!" he called out excitedly to her.

The sudden cry snapped Hailey out of her daydream, drawing her lingering gaze away from the mesmerising, caramel-skinned beauty, and back in the direction of her old classmate. Hailey unexpectedly found herself fighting back the urge to smile as she came face-to-face with her friend. Hailey had actually forgotten how attractive Alex was.

Refocusing herself, the young woman stiffened as she approached him, trying not to let his youthful good looks weaken her resolve.

Before the young woman knew it, she was chest to chest with the man who had harangued her into coming to Florida. Never in a million years did Hailey think that her reunion with Alex would be overshadowed with such deep-seated feelings of animosity (at least on her part). Noting Hailey's serious demeanour, Alex's smile quickly faded. He wasn't getting out of this one unscathed it seemed. As such, he quickly braced himself.

"Let's get one thing straight, shall we?" Hailey's gleaming jade eyes bored into Alex's. "That shit you pulled- all the guilt tripping- was total bullshit!"

"Hai-"

"Don't *dare* speak over me!" A cold anger flashed across Hailey's smooth features, her voice slightly shaky.

Nothing was going to deter her from giving Alex a piece of her mind. Indeed, she had spent the entire flight planning just exactly what she was going to say to him.

"What you did was wrong! So, don't you think for one second that everything is good between us. For some reason you've got it in your head that I am the solution to this problem. Well, I'm not! But I'm here now, regardless of that fact!"

Antoine and Tahlia, along with several others inside the airport, looked on dumbstruck as Hailey verbally destroyed her old friend. A mixture of nervous embarrassment and pure nosiness stopped them from interrupting Hailey's heated diatribe. After all, it made for good viewing.

"You are on thin fucking ice, my friend!" Hailey barked. "*Thin fucking ice!*"

Alex stood stock-still, his lips seemingly sewn shut and the colour all but gone from his handsome face. Antoine looked on with a smirk, utterly enraptured with Hailey Benson. She was one tough cookie it seemed. Tahlia on the other hand was much like her mentor: in total shock, and even a little frightened if she was honest about it.

Hailey's demeanour quickly changed as she remembered the other two people standing there waiting on her. Blushing, she turned to face them.

"Nice to meet you," Hailey extended her hand to Antoine Jackson. "Doctor Hailey Benson. Please forgive me."

"The pleasure is all mine," the game warden laughed with a warm smile. "Antoine Jackson. Florida Wildlife Commission."

Tahlia's introduction was a little more sheepish as she took Hailey's proffered hand. "Tahlia... Tahlia Mohan," she stammered shyly.

"What do you say we get something to eat?" Hailey smiled warmly, her gaze shifting between the three of them. "Alex's shout."

Not long after leaving the airport, the foursome found a quiet restaurant about a five-minute jaunt from Hailey's motel. Famished and running on fumes, Hailey failed to take note of the restaurant's name as she and her companions entered. Exhausted after her frenetic day, the young woman was struggling to function on the most basic of levels, never mind pay attention to such trivial things. Still, upon entering the eatery, Hailey couldn't help but be taken aback by the eclectic décor inside. Her friends responded in much the same way. It was nothing short of an assault on the senses. In addition to brightly-lit neon signs, the walls of the restaurant were covered in memorabilia from all over the world, made up mostly of license plates and street signs, albeit peppered with the odd taxidermist's project and autographed picture of a long-dead celebrity. It was tacky, but it would do.

Recovering from the sensory overload, they found a quiet, semi-circular booth nestled into a corner of the restaurant. Squeezing themselves in, the quartet got down to ordering almost right away. Hailey, it seemed, wasn't the only one who was dying from starvation. Perusing the menu, they made the usual chit-chat which one might expect, working to settle themselves in before moving onto more serious matters.

"Alright," Hailey spoke up as their waitress left to pass their orders to the chef, "let's get down to business."

From across the table, Tahlia watched Hailey somewhat nervously, which the latter hadn't failed to notice. Hailey was used to it though, for the most part. Not so much these days, but certainly in the weeks and months after Lake Minerva; it was something she had encountered more than she would have liked. Doctor Benson had grown used to being recognized as 'that woman who fought the shark in the lake'. So, when Tahlia proceeded to shoot sideways glances at her, Hailey paid it next to no mind (as irritating as she found the behaviour).

"Are we still working under the assumption that our predator is a Bull shark?" Hailey enquired of her companions.

"That's correct," Antoine replied, taking on the role of spokesperson for the group.

"And still only the one human victim?" Benson sought further clarification.

"Yes," the game warden told her. "As far as we are aware, there has only been one human fatality."

"Well, that's something I suppose." Hailey grimaced inwardly at her morbid reasoning.

Interrupting momentarily, the smiling waitress returned with their drinks, hushing the conversation.

"Based on the locations of all three kills," Hailey started again as the waitress left them once more, "I have identified an area of the wetlands that I believe our predator frequents. I would like to visit this area first thing tomorrow and perform several sweeps of it. Who knows, we might get lucky."

"What do you think, warden?" Alex spoke up for the first time in a while. He seemed to be slowly regaining some of his confidence after his very public tongue-lashing. "Up for a little expedition?"

"Fine by me," Antoine shrugged.

"Excuse me," Tahlia suddenly got to her feet and stepped away from the booth. "I have to use the little girl's room."

The others watched as Miss Mohan slipped out of the curved booth. Hailey in particular kept an inquisitive eye on the girl. She was still trying to figure out if she knew her from somewhere else. A faint, nagging feeling in the back of her mind told Hailey she did. Even so, she still came up blank. Watching the girl disappear deeper into the restaurant, Hailey decided she would ask Alex about his student later when she got a chance.

Meanwhile, Tahlia made sure to take her handbag with her, leaving the others behind to continue making their plans for the following day. She quickly found the female restroom at the opposite end of the quirky little restaurant.

Sliding inside one of the graffiti-littered cubicles, Tahlia closed the toilet seat over beneath her. In truth, she had absolutely no intention of using the toilet itself. Next, she hurriedly pulled her cell phone from her handbag. Hands shaking, her fingers danced over the touchscreen as Tahlia urgently composed a message:

`Hailey Benson is HERE in F.C.!`

Phone clutched in one hand, Tahlia waited for a response. If she didn't get one within the next few minutes she would have to return to her companions, lest they get suspicious. Struggling to occupy herself, Tahlia began chewing at the nails belonging to the fingers on her free hand. Unable to keep her nerves in check, the student's legs bounced up and down like a tweeker awaiting their next hit. For a moment, it felt like her entire body was vibrating.

"C'mon, c'mon!" Tahlia breathed impatiently, staring at the little screen, begging it to light up.

Tahlia almost jumped out of her skin when the reply finally came through a second later. Squeaking with excitement she scanned the message:

```
We are on our way.
Be ready and keep an eye on her.
```

THURSDAY

11.

Trina Michaels was a brat… among other things. Thirteen years old and spoiled rotten, her parents, John and Barbara, were almost incapable of disciplining the belligerent little shit. This situation was made worse by the fact that they had no issue penalizing her older brother Tommy for the slightest of infractions; which resulted in a serious amount of friction between the two siblings. Needless to say, and not surprisingly in stark contrast to her brother, Trina wasn't used to hearing the word 'no' a lot. Still, once in a blue moon it did happen.

In this instance, everything came to a head after John Michaels informed his family he was taking them to the Everglades for their yearly vacation. Of course, Trina wasn't impressed at this news ('Florida was for old people and children!'). Disappointed with her father's choice of destination, young Trina made it known she wanted to go to Los Angeles instead. The teenager was even less impressed when- after throwing the typical adolescent bitch-fit- her father didn't cave in to her demands. In rather uncharacteristic fashion, John even went as far as to confiscate the girl's iPhone, something which he hadn't done in years. Well, not totally. He gave it back to her in the evenings after the family had completed their scheduled outing for that day.

On that note, today's outing was a sight-seeing trip to the Southern Glades on an airboat. Tomorrow they were pencilled-in to go to an alligator farm. Trina couldn't decide which of these she hated more. So, as fate would have it, there she was hitching a ride on an airboat down the middle of a swamp.

This is such basic bullshit. The girl scowled inwardly.

Despite its size, the wide-bodied craft deftly skirted the undulating length of the meandering slough. Flanked on either side, the waterway was enclosed by densely-knitted tracts of sawgrass. Broad and flat, the waters of the channel were otherwise undisturbed, save for the rippling wake generated by the hulking vessel proceeding down it.

Seated on a bench-style seat toward the aft of the airboat, just in front of the vessel's skipper, and the massive vertical rotor blade assembly that powered it, Trina gazed into oblivion, totally uninterested with life in general. On the other hand, Trina's parents along with sixteen-year-old Tommy sat to the fore of the vessel, clearly much more interested in the Floridian wildlife and landscape than Trina could ever be.

Losers. Trina chided them silently.

Unlike Trina, Tommy was in his element- the boy loved animals and nature. So much so in fact, that it was the lad's ambition in life to become a conservationist. Indeed, he even had his eyes set on an Ivy League college. As for Trina, not so much.

Brushing silky, dirty-blonde strands out of her vision, Trina reorientated her line-of-sight, staring daggers at her preoccupied family. The rake-thin blonde looked as if she was trying to bore holes into their backs with the small, azure spheres flanking her thin pointed nose.

"Look another one!" her father shouted animatedly, pointing off to port and into the channel with one of his short, flabby arms.

An ad executive from New York City, John Michaels was a balding, tubby fellow with big goggle-like glasses at the end of a tiny, button nose. He looked like such a tourist in his brightly-coloured Hawaiian-style shirt, cargo shorts and sandals, at least Trina thought so anyway.

"I think I see it!" Trina's mother bawled as she put a hand to her brow, shielding her eyes from the sun's vibrant rays.

Barbara Michaels was an older, more wrinkled version of her daughter. A warning of things to come, perhaps. Slim and blonde, she was also possessed of a cringe-worthy artificial tan. Indeed, the latter was on full display for all to see in her black strapless top and pair of tiny, butt-hugging, white shorts that failed to conceal her veiny thighs.

"Amazing!" John cried with obvious excitement.

John Michaels had hired the airboat exclusively for his family, complete with a personal tour guide for the entire day. Their guide, Larry Krasinski, an overly tall and muscular type, promised them alligators galore. Yet, things hadn't quite gone that way thus far, despite the Michaels family (except for Trina, that is) thinking otherwise. Larry didn't have the heart to tell them they hadn't actually sighted an alligator yet. Rather, the family were pointing at sticks and larger pieces of floating driftwood bobbing along on the current. In all, Larry and the rest of the Michaels posse had been on the water for almost two hours now, and for some reason the usual plethora of wildlife was unnaturally few and far between. Needless to say, it wasn't a good sign.

"Is that an alligator?" Tommy asked, wrinkling up his face and pointing directly ahead of them at a second object.

Probably another stick, dipshit, Trina thought venomously to herself, hearing her brother's excited question.

Tommy was a gawky teenager. Like his father, the lad was short and rotund. Although, he didn't have the same thick-framed spectacles or lack of hair. Instead, his hair was a knot of sheening black strands like his father's used to be, once upon a time. Still focused on the unidentified profile hovering in the water, Tommy leaned forward in an attempt to get a better look at the object, his ass leaving the seat and coming to all but fill Trina's view.

"Ew!" she whined loudly.

The teenager had to fight back the urge to plant her foot between his massive cheeks.

"Sit down!" Trina snapped angrily. "You fat shit!"

"Language!" John Michaels yelped at her.

"Please don't talk to your brother like that, sweetie!" Barb scowled at her daughter before making sure to tack a smile on at the end. "You know he has glandular problems."

When her parents were no longer looking, Tommy flipped Trina off with a sneer.

"Hey!" Trina screeched, trying to kick him.

John Michaels' blubbery, Walrus-like frame pivoted unnaturally fast in his seat, managing to catch Tommy flashing his sister the rude gesture. He wasted no time in whacking his son over the side of the head.

"Ow!" Tommy clutched a handful of his lush black hair.

"Be nice to your sister!" his father ordered, narrowing his eyes ruefully.

"She started it!" Tommy protested, waving his arms at the girl.

Trina sneered triumphantly at her sibling. Unable to do anything else in response, he mouthed the word 'bitch' to her and turned away. As Tommy returned to his seat, a gap appeared between him and his father, giving Trina a view of the object Tommy had pointed out. Narrowing her eyes to slits, Trina tried to focus in on it. All she could make out was a dark, motionless hump, seemingly floating about thirty meters up ahead, surrounded by glimmering, jade-coloured water.

"Hey boat-dude!" Trina shouted over the noise of the spinning rotors as she turned to face Larry. "Is that an alligator?" Trina pointed past her family at the fore of the airboat, toward the mysterious shape beyond.

Larry instinctively cut the engine, wary that the noise might scare the animal off, if indeed it was a gator. Next, the robustly-built guide grabbed a pair of bulky, black binoculars tucked down the side of his 'captain's seat'. The big chair was perched a little higher than the other bench-seats lining the craft, giving him a better view of the channel ahead.

Krasinski zoomed in on the shadowy profile, expecting to see the rugged, knotted hide of an alligator. Yet, peering into the binocular's twin lenses, what Larry found instead was something totally alien to his icy-blue eyes. Krasinski had been hosting these kind of tours for almost ten years now. He must have covered the Everglades a hundred times over, top to bottom, east to west. All that experience hadn't prepared him for the unusual sight now before him.

Blurry at first, the sinister object quickly grew clearer. Like a gator, albeit only running down either flank, its hide was ridged and rock-like in appearance. However, the similarities stopped there. Right through the centre, a line of quill-like spines ran the length of its ugly back; the jagged procession connected via a thin, pinkish-red and semi-transparent membrane.

Larry only saw it for a few seconds before the thing disappeared under the surface, its swift departure shattering the slough's tranquil façade. A foaming spout went up as the creature arched its spiny back and proceeded to dive deep. Curling its great length over, the last sign of the animal was its paddle-shaped tailfin; the appendage also ringed with needle-like vertebrae; smaller versions of those skirting its back.

"What the hell?" Larry breathed with some shock.

"What is it?" Trina queried, suddenly interested in developments.

"I'm not sure, sweetheart," Larry admitted apprehensively.

Larry couldn't be sure how much of the unidentified creature he had actually sighted.

Six feet? Eight feet? More?

Focused ahead, neither Larry Krasinski nor the Michaels family spotted the two smaller spectral profiles closing on them from the rear. Moving on a diagonal, the slender silhouettes scythed through the still water like a pair of torpedoes after an enemy ship.

12.

Monotonous and unrelenting, the pair of outboard motors reverberated noisily. One in front of the other, the two aluminium-hulled dinghies, complete with FWC logos stencilled along their corrugated sides, raced down the winding channel.

At the helm of the lead vessel was the resolute figure of Antoine Jackson, attired in his trademark skip cap and a heavy-duty pair of dark green dungarees. Not far away, and similarly-dressed, the fire-haired Doctor Benson rode shotgun, the woman's glossy hair floating on the breeze. Trailing some distance behind them, Doctor Scott and Tahlia Mohan were doing their best to keep up, both decked out in the same physique-flattering apparel as their companions.

Nervous and alert, Hailey sat near the centre of the small boat she shared with the handsome, dark-skinned game warden. Somewhat on edge, the biologist scanned her surroundings warily, watching the stretching sections of sawgrass, punctuated by the occasional hardwood hammock, dart past before disappearing into oblivion, only for another to suddenly appear and repeat the cycle all over again. It felt a little strange being back in the field- not to mention out on the water. After all, it wasn't like Hailey's life was that exciting anymore. Not since Lake Minerva anyway. Other than exercise and her weekend job, she didn't really have much going on. She had no social life that's for sure. No boyfriend to keep her warm at night. Nothing. It was kind of sad, really. In fact, just thinking about it made her depressed.

If the young woman was honest with herself, she was actually a little excited about being out on the water. Indeed, in terms of her overall mood, Hailey felt much clearer than she had the day before. It was amazing what a good night's sleep could do for a person. After rising early, she had expected to feel somewhat sluggish, but soon found that this was not the case. Perhaps it was the adrenaline coursing through her body that had the young woman feeling bright-eyed and bushy-tailed. Then again, maybe it was the fact that she had a purpose once more. That is, a purpose beyond simply making it from one day to the next.

Gazing out over the shimmering landscape before her, Hailey's thoughts periodically wandered back to her confrontation with Alex at the airport. She found herself see-sawing between two distinct emotions: guilt and anger. The doctor's guilt stemmed from having chided Alex so vehemently, and in such a public manner. Whereas her anger resulted from what he had done to get her to Florida. No matter how much the young doctor might have wanted to, she was struggling to forgive him for his actions (however well-intended they may have been). Of course, Alex claimed that his actions were in the interests of saving peoples' lives. Still, Hailey couldn't help but feel there was something more to it. Something a little more selfish. She remembered full-well during their time at university he was ambitious.

Twisting slightly, Hailey peered over her shoulder, looking back at the second boat skimming along the water's surface behind them. She could just make out Alex crouched by the motorboard, gripping the throttle.

Asshole. Hailey felt a knot tighten in her chest. *But a handsome asshole, nonetheless.*

Shifting her gaze away from Alex, the biologist was instantly taken aback when she spotted a blurry, pallid, elongated object bobbing gently in the water off to starboard. With that, the sudden burst of excitement she experienced quickly ushered away the lingering spectre of Hailey's previous ponderings.

"Jackson!" Hailey twisted her body to face the warden. "Over there!" she pointed across the slough. "Do you see that?"

"I see it!" Antoine nodded after taking a moment to follow her finger.

The big warden quickly proceeded to signal their companions to follow, waving his arms animatedly at them as he tried to grab their attention.

"Over here!" Jackson shouted, his voice full of bass.

Drawing nearer to the swollen, ashen-coloured outline, Antoine eased up on the throttle, slowing the silver-bodied vessel to a mere crawl. Whatever the thing was, it was big and long; each end tapering to a point; the two sections connected via a thick trunk, off of which four short, roughly L-shaped appendages sprouted. By his estimation, the creature was close to ten-feet in length. It immediately became evident to both of them that the figure was upside-down.

"Holy shit!" Hailey cursed as their dinghy pulled up alongside it.

The overturned shape had been sawn almost in half, its trunk held together by little more than a tendril of flesh. Off-white, with hints of yellow, the thing's belly had clearly been gored. The subsequent wound was roughly hemispherical in shape, the edges of it ragged. Wide-eyed, Hailey noted a pattern of squared scales ran the length of what was left of its distended torso. Zeroing in on the wedge-shaped jaws, lined as they were with small conical teeth, Hailey's first thought was: *alligator*. Inspecting it a little closer, the biologist realized the jaws were in fact too narrow for this to be the case. It wasn't an alligator, but it was definitely some species of crocodilian.

Another introduced species perhaps? Hailey wondered to herself.

Wasting no time, Benson stretched out an arm and grabbed a hold of the scaled cadaver, much to her companion's surprise. Heaving loudly, the biologist tried to roll the animal over in the water, but soon found it was a little too heavy for her to manage alone, at least without risking falling out of the boat.

"A little help?" Hailey asked Antoine in a shrill voice as she dangled precariously over the side.

"Sorry!" Jackson apologized before rushing to aid the young woman.

Together they rolled the reptile over, revealing its mottled and ancient-looking, dark green-coloured hide. In silence, the pair looked over its armoured corpus, their brains processing the more intimate details of the gruesome sight before them. Hailey began mentally comparing the wound to those inflicted on the poor animals in Alex's pictures.

Then, racing up from behind, Alex and Tahlia's boat peeled in on a wide angle, coming to a halt on the other side of the reptile's decomposing remains. Both Alex and Tahlia let out cries of astonishment as they manoeuvred their vessel into position. Sandwiched in between the two vessels, the respective crews looked over the bloated carcass. Neither of them said very much.

In addition to the gruesome spectacle, a faint smell wafted off the corpse, almost like rotten eggs. Furthermore, there didn't appear to be much blood left inside the pale form. This was evident from the flesh around the edges of the curved injury which had turned bone-white, as well as the shredded, noodle-like organs and stringy tendons that accompanied it. Upon looking closer, Hailey found that the edges of the abused tissue had a fuzzy appearance to them. This, coupled with the growing smell, clearly meant that the tissue was in the early stages of putrefaction. The animal had been here for a while it seemed.

Hailey was a little shocked when she heard Tahlia speak up before either Antoine or Alex- or herself for that matter. In the biologist's experience, it was quite out of character for Tahlia to be so forthcoming. After all, the girl had been especially quiet around Hailey.

"*Crocodylus niloticus*," Tahlia said aloud and not necessarily to anyone in particular. "It's a Nile crocodile! Look at the markings! It's gotta be! Right, doc?"

Directly across from Hailey, on the other boat, Doctor Alex Scott smiled at his student, obviously impressed with her astute observation.

"A Nile crocodile?" Hailey gasped. "In the Everglades? Really?"

“Nile crocodiles have been resident in the Everglades since at least 2009,” Alex explained. “Although, so far only three specimens have been positively identified as such.”

“I guess this makes four,” Antoine Jackson added. “Looks like a younger specimen, too. Adults are much larger, if I’m not mistaken.”

“That’s right,” Alex agreed, chewing his bottom lip nervously.

The aroma, rather than the sight itself, was starting to make Hailey feel slightly queasy. Turning her back on the putrefying reptile and her companions, the doctor gasped with shock at the sight awaiting her.

Three pairs of watery, sheening, onyx eyes watched Hailey and her companions from across the channel. They belonged to a looming, silhouetted trio who were staring intently at them from behind a semi-transparent partition of swaying reeds. Two of the silent, hairy figures were in the region of six feet tall. Standing slightly apart from them, and off to Hailey’s left, was a smaller one about half this size.

A baby, Hailey silently realized. *A cub*.

The group was a family of bears; a mother, a father and their child. They were Florida black bears; a distinct subspecies of the American black bear. They had most likely been attracted to the area by the smell of the rotting croc, Hailey surmised.

Wide in the shoulders, not to mention the remainder of their bodies, the family of bears were husky and impressive specimens. Indeed, standing upright as they were, they looked a lot like Rottweilers on two legs, albeit much shaggier. Even the smallest one was a hulking brute and close to one-hundred-and-fifty pounds in her impromptu estimation. As for the parents, they were closer to three-hundred pounds. Together, their ears, rounded at the tops, stood erect as they listened intently to the world around them. One of the larger bears was slightly closer to the water’s edge than the others. Hailey wasn’t sure if it was the mother or the father as she couldn’t make out any sex organs. She noted that the top of its left ear had been sliced in two, no doubt a token from some previous battle.

“Whoa!” Hailey heard Tahlia exclaim from the other boat.

Soon Alex and Antoine became aware of the bears’ presence as well, squeaking out similar cries of astonishment. As one, the foursome watched the furry interlopers. Or was it the other way around? In either event, for their part the brawny titans simply watched the humans right back.

“What do we do?” Hailey asked, the smallest suggestion of concern in her voice.

“Don’t make any sudden movements,” Antoine warned, his body going rigid.

"If we start the engines, will that spook them?" Tahlia asked worriedly, eager to just flee.

"Maybe," Antoine replied, his voice low.

"You brought your rifle along didn't you, Jackson?" Hailey asked nervously, shooting him a sideways glance.

"Rifle on deck," Antoine reassuringly tapped the long, black rifle case at his feet with his boot.

A sudden *bang!* sounded somewhere off in the distance, causing them all to jump, whilst simultaneously redirecting everyone's attention, bears and humans alike. The sharp noise echoed down the slough, seemingly carried along the top of the water itself. Startled, the bear closest to Hailey and the others snapped its head in the direction of the commotion. Sniffing the air with its blunt snout, the massive animal stared down the length of the channel as if waiting for something to happen.

"What was that?" Hailey asked. "A gunshot?"

"I'm not sure," Jackson answered.

"We should check it out," Alex spoke up.

"He's right," Hailey added softly.

Glancing back in the direction of the furry behemoths, Hailey noted that all three of them had turned their heads now to look further up the slough. Alert and intrigued, the bears searched for some sign of the cause of the tumult, no longer interested in Hailey or her group.

Whatever the source of it was, it didn't appear to be forthcoming. Hailey wasn't sure if that was a good thing. Apprehensive, the young woman could feel the butterflies forming in her stomach.

"Let's go," Antoine said as he cranked the choke, starting the engine to his and Hailey's boat.

13.

Some minutes before…

"Where'd it go?" Barbara Michaels asked her husband, jerking upright as she scooted her skinny frame out of the bench-seat she shared with him.

Pushing his glasses back along the short bridge of his nose, John said nothing as he followed his wife half-a-second later. Somewhat intrigued by events, Trina got gingerly to her feet as well. Even the giant figure of Larry Krasinski was up and about. The big man moved curiously towards the fore of the craft. Stopping by Trina's side, the girl noted the hard grimace etched into Larry's worn and scruffy features. Tommy however, still smarting from his smack over the head, chose to stay seated, pouting away to himself.

"It's gone," John Michaels blurted out as he perused the now calm portion of water. "Vanished." Like a ghost.

"It'll come back," Tommy mumbled rather unhappily (and pretty much to himself).

An eerie and uncomfortable quiet descended upon the scene then. Not even the usual background noise made up of calls from the local bird population, or the myriad insect species that called the Glades home, were to be heard. What's more, the area had grown ever so still- there was simply no breeze anymore. It was almost as if Larry and the Michaels family had entered some kind of void. A dead zone.

"Something's not right," Larry whispered, a little louder than he initially intended.

All of the Michaels family heard his comment, the group turning in unison to look at him as he edged back towards the stern. The fear was evident in their wary, almost pleading stares. Larry knew he shouldn't have said anything, but he couldn't help it. Indeed, if Larry was honest with himself, he was just as frightened as they were. Then, barely a second later, the world around Larry and his companions descended into total chaos.

Out of nowhere, something- or *things*- battered unforgivingly into the boat's stern, causing the vessel to pitch frighteningly in the water! The noise that accompanied the bone-jarring collision was thunderous; like a wrecking ball smashing against reinforced concrete. Indeed, the horrendous sound reverberated for miles up and down the length of the meandering slough. The force of the impact was such that it caused the boat to lift ass-up out of the water, whilst forcing its prow to dip below the surface! As a result, the vessel began to take on water. At the same time, everyone- save for Tommy, who was still seated- was thrown clear from the beleaguered airboat.

One after the other, their flailing bodies crashed clumsily into the green water below, sending up shimmering fountain-like geysers as they landed unceremoniously. Each spout was near-hypnotic in its beauty, the crystalline droplets scattering in helter-skelter fashion to the wind; a sight reminiscent of glimmering shards of glass breaking away from the frame of a shattered window.

Still inside the teetering, semi-airborne vessel, Tommy tumbled from his seat. Rolling about the belly of the craft, water crashing over him, the terrified teenager threw out an arm, his hand desperately clawing for some kind of purchase. Grabbing a hold of the rim of his former seat, Tommy managed to keep himself inside the airboat- but only just. With that, gravity kicked in a split-second later and the rear of the boat came plummeting back down. Subsequently, the vessel landed with a harsh *craaack!* as its belly slapped hard against the surface of the slough.

Flat on his back now, the chubby teenager panted heavily, his mind playing catch-up. Flustered, Tommy lay there for several seconds, gathering himself... until he heard the high-pitched screams and panicked shouts of his loved ones.

"I've got a bad feeling about this," Hailey shouted over the near-deafening noise of the outboard motor positioned to her rear.

Antoine Jackson didn't respond. Rather his stony demeanour said all the young doctor needed to know. It was obvious that the warden was just as concerned as the marine biologist. In fact, Hailey's words seemed to stoke a fire somewhere deep within the brooding man. Cranking the throttle, Antoine gunned the engine, pushing the machine to its limit.

Hailey's stomach clenched as the small vessel jerked forward a split-second later, her heartrate fluttering in unison with it. Picking up some serious speed, the boat's thin chassis proceeded to tremble under the strain, the rhythm penetrating her body. Unblinking, the young woman watched the line of the horizon, both uncertain about and terrified of whatever it was that lay ahead.

Falling face-first into the water, John Michaels' tubby frame sank like a brick, at first. Then, kicking and thrashing like he was caught in the throes of an epileptic fit, John scrambled for the surface as his survival instincts kicked in. Eyes clamped shut like a frightened child, John had no idea how far off the surface was. Still, he powered on, fighting through the darkness, his heart thumping furiously inside his body.

Letting out a desperate gasp, the terrified man broke the surface a moment later, thankful for the rush of much-needed oxygen that filled his sore, cigarette-ravaged lungs. Yet, the sense of relief he felt proved fleeting. Water cascading off him, John snapped his beady eyes open only to be greeted by a most unholy sight.

The New Yorker froze with fear, paralyzed by the unexpected view of the fang-ridden maw that awaited him. Closing on its prey, the primeval nightmare emerged almost seamlessly from the liquid arras, the emerald-coloured water appearing to recede from its dark and scaly armoured corpus. John had a front-row seat as the hulking abomination all but blocked out the view of the airboat behind it. He instantly realized there was no getting past this thing, positioned as it was between his family and their wayward vessel. As the beast's jaws wound open, revealing a ribbed, purple-pink gullet beyond, slick with myriad viscid fluids, John Michaels simply bobbed in the water waiting for his end to come.

Eager to feed, the beast wasted no time. Like some kind of missile, the ruby-eyed monster bowled into its prey, the gruesome thing's broad orifice engulfing the man's upper body in an effusion of blood; the red liquid spewing forth, thick and treacle-like. Next, with its helpless quarry held in a bear trap-like grip, the creature slid swiftly beneath the surface in an eruption of froth and foam, disappearing from view amidst the jade-tinted waterscape.

Only a short distance away- less than a dozen feet, in fact- Barbara Michaels' whole body shook with fear as she floated there in the middle of the slough. Tears, mingled with mascara, streaked down her colourless, weathered face. Snivelling to herself, the horrified woman tried to comprehend what she had just witnessed. It was like some dweller of the Underworld had risen to snatch her husband, only for it to disappear a moment later as the fiend dragged him back to Hell with it.

Suddenly, there came a loud voice from somewhere to her rear. "Mom!"

Her son's cry managed to re-focus Barbara's attention. Zeroing in on Tommy's voice, Barbara steeled herself, making to push off in his direction. Struggling to make her limbs cooperate, the shaken woman clumsily shifted her weight in the water. Reorientating herself, Barbara angled her body to find Tommy, soaked and looking somewhat dishevelled. He was screaming at her from the safety of the beat-up airboat. For some reason, the vessel appeared to be floating away from the woman. Barbara assumed its creeping retreat was simply the result of the momentum generated by the collision before, since its engine had not yet been re-engaged.

"Mom! Over here!" Tommy waved her on, leaning precariously over the prow of the boat. "Come on!"

"Tommy!" Barbara shrieked, starting towards him, her arms slicing determinedly into the lime-tinted water.

Fixated on her son and the airboat, Barbara only spotted the menacing, serpentine shadow wending its way towards her when it was already too late. Distorted by the rippling surface, the monster's ethereal profile was made all the more terrifying. Mere feet from the airboat- and her son's waiting arms- Barbara cut short her advance mid-stroke. She recoiled in terror as her eyes finally locked onto the sinuous, submerged shape thrusting towards her. At somewhere in the region of seven-feet-long, the sight of the ominous, serpentine silhouette sent an ice-cold shiver down her spine.

"Mom!" she heard her son cry out once more. "What are you doing?" Tommy, it seemed, hadn't spotted the oncoming horror stalking towards his helpless mother.

Panicking, Barbara kicked out hard with both feet. Next, the woman spun in-place as she tried to dodge the encroaching fiend. Unfortunately for her it didn't work. The sabre-toothed monstrosity powered on. Swift and cat-like, it deftly evaded the majority of the screeching woman's blows, and even wore those few, petty strikes Barbara did manage to land, treating them as if they were nothing.

Closing to within inches of the shrieking female, the beast tensed its snaking length before letting loose with a powerful snap of its blade-enshrouded caudal fin. The creature smashed into Barbara's abdomen, the brutal collision driving the air from her lungs! Jaws splayed wide, the horror's blade-like fangs sunk into the helpless woman's flesh, instantly drawing a stream of coppery-scented blood. Surging forward, the scaled fiend burrowed deep into Barbara's belly, feverishly tearing free sections of flesh and viscera. Lost in its bloodthirsty frenzy, the monster kept tunnelling right up until its rounded snout hit Barbara's spinal column. Only then did it stop.

For her part, Trina managed to catch only fleeting glimpses of the savage creature thrashing about wildly as it eviscerated her fleeing mother (Trina was fully aware that the woman she called 'mom' had forgotten her, leaving the teenager to her fate, in order to save herself). Rather, the girl's focus was drawn to Barbara's face, and the expression of sheer terror etched across its ghostly, ashen façade. The worst part of it all was the moment when their eyes met. Shocked to her core, Trina watched helplessly as blood- copious and scarlet- spilled over her mother's Botox-augmented lips, the end result similar to ocean waves crashing against sandbags. In the end, Trina witnessed the light go out in her mother's eyes, all before the woman's now limp body was seemingly swallowed up by the emerald waters around her.

"Faster!" Tahlia yelled as she looked back in Doctor Scott's direction, eyeing him intently.

"I'm trying!" Alex responded heatedly, the academic more than a little exasperated with the young woman's version of encouragement.

Antoine on the other hand was proving to be much more adept in his boating skills than the struggling herpetologist. So much so, that Alex and Tahlia were trailing behind Hailey and Jackson by approximately a hundred metres. Still, Alex wasn't about to give up. Gripping the throttle, he gunned the engine, fighting against the vibrations that rode up his tensed arm the whole time.

Shaking with each laboured breath, Trina wept as she fought to stay in control. This proved difficult as images of her mother's death replayed in her mind's eye; the subsequent psychical assault threatening to undo the girl's fragile state of mind completely. Yet somehow, she held on. Fighting through the terror of it all, Trina looked about herself, trying to work out a way of escaping the madness unfolding around her.

It was at this point the teenager realized she couldn't locate her father. Although, she could see her brother's plump, bushy-haired outline. He was just up ahead in the airboat, floating not far from where their mother had been killed. Trina thought Tommy may have been calling to her, but she couldn't be sure. A mist-like haze played at the edges of her vision, making it difficult to focus, and her ears felt like they had been stuffed with cotton wool. The teenager didn't realize it herself, but she was going into shock.

"*Daaaaaaad!*" Trina bawled, the word sounding muffled.

All of a sudden, something popped inside her skull, as if a pressure had been released. This sensation was followed by a sharp, high-pitched whine sounding in her ears. It took Trina a moment to realize her hearing had returned.

"We have to try for the boat!" came a man's voice, deep and commanding, from somewhere close behind her.

Surprised, Trina twisted nervously, expecting- or perhaps more so *hoping*- to see her father there. However, the unidentified male wasn't John Michaels. Instead, Trina came face to face with the dripping wet figure of Larry Krasinski. Still, despite the fact that it clearly wasn't her father, a wave of relief quickly overcame the girl. The fact that she wasn't alone in the water brought her a small measure of comfort, and not to mention hope.

"C'mon!" Larry tried to grab the girl. "Make for the boat! It's not that far!"

Unfortunately, Larry's attempt to take hold of Trina and guide her to safety was cut unexpectedly short. Out of nowhere, a row of webbed spines, riding down the centre of an elongated and rock-like hide emerged from the chaos that was the swirling slough. The scythe-like protrusions proceeded to slice through the emerald-coloured water; the creature's unique anatomy producing a dramatic, effervescing wake as it went- all before colliding with the unsuspecting man's robust frame.

The tubular-bodied being hit the tour guide square in the sternum, driving him backwards in the water whilst producing an oversized wave that inundated Trina, working to momentarily blind her. Amidst the spraying tumult, the teenager thought she might have spotted something metal hanging from the predator's jaws, but she couldn't be sure.

Wiping the irritating liquid from her eyes, poor Trina could only watch as Larry was ripped unforgivingly from her side. Skewered just below his ribcage, the big man was held aloft by the demon's haphazard array of steak-knife-like teeth. Eyes wide with fear, Trina watched dumbstruck as hints of cerise leaked down the curved, yellowed incisors. Krasinski screamed the whole time, spitting up blood and phlegm, his pained screeches cutting through the air as he was forcibly propelled aftward through the water! Next, the half-submerged beast forced the man to go under with it as the thing arched its spiked back, diving deep.

Even with its succulent prize claimed, the creature continued to ravage the helpless tour guide. Plunging deeper, the monster snapped its head from side to side beneath the green waterline, the underwater fracas causing the agitated surface overhead to bubble and fizz. Petrified beyond belief, Trina screamed when blood appeared, staining the churning body of water a nauseating hue of crimson. Combined with the roiling, foamy liquid, the rising fountain of fluid looked like the end result of some grotesque potion brewed up inside a witch's cauldron. Vomit crawled its way to the back of Trina's throat at this point, the acidic liquid fermenting inside her and working to burn the girl's oesophagus.

"Trina!" Tommy's voice sounded once more.

Tommy's panicked voice thankfully took his sister's attention away from the gruesome sight playing out before her. Swallowing back the fiery vomit lingering at the periphery of her throat, Trina took off, firing her arms into the murky waters.

Hunger abated for the time-being, the two smaller creatures peeled off in different directions as they sensed their parents' measured approach. Quickly, they proceeded to finish off what morsels they still held onto, working their jawbones vigorously.

The larger beasts, although protective of their offspring, were not averse to throwing their weight around when it came time for feeding. They were the matriarch and the patriarch of the family unit, after all. As such, they sat at the top of the pecking order and would settle for nothing less than the best for themselves.

Snake-like, the adult creatures wended their way nonchalantly through the green water. Side by side, the hulking predators cruised just shy of the slough's debris-littered floor. Unlike their progeny, the pair didn't bother to duck and weave amongst the maze of driftwood and other refuse, rather they relied on their massive physiques, simply barrelling right through whatever might lie in their path.

Powering towards the airboat and the figure of her shouting sibling, Trina focused her gaze straight ahead, trying not to think about the horrors that occupied the slough alongside her. Tommy continued to yell to her, doing his best to encourage his sister to keep going. Even with her lungs on fire and the lactic acid building up in her joints, Trina refused to give up. She had witnessed first-hand what these things could do. Therefore, she was determined to get back inside the airboat, where at least she had a chance… maybe.

"You can do it!" Tommy bellowed, the boy's long strands of black hair framing his flushed face. "Keep going!"

Cruising at a leisurely pace, the two goliaths glided smoothly through the swirling green realm, all the time making sure to remain close to the bottom. Hanging above them, a single, small figure stood out, silhouetted by the sun's rays shining through the surface. A mess of gangling limbs thrashed wildly as the tiny shape cut through the water, heading towards a larger more pronounced profile situated a little further out.

Initiating their attack, the patriarch cut to the left, whilst his mate maintained her course, albeit pulling away from the slough's floor and making for the surface.

***

Trina's sprint to the bobbing vessel was a strange experience. No matter how hard she tried for the broad craft it seemed to be far-off and ultimately out of reach. Until all of a sudden, the boat was no longer out of reach anymore. It seemed to appear almost miraculously right there in front of her.

The looming figure of Tommy extended a hand towards her. Smiling ecstatically at her brother, Trina reached for it-

-only for her to miss by mere millimetres.

Suddenly, it was as if she was falling away from Tommy. No wait, she wasn't falling. Rather Tommy was the one who was on the move. Trina watched, utterly astonished, as her brother rose into the air- the airboat going with him! Her mind did a double-take: it just didn't make sense. Tommy and the boat were somehow being launched into the sky.

What the hell? Screamed a voice inside Trina's head. *This can't be happening!*

Yet, it was happening... kind of. Her mind just wasn't processing it properly.

The vessel continued to rise into the air as if it was levitating. Only it wasn't levitating. As the boat rose higher and higher it became apparent that something was holding it aloft, forcing it upwards into the air and *out* of the water! That something soon revealed itself.

Bowed teeth, long and sharp like butcher's knives, were dug deep into the vessel's metallic frame as a creature- much larger than those responsible for killing her parents and Larry- emerged triumphantly. Like an arrow snagged in a gambeson, the beast's snout was lodged firmly inside the boat's metal frame. Somewhere up above, Trina could hear her brother screaming for help... but there was nothing she could do for him, not from down in the water.

There soon emerged a large, cherry-red eye situated under an arched, angular and bony brow. Said eye was bisected by an oil-black pupil that sat just behind the spade-shaped snout, the latter complete with a pair of prominent, knobbed nostrils. Trina swore the glistening sphere flicked in her direction, almost as if the creature was surprised to see her floating there. Then again, perhaps it was just curious.

Next, came the monster's gills- or more accurately, one of them. Unlike the rest of the creature's upper-body, the gill wasn't covered in a stony epidermis. Rather, it was easily distinguishable from the rest of its anatomy due to its pink, fleshy and frilled appearance. A trunk-like abdomen, thick like a redwood, slowly appeared thereafter, shimmering streams of water falling away from it.

Mere feet from the behemoth, Trina couldn't help but feel like an ant next to its great girth. What's more, the sight of the fearsome beast rising from the slough reminded Trina of pictures which Tommy had shown her of leaping sturgeon- only the thing in front of her was much more terrifying than any sturgeon could ever be.

Just when Trina thought she had seen it all, a second creature exploded from the water! Rising on a sharp angle, the monstrous denizen fired towards the airboat's stern. Lathering water dispersed chaotically about its titanic frame, before the impressive predator smashed face-first into the vessel's rotor-assembly, spearing it with its teeth. Several of the fangs protruding from its bottom jaw became wedged in the metal guard encompassing the powerful fan. As metal and teeth ground against one another, a noise not unlike nails running down a chalkboard assaulted Trina's defenceless ears, sending a hauntingly cold sensation through her entire body.

The two scaled titans hung in the air for what seemed like an age, appearing to fight over the craft containing Trina's helpless brother. It was as if they were playing a game of tug-of-war with the airboat. Then without warning, the frame of the suspended vessel snapped.

Unable to withstand the pressure exacted upon it by the two competing beasts, the metal frame came apart in two pieces, breaking roughly at the point where the first brute had punctured the craft below with its wicked-looking fangs. The airboat cracked like a breadstick, after which the creatures let gravity do the rest. Both monsters veered off in different directions, rolling over before crashing into the waters below, similar to a Great White snatching a seal. Splashing down, the monstrous pair vanished beneath the soaping waves once more. Meanwhile, the boat plummeted down in two sections, forcing poor Tommy to lunge desperately overboard!

Down below, small shards of metal, combined with an array of wood splinters and other debris, rained down on the helpless Trina. The girl did what she could to shield herself with her stick-thin forearms. Yet, these fragments proved paltry compared to what came next.

Tommy- all one-hundred-and-eighty-five pounds of him- came crashing down on top of the spindly-limbed Trina. The force of the subsequent impact drove the boy's sister below the waterline. As she was forced under, the poor girl inhaled a gutful of swamp water, some of which entered her wearisome lungs. This, and the weight of her sibling on top of her, proved too much. A dense blackness took hold of Trina; a blackness made worse by the dark, liquescent milieu that enshrouded her. Losing consciousness, the struggling girl sank further, all but swallowed by the slough itself.

Out of nowhere, and very much to her surprise, the girl quickly felt herself rising. At the same time, Trina felt something press against her back. She didn't realize it right away but it was Tommy. The elder sibling hooked his flabby limbs under his sister's armpits and proceeded to kick for the surface with everything he had, dragging her along with him.

Together the siblings breached the sloshing surface. Tommy looked at his sister through a dark veil of wet hair hanging in front of his eyes, the soaked strands working to obscure his vision. Wiping the clinging strands aside, Tommy quickly found his sister was in trouble. Besides Trina's head, which was lolling to one side, the colour was all but gone from her youthful face. In short, she didn't look good.

"Trina!" Tommy shook his sister vigorously, trying to wake her. "C'mon! Stay with me! Please! God, please stay with me!"

The girl's eyes flickered open and shut several times in quick succession, green water dribbling from her mouth and down over her bluing lips.

"T-Tom-Tommy," she whimpered, coughing up more water.

"Trina!" the lad pulled his sister close, awkwardly hugging her as he tried to stay afloat.

Using a thumb and forefinger, Tommy pried opened one of Trina's eyes at this point. He instantly noted that the pupil was dilated, before the lid quickly closed over again. Not only was she struggling to focus, she was on the verge of complete unconsciousness. He shook her again, this time with more force. Tommy watched both his sister's eyes flash open and her pupils thankfully begin to shrink.

"That's it," Tommy smiled. "Stay awake! Stay with me!"

Holding on like grim death, Tommy could feel Trina quivering in his arms. Then he heard her gasp. Checking her eyes again, he noted that the pupils were much smaller than before. She was locked onto something, staring hard at it. That something was *behind* Tommy, outside his line of sight.

Tommy spun franticly, both terrified and curious. He turned just in time to witness one of the hellish creatures responsible for terrorizing him and his family rise from the emerald depths, barely ten feet away from him.

Eyes wandering over its huge, brawny mass, Tommy took in the monster in all its terrifying glory. Its hide was akin to the scarred and desolate landscape of some far-off alien world, punctuated by towering tusk-like spires that resembled citadels for the extra-terrestrial inhabitants, the wicked procession knitted together by a fleshy membrane.

Most terrifying of all however, a pair of crimson irises tinged with shades of ochre and lemon, each of them divided by a thin, cat-like, onyx pupil, stared back at the boy and his sister. A noise- a hissing gaseous expulsion of some kind- issued forth from the animal's protuberant, gnarled nostrils that poked out just above the waterline like a crocodile's. Its demonic eyes stared back at the siblings, calm and collected. It had them dead to rights. What's more, the beast knew it. They were fucked.

Then it lunged for them.

14.

Long, curved, blade-like teeth followed by a cavernous, fleshy gullet came to fill the siblings' world as the living horror flew straight at them. In mid-flight, the creature began listing slightly to its left as if preparing to roll over. The peculiar movement worked to expose the length of semi-reflective, steely scales that lined the beast's rounded underbelly, as well as offering a fleeting glimpse of a large, clamshell-shaped pectoral fin that looked to be made of calcified bone.

Crack! an ear-ringing shot unexpectedly sounded as the monster closed to within less than a foot of the two terrified teenagers.

The resulting bullet tore a sizeable wound open across the creature's flank; just along the line where the monstrous animal's ridged hide fused with its scaled underbelly. Within a fraction of a second, a gout of dark-red blood issued forth from the ragged-looking injury, the liquid leaking over the demon's ugly epidermis. Still, seemingly undeterred by the freshly-opened wound, the fiend kept coming for them, the hunger evident in its glowing eyes.

Crack! a second shot rang out quickly thereafter.

This was followed by another streaming fountain of red sprouting away from the creature's dark skin, not far from the first. A split-second later, the two confused siblings were engulfed by a foaming wave as the wounded beast fled the gunshots.

Seeking refuge below the surface where it knew it was safe, the monster swiftly returned to its stygian underwater realm. Concerned for it, the animal's mate quickly joined it, seeking to comfort the injured beast. Together, the pair retreated from the scene, leaving their offspring to fend for themselves.

Surprised to still be alive, Trina and Tommy hesitated for a few seconds before looking over their shoulders. Thankfully, the sight that awaited the brother and sister was a welcome one.

Standing toward the prow of his vessel, the stoic figure of Antoine Jackson loomed large. Barrel smoking, the towering male had his rifle levelled at the glistening stretch of water. Looking through the scope, he scanned cautiously for some sign of the horrific creature he had just shot at. As far as the man could tell, it was gone. He just hoped it wouldn't return anytime soon. However, a faint nagging voice residing somewhere in the deep, dark recesses of his mind told Antoine he might not be so lucky.

What in the hell was that thing? Jackson wondered silently. *It's not like any shark I've ever seen.*

By the man's side was the auburn-haired beauty, Hailey Benson, her piercing green eyes appraising the pair of distraught teenagers bobbing in the water, about twenty feet out. Just as she was about to call out to the two youngsters, the woman's voice caught in her throat. A sleek, haunting profile suddenly appeared at the periphery of Hailey's vision. Situated off to her left, the speeding silhouette sliced through the emerald water, closing rapidly on the unsuspecting kids.

"Jackson, look!" Hailey pointed. "Another one, over there!"

Antoine obediently swung his upper body into position, rifle and all. Raising the weapon, he tracked the object through his scope, gauging its speed and trajectory. Finger hovering by the trigger, he lined the beast up. Next, the game warden made to pull the trigger-

-but nothing happened.

Click!

"What the-" Antoine snarled at the rifle. "You have got to be kidding me!"

The man was sure it couldn't be empty. By his count he had at least another three shots left. Or so Jackson hoped. Turning the rifle over, Antoine quickly inspected the impotent weapon. It immediately became evident that his rifle was jammed.

"God damn it!" Antoine set about trying to pry a skewed casing from the chamber.

Hailey looked on in horror as the missile-shaped demon continued to close the distance between itself and its exposed prey. Now well-aware of its presence, both teenagers were screaming to the heavens at the approaching danger, splashing manically in the glimmering water as they futilely attempted to escape it.

"Jackson!" Benson screeched at the warden. "What are you doing? *Shoot it!*"

"My rifle's jammed!" he snapped back at her. "Gimme a second!"

"You've had five too many!" Hailey answered brusquely.

Butterflies vibrating sickeningly in her stomach, the biologist was on her feet in an instant, the cries of the two petrified kids ringing hauntingly in her ears.

"Hold on!" Hailey told the siblings in a shrill voice. "We're coming for you!"

Hailey quickly scuttled past Antoine, pushing him out of her way as she moved towards the waiting motorboard. Planting her butt a second later, Hailey took hold of the outboard's throttle and gunned the engine with a flick of her wrist. As the small vessel lurched forward, Antoine

Jackson- still clutching his useless rifle- fell on his ass, quite unceremoniously.

"God damn women drivers!" he yelped, landing on his back with a solid thump.

Hailey ignored him. The warden's fragile male ego would just have to deal with it. There were more pressing concerns to address.

"C'mon!" Hailey urged herself on under her breath as she eyed the sinister profile.

Nauseous and weak-kneed, the young woman's heart felt like it was in her throat as she watched the coursing terror gaining on its helpless quarry. The fear set in immediately, pins and needles spreading through her fingers and toes. Hailey suddenly became aware that she was feeling rather light-headed, as well. The world around her dimmed for a second, before she snapped back to reality. Panicking, Hailey sucked in a deep breath, fighting to compose herself.

"Keep it together!" she commanded herself.

With everything the young woman had she refocused her energy, eyeing the meandering spectre in the water. Flicking her eyes nervously back and forth from the stealthy, sleek profile to the pair of floundering teenagers, the distance between the two quickly shrank, working to unnerve her further.

NO! screamed a voice in Hailey's head. She wasn't going to let them die. *I've got to do something!*

The graceful wake the demon cut through the slough was made much more terrifying by the series of rising spikes jutting out amidst the lathering water. What's more, the tract of webbing interlacing the spines appeared to almost glow as the morning sunlight penetrated the thin stretch of membrane.

Powering on, the animal ignored the irritating reverberations generated by the thrumming motorboard that permeated the murky body of water. Clearly, it was determined to have its prize… both of them.

"You're mine, fucker!" Hailey snarled at the nightmarish shape through gritted teeth.

For the briefest of seconds, the scene transformed before Hailey… if only in her mind. In the blink of an eye, Doctor Benson was transported back to Lake Minerva. The slough's waters lost their lime hue, morphing instead into a sparkling, azure panorama. What's more, the creature's marauding silhouette melted away, only for it to be replaced by a tall, menacing, triangular fin.

Snap out of it! Hailey's mind screamed. *Get your head in the game, girl!*

With a vigorous flick of her head, the young marine biologist returned to the here and now. Refocusing, she revved the engine and gave it one more spurt. With a deftness the young woman wasn't even aware she possessed, Hailey skilfully navigated the boat in between the oncoming killer and the Michaels siblings. With only seconds to spare, Hailey cut the monster off mid-attack!

Stalled, the creature hovered in the water for a moment. Hesitating, it flicked its paddle-shaped pectoral fins back and forth. Ultimately, this instant of indecision was the beast's undoing as it gave Hailey the opening she needed.

Yanking hard on the throttle, Hailey swung the boat's rear-end out in an exaggerated arc, throwing the craft into a gut-wrenching ninety-degree spin. Meanwhile, Antoine let rip with a string of obscenities as he held on for dear life. The boat came to an abrupt stop as the outboard's propeller smashed brutally into the hitherto advancing predator, catching it just behind one of its fibrous gill slits!

The spinning collection of blades proceeded to chew through flesh, muscle and ligaments like they were warmed butter. Flecks of bloodied flesh, combined with sparkling droplets of water, scattered to the wind. Amidst the churning torrent, a scarlet-coloured cloud oozed free from the creature's mutilated body and into the channel, forming what looked like a blood-red oil slick around it.

Satisfied the animal was dead, Hailey cut the engine a second later and the slough grew silent once more. Slowly, the creature edged lifelessly away from the vessel. Carried by the water, it floated further out into the channel, its stubby head attached to its trunk-like body by nothing more than a thin stem of mangled flesh. Hailey sat by the outboard for what seemed like forever, watching the floating horror creep into the distance. Up so close, the biologist mistakenly thought she would be able to appreciate it in much greater detail, but her examination was cut short by the noisy arrival of Alex and Tahlia in their FWC boat.

Shaking her head, Hailey diverted her attention to her newly-arrived colleagues. The pair swept in gracefully on their vessel, bringing it to a halt virtually parallel to Hailey and Antoine's craft. Sandwiched between the two boats, the shocked siblings simply sat shivering in the water, their eyes wide with fright.

"Are you okay?' Alex shouted at Hailey from the other boat.

"I'm fine," Doctor Benson responded curtly. "Don't worry about me." Then she pointed at the kids still in the water. "Help them!"

"I'm just fine," Antoine grumbled, staggering to his feet. "Thanks for asking."

Alex and Tahlia both offered the girl a helping hand. Whereas, Hailey and Jackson moved to help the boy. Each grabbing an arm, Doctor Scott and his assistant easily retrieved the tiny female from the slough, dragging her soaked and quivering frame over the lip of the boat and into the vessel proper. Meanwhile, Hailey reached over, grabbing onto the waiting lad's hand. Looking on, Antoine slung his rifle before moving to help his companion.

"Are you-" Antoine's question died in his throat.

Jackson swiftly recoiled in horror as the water behind the boy erupted in a tornado of foaming spray! Teeth like freshly sharpened palisades stood out, protruding from a short, rounded mouth. Snapping shut akin to a spring-loaded trap, the mouthful of tines clamped painfully down around the helpless boy's left ankle. The poor lad let out a horrendous, agonizing shriek before the monster forcefully tried to drag him under with it. Yet, halfway through helping him into the boat, Hailey- shocked as she was- somehow managed to hold onto him.

Gritting her teeth, the young woman anchored herself by planting the soles of her feet against the insides of the craft. Giving it everything she had, Hailey refused to let go of him. All the while, the lad continued to scream with a mixture of pain and terror, slowly slipping from Hailey's grasp, bit by bit. Groaning from the exertion of it all, the young woman leaned back, trying to pull the boy back with her. Still, she could feel herself losing him, slowly but surely. It was only a matter of time before the monster would have him for itself.

The young woman looked the struggling kid dead in the eyes for a moment, and a memory flashed somewhere in the back of her mind. Hailey saw the face of her friend and colleague Ashlee. The petite blonde's big blue eyes were pleading with Hailey to save her as she scrambled to get inside the boat with her. Not wanting to remember what came next, Hailey shook her head, the action working to return her to the present. Yet, the boy in the water wore that same desperate, beseeching expression as Ashlee had. Hailey told herself then and there he wasn't going to die like Ashlee.

"Help meeeeeee!" the teenager screamed.

"Ja-" Hailey's cry was cut short.

As she turned to call for his help, Antoine appeared at the young woman's side. Rifle raised, the game warden aimed the weapon, its barrel pointing down on a sharp angle into the water. He squeezed the trigger-

-and this time it worked.

Crack! the shot echoed down the slough.

Hailey witnessed one of the fanged horror's garnet-coloured eyes explode, the organ bursting something like a fluid-filled balloon. Next, the bullet exited the creature's head, erupting out the back of its cranium in a shower of craggy epidermis and blood. The putrid mixture of fluids filled the air momentarily, almost like a vapour, some of the particles hovering in a mist-like fashion before dispersing completely.

Even so, it wasn't over, just yet.

The wounded teenager continued to screech, the now dead animal still attached to his lower leg. Unexpectedly, the beast spasmed involuntarily, as if electrocuted, causing it to bite down harder still! Unaware it was no longer alive, incomplete messages continued to be relayed to its muscles from the thing's primitive and still partially-functioning brain.

"Help me get him inside the boat!" Hailey roared at Jackson. "Before it bites his leg off!"

On board the other craft, the rake-thin blonde shrieked hysterically, her cries adding to the urgency of the situation. At her wit's end, the young girl proceeded to rock back and forth, holding her hands to her ears and burying her head into her knees. Too afraid to look any longer, the girl had finally caved.

Together, Hailey and Antoine pulled the boy from the water, dragging the scaly predator with him into the vessel, the pair struggling the whole time. Once inside, Antoine began working on trying to pry the beast's jaws from the boy's gushing leg, one half of its serpentine mass hanging limply over the side of the boat.

"Get the other one!" Hailey suddenly shouted to Alex, pointing at the floating corpse drifting down the slough and away from them.

"The other one?" Alex asked, perplexed. "Why?"

"You're a biologist for Christ's sake!" Hailey shot back. "Figure it out!"

Alex wore a less-than-flattering expression as he tried to figure out where Hailey was going with this. Then something clicked.

"Necropsy!" he pointed at her.

"Exactly!" she cried in reply, exasperated.

"Forget the remains!" Jackson snarled at them both. "We have to get these kids to a hospital!"

"She's going into shock!" Tahlia yelled from the other boat, appearing to back up Antoine. Tahlia was huddled next to the girl, her arms wrapped around the lass in a comforting embrace.

"We need those remains- *as proof!*" Hailey barked at the warden. "If not for a necropsy, then at least for that! The more evidence the better! Isn't that how it works?"

Antoine hesitated for a second. He looked from the boy, who was soaked, pale and bleeding, to the monstrous thing dangling from him. Then to the girl. And lastly to what was left of the other creature disappearing down the channel. After a few moments more consideration, he eyed Hailey before glaring in Alex's direction.

"Make it quick!" Antoine told him forcefully. "We have to get these kids medical attention!"

15.

A single red eye stood out like a freshly unearthed ruby as the sheriff examined the mangled remains of the ugly creature in front of him. Blank and emotionless, the crimson, golf ball-sized sphere stared back lifelessly at the shocked lawman. As for the other organ, it was gone. Instead, all that remained was a putrefying crater, accompanied by a grotesque exit-wound positioned towards the rear of the beast's hardened cranium. Close by, lying parallel to the one-eyed fiend, was the second mysterious animal, its head barely still attached to its rigid, elongated body.

"Jesus…" the sheriff rasped, the shock written clear as day on his ruddy face.

Unblinking, his cold grey eyes refused to leave the pair of monstrous creatures sprawled out and on display. Even dead, both animals were impressive (and not to mention frightening) specimens, at least in the sheriff's opinion. Quite frankly, just the thought of seeing them alive and in action scared the shit out of him. If truth be told, Walter Crawford had a newfound respect for Antoine Jackson and his friends. The fact that they took on these things and won, as well as managing to rescue two children in the process, said a lot about them and their respective characters.

After being made aware of the incident involving the Michaels family, Sheriff Crawford rendezvoused with Doctor Scott and the others back at FCU's biology department. This was following the latter's trip to the local hospital. Monsters aside, the lawman's eventual arrival at the university ultimately proved to be rather anti-climactic. Indeed, Crawford had spent much of the ride to FCU preparing to chew-out the game warden and his cohorts for abandoning a potential crime scene. Things soon took an unexpected turn, however. As a result, Crawford was forced to eat his words and swallow his pride.

Now inside one of the university's laboratories, the sheriff was up close and personal with the monster- or rather *monsters*- Jackson had warned him about only days before. Yet, even with the evidence right there in front of him, a part of the sheriff still struggled to believe it all. Quite simply, this type of thing was well and truly above his pay grade.

"I'm sorry I doubted you," Sheriff Crawford apologized to the group with a serious degree of embarrassment. Humility clearly wasn't the man's strong suit.

In the end, Jackson and the others didn't say anything. Rather they just nodded their acknowledgement of the sheriff's apology. By now it was quite late in what had been a very long day for them all. Not surprisingly, the group was too exhausted to give him the 'told you so' treatment. In truth, they were just happy to still be alive and in one piece. After their adventure, Hailey and the others had left the two teenagers (who they now knew were siblings) at the local hospital. It had been a dramatic entrance into the emergency department, to say the least. Screaming and shouting, they pleaded for assistance from anyone who would listen. The chaotic scene eventually ended with the hysterical Trina being sedated, and Tommy- still bleeding profusely- being rushed off to surgery on a gurney.

By now, the brightly-lit FCU laboratory, littered with tables, equipment and various scientific instruments, had descended into an uneasy silence. Positioned towards the centre of the brightly-lit room, the quintet stood at various points of the compass around two long, sheening, steel tables which they had pushed close together. Prostrate across these tables, were the two dead predators hauled back from the Glades. The sheriff hovered at the head of the shining metallic slabs, whereas Hailey and Antoine stood on the left and right flanks respectively, and lastly, Tahlia and Alex stood off towards the bottom.

"So, just what the hell are these ugly mothers?" Crawford asked, coolly appraising the one-eyed monster in front of him, before he quickly switched his gaze to its nearly-headless companion.

"We're not entirely sure," Alex told him quietly, "to be totally honest with you."

"A preliminary examination would suggest some species of predatory fish," Hailey added her voice to the conversation. "As to what species, I couldn't say. I haven't seen anything like this before. Actually, I doubt anyone has. Tissue samples will have to be taken for DNA analysis, and necropsies performed on them both, before we can tell you anything with a decent degree of certainty."

"At least we can rule out a Bull shark," Antoine spoke up, looking in Hailey's direction.

Benson noted that the game warden's dark features looked slightly haggard. In particular, his eyes were glassy and his shoulders stooped. Clearly, the day had taken its toll on Jackson as well. Watching him a little more closely, she suddenly realized that Jackson's pale-coloured uniform shirt, as well as his blue jeans, were splattered with myriad slicks of dried blood, like some Avant Garde art project. Looking around the room, the doctor quickly discovered all of them, herself included, were in a similar state of dishevelment (except for the sheriff, of course). Hailey couldn't help but feel that their FWC-issued overalls, dirtied and bloodied as they were, gave them the look of abattoir workers.

“This is a whole different ballgame, I’m afraid,” Benson responded, briefly making eye contact with the game warden across from her.

Alex and Tahlia continued to linger at the feet of the two tables, quietly spectating. Apart from Alex’s previous comment, neither of them had said much at all since the hospital. Hailey assumed they were suffering from a mild case of shock, which was understandable considering the circumstances. Even so, there wasn’t much anyone could do for either of them: they would just have to ride it out. The worst was over, for now anyway. Still, Hailey made a mental note to keep an eye on them, just in case they got any worse.

Walter Crawford stretched out one of his flabby, tattoo-covered arms and flicked at the end of the barbed hook lodged in the one-eyed creature’s mouth. “I spoke to some folks in town,” he told the others, “a few of them said Delacroix was fond of using these kind of snares.”

Hailey zoned out at this point in the conversation. For what seemed like the hundredth time, the young woman inspected the two predators, trying to make sense of them and their unique biology. All in all, the young biologist found their physiology to be rather chimeric. Certainly, their diverse array of features helped lend a degree of mystery as to their origins.

What are you? Hailey wondered to herself.

Armour-plated, the entire corpus on both fish, save for the underbelly and gills, appeared to have been chiselled from granite. They were like some unholy amalgamation of a coelacanth and a crocodilian: a near-perfect fusion of fish and reptile. Looking at them in more detail, Hailey Benson couldn’t help but feel like they were a relic from some bygone age. Indeed, the beasts’ armour-plated scales, along with its lobed, clamshell-shaped pectoral fins and vestigial pelvic limbs endowed them with an almost prehistoric aura. In place of a true dorsal fin was a fearsome, towering arrangement of bowed spines, complete with interlocking webbing, running down the length of their backs. This particular feature reminded Hailey of a Stickleback fish, but that was where the resemblance ended. Furthermore, at the end of their prehistoric-looking lengths could be found paddle-shaped caudal fins. Rimmed with curved spines of their own, they resembled the blade on a buzzsaw. Next, eyes trailing across the semi-decapitated monster in particular, Hailey zeroed-in on its spade-shaped head. Its protuberant eyes sat under ridged, menacing brows, located behind a set of knotted, bony nostrils. Worse still were the ferocious-looking, sabre-toothed jaws that reminded Hailey of a bear trap- albeit one encased in rough, hardened flesh. Indeed, the teeth seemed to emerge seamlessly from the mouth. The lips for that matter were almost non-existent. Finally, in terms of overall size, the nearly-decapitated creature was the smaller of the two at just over six-feet in length. Whereas, its cohort was just shy of eight feet. Although slender, the animals' bodies were pure muscle like an anaconda, or similar species of large python. In her impromptu estimation, they were biological marvels: the perfect predators it would seem.

Killing machines, Doctor Benson thought grimly.

Hailey's brain was going into overdrive at this point, her synapses firing one after the other as a rush of ideas flooded her mind. Indeed, it wasn't long before she became lost in her own head, forgetting about the others present around her. The biologist didn't realize it then, but she was staring determinedly at the pair of cadavers. Although, she wasn't really seeing them, at least in the conventional sense. Whilst Hailey may have looked like she was staring *at* the creatures, she was really looking right *through* them.

"*Machaerodontis carnifex*," Hailey blurted out absentmindedly, her pupils somewhat dilated.

"What did you say?" Crawford asked, rather bewildered. "I thought you said you didn't know what these things are?"

"I don't... well... not really, anyway," Hailey answered, stumbling over her words. "I just named them... I guess."

"You think they are a previously undiscovered species?" Antoine asked, stroking his chin.

"Yes, I think so." Benson nodded a little nervously. It felt a little strange acting like a biologist again.

"What does it mean?" the sheriff asked sheepishly, clearly a bit confused by this revelation. "What you just said." He pointed at Hailey and then at the decomposing fish.

"It's an amalgam of ancient Latin and Greek," Alex interjected, explaining the name's origins in a low, serious voice. "Roughly translated, it means 'sword-toothed butcher'."

"Impressive," Crawford grunted, his lips contorting into a half-smile. "And quite fitting, I have to say."

Nodding, Hailey shot Alex a quick smile, which he instantly reciprocated, his freckled face almost glowing with the action. What's more, Benson noted a gleam in her old friend's eyes as the smile spread across his full, welcoming lips. Quite unexpectedly, a strange feeling came over her in that moment. Hailey felt like she was only just seeing her friend for the first time since arriving in Florida City. There was something in his face...

A glimmer of the old Alex perhaps?

For his part, Alex held Hailey's gaze, and with this the atmosphere in the room grew uncomfortable for the others in attendance. Thinking fast, it was the sheriff who thought of something to say.

"Quite a shot!" Hailey heard Crawford exclaim, his words bringing her back to reality. Drawing her eyes away from Alex's handsome features, the young woman quickly realized the sheriff was talking about the bullet-wound bored into the larger of the two fish.

"Thanks," Antoine murmured, looking over his work.

"Was this one your handiwork too?" Crawford pointed to its slaughtered companion.

"No," Hailey stared at the sheriff. "That would be me."

Crawford was visibly taken aback by the doctor's admission. At first, he was simply impressed with the young woman's method of execution. However, the expression on his bearded face changed somewhat as a suggestion of recognition inched across its scruffy, plump façade.

"Forgive me for saying, but you look kinda familiar, Doctor Benson," the sheriff smiled.

"I get that a lot," Hailey clenched her jaw, waiting for what she knew came next.

"Wait a minute!" Crawford pointed at her. "Ain't you the gal who hunted down and killed that shark in Lake Minerva?"

Hailey visibly stiffened at the mention of the killer Mako and the lake. "Unfortunately, yes that was me," the biologist responded, rather unenthusiastically. "It's not really something I like to talk about, though."

"I see," he bobbed his square-shaped head. "So how many of these things are out there?" Crawford asked with a vague smile, his pale eyes lingering on the auburn-haired woman. "It can't just be these two of them, can it?"

"There's no real way of knowing," Antoine told him, cutting in. "At least yet, anyway."

"The Michaels girl claims her family was ambushed by four of them," Hailey added. "Two larger specimens and these smaller ones," she pointed at the remains stretched out across the pair of tables.

"A family unit, perhaps?" Alex suggested.

"I would say it's a distinct possibility," Hailey replied sombrely, crossing her arms. "Based on how well they worked together."

"Fuck me…" the sheriff breathed, running a hand over his moustache. "Can you verify her story? About the big ones, I mean."

"We have no reason to disbelieve her story," Antoine quickly answered the lawman. "Tommy, the brother, corroborated it, after all."

“Not to mention we saw one of the big ones for ourselves,” Tahlia added in a low, nervous voice.

Miss Mohan’s doe eyes were wide with fear at the recollection of the monster. The caramel-skinned lass took a tentative step forward, inching closer to the remains of the killer fish perched on the cold metal slabs. Running her small hands up and down her skinny upper arms, Tahlia was hugging herself in a slightly pathetic attempt to comfort herself. Noting Tahlia’s distress, Alex placed an arm around her nimble shoulders and pulled the girl closer to him.

“Sheriff, don’t you think it’s about time we closed down access to the Southern Glades?” Antoine asked the lawman.

“Yeah, I think that’d be a good idea,” Crawford responded, albeit with a visible lack of enthusiasm. “It’s gonna be a pain in the ass. But it has to be done.”

“What about SGGC?” Antoine asked next. “Casey’s holding his fiftieth anniversary celebrations over the weekend.”

“Shit,” the sheriff spat. “I forgot about that.”

“Wait,” Hailey looked puzzled. “What’s SGGC?”

“It’s the local golf course,” Antoine explained. “Where all this craziness started. It backs right out onto the Southern Glades. Casey’s celebrations and the complex’s proximity to the Glades is something we should probably take into account, considering everything that has gone on, of late.”

“Right,” Hailey nodded. “Gotcha.” She quickly remembered something about the golf course in one of Alex’s original emails.

“We have to close down access to the course as well,” Antoine eyed the sheriff. “You understand that right, Crawford?”

“You’re forgetting two things,” Crawford held the game warden’s stern look. “Firstly, William Casey has more money and power in this town than I could ever dream of. Secondly, his golf course is private property. There is literally nothing I can do, unless he his breaking some kind of law, and even if he was, Casey has enough friends in this town to make me reconsider going after him.”

Words failed Antoine Jackson at this point. Unfortunately, Crawford was right. They had to approach this situation differently.

“Shit!” Jackson rasped with frustration.

“Don’t worry,” Crawford held up a hand. “I’ll send some of my deputies out there to keep an eye on things. Just in case.”

“I should probably send some of my people, too,” Antoine replied.

“I’d appreciate that,” Crawford nodded with an uncharacteristically warm smile.

At that very moment, a sudden, sharp blast of static cut through the quiet room, startling everyone and causing them to jump with fright. They soon discovered it was the walkie-talkie sitting on Antoine's hip.

"Boss, it's Nicholls," came a tinny voice from the other end. "We've got a problem over here at SGGC that needs your attention."

"Speak of the devil," Hailey glanced in Antoine's direction.

"I'm listening," Antoine responded as he hesitantly placed the walkie-talkie to his mouth.

16.

Looking out over the close-cut golf course, Robbie Nicholls absent-mindedly slid his walkie-talkie back onto his hip, securing it to his belt. Thankfully, Antoine was on his way; it shouldn't be too long until he got there. For now, all the junior warden could do was stand guard, as it were. At least, until his superior arrived, that is. There was nothing else for it, as far as he could figure.

Jackson will know what to do. Or at least that's what young Nicholls told himself.

The game warden's usually small, blue eyes were as wide as saucers; the shock of the sight unfolding before him yet to wear off. Moreover, Bill Casey's angry voice, coming from somewhere behind him, continued to resonate annoyingly in the game warden's ears. Accompanied by his bodyguard and a slew of underlings, Casey was lost in one of his famous rages. In fact, the course owner had been in this state for close to half-an-hour now. It was starting to get a little old in Nicholls' opinion. For his part though, Nicholls was just trying to block the guy out. Unfortunately, it was proving rather difficult, loud as he was.

"I want these wretched things gone from my course!" Casey screamed at Nicholls, the veins bulging in his reddened, bird-like neck. "As in yesterday!"

"Sir," Nicholls turned to face the irate man, "as I've already told you, my superior is on his way. Things are under control." As he spoke, Robbie gestured with upturned and opened hands, trying his best to keep Casey calm. As one might expect, it didn't work.

"Under control, my ass!" Casey spat, before turning his back on young Robbie. "Your boss, Jackson, doesn't know his asshole from his elbow!" Bill continued to rant as he walked back towards SGGC proper, his gaggle of lackeys flocking to him like flies moving in on a freshly-pinched turd.

With that, the game warden went back to studying the unusual scene before him. Where Nicholls stood (only a short distance from the ninth hole), the lay of the land gradually fell away from him, delving into a gentle slope. This particular feature gave him an excellent view of the sprawling course.

Directly ahead, a little further out there was a shallow bunker, just shy of the small hill's base. Beyond this, the course stretched for a few hundred feet before merging with a small pond. In addition to this, just off to Nicholls' right, on a diagonal, a densely-packed collection of trees stood out. Whereas, to his left, the course rose and fell into infinity, dotted here and there with more holes and bunkers. However, it wasn't the small wooded area or the beautiful sheet of shimmering water, or the undulating knolls for that matter, which had managed to grab his undivided attention. Rather, it was the swelling carpet of wildlife- a surging mass of fauna- that had him fixed to the spot in stunned amazement.

"What in the hell?" Nicholls ran a veiny hand over his close-cropped head of blonde hair. "This doesn't make any Goddamn sense!"

The teeming collection of wildlife seemed to go on forever, saturating almost the entirety of the green tapestry stretching out before him. At first glance, one could be forgiven for thinking it was a single organism. Upon closer inspection however, it became evident that this was not the case.

What's more, once Nicholls' eyes actually managed to decipher what was unfolding in front of him, he mistakenly thought the stampede was composed entirely of reptiles. Indeed, its choked ranks were filled with both Green and Spiny-tailed iguanas, Cuban anoles, Burmese pythons, the odd African rock python, as well as a smattering of lumbering tegus and many other scaly forms of biota. He soon found it didn't end there, though. The junior warden had spotted dozens of Gambian pouched rats, Black rats, boars, Macaque monkeys and even some deer bringing up the rear, as well.

"Did Noah's Ark beach here or something?" Robbie blurted out whimsically to himself, scratching the back of his head and scrunching up his smooth, youthful features.

As Nicholls watched the multitude of species scampering and slithering across the emerald landscape, another more serious thought occurred to the young man. Not a single species in attendance was native to the region, at least as far as he could tell. He thought about that for several minutes. Then another more shocking thought occurred to the warden.

"It's a Goddamn exodus," the deputy realized to his horror.

Bill Casey looked on scornfully as the last of the FWC trucks made for the adjoining highway. Moving in single-file, the small convoy of pick-ups led by Antoine Jackson (who had arrived some hours before) edged down the wending, tree-lined lane towards the course's towering, gated entrance.

Less than a minute later, loaded with a plethora of dead and captured animals, the quartet of grey-bodied vehicles left the course grounds behind; and Casey couldn't have been happier to see the back of them. In fact, he was ecstatic.

"Good riddance," he snarled venomously.

The sun was setting by now, and yet another day of business had been lost due to wildlife wandering onto his golf course. In Casey's opinion, things were getting beyond a joke. Honestly, how many times could this kind of thing happen in just one week? Seriously, what were the chances? Clearly Jackson didn't have a handle on the situation. As such, Bill would have to remedy it himself, he decided. His father wouldn't have stood for such ridiculous crap. It stood to reason then that nor could he.

"Useless pricks," William Casey muttered as he placed a fresh cigarette to his pursed lips.

Along with his burly security advisor, former Staff-Sergeant Jerome Hawkins, Casey stood just outside SGGC's reception area. Hovering just shy of the gutter, the severe-looking pair stood guard outside the area that made up the entrance to the compound's country club section. Their figures were silhouetted against a series of overly tall, sparkling glass doors which were framed by two tall, crème-coloured Romanesque pillars. Said entrance sat on one side of a wide roundabout, complete with pristinely manicured hedges atop beautifully crafted stonework ringing the base, and a lone palm tree placed there for good measure. On the other side of the impressive man-made island, the tarmac enshrouding it merged with the lane which fed all traffic in and out of the SGGC grounds.

"I've had word from my contact down at the Sheriff's Office," Casey grumbled as he lit the smoke dangling from his mouth.

"What did they have to say?" Hawkins asked, his icy eyes flicking in his boss' direction.

"Word is, there is some unidentified predator on the loose," Bill Casey told the ex-marine as he took a drag of his smoke. "That information hasn't been released to the public yet either, by the way. They don't want to start a panic… or some shit like that."

"So, this 'unidentified predator' is supposed to explain all the dead and displaced critters?" Hawkins asked, rather disbelievingly.

"Apparently," Casey exhaled, narrowing his green eyes.

"Do you believe your contact?" Hawkins asked with a sideways glance.

"How else would you explain all the weird shit that's been going on around here lately?" Casey eye-balled his bodyguard, smoke wafting from his thin nostrils.

"Point taken," Hawkins conceded with a slight grimace.

“I need you to do something for me,” Casey flicked his still-burning and barely touched cigarette out onto the tarmac at his feet.

“What did you have in mind?” Hawkins asked, his curiosity piqued.

“Not here,” Casey replied. “We can discuss it in my office. Come on, follow me.”

FRIDAY

17.

Punctuated by brief silences, a series of deafening cracks filled the humid, fog-filled air hanging over the Southern Glades. The thunderous reverberations travelled for miles up and down the length of the swamplands. What's more, the hellish tumult could be heard both above and below the water.

Of all the fauna affected, those species that inhabited the intricate maze of interwoven sloughs fared the worst. For those poor, unfortunate animals residing below the waterline it was as if some great cataclysm was unfolding around them.

"Go! Go! Go!" Jerome Hawkins roared at his spindly-limbed companion. "Move it!"

On cue, the airboat Hawkins was riding in staggered forward as its teenaged skipper gunned the throttle yet again. A few, short seconds later, an enormous frothing geyser spewed skywards as another raucous explosion sounded, resulting in a cascade of soaping waves radiating outwards from its point-of-origin. Crystalline droplets of aqua rained down briefly thereafter, spreading out over the scene in a thin mist.

When Jerome set out that morning, the world had been much darker. In particular, the fog was denser, almost impenetrable in fact. By now however, the sun hung visibly in the sky. Indeed, the molten sphere brought an inescapable and almost suffocating heat with it. Wisping tendrils of mist curled away from the water's surface as the sun's rays worked to dissipate the foggy veil hanging over the swamplands.

Setting out just after dusk, Jerome hadn't wasted any time in setting about his assigned task. After all, if Casey's contact inside the Sheriff's Office was right, then access to the Glades would be closed down completely before they knew it. They wouldn't have another chance at taking out whatever it was that was carving its way through the local wildlife population. Funnily enough, Hawkins didn't stop to consider how his actions at that very moment were impacting on the local fauna as well. Then again, Hawkins wasn't doing it for the local wildlife. He was doing it for William Casey.

"Only another couple to go," Hawkins told his pilot, "and we're done!"

Sweat covering his wrinkled brow, the former soldier scanned the scene with his ice-blue eyes, watching for anything unusual. Unsurprisingly, the big guy came up short. Besides the fact he'd no doubt managed to chase off every living thing for miles around, he didn't really know what he was looking for. As usual, Hawkins was just following orders: if his boss told him to dynamite the sloughs, then that was what Hawkins was going to do. So, he did. No questions asked. Despite the fact that he was just doing what soldiers do best, Hawkins also knew just how important his task was. He was well-aware the last thing his boss could afford was for another horde of beasts to make a surprise appearance at his boss' forthcoming shindig. Therefore, it was left to Jerome to sort it out.

Things need to go off without a hitch. He remembered Casey telling him back in his office. *I've got a lot riding on this. Money... my reputation... everything.*

If Hawkins was honest with himself, he didn't really want to chance upon this 'unidentified predator' he'd been told about. The fact that no one could tell him exactly what it was, made the thought of encountering it that much scarier, even for a battle-hardened grunt like himself.

"Slow down," Hawkins told his skipper as he reached for another stick of dynamite.

Retrieving a dull, red-coloured cylinder from the wooden crate at his booted feet, Hawkins sparked the silver lighter held in his off-hand. Engraved with the words *Sempre Fidelis*, the sheening item was a keepsake from the Corps, given to him upon completion of his service some years back. Placing the flame at the end of the fuse, he watched as the latter began to spark and fizzle. Waiting a few seconds, Hawkins let the fuse shorten as it burned bright and hot, before he lobbed the dynamite stick into the air and behind the wide-bodied boat.

"Go!" he shouted once more to the young lad at the helm.

As always, Richie O'Donnell, his chauffeur obeyed without hesitation. Richie was a kid from the golf course. The lad was working there over the summer, as he was in desperate need of money for a new car- otherwise he was never going to get laid. His girlfriend Donna was a classy kind of girl: she refused to do it in the back of his clapped-out and cramped WB. So, when Hawkins approached him, asking if he wanted to earn some extra cash, the kid pretty much jumped at the chance.

That being said, there was one other important consideration for young Richie. At eighteen years old, greasy-haired, covered in pimples and skinny as a rake, he didn't really feel all that confident about telling the muscle-bound Hawkins 'no'. Somehow Richie didn't see that going down too well with the ex-marine.

Doing as he was bid, the boat under him lurched forward, slicing through the green body of water. For several hours now, this had been the pattern: stop; dynamite; go; repeat. With every explosion, Richie felt the anxious knot in his stomach tighten further.

BOOM! Another humungous spout went up behind the fleeing craft.

"Holy shit!" Richie cursed, his expression a mixture of shock and excitement.

Hawkins looked on, a slight grin playing at the edges of his thin lips. He had been a demolitions expert during his time in the Marine Corps. Nothing got his rocks off like a good old explosion.

"Come on," Hawkins told the lad, "one more to go and we are done. The cops will be crawling all over this place before you know it! Someone must have heard the explosions by now, surely."

"You don't have to tell me twice," Richie smiled as he twisted the throttle, thinking of the five-hundred bucks he'd been told was waiting for him back at SGGC.

Together, the two beasts hovered in the water, their lobed fins gently swaying back and forth. Drawn from their lair and away from their newest brood by the roaring eruptions, the duo watched the airboat from a safe distance. They had been trailing the vessel for almost an hour now, trying to stay out of the blast radiuses whilst maintaining a watch of the bothersome craft.

Needless-to-say, the creatures were angered. Furthermore, their remaining offspring were petrified- which only angered the adults more. They had to do something about this invasion into their domain. It could not go unaddressed. To do so, would mean they had relinquished their claim to it. This was a challenge that must be met with force.

As one, the mighty predators dove beneath the surface. Plunging into the emerald depths, the enraged killers glided onward side by side, cautiously stalking the noisy, metallic craft. Keeping to a safe distance, the pair of hunters formulated their plan of attack, communicating back and forth with a series of subsonic clicks and whistles.

Their progeny would be protected… at all costs.

18.

Immersed in her work, Hailey Benson's day disappeared before her eyes. By now, the ochre haze cast by the sun was visible through the series of windows situated at the opposite end of the stretching lab. Gradually, over the course of the day the fiery glow seeped into the long room, saturating it. Despite the grotesque nature of the goings on inside the laboratory, the latter helped to provide the space with somewhat of a calm aura.

Together with Alex, locked away deep in the bowels of FCU, Hailey got to work dissecting the two monstrous creatures. Clad in overly large, butcher-style aprons that sat over the top of their laboratory coats, along with Latex gloves and Perspex goggles, the biologists set about inspecting the carnifex pair. Peeling back skin and cracking through bones and cartilage they worked to unravel the mystery of the creatures' origins.

Meanwhile, not far from them, attired in all black, Tahlia took notes on her laptop. Perched on a stool, seated behind a long workbench, she diligently recorded the biologists' observations as they relayed them to her.

By the end of the dual-necropsy, both dissection slabs were bloody messes, littered with various organs, small puddles of bodily fluids and strips of excised flesh. On top of taking tissues samples, each fish was gutted and its stomach contents removed for further examination.

In addition to having swallowed a whole chicken carcass (plucked and all), the one-eyed beast had also managed to gobble up a Gambian pouched rat and a Nile monitor, around the same time as the former. As for its companion, the second monster's stomach contents included a juvenile Burmese python, some Cane toads and a Crested Basilisk.

Finally, the partially-decapitated fish had its cranium cracked open and scrutinized. What Hailey and Alex discovered inside was quite a surprise to them both. More specifically, they found a long, tubular organ, similar in appearance to a human intestine, connected to its nostrils which extended backwards into its body proper.

"This is a labyrinth organ," Hailey said loudly, using her bloodied scalpel to point at the sausage-like body part.

"You're going to have to jog my memory of Biology 101," Alex replied, a little ashamedly. "Remember, I'm a herpetologist. Fish aren't exactly my speciality." Doctor Scott flashed Hailey a quick and slightly bashful smile.

"It works kind of like a human lung," Hailey explained, placing her glistening scalpel parallel to the beast's toothy, bullet-shaped head.

"But it has gills," Tahlia interrupted, looking up from her laptop.

In that moment, Hailey noted the young woman's sharp, exotic features were accentuated by the glow from her computer screen- as was the decidedly confused look she wore.

"Why would any species need gills *and* a lung?" Alex asked, rather perplexed by the discovery.

"Fish with such an organ generally come from still, oxygen-depleted waters," Hailey informed her companions. "Therefore, the possession of a labyrinth organ is an adaptation which allows them to survive in low-oxygen environments, when their gills can no longer extract enough oxygen from said waters. All they have to do is break the surface and inhale air directly. It also means- as long as they remain moist, mind you- they can actually survive outside of water. At least, for brief periods."

Tahlia let out an audible gasp at this. Hailey couldn't tell if the girl was impressed, or scared, or maybe a bit of both. After all, she certainly was.

"You're telling me these things can survive out of water!" Alex exclaimed, staring in disbelief at the two creatures. "What the hell are these monsters, Benson?"

Alex's question seemed to spark something inside Hailey. Whilst she didn't answer him right away, her mind had by no means checked out. It was still very much working away, trying to form some kind of a conclusion.

Doctor Benson's eyes trailed from the beasts themselves to the remains of the prey taken from inside their stomachs. Next, in her mind, she returned to the day before. Hailey briefly considered the potential importance of the Nile crocodile's corpse which they had stumbled across whilst out on the sloughs. In addition to this, Hailey thought back to her first night in Florida City. In particular, she recalled that quirky little restaurant they had all eaten at. She remembered a little later in the night, Antoine mentioning a strange incident which happened a short time before Hailey's arrival. As the story went, the warden had responded to an older woman's residence. For some unknown reason, her backyard was infested with Cane toads, if Hailey remembered correctly. Benson was also aware of the circumstances surrounding the game warden's latest visit to SGGC. In the end, the latter incident involving the peculiar faunal evacuation did much to confirm the young woman's suspicions. As a result, a theory began to take form in Doctor Benson's mind.

"I have an idea," Hailey spoke up, albeit with some hesitation.

"I'm all ears," Alex threw his hands up, the man's eyes wide behind his Perspex goggles.

"As far as we can tell," Hailey started, "these two juvenile specimens belong to a previously undescribed species."

"Okay…" Alex waited to see where his colleague was going with her train of thought.

More than a little intrigued, Tahlia made her way from her bench towards the others. Coming to stand beside Alex, the young woman crossed her arms as she waited to hear Hailey's theory. Tahlia watched the biologist intently, clearly just as eager for answers as her companion. The look she gave Hailey seemed to suggest the young woman was possessed of a confidence which had yet to fully manifest itself. In fact, Hailey was beginning to think she might actually like the girl.

"Even if we take the alligator and cougar that were killed into account, the common denominator in this case seems to be introduced species." Hailey waved her hand towards the collection of mouldering wildlife lined up alongside the two predatory fish.

"Wait. You just finished saying they were an undescribed species," Alex reminded her, pointing at the carnifex duo. "Have you changed your mind? Are you now saying, we are dealing with an introduced species?"

"No, actually," Hailey responded bluntly, removing her goggles and placing them on the slab closest to her. "I think we are most definitely dealing with a previously undescribed species. I think there is no question about that."

"Then why do we keep returning to the issue of exotics?" Alex probed further, obviously confused.

"Think about it," Hailey said. "Florida- the Everglades especially- has been exposed to a multitude of introduced biota in the last five or six decades."

Alex looked at Hailey as if to say, 'Tell me something I don't know!'

"Added to that," Hailey went on, clearly unperturbed by his thinly-veiled condescension, "the Everglades region has experienced a massive amount of anthropogenic manipulation; the clearing of swampland; the construction of roads and cities; pollution; the list goes on and on."

"I'm sorry, Benson," Alex shrugged, "but I'm not following you."

Even Tahlia looked on vacantly at this point.

Keeping her composure, Hailey went on anyway. "What if, this species- in order to survive in one form or another- emerged as a response to the different kinds of human-induced change exacted upon this area?"

"An evolutionary response?" Alex shot her a sideways glance.

"Exactly!" Hailey smiled excitedly. "An evolutionary response to the influx of all these introduced species- in conjunction to the other environmental factors I mentioned, of course. When conservationists and environmental scientists discuss the Everglades- or any area affected by the arrival of exotic species- they almost always seem to focus on the negative effects exacted upon the indigenous species, but never the positives. What if *Machaerodontis carnifex* literally turned the tables on the introduced species by using them as a food source?"

"Interesting..." Alex spoke softly. "So, in order to compete, this species developed mechanisms that would give it the best chance of survival under these circumstances." His eyes trailed over the beasts' armoured hides and fanged jaws.

"But what did it evolve *from*?" Tahlia added her voice to the conversation.

"That's the million-dollar question," Hailey told her, removing her apron and placing it alongside the dead fish closest to her. "The only way we are ever going to know is by running genetic tests. That way, we can be certain of this species' origin."

Following suit, Alex set about removing his apron as well. He didn't say anything as he set the garment down, folding it over the back of a laboratory stool. In fact, Alex remained quiet, speaking to neither Hailey nor Tahlia. The man was clearly thinking hard about everything Hailey had told him.

Unexpectedly, a door clicked somewhere behind Hailey and Alex. Their attention suddenly diverted, the group waited for their visitor or visitors to make an appearance. Coming into view a second later from behind a corner, both Antoine Jackson and Sheriff Walter Crawford appeared, each looking rather haggard.

Talk about the odd couple, Hailey thought. "How goes the monster hunt?" she asked them both.

"Don't ask," Crawford grumbled, his jowls jiggling with each syllable.

"That bad, huh?" Hailey zeroed-in on Antoine instead.

"That bad." The game warden noticeably chewed his bottom lip.

"Some fucking moron has been letting off dynamite!" the sheriff barked suddenly.

"Wait!" Hailey gave the man a puzzled look. "What?"

"We got reports of someone dynamiting the sloughs," Jackson explained.

“Are you serious?” Hailey asked.

“I’m afraid so,” Jackson nodded. “Apparently the explosions started sometime this morning.”

“Did you catch whoever it was?” Hailey queried.

“It was fucking Casey!” Crawford snarled. “I know it!”

“So, you arrested him?” Hailey eyed the sheriff.

“No,” Antoine interjected, a little angrily. “We didn’t catch anyone. We can’t even prove it was him.”

“Crafty bastard,” Walter Crawford muttered. “We must have covered the Glades twenty times over.”

“Why would this Casey be dynamiting the sloughs?” Hailey asked.

“He owns SGGC,” Antoine explained. “My guess is he is trying to kill or scare off our friends here,” Jackson pointed to the dead fish.

“The arrogant fuck!” Crawford added.

Ignoring the sheriff, Antoine continued to focus his attention on Hailey. “Enough about our day. What can you tell us about these wretched things?” Jackson motioned to the butchered fish.

“Where do we even begin?” the biologist responded, tilting her head and rolling her eyes.

19.

With a lit cigarette dangling lazily from his lips, William Casey III listened to the comings and goings of his guests around him. Much to the man's satisfaction, the periphery of the golf course and its adjoining complex was alive with a mixture of excited chatter and hearty laughter. It had been this way for several hours now. By all accounts, things appeared to be going smoothly. Bill couldn't help but feel it had the makings of a good night.

Taking a moment to look up at the night sky, he noted a collection of grey-coloured, cotton-bud-like clouds approaching. Hopefully, the rain would hold off for another while still. Even if/when it did hit, he and his guests still had the function room to retreat to. Watching the creeping, heavenly procession, Casey decided it wasn't anything he and his employees couldn't handle.

About time I had some good luck, Casey grumbled inwardly, thinking of the peculiar interruptions to his business of late.

Dressed in a tailor-made, navy-blue, pin-striped suit, Casey stood just outside the entrance to his complex's expansive function room; a wide conservatory-style building that looked out onto the course proper. Bill had pulled out all the stops for the Club's fiftieth anniversary celebrations. Indeed, no expense was spared.

Inside, an army of caterers flitted from table to table and person to person, keeping them plied with drinks and nibbles. What's more, a band was playing, and thankfully the dancefloor was packed with bustling bodies. Whereas outside, fairy lights lined the exterior of the greenhouse-like structure housing them all, endowing the already festive scene with an intense crystal-like glow. Although, the full effect of this wouldn't be felt until the sun had retreated behind the horizon.

If Casey had any qualms about his festivities, it was the presence of a handful of sheriff's deputies and FWC wardens smattered amongst his guests. Beyond that however, things seemed to be going well. Hopefully things would remain that way.

As always, by Casey's side, keeping guard was Jerome Hawkins. Staunch and muscular, the big guy hovered silently next to his employer. Attired in a pair of dark slacks and a matching, tight-fitting T-shirt tucked in at the waist, the ex-marine looked every bit the bouncer- just like he was supposed to.

"Good work today, Hawkins." Casey congratulated his underling, exhaling a heavy lungful of smoke. "Hopefully your little operation did the trick."

"I hope so, sir," Hawkins replied with almost no emotion, his eyes morphing to mere slits as he surveyed the steadily darkening scene.

As if appearing out of nowhere, Casey caught movement off to his left, further out on the course itself. He wasn't entirely sure, but there appeared to be two figures- a male and a female- traipsing across the green, hand-in-hand. Apart from these two individuals, there was only a handful of others dotted about the place, albeit all of them much closer to Casey. Bill smirked when he saw what he believed to be the female profile almost fall flat on her face, the woman's ankle appearing to bend underneath her own weight. Someone was obviously a bit tipsy.

"Well," Casey chuckled loudly, "looks like someone's getting lucky tonight."

Hawkins didn't say anything in response to this. He just watched the two figures with those predatory, ice-cold eyes of his. Silhouetted against the shadowy contour of a dense, towering nest of trees, the distant pair appeared to slowly merge with the dark sentinels, before eventually disappearing from view altogether.

"Come on," Casey croaked, "we should go back inside… mingle… all that shit."

With this, the course owner casually flicked his cigarette out onto the green in front of him. Next, Casey turned on his heel to face the yawning entrance to his brightly-lit function room and the busy mass of bodies inside. For the briefest of seconds, the light emanating from it stung his pale green eyes.

"Find Richie," Casey told Hawkins grumpily, trying to ignore the irritating glare. "Get the little retard to start cleaning this shit up." Casey waved his arms at the collection of debris littering the green about his feet.

"Will do, boss," Hawkins answered, dutifully following his employer inside.

The concussive force generated by the earlier explosions had made the two brutes hesitant. Together, they lingered at the periphery of the swampland, their rocky hides poking through the shadowy surface like submarines recharging before another dive into the abyss.

A strumming, bass-filled sound continued to reverberate, emanating from somewhere on dry land. Still, it managed to work its way down into their marshy habitat, disseminating aggressively throughout- much to their annoyance. Although much softer than the raucous eruptions they had been exposed to earlier that day, said experience had left the creatures cautious as to how to proceed. In effect, the continuous noise and the haunting memories it conjured up for the two animals worked to keep the beasts at bay.

Even so, the carnifex pair wouldn't bide their time much longer.

***

Kirsty Montgomery's world was spinning around her, so much so that the sensation was on the verge of sickening. Champagne always went straight to her head. It wasn't a surprise then that the young redhead was struggling to stay upright, let alone walk in a straight line. At her side, Kirsty's beau, Liam Livingstone, held onto one of her dainty, freckled hands, helping to support the struggling girl. Every so often Liam would cast a backwards glance, trying to ensure they weren't being watched.

"Are you sure you're okay?" the older gentleman asked tenderly.

"Yep," Kirsty hiccupped in reply, smiling warmly at Liam. Even in the dimming light her azure eyes seemed to sparkle invitingly to him.

"You haven't had too much?" he probed further.

In response, Kirsty shook her head rather than risk opening her mouth.

The two had been seeing one another (in secret) for several months now. They had met at SGGC not long after Kirsty started working there, and like any great love affair the attraction was instant. Actually, it was William Casey who had introduced them to one another.

Liam was a local business man, and twenty-two years Kirsty's senior. Still, he had aged well as far as Kirsty was concerned. She loved his broad, rounded shoulders, not to mention his Rock Hudson-style square jaw and deep hazel eyes. The young woman also loved his thick head of sable-coloured hair, which Liam kept slicked back. To be honest, Kirsty loved everything about him. In fact, she loved the man so much, the young woman didn't care that he was married with three kids. Liam had promised he was leaving his wife soon anyway, so it didn't really matter. Kirsty might have felt differently however if she knew he was still fucking his wife.

"A little further out is where we found the alligator," Kirsty pointed with an unsteady limb as they navigated yet another knoll. "Me and the warden," she added.

Liam smiled, but beyond that he didn't say anything. To be honest, he didn't really care. The man was too horny to be worrying about a dead reptile of all things. To put it simply, Mr. Livingstone just wanted to get down to business before Kirsty passed out, or threw up… or both.

"Look at the water!" Kirsty pointed ahead of them this time. "It's *sooooo* beautiful!"

At least a couple of hundred meters out and partially obscured by the series of rising and falling hummocks that dotted the course, a sheening, obsidian carpet caught what was left of the day's drastically diminishing sunlight. All that remained was a pair of fading red-orange strips shimmering hypnotically across the slough's flat, seemingly even surface. It was here where the Southern Glades merged with the grounds of SGGC.

"Yeah," Liam muttered as he watched the lissom redhead try to stay upright. He loved the way she looked in her skin-tight, knee-length, black evening dress, complete with matching high heels.

Very fuckable.

"C'mon!" Kirsty yelped, suddenly yanking her hand free from Liam's grasp.

Caught off-guard, Livingstone watched somewhat confused as his bit-on-the-side started pulling off her heels. Kirsty swayed drunkenly as she awkwardly set about performing the task. Yet, against all the odds, she somehow managed not to fall flat on her face.

"What are you doing?" Liam asked, his voice slightly hushed.

Kirsty didn't answer him. Instead- much to her lover's surprise- the girl turned and sprinted as fast as her skinny legs would carry her down the length of the undulating green, the fancy shoes Liam had bought her dangling from her curled fingers at her side. Even in her drunken state, Kirsty could feel the trimmed blades of grass between her toes. Admittedly, the sensation felt good, but not as good as Liam would feel. The young woman had been aching all night to get some alone time with him.

"Kirsty!" Liam barked, rather perturbed. "*What are you doing?*"

Stopping mid-stride, the redhead turned and gave him that one-sided smile he loved: the one full of mischief… and unbridled lust. Kirsty could be a real handful when she got into just such a mood. Still, as much as her girlish playfulness annoyed Liam at times, a part of him loved it, too. After all, it made things interesting, especially in the bedroom (where they spent most of their time).

"Come and get me!" Kirsty yelled, taking off once more into the encroaching darkness.

"Fuck it!" Liam told himself in a low voice, before bolting after her.

The mischievous Miss Montgomery suddenly disappeared from view, dipping behind the peak of an outlying hillock. Concerned he might lose her completely, Liam instantly sped up. His heart began to thump wildly in his chest from the exertion. The sun was gone by this point and the moon was on the rise, which didn't make it any easier for Liam to keep an eye on his wandering lover.

As Livingstone crested another hummock, he heard Kirsty well before he actually managed to catch sight of her again; she was laughing and calling his name, enticing the man to come and find her.

"Where'd she go?" Livingstone asked himself.

Panting with each laboured breath, his eyes desperately scanned the gloomy world around him for some sign of the young woman. Then, as Liam mounted another knoll, Kirsty reappeared; the girl giggling hysterically to herself. There were no more mounds for her to dart behind, at least in the immediate vicinity. Instead, the land fell away here, before levelling out a short distance away from the marsh they had spotted earlier… and there was Kirsty barrelling along, right out in the open.

What is she doing? Liam pondered, more than a little annoyed with how things were going.

The young woman shot towards the water's edge without so much as a backwards glance. For his part, Liam was still trailing some distance behind, but nonetheless gaining on her. Determined to get to Kirsty before she made it to the water, Livingstone gave it everything he had to catch up to her. Locking onto her with those hazel eyes of his, he made a beeline. Panting hard, Liam quickly covered the distance between them. Then, just when he thought Kirsty was about to dive into the stagnant pool of water ahead, the young woman spun sharply on the spot, her movements reminiscent of a drunken ballerina. Frightened he was going to bowl her over, Liam was forced to stumble to an awkward halt.

"Whoa!" Livingstone threw his hands up as he dug his heels into the damp ground beneath him.

Now face-to-face, Kirsty simply sniggered at her lover, clearly unconcerned with their near-collision. Bathed in the freshly-risen moonlight, the darkly-clad pair stood for a moment, each silently watching the other. It was perfect, or so Kirsty thought in her drunken state.

Staring adoringly into Liam's eyes, Kirsty casually threw her heels onto the ground beside her. Next, she leaned in to kiss him. Arching her neck, she grabbed the lapel of his suit, black like the man's hair, and moved to place her tongue into his waiting mouth.

The alcohol was heavy on Kirsty's breath, but Liam barely noticed this detail as he became lost in the moment. Their tongues clashed as Liam dipped his head so that Kirsty, who was a full foot shorter than him, might reach his parted lips. Holding her close, he pressed himself firmly up against her. Locked together in their passionate embrace, the pair stood for several moments, young Kirsty up on her toes the whole time.

"Get on the ground!" Kirsty cut their kiss short to whisper in Liam's ear.

"What?" Livingstone wrinkled up his face in confusion.

"Just do it!" Kirsty commanded forcefully, taking a step back.

Not thinking about what it would do to his expensive new suit (or what his wife might think if she noticed the grass stains), Liam obeyed his mistress and plopped down on his rump with a laugh. Kirsty stood over him, looking down mischievously, her ginger head of carefully-crafted curls cascading over her small shoulders.

"Lie back," the redhead issued another command, grabbing at the hem of her figure-hugging outfit.

Next, as Liam lay back, stretching himself out, Kirsty fell on top of him. Hiking up her dress, she came to straddle him. Tenderly, she placed a hand to one of the man's freshly-shaven cheeks. Her lips full and wet, she kissed him again with just as much conviction as before. As for her other hand, it wandered down to Liam's groin, the girl's nimble fingers searching eagerly for his zipper. As the young woman's travelling hand brushed over her lover's engorged crotch she heard him issue forth an exhilarated gasp.

"You like that?" she purred enticingly, a wicked smile inching across her lips.

"Yeah," Liam moaned, staring into her glistening, cobalt eyes.

"Well, you're going to like this even bet-" Kirsty's words were unexpectedly cut short.

To Liam's utter horror, the young woman was peeled right off him, torn away by something powerful and unseen! In the blink of an eye, it was as if Kirsty was absorbed by the very darkness that enshrouded them. For a fleeting moment, Liam actually thought the night had come to life and swallowed her whole! So swift and violent was the action, it was like watching someone on the return leg of a bungee cord being yanked back into the air. Travelling backwards into the black, Kirsty screamed, high and sharp, only for the terrified screech to be cut short a second later as it was replaced by a harsh *splaaaash!*

"Kiiiiiirsty!" Liam cried out in dismay, his piercing voice cutting through the still night air.

Sitting up, the man looked about for his dirty little secret. His eyes went wide as they locked onto the struggling figure of young Kirsty positioned at the water's edge. Flanked either side by knots of stringy vegetation, the girl lay flat on her front, pressed against the wet soil, half-in and half-out of the water. She was clawing desperately, trying to drag herself out of the stagnant marsh and back to safety.

What the hell happened to her? Liam's mind raced.

Behind Kirsty in the water, a large hump, shaped like an overturned boat approached. The menacing profile cut a distinct V-shaped wake through the oil-like surface of the water, the moonlight bouncing off the subsequent ripples. As it drew nearer, Liam noted several tall, spire-like protrusions rising away from the jagged, uneven corpus. In that moment, Livingstone didn't know what he was looking at. Still, he knew- whatever this thing was- it was *alive*.

"*Help meeeee!*" the young woman shrieked, extending a hand towards Liam.

"I-" Liam's words caught in his throat.

Doused in ghostly moonlight, every detail of the chilling scene was accentuated in that one terrifying moment for Liam Livingstone. The thing behind Kirsty came into full view, its presence sending a haunting sensation down the terrified man's spine. He tried to scream... to say something... anything... but whatever the words were, they perished in his throat.

Paralysed, Liam watched the monstrous entity draw nearer, the man totally and utterly awestruck at the sight of it. Switching his gaze to Kirsty, who was still struggling to exit the marsh, he could only surmise that as the beast had initially tried to snatch her, either Kirsty had somehow struggled free or it had inadvertently lost its grip on the lass whilst trying to abscond with her.

Either way, it hadn't given up. Its intentions were clear.

Liam suddenly became aware of the creature's eyes, a detail he hadn't picked up on before. The orange-red spheres loomed large amidst the darkness of the night. They didn't glow, rather they *burned*- like hellfire. Sitting there frozen with fear, Liam couldn't help but feel like he was watching some demonic denizen from some otherworldly realm emerge to feast upon the souls of the damned. Eyes blazing with a primal fury, the creature closed on Kirsty, its broad jaws and gnarled snout suddenly breaking free from their liquid prison in an eruption of foam and sparkling droplets that caught the heavenly gleam radiating from above in a mesmerising display.

"Kirsty!" Liam screamed, futilely extending his hand towards her.

It was no use. It was all over in a matter of seconds.

Closing to within only a few feet of the young woman, the scaly, sabre-toothed demon pitched to one side, arching its massive, prehistoric-looking jaws wide in anticipation for the inevitable. Even in the subdued light, its fearsome collection of bowed fangs appeared to glisten. A second later, the creature crashed into poor, helpless Kirsty.

Coming down on top of the young woman, its jaws snapped shut around her skinny, prostrate frame. Locked to the spot by his own sense of powerlessness, Liam witnessed the beast take hold of Kirsty, its tusk-like teeth sinking into her supple, white flesh, resulting in a grotesque expulsion of blood. In that moment, Liam and Kirsty's eyes locked. The young woman still had her hand extended expectantly towards her lover. In fact, Liam's own hand still hovered in front of him as well. Tears rolling down her cheeks, Kirsty mouthed the words 'I love you' as blood, copious and crimson, spewed forth from her mouth, rolling down her pallid chin.

And then she was gone.

With little more than a twitch of its muscles, the armoured killer pulled the young woman beneath the pearl-black waterline, sending up a fountain of spray as it retreated with its struggling quarry.

"No!" a single tear streaked down Liam's shocked face. "Kirsty! No! God, no!"

Quivering like a frightened child, Liam Livingstone sat at the edge of the marshy boundary to the slough. He proceeded to shake with each haggard breath that escaped his lips, adrenaline pulsing through his traumatized body.

I've got to get out of here! A voice suddenly told him.

He hesitated for a second, unsure what to do. Then, realizing there was nothing else to do but run for his life, Liam made to stand up. Pushing off with the heels of his hands, Liam struggled to gain traction, his feet sliding underneath him on the wet grass. Ultimately, something forced him to stop short of making it to his feet. The man's ears pricked up as they registered a low, menacing *hiiiiiiss!* emanating from close by, somewhere off to his left.

"What the hell?" Livingstone breathed, his whole body tensing at the eerie sound.

Liam cricked his neck to the side-

-and was greeted by a waiting set of yawning jaws. Viscid fluid dripped from the savage array of discoloured fangs, spilling sickeningly over a rugged bottom lip. Beyond this lay a cavernous, ribbed gullet just waiting to be fed. In the end, Liam didn't even get the chance to scream as the second cerise-eyed monster launched straight at him.

20.

Richie O'Donnell stabbed away furiously with the aluminium litter spike gripped in his right hand. Grumbling to himself, he poked determinedly at the pieces of refuse strewn about the grass at his feet. Held in his other hand was a garbage bag which he used to collect the various articles of rubbish which had been thoughtlessly discarded by Casey's guests.

Dressed in a suit that was one or two sizes too small for him, the lad looked less like a golf course attendant and more like someone's eccentric uncle left to wander about at a funeral. Working his way along, Richie gradually distanced himself from the complex's function room located to his back, edging further out onto the course proper as he followed the thinning trail of debris.

"This is bullshit!" Richie fumed in a low voice, afraid that one of Casey's guests might hear him. "Cleaning up other people's shit! Lazy motherfuckers!" he went on angrily with his hushed tirade.

Richie turned his skinny frame to look back in the direction of the sprawling conservatory for a moment. Music blared over the top of nattering and laughing guests, their figures silhouetted against the glow of the brightly-lit room. Disgusted by the jovial sight, the young man quickly turned away, cursing them all for the umpteenth time.

"Fuck this!" Richie finally snapped, throwing his litter spike and bag full of trash at the ground. "Time for a break."

Richie proceeded to take off at a brisk pace, making his way down the green and off into the night. Once he felt like he had put enough distance between himself and SGGC, Richie began tapping at the breast pocket of his suit jacket, feeling about for the joint he'd stashed there earlier.

"Come to papa!" the lad crowed as he retrieved the hand-rolled cigarette from his pocket.

Next, after brushing a curtain of greasy, shoulder-length hair out of his eyes, Richie grabbed his lighter from another pocket and sparked it. The end of the cigarette glowed in the night, standing out like a lone firefly set against the obsidian arras surrounding him. Inhaling a lungful of smoke, Richie interrupted his walk to savour the moment.

Arching his neck, he looked up at the night sky. A seemingly solid mass of thick grey clouds moved in, rolling over the Southern Glades like an inverted tidal wave. More concerned with smoking his doobie, young Richie didn't pay the angry-looking formation much attention.

"Ah!" the young man smiled as smoke, thick and heavy, curled away from his thin lips. "That's the shit!"

Taking off once more, Richie kept moving down the length of the green, trying to put as much distance between himself and the SGGC complex as possible. After all, the last thing he needed was for Casey- or worse still his goon Hawkins- to catch him smoking a joint out in the open.

Fuck them, he thought bitterly to himself. *The dicks haven't even paid me for that little 'assignment' of theirs, yet. The assholes.*

These were the thoughts that occupied Richie's THC-riddled mind as he continued on into the darkness, navigating his way over knolls and through sand-filled bunkers. If not for the burning end of his lit cigarette, Richie was virtually one with the night, attired as he was in his black suit and dress shoes. As for the world around him, it was quiet, much like a graveyard. Not to mention, the air remained hot and uncomfortably still. Trudging along with his head down, the lad wasn't really paying attention to where he was headed. All Richie really knew was that he didn't want to be anywhere near Casey and the slew of pretentious socialites he had gathered together for his weekend of celebrations.

Out of the blue, thunder cracked overheard; the sound like a hammer smashing against an anvil. Jumping with fright, the noise momentarily drew Richie's gaze skyward once more. Heart racing, Richie paused for a second, unsure whether or not to proceed. Taking a deep breath, the lad tried to calm himself as best he could. He craned his neck, looking back in the direction of the SGGC. The conservatory was little more than a glowing ball in the distance, perched on the horizon. Hesitating for a second, the young man shifted his gaze to the joint still burning between his fingers. Deciding he still had a bit left to smoke, Richie took off once more.

He didn't get far.

Dipping behind the crest of a small hummock, Richie abruptly stopped short. The young man's heart skipped a beat as his mind struggled to comprehend the chilling sight before him. Digging his heels in against the incline of the slope, Richie staggered, throwing his arms out like a tightrope walker in an attempt to keep his balance. It didn't work. Instead, he landed hard on his coccyx before sliding down the incline of the hill and skidding to a halt.

"What the?" Richie gasped, his eyes growing wide with shock.

At the bottom of the slope sat three shadowy figures- only one of which looked even vaguely human. As for the other two, Richie was at a total loss. At first, he thought the two larger, scaled shapes- each of which were close to twenty-feet long- might be gators. That was until his eyes registered the presence of a sail-like row of webbed spines running down each of their armoured, rough-skinned backs. Silvery moonlight bounced off their scaly sides, sheening hypnotically amidst the gloom. Using their bony, paddle-shaped forelimbs, the hulking beasts held themselves aloft, their postures akin to those of seals. Next, Richie noted their molten, glowing eyes. Needless to say, it wasn't long before Richie's gaze shifted to their wide, spade-shaped jaws complete with an array of steak knife-sized fangs. He quickly realized that they weren't gators at all.

Not even close, said a scared voice.

These were something much worse.

Perhaps the only thing more frightening than the creatures themselves was the ravaged set of human remains sandwiched in between the two behemoths. Indeed, the humanoid figure was little more than a skeleton with only a few patches of flesh and muscle still attached to it. What's more, the profile was clad in the remnants of a shredded suit; the garment soaked in blood.

"*Fuuuuck meeeee…*" Richie's jaw dropped, the joint falling from his lips and bouncing off his chest.

Richie's outburst, quiet as it was, still managed to give him away. One of the tubular-bodied beasts, positioned to Richie's left, snapped its broad head in the young man's direction, violently wrenching free a bloodied strip of pink flesh from its brutalized quarry in the process. The monster's eyes instantly turned to slits as it zeroed in on young Richie. Meanwhile, the other creature arched its head back before it began loudly clacking its jaws together, swallowing something that Richie couldn't identify.

Sssssss! The fiend to his left let loose with a savage hiss, emitting a sound not unlike steam escaping from a cracked pipe. Salivate spilled from its parted jaws as the piece of flesh it had acquired fell clumsily from its gaping mouth, landing with a sickening *plop!* on the grass in front of it.

At this point, the second animal off to the right suddenly became aware of the lad's presence. Splaying its fanged jaws wide, the beast issued forth a hellish screech quite unlike anything Richie had heard in his short life. Its neck vibrated with the reverberations whilst simultaneously letting spittle fly in all directions. Even more sickeningly, Richie caught glimpses of what he assumed were ragged chunks of decaying flesh lodged between its bowed teeth. He suddenly felt quite sick. The young man's stomach churned as his mind struggled to process his dire situation.

This can't be happening! Richie's mind screamed in terror.

It was at this point that young Mr. O'Donnell realized he had made it all the way to the boundary of the SGGC grounds, high as he was. Just beyond the two primordial terrors and their meal lay a marsh, which he knew from memory led out into the Southern Glades. A dark, glistening trail- which could only be blood, Richie surmised- snaked away from a section just shy of the water's edge, all the way up to the monsters' current position. To his horror, the moon's pale rays of light reflected off the slick, liquid track, giving it a haunting sheen.

I have to get out of here! Richie told himself.

The goliath to his left remained where it was, watching him intently. Whereas, the other beast shifted its weight slightly, reorientating itself towards young Richie, the thing's cumbersome movements reminiscent of a sea lion. Richie noticed that the monster's craggy flank had two grotesque holes bored into it- wounds of some sort. Beyond this however, he couldn't tell the difference between the two.

What am I still doing here? A voice screamed in the back of his head. *Move, you moron!*

Richie sprang into action, getting to his feet quick-smart. The sudden movement startled the monstrous pair, but before they could respond Richie was clambering up the small incline. A moment after that, he was gone.

The female carnifex was slower off the mark than its mate. Although roughly the same size and weight as its male counterpart, the female creature was slower on account of the pair of bullets holes that had been drilled into its flank. As such, the male carnifex took the lead in the subsequent pursuit.

Leaving behind their previous meal, the beasts trailed after the fleeing human, their wending movements similar to an eel or serpent. Although, whilst they may have been swift underwater, their speed was significantly reduced on land. Still, half-sliding and half-thundering along, the duo made for a fearsome sight nonetheless. Grunting, hissing and shrieking like banshees, the ruby-eyed twosome barrelled after their fleeing quarry with a vengeance.

Giving it hell for leather, Richie bolted as fast as his skinny legs would carry him. The lad didn't realize it at the time but he was screaming and cursing, his voice embarrassingly high and shrill. Overhead, thunder continued to crack and boom, albeit much louder than before; the hellish noise working to drown out his desperate cries.

I've got to keep moving! he told himself. *Put as much distance as possible between me and those things!*

Distracted amidst his frenzied ponderings, Richie didn't feel the first few drops of rain right away. In fact, it took him the better part of a minute to register the presence of the cool liquid on his pimple-ridden cheeks and forehead. Instinctively, he looked to the sky just as another burst of thunder abruptly sounded; the powerful note ripping through the night air with a fury.

A split second later, a shimmering torrent of crystalline droplets plummeted from the obsidian heavens, inundating the scene around him. Rain hammered hectically into the ground, saturating the jade course. With each subsequent step, Richie kicked up miniature geysers about his feet and ankles. The grass at Richie's feet quickly grew slick, making it difficult to traverse. With this, the soles of his shoes began to slide wildly underneath him. Unable to maintain traction, Richie was thrown off-kilter-

-only to recover his balance at the very last second.

That was close! said a voice.

By now it wasn't simply Richie's lungs that were weary, the muscles in his legs burned too. Even so, the young man wasn't about to quit. Richie knew he had to keep running. He had to make it back to SGGC. Richie had to tell someone about what he had seen… anyone.

Whether they would believe him though was quite a different story.

Casey will know what to do! Richie decided in his manic state. *Wait... are these the things Casey wanted Hawkins and I to kill?* he asked himself, experiencing a moment of clarity amid the madness.

Squelch!

Richie's feet suddenly slid out from underneath him. Falling face-first into the soaking soil, his twiggy body splashed down with a solid, bone-jarring thud. Landing in a heap, Richie cried out as his cheekbone collided with the ground, the force of the impact snapping his head backwards on a sharp angle. For a few fleeting seconds, stars danced in front of the young man's eyes. What's more, pain pulsed under the skin around his cheek, the sensation hot and angry. Still, he was able to recover; his vision settling as the accompanying pain faded into nothingness.

Chest heaving, Richie lay prostrate with his hands pressed flat against the wet grass, attempting to catch his breath. Trying to steel himself before he intended to make another run for it, a strange sensation unexpectedly overcame him. Something- a sixth sense perhaps- drew Richie's gaze aftward.

Slowly, he twisted his neck, peeking over his right shoulder. Behind him, Richie could make out the smooth hump of a hill. Indeed, the mound's silhouette loomed large, highlighted as it was by the pale light cast from the heavens. However, the hillock wasn't the thing responsible for holding the young man's attention.

Despite the curtain of pouring rain, Richie was still able to distinguish the monster's slinking profile, warped as it was by the gushing liquid torrent. First, its spines appeared at the lip of the mound. In that moment, Richie felt like a swimmer watching a shark fin emerge from the surf. He felt his stomach begin to knot as more of the beast's hulking frame appeared. Wending its massive girth towards him, it had the appearance of an anaconda on steroids. Next, cresting the hill, the tubular, serpentine figure glided down the grassy incline, leaving a glimmering, slimy trail in its wake.

Go! Go! Go! Richie's mind screamed at him to get moving.

Yet, for some reason, the young man couldn't find it in him to get back on his feet. Lying there, Richie's temples pounded relentlessly, each throb painfully uncomfortable. Watching the gargantuan monstrosity draw nearer, the young man's breathing came out ragged and shallow. Richie could feel his entire body shaking. Then, as the first creature levelled-out at the base of the hummock, the second animal appeared. The latter beast stopped for a second, perched atop the knoll like a lion surveying its domain, its bulky body held aloft by its petrified, clam-shaped pectoral fins.

Is this really happening?

Once more, thunder cracked like the snapping of a giant's bones. This was quickly followed by a vibrant blast of lightning, one which managed to light up the entire scene. In that moment, the flickering skyward flash seemed to amplify the stony figure's ghastly features, if only briefly. Its fearsome collection of talon-like teeth stood out amongst the blackness of the night, displayed in a wicked, haunting smile. What's more, Richie swore the horrific thing was looking right at him, its wine-coloured eyes locked onto his quivering outline.

A delayed jolt of adrenaline shocked young Richie's system as he took in the sight of the second beast, its rapacious sneer seeming to prompt something deep within him. It was then he realized just how close the other creature had gotten. Distracted by the arrival of its companion, Richie had forgotten all about its counterpart. The monster was charging right for him, its jaws cranked wide and expectant!

"Holy shit!" he yelped, pushing himself up off the sodden bed of grass.

Stumbling to his feet, Richie almost went face-down again right off-the-bat. Luckily, he kept his balance, however awkward his take-off may have been. The approaching fiend's maw snapped shut mere inches from his right ankle, the two sections of its powerful jaw clamping shut on thin air with a very audible *whump!*

"Fuck!" Richie squeaked, looking back in the direction of the lumbering, scaly horror.

Richie stumbled onward, barrelling into the night. Too afraid to look back now, the lad focused his gaze ahead. In between the rumbles of thunder, Richie could hear the guttural grunting of the predator on his heels. Each grumble from the trailing monstrosity worked to encourage the terrified youth to keep going.

Then, out of the blue- or rather the black- another embankment appeared up ahead. Richie sprinted towards it, his lungs fit to burst at this point. Reaching the hummock's base, he fell forward slightly. Using his hands and feet, he clambered up the incline and over the brow… and hopefully to safety. Richie was unexpectedly greeted by a shining ball of light, the glare of which momentarily stung his eyes. Blinking profusely, the object gradually came into focus.

The conservatory! Richie realized.

Overall, the atmosphere inside the function room was cheerful. Without a doubt, things were going rather well. So much so, that William Casey wasn't all that bothered by the horrible noise resulting from the storm brewing outside, or the presence of multiple sheriff's deputies and FWC wardens dotted amongst the festive crowd.

Glass of bourbon in hand, Bill Casey began navigating the throng of people choking the dance floor (law officers and game wardens included). Scanning the room, he performed his usual routine of smiles and small talk, coupled with handshakes and hugs. Off to his right, about midway down the length of the room was a small stage, on top of which was situated the band he had engaged for the night. Catching a glimpse of the lead singer gyrating on stage, he struggled to remember the band's name. In any case, they were good at what they did. As long as they kept his guests happy, they could call themselves whatever they liked.

Starting at the top end of the conservatory, Casey slowly worked his way to the building's rear. Keeping his eyes on the wide set of wooden-framed doors leading out onto the lawn overlooking the course, he manoeuvred deftly from person to person, never failing to exchange the expected pleasantries. His father had taught him well, after all. Still, it didn't mean he liked having to do it. The way Bill saw it, he simply had a role to play. In the end, keeping his patrons happy meant keeping himself in business. Like any true businessman, he wasn't doing it out of the kindness of his heart.

Finally making it to the end of the sprawling room, Casey felt the knot that had been forming in his chest begin to dissipate. Feeling rather wearisome, he expelled a lungful of air before draining his glass of the remaining bourbon.

"Thank God for that!" Bill breathed, letting the empty glass leave his thin, purpling lips.

Peering back over his shoulder at the swarm of people, Casey felt a real urge to slip outside for a breath of fresh air, rain be damned. As such, his eyes were instinctively drawn to the conservatory's entrance/exit. By now, the function room's doors were shut on account of the rain and wind. With the storm raging, Bill couldn't make out much beyond the building's vast array of segmented, white-framed windows, splattered as they were with rainwater.

Occasionally, a burst of lightning would punctuate the night, briefly lighting up the darkened scene yonder. Still, this really didn't do much in terms of overall visibility; one was given but a fleeting glance at the green landscape, only for it to descend into pitch blackness once more. Even so, something drew Casey away from his guests and over to the windows.

As he separated himself fully from the collection of bodies and various furniture, Bill placed his empty glass on a nearby table and headed to the periphery of the function room. Looking out into the night, Casey surveyed the near-impenetrable scene. In fact, with his face hovering only inches from one of many water-laden windows, all he could make out was his reflection: the man's signature blonde comb-over and hooked nose appearing to float in front of him. All of a sudden, lightning sparked yet again and for a fleeting instant William Casey thought he might have seen a figure- a man, he guessed- running down the length of his golf course.

Who'd be mad enough to go out in this kind of weather? asked a perplexed voice. *I must be seeing things,* he told himself.

When he looked again, darkness had returned to reclaim the world beyond the window, and Casey was left inspecting his pallid and gaunt reflection once more. Thunder boomed unexpectedly, drowning out the music filling the room and causing Casey to jump nervously.

"Get yourself together!" Casey scowled at himself under his breath, before looking around to check if anyone had witnessed him making a fool of himself.

If anyone had noticed, he certainly couldn't tell. For the most part, people were clustered around tables chatting away, whilst others danced and frolicked as happy people do. Turning back to look out into the night, this time Bill was greeted by another crackle of lightning-

-and a face that wasn't his own.

"Jesus H. Christ!" Casey cried aloud, backing away from the glass.

Tiny streams ran down the length of the ghoulish visage on the other side of the glass. A mop of hair, drenched and matted, hung in glistening strands down to the person's hunched shoulders. The individual outside - definitely a man- was screaming something that Casey couldn't quite make out over the noise of the storm, in addition to that of the band playing to his rear. A second later, Bill's lime-coloured eyes shifted to the set of doors located a few feet off to his right. Moving quickly, he reached for both handles and yanked the doors open.

"Wha-" Casey's words were drowned out before he got the chance to finish them.

A chilling gust of wind, peppered with icy droplets, assailed William Casey. Stepping back from the entrance, he raised a hand in front of his face, trying to shield himself from the elemental assault. Taking a step back, the tails of his suit-jacket fluttered wildly as the icy wind battered into him. Next, sopping-wet and shivering, the dark figure staggered to a halt less than a foot from Casey. The music instantly cut out, with the excited chatter of Casey's guests following suit almost immediately thereafter.

Bill looked the unfortunate figure up and down as the conservatory doors swayed shut, drawn closed by nothing more than their own momentum. With this, the noise from the storm softened once more. Casey was certain it was a man standing before him, although as to his age Bill couldn't say. Completely water-logged, the mysterious stranger's suit was pressed against his skin, accentuating his skinny frame. He was soaked to the bone it seemed, dripping water all over Casey's freshly-polished floor. Furthermore, the individual's face was hidden behind a veil of dark, scraggly hair. Indeed, the man was staring at his feet, almost as if he was ashamed to look Casey in the eyes.

"Are you okay?" Casey reached tenderly for the dishevelled figure.

Out the corner of his eye, Bill noted Hawkins' bulky physique bounding towards him, pushing his way through the now hushed crowd.

"M-m-mm…" murmured the quivering male, cricking his neck ever so slightly towards Casey.

"Richie?" a flash of recognition inched across William Casey's face. "Richie what's the matter? Has something happened?"

Hawkins quietly joined his boss at this point. Slipping in beside him, Hawkins had a stern expression etched into his already grim features. Saying nothing, he appraised the rather pathetic-looking Richie.

"M-m-mon…" Richie O'Donnell stuttered on.

"C'mon, Richie what's wrong?" Casey placed a tentative hand to the lad's shoulder, showing an uncharacteristic degree of concern for his employee.

Richie's head unexpectedly snapped upwards, numerous drops of water flying everywhere as he recoiled from Casey's touch. Side-stepping, he distanced himself from Bill, the lad's eyes wandering erratically, struggling to focus.

"Monsters!" Richie barked, the veins bulging in his gangly neck. "Two of them! Outside!"

"Monsters?" Casey tried to laugh it off. "Richie, be serious," he added sternly.

"I am being serious!" Richie squealed.

Nervously, the club's owner looked around at the faces of his guests, all of whom looked rather worried. He knew some of them had heard the stories about what was going on out on the Glades. It was Florida City's worst kept secret at this point. Craning his neck back around towards his dishevelled employee, Casey made to speak.

"Rich-"

The conservatory doors blasted open again… and this time the wind wasn't responsible.

Standing there in the doorway, with its wet corpus glistening, was one of the foulest and most terrifying things William Casey had ever laid eyes on. His eyes were drawn first to its webbed dorsal spines, before they shifted to the monster's armoured flanks. Bill very quickly realized he didn't understand what kind of animal he was even looking at. Multiple possibilities went through his mind, one after the other in rapid-fire succession as he took in the remainder of its tortuous and hulking physicality.

Snake? Eel? Croc? Mutant? He asked himself. *What the hell is it?*

Hiiiiiiiissssssss! The fiend expelled a savage warning from somewhere deep in its throat as it narrowed its voracious gaze at Bill Casey.

Screams filled the function room at this point, Casey's patrons becoming aware of the prehistoric-looking entity now within their midst. Their resulting high-pitched shrieks bounced off the walls horrifyingly. Next came the clamber of peoples' feet as Casey's guests descended into an outright panic, trying to stampede their way out of the room.

"We've got to get out of here!" Casey heard Hawkins telling him.

Registering one of Hawkins' large paws curling around his bicep, Casey spun on his heel to leave-

-only for his feet to be swept out from underneath him! Throwing his arms out, Bill grabbed desperately for Hawkins. Their fingertips brushed together briefly, but it was ultimately to no avail. Casey landed with a resounding *thud!* on his front, the air all but forced from his lungs by the impact. Almost immediately, a scorching pain tore up his left leg, starting just above the ankle. Before he could react, Casey felt himself being dragged along the floor. Clawing with his hands he tried to gain some purchase, but the polished floorboards provided none whatsoever.

"Help me!" Bill howled.

Screeching, Casey spun onto his back, his suit jacket flapping wildly about the place as he was yanked backwards against his will. Looking down at his legs, he was met with an utterly bone-chilling sight. It was like looking into a mouthful of butcher's knives... knives greased in dripping, viscid, bacteria-ridden fluid. Casey noted some of the predator's teeth were slick with blood- *his* blood. Bill's eyes quickly darted to his wounded ankle. His pant leg was torn and the leather of his Versace shoe shredded. Blood pooled around Casey's foot, staining the sheening floor.

"Come on!" Casey heard Hawkins' voice amidst the chaos.

Hawkins grabbed hold of his boss, hooking his brawny arms under the older man's pits. Groaning, he prepared to remove him from the danger zone.

"You're coming with me!" Jerome Hawkins grunted as he began dragging his boss to safety.

William Casey's sense of relief was promptly ushered away by the guttural roar emanating from close by his feet. Eyes wide, Bill redirected his gaze to the scaled beast clambering after him. In that instant, he felt like he was looking at a dragon without wings. Its scarlet eyes loomed large as the demon slithered after him. Suddenly, hyperextending its jaws, the monster lunged as it let loose with a vicious hiss.

"Fuck off!" Casey panicked.

Working on pure instinct, Casey kicked out with both legs, striking at the advancing creature. In the end, it didn't work. William Casey watched dumbstruck as his legs disappeared down the beast's broad gullet, its rancid breath washing over him. A nanosecond later, its maw snapped shut, the fiend's teeth slamming into him just below the groin!

"Aaahhh!" Bill cried out. "Hawkins! Help me!"

With a savage tug, the beast tried to yank its quarry backwards. Hawkins however held on. Clenching his jaw, he let out a strained growl as he gripped Casey harder, determined not to let go of his charge. Momentarily switching his gaze from the terrifying beast to his employer, Jerome realized Casey was coughing up blood.

"*Haaaaawkiiiiiins!*" Casey screamed.

Then, with a flick of its stubby head and neck, the sabre-toothed demon readjusted its hold on the bleating prey item held between its gruesome jaws. Working its way forward, the killer jammed more of the struggling man down its broad, corrugated gullet. By now its teeth were up to Bill's navel, firmly lodged in his flesh. Biting down harder on him, Casey responded by hacking up another mouthful of crimson, syrupy blood, the thick liquid running down his shirt.

Still, Hawkins refused to let go. Rather than quit, he dug his heels in, trying to stabilize himself. Throughout it all, Hawkins hadn't stopped to consider the fact that he was literally playing tug-of-war with his boss' life!

"You're tearing me apart!" William Casey suddenly coughed, his voice growing weaker.

The realization came too late for Jerome Hawkins.

With a sudden, unforgiving jerk, the massive predator wrenched all its weight aftward, pulling Casey with it. Falling backwards, Jerome landed on his rump, pain dispersing throughout his lower back, starting at his coccyx as he plopped down. Still gripping his boss determinedly, Hawkins could only watch the gruesome scene unfold before him.

Bill let loose with an ear-piercing howl as his lower half was separated from the rest of his body! Stunned, Hawkins watched as his boss' body was stretched- literally to breaking point! First, Casey's skin tore in strips just above the waist, exposing raw flesh and viscera beneath. Blood proceeded to spray in multiple directions, like a series of burst pipes going off all at once. Wide-eyed and dumbfounded, Hawkins witnessed Casey's organs spill outwards from the grotesque, gaping cavity created by the bloodthirsty monster. As such, the sausage-like innards spilled onto the floor, accompanied by a heavy torrent of scarlet blood.

"Bill…" Jerome breathed, his arms still hooked under Casey's armpits.

Looking up at his bodyguard, William Casey's eyelids flickered before his eyeballs rolled back in his head, going white. It was at this point Hawkins knew Bill was gone. Jerome sat there silently, William Casey's top-half nestled in against him, blood leaking out across the floor, forming into a glossy, dark red puddle. Shocked into a stupor, the brawny ex-marine began to shake uncontrollably. In fact, he even forgot about the murderous predator only a few feet away.

That was until the goliath produced a low, rasping hiss, signalling its intent to attack.

Snapping his eyes up, Hawkins found a slightly parted maw, rimmed with an arsenal of bowed sabres for teeth, waiting patiently for him. Salivate fell from the beast's lips in gelatinous, stringy tendrils, a hungry, expectant look in its devilish eyes.

"Come and get me!" Hawkins snarled. "Motherfucker!"

21.

Robbie Nicholls watched the horrifying scene unfold from the other end of the conservatory. Panic was at fever-pitch levels by now, and as such the function room had descended into total chaos. Screams of terror filled the air, coupled with the hectic rhythm of stampeding feet as people made to flee the scene.

Madness… whispered a voice inside Robbie's head.

Yet, whilst others fled the scene, the young FWC warden fought against the tide of human bodies rushing towards him. Each step was a battle in itself, as person after person smashed into him in their individual attempts to escape the dreadful situation. Even so, Nicholls wouldn't be deterred from trying to help.

In between being buffeted from side to side by frightened patrons, Robbie did his best to keep his eyes on the figures of Casey and his minder… and not to mention the goliath-sized creature the pair continued to struggle against.

What the hell is that thing?

Peoples' screams, sharp and unrelenting, reverberated in the warden's ears, the noise working to disorientate him. Indeed, the racket was nigh-on maddening. Trying to block it out, Nicholls pushed on, drawing closer.

Out of the blue, Nicholls felt a hand slap hard against his right shoulder. Snapping his neck to the side, he came face to face with a blonde-haired sheriff's deputy with dark eyes. Nicholls got the impression the officer was only a few years older than himself. What's more, Robbie instantly noted the matt-black revolver gripped firmly in the officer's right hand.

"Do you have a weapon?" the deputy asked, his features desperate.

In his haste to help Casey and his employee, Robbie had forgotten all about the rifle secured in his truck, outside in the parking lot. It was standard practice for FWC wardens to keep a rifle in their vehicle, in the event that they would have to deal with dangerous and out-of-control wildlife. This was clearly one such situation.

Surprisingly, Robbie found he couldn't speak, so he simply nodded in the affirmative.

"Go get it!" the deputy said forcefully. "We'll take care of this." The lawman nodded in the direction of a colleague over on the opposite flank of the room. "Hurry back. I think we're gonna need all the help we can get."

With that, Robbie Nicholls turned to join the fleeing crowd. His last image of the sheriff's deputy was of the officer reaching for his walkie-talkie with his free hand. As for the feasting abomination beyond, Robbie couldn't bring himself to look. Perhaps if he had worked up the courage to look, Nicholls might have noticed something else.

Like so many others present, Robbie failed to notice the second looming shadow hovering at the periphery of the conservatory's entrance. Unlike the beast attempting to swallow Casey, the second animal seemingly refused to enter. Instead, it slinked off into the darkness, disappearing into the night.

A short time before…

"So, what exactly are you trying to tell us Doctor?" Sheriff Crawford signalled to the two beasts. "That these ugly bastards could eclipse the Alligator as the region's apex predator?"

"It's a distinct possibility," Hailey Benson nodded, her green eyes failing to waver under the lawman's hard-set stare. "As far as we can tell, they are a new, emerging species," Hailey added, "with a lot of potential, in my opinion… and very few weaknesses." Her eyes momentarily wandered to the creatures' exposed, pink, fleshy gills. "They have done a great job of clearing the Southern Glades of noxious species. In addition to this, they have shown a willingness to prey upon some of the region's top-line predators- alligators included."

"And I thought removing Burmese pythons from peoples' backyards was bad enough," Antoine Jackson scoffed, rubbing the back of his thickset neck.

"The entire ecological balance of the Florida Everglades stands to be disrupted," Benson shifted her gaze to Alex. "Potentially beyond repair," she emphasized further. "I mean, we actually have species *fleeing* the region. It can't just be coincidence. Can it?"

No one in the room could dispute Hailey's conclusions. All but one of them had witnessed with their own eyes what these creatures were capable of. Moreover, the two specimens sprawled out in front of them were only juveniles. Just that in itself was a frightening thought to contemplate.

"What do you propose we do then?" Alex asked Hailey gloomily from his side of the lab.

A harsh blast of static from the sheriff's walkie-talkie cut through the room, denying Doctor Benson the opportunity to respond.

"*Sheriff!*" came a tinny voice. "*It's Daniels! We've got a serious situation over here at the golf course!*"

"Talk to me, Daniels!" Crawford grabbed his walkie-talkie.

"*One of those things is here!*" the deputy's panicked words were accompanied by screams and shouts in the background. "*William Casey is dead!*"

Crawford didn't respond to his deputy right away. Instead, his eyes wandered from Hailey and then to Jackson, and finally to the figures of Alex and Tahlia.

"*Sheriff?*" Daniels' dismembered voice returned to prompt his superior.

"I'm on my way!" Crawford growled into the device.

"I'm coming too," Antoine Jackson added quickly.

Crawford nodded curtly before spinning on his heel to leave the laboratory. Skipping swiftly around the periphery of the two shining metal tables that housed the dead fish, Jackson was only a few steps behind the sheriff.

"We should go too," Hailey found herself saying to Alex. Indeed, the woman's bold statement shocked even herself. Hailey didn't want to go, but the doctor felt that she had to.

"You're right," Alex nodded before starting to remove his lab-coat.

"No! No! No!" Antoine turned to face them, putting his hands up. "It's too dangerous. You're civilians."

"I don't have time for this!" Crawford snarled, his face red and flustered. "We need to move, Jackson!" He was almost at the door.

"You need us," Hailey told the sheriff calmly before he had a chance to leave. Taking her lead from Alex, she began unbuttoning her laboratory coat to reveal a black singlet top over a pair of skin-hugging blue jeans.

Rather than answer the biologist, Crawford simply let his grey eyes bore into hers.

"You're wasting time, sheriff," Hailey told him flatly, still not intimidated by him.

"Then it's on your head," he replied forcefully, before turning to exit the room.

"Let's get going," Antoine prompted them.

Hailey fell in beside Antoine. It took her a moment to realize Alex hadn't joined them, and neither had Tahlia for that matter. The young woman had returned to her desk, hovering tentatively by her laptop. Alex wasn't far from her, standing on the opposite side of her bench.

"You should stay," Alex told Tahlia softly as he edged closer to her. "You're my student and it would be remiss of me to ask you to come along," he said moving around the bench to place a tender hand on the girl's shoulder. "I've put you in too much danger already. Please forgive me. It was reckless of me."

“Thank God!” Tahlia breathed out, deep and slow. “I didn’t want to be the one to say it. Sorry doc, but I don’t think I have what it takes for this kind of work.” Tahlia flashed him a quick, bashful smile.

“You stay here, where it’s safe.” Alex smiled back warmly. “We’ll keep you appraised of events if and when we can.”

“Thanks,” Tahlia smiled at him, her big eyes gleaming at the herpetologist.

“C’mon,” Antoine interjected from behind Alex. “Let’s do this.”

Cramming themselves into the cabin of Jackson’s FWC pick-up, the trio were on the road within a few minutes, racing after Sheriff Crawford. Antoine of course was driving, with Hailey seated in between him and Alex.

“Man, what a night,” Antoine remarked, scowling at the weather through the windscreen.

Rain continued to fall in buckets from the heavens. Pelting furiously into the tarmac, the torrent proceeded to flood the darkened scene around the speeding vehicle. Barrelling down the multi-lane highway towards SGGC, the truck’s headlamps cut dazzling twin paths through the liquid veil hanging in front of it. For his part, Jackson skilfully manoeuvred the vehicle despite the wet conditions, weaving gracefully from lane to lane. Even so, he was no match for Crawford, whose flashing red-and-blue lights had disappeared into the distance.

“Where the hell is he?” Alex murmured as he peered into the watery panorama.

“Goddamnit, Crawford!” Antoine Jackson growled, leaning forward in his seat.

Unlike her two male companions, Hailey said nothing. In fact, the young woman stared straight ahead. Gazing at nothing in particular, she focused all of her energy into trying to calm herself. Doing her best to regulate her breathing, Hailey did what she could to prepare herself for whatever might lie ahead.

22.

Yanking his steering wheel hard over, Sheriff Walter Crawford's pick-up truck responded by turning sharply. Tyres sloshing underneath the heavyset vehicle, the sheriff moved his truck off the highway, hurriedly making for SGGC.

"All available deputies to Southern Glades Golfing Complex!" the lawman barked into his radio. "On the double!"

The course's wide, gated entrance appeared before him, lit up by his pick-up's powerful hi-beams. Much to his surprise, the massive iron-wrought entryway was lying wide open, almost as if he was expected. Yet, if that was the case, no one was there to welcome him. Rather disconcertingly, there didn't appear to be a security guard on duty. Indeed, although the light was on inside, the little cuboid booth situated just outside the entry was clearly unoccupied.

Deserted… Walter Crawford surmised grimly from behind his windshield.

Inching his vehicle forward, the sheriff crossed the threshold into SGGC. Trepidation filled his body, causing his heart to race. Scanning the scene, a shiver ran down Crawford's spine, blood pounding in his temples.

Ominously, a collection of towering, sentinel-like palm trees lined the road ahead on both sides. If memory served the sheriff correctly, they led almost the entire way up to the reception area. Even so, as familiar as he was with these palms, Crawford still felt the hairs on the back of his neck stand on end. Nervously, he took in the foreboding silhouettes of the trees on either side of him and his pick-up. Dark and imposing, he couldn't shake the feeling that they were looking down at him. Crawford knew he was being stupid, but the lawman found he just couldn't help it.

Harden up, pussy! Crawford told himself sternly. *You need to be worrying about those things. Not some friggin' overgrown palm trees.*

Travelling on a slight incline, the sheriff slowly manoeuvred his truck along the little road, drawing closer to the course's reception area. Thankfully, the rain was beginning to ease off by now, which meant visibility was a little better. Rather than streaming down from the sky, the rain simply trickled. All the same, Sheriff Crawford remained unsettled. If not because of the weather, then on account of the ever-darkening night enveloping the world around him, and the horrors dwelling somewhere out there in it.

"No turning back now," the officer muttered to himself apprehensively.

Moving forward, a familiar roundabout, ringed by brickwork and manicured hedges, and topped by a lone palm tree, all of a sudden came into view, a little off to his left. A second later, Crawford's headlights were reflected back at him, the vibrant beams of light bouncing off the tall glass doors that made up the reception's impressive façade. Momentarily blinded by the glare, the sheriff flicked his hi-beams off, grimacing irritably.

Walter Crawford brought his truck to a stop right there in his lane, barely bothering to pull over to the curb. Leaving the engine running, the sheriff stepped out of the vehicle briefly thereafter. Immediately, Crawford went for his revolver, followed quickly by his flashlight. He wasn't taking any chances.

"All right then," Walter told himself, knocking the driver's side door shut with his hip. "Let's do this."

Edging away from his pick-up with cautious, calculated steps, the sheriff drew closer to the roundabout on his left. Gun and flashlight pointed ahead, the lawman hugged the periphery of the roundabout, his back to the wall of rough masonry and densely-knitted bushes.

Crack! Crack! twin gunshots, albeit slightly muffled, sounded from out of the blue. These were accompanied by a pair of dim flashes, visible through the glass doors leading inside SGGC's main building.

"Shit!" Crawford cursed, jumping with fright at the unexpected shots.

Holstering his pistol, the sheriff hurriedly reached for his walkie-talkie.

"Daniels!" Crawford barked into the device. "Do you read me? Over."

Sheriff Crawford stood frozen on the spot, gripping his walkie-talkie like grim death, waiting for Daniels' response. But it never came.

Unbeknownst to the lawman, hanging just over his shoulder, a pair of garnet-coloured orbs appeared to float amongst the tangled and darkened collection of leaves and branches flanking him. Haunting in their brightness, the ominous twin spheres stood out like the last embers of a dying campfire.

Silently, the female carnifex watched the sheriff from the shadows, sizing him up. Gripped with anticipation, its lips parted slowly, salivating heavily at the sight of a potential meal. Creeping forward, the monster's snout nudged up against the hedge in front of it, parting nuisance branches and leaves out of its way. Drawing closer, its callused nostrils twitched ever so slightly as they inhaled the unsuspecting lawman's scent, the fiend's body tensing with expectation.

Snap! Unexpectedly, something broke underneath it as the creature's wending mass surged toward its quarry, giving away its position.

Crawford's stomach dropped when his ears registered the sharp, but no less portentous sound to his rear. Spinning about-face, he was greeted by a sudden eruption of leaves and branches. Stray twigs and pieces of bark proceeded to assault his face, bouncing off his plump, ruddy-coloured cheeks. Then to his amazement, out of the maelstrom emerged a bared maw, sporting a savage array of dentition that would have put a Great White to shame.

Like a deer hypnotized by headlights, Crawford froze at the sight of the beast's splayed fangs, slick as they were with saliva. What's more, he almost vomited as the fiend's rancid breath washed over him a split-second later.

"God, no…" Walter gasped in a low voice, watching awestruck as the monster's yawning gullet descended upon him.

He reached for his gun a second too late.

With the speed and ruthless efficiency of a cheetah, the carnifex clamped its massive jaws shut around the man's head and neck area! Subsequently, the man's cranium disappeared in the blink of an eye down the monster's throat, muffling his frightened and desperate cries.

Cruuuuunch! The predator bit down hard, its curved incisors piercing the flesh about the sheriff's chest and back.

Blood ran in thick streams down Crawford's torso, front and back, staining his tan uniform a sickly burgundy. Next, straining its neck, the beast lifted Sheriff Crawford into the air, before retreating swiftly into the brush with its panicked and struggling prize. Legs kicking and arms thrashing about wildly, the sheriff's form proceeded to meld with the nest of shrubbery a moment later.

In the end, it was as if Walter Crawford hadn't been there to begin with. Save of course for a few broken branches and leaves, accompanied by the sheriff's discarded flashlight and walkie-talkie, both knocked free amidst the bloody but not less brief fracas.

Antoine slowed his truck to a crawl the instant his headlights danced across the tailgate of the Florida City Sheriff's Department vehicle.

"That's Crawford's truck," Alex breathed. "What's it doing just sitting in the middle of the lane like that?"

"Forget about the truck," Hailey told them. "Where has Crawford got to?" she pondered out loud. "Did he go on ahead? Inside the complex, I mean."

"Maybe..." Antoine breathed, unsure of what else to say, leaning over his steering wheel.

"Why didn't he wait for back-up?' Hailey asked the others.

Neither of her companions could offer up an answer, and with that the cabin was overcome with an uncomfortable silence.

Slowly, Antoine made to manoeuvre his pick-up around Crawford's seemingly abandoned vehicle. Carefully, he rotated the steering wheel between his hands, trying to give the sheriff's truck a wide enough berth. All the while, he perused the gloomy scene, gripped by a mixture of curiosity and concern.

"I don't have a good feeling about this," Hailey told her companions apprehensively, her voice shaking with each word. "His truck's still running…" her voice trailed off as she snatched a quick glance at the pick-up.

Neither man responded to her. Even if Alex or Antoine had wanted to, they probably wouldn't have had the chance. As Jackson brought his pick-up's tray parallel to the hood of the sheriff's vehicle, the world around the warden and his companions went to shit. What's more, time seemed to slow as events took on a dramatic life of their own, spiralling completely out of the trio's control.

Up ahead, a single dull flash sparked to life, emanating from somewhere beyond the glass entrance to the reception area. Within seconds of this, from behind the transparent partition, two tan-coloured and slightly dishevelled figures suddenly appeared.

"Are those sheriff's deputies?" Alex squinted at them through the windshield.

The two figures- both apparently male- burst unceremoniously out into the wet night, one man with his arm flung over the other's shoulder. It was immediately evident that they were fleeing from someone… or more likely some*thing*.

"I think he's injured!" Alex cried out, watching the two hobbling figures.

"Oh my God!" Hailey raised her hands to her mouth.

The marine biologist wasn't in shock at the sight of the two fleeing sheriff's deputies however. Rather, her sense of horror was reserved for the lumbering, scythe-backed silhouette trailing menacingly behind them. Hailey watched in awe, as just beyond the glass frontage, a massive, sinister shape appeared, thundering after the retreating deputies.

They don't stand a chance… Hailey thought to herself.

Eyes trailing across the fearsome profile, Hailey watched in horror as the figure, long and sleek, crashed through the transparent façade, shattering it into a million, tiny pieces! The subsequent mixture of crystalline debris and falling raindrops was left to scatter to the wind, nigh-on hypnotic in its beauty. Amidst the glistening display, the scaled behemoth roared and hissed, splaying its jaws furiously as it inadvertently collided with the Romanesque-style pillar to its left. Slamming into the thick-bodied support, the column cracked on impact, denting slightly. Furthermore, a cloud of dust exploded from the wound as the injured section of stone crumbled.

The jarring collision halted the beast's advance… barely.

Stopping for what could have only been a fraction of a second, the carnifex shrugged off the pain, its dorsal spines involuntarily standing to attention as its wine-red eyes locked onto its elusive prey once more.

Seemingly reinvigorated at the sight of the two lawmen, the armoured goliath clambered after them, using its hardened pectoral fins to clumsily propel itself forward. Hot on their heels, it launched its full weight at them, its great girth momentarily lifting into the air in a surprising display of agility. Slamming its blunted snout into their backs, the two men went down *hard*, face-planting into the tarmac, their figures proceeding to slide for a short distance across the wet surface.

"We have to help them!" Hailey bawled.

But it was too late for that now.

The injured deputy was the luckier of the two. He was thrown off to the side, offering him a brief reprieve from the beast's vicious onslaught. In fact, as soon as he hit the deck, the lawman started scampering across the slippery surface on his belly, in an attempt to escape the bloodthirsty beast behind him, leaving his comrade to his fate.

As for the more mobile deputy, the enraged carnifex came down squarely on top of him- all one-thousand-plus pounds of it! Ultimately trapped between the scaled monstrosity and the hard, unforgiving bitumen, the poor deputy had nowhere to go. He was crushed to death instantaneously, his body going limp underneath the immense weight of the enormous creature.

For a moment, the carnifex stood over the downed deputy. Seemingly revelling in its victory, the fiend loomed menacingly over the crumpled cadaver beneath it, the subsequent sight akin to a lioness defending its kill. Lingering there, it took a second to appraise the scene around it, before it shifted its steely gaze to the other tan-clad figure making his escape.

The second deputy had yet to regain his ability to walk; still moving about on his front. As such, he didn't get far in his attempt to escape the rampaging animal to his rear. Jerking its wending length to the side, the carnifex latched onto one of the terrified man's legs, its teeth clamping shut around the limb, just above the ankle. Then, yanking him backwards, the still-struggling lawman was thrown about like a ragdoll, momentarily falling from the killer's jaws.

For the briefest of seconds, it seemed he was free. Alas, this proved not to be the case.

Clambering about on all-fours, the deputy made a break for it once more, only for the carnifex to strike out at him again. Quick as a flash, it grabbed a hold of him, this time around his torso, its sabre-like incisors skewering him firmly in place. With that, the fiend wasted no time in shaking him like a terrier snatching up a rodent, before casually flinging him to the side and out of view of Hailey and the others.

All of this unfolded within less than thirty seconds.

Hailey's bottom jaw hung loose, the young woman stunned into silence by the brutality of what she had just witnessed. These monsters weren't feeding. Rather, they were simply killing their victims and leaving them. It struck her then that they were making a statement.

Marking their territory… Hailey realized. *Eliminating all potential adversaries in an attempt to solidify their position.*

No one else in the cabin uttered a word, either. That was until the truck they were riding in was buffeted forcefully to the right, as something unexpectedly collided with it! Such was the force of the impact that the pick-up's entire frame jerked nauseatingly, terrified screams and confused shouts coming to fill the cramped cabin within. At the same time, the window to Antoine's left exploded, glistening debris coming to fill the air. With the world shifting around them, jagged slivers of glass showered the occupants, assaulting their exposed faces.

And with this, Doctor Hailey Benson's nightmare began in earnest.

23.

Without warning, the female carnifex burst forth from its hiding place atop the roundabout. Fragments of brick, together with leaves and sticks, came to fill the air, knocked loose by the marauding fiend as it launched itself at its unsuspecting target.

Jaws arched wide, an unholy shriek pierced the night as the beast- a living missile, no less- soared through the air, sheening droplets of rain bouncing off its granite-like hide. Coupled with this, its webbed spines were spread wide like a ship's sail, adding to its already unholy and fearsome presence.

Launching towards the FWC pick-up, the monster battered unforgivingly into the big-bodied vehicle. Its broad snout, fangs and all, rammed into the truck's driver's side, puncturing and crumpling in the metal chassis on contact! The end result saw the doorframe bend inwards, the adjoining window shattering in chorus with this under the force of the thunderous collision!

Resulting from a combination of the momentum generated by the impact, and the slick surface upon which it sat, the FWC truck began to slide wildly out of Antoine's control. Even so, it proved to be a short-lived journey. The pick-up came to an abrupt and bone-jarring stop, its tray smashing into the hood of its Sheriff's Department counterpart. Inside, the vehicle's cabin was filled with terrified shrieks and angry shouts from the beleaguered occupants as they struggled to comprehend just what was happening to them.

Despite no longer being mobile, the carnifex's teeth remained lodged in the truck's abused chassis, speared firmly inside the metal doorframe. Clumsily, the female tumbled from its position atop the roundabout, its scaly underbelly slapping wetly against the bed of tarmac below. The force of the subsequent impact was evident in the ripples that dispersed across the beast's gigantic frame, its scaly skin appearing to undulate and shimmer as it landed.

Then, with a vigorous shake of its broad head and neck, the animal wrenched itself free from the truck. With this, it was able to make its next move.

Hailey looked about the cabin, feeling slightly dizzy, taking in her tight surrounds. Alex wasn't moving, the herpetologist's head lolling to one side. As for Antoine, the game warden was clutching at his leg. Hailey noted the man's left pant leg was ripped, the exposed skin beneath seemingly slathered in blood. Next, her eyes travelled to the mangled door. A mixture of metal and plastic jutted inwards, slick with blood and clearly the reason for the warden's injury. She could hear him groaning and mumbling incomprehensibly to himself as he laid there.

Checking on herself, Hailey raised her shaking hands to her face, feeling for any cuts or abrasions. The young woman quickly came across several chunks of glass embedded in her skin, mostly about her left cheek and temple.

Great. More scars. Hailey started plucking at the bits of glass, pulling them from her skin.

"What the hell just happened?" Alex croaked, coming to after a few seconds.

"My leg..." Antoine grimaced, clutching at the wounded limb, seemingly roused by Alex's question.

"We have to get out of here," Hailey told them worriedly.

"My door's busted," Antoine fidgeted with the door handle to no avail.

"We can use mine," Alex replied.

Hailey's jade-coloured eyes wandered momentarily to the reception area's exterior. She soon discovered that the original carnifex- the individual responsible for killing the deputies- was gone. Indeed, all that remained were the deputies' ravaged and tan-coloured carcasses.

"No, wait!" Benson tried to grab Alex by his shoulder.

But she was too slow off the mark.

Heaving, Alex pushed the door open, only to be greeted by a waiting set of jaws, rimmed with rapier-like tines! Beyond these lay a hungry, corrugated gullet, dark and cavernous. In that moment, Alex felt like he was looking into some kind of fleshy abyss; the walls of the throat beyond lined with viscid fluid.

"Close the door!" Hailey screamed at him, her voice shrill and scratchy.

Throwing all of its weight behind it, the scaled fiend fired towards poor Alex-

-who still had his hand on the door handle. Quick as a cat, the herpetologist yanked the door shut with barely a second to spare. The carnifex crashed head-first into the truck's door, denting the chassis inwards, the metal screeching like a nun's nails on a chalkboard as the monster's teeth pierced and scraped it!

Inside, Alex and Hailey backed away from the door, crying out in terror as the only barrier between them and the waiting horror beyond began to give way.

"What do we do?" Alex yelled, panicking.

Before Hailey could answer, something else happened. Benson felt her stomach sink nauseatingly, as the entire truck suddenly dropped closer to the ground, accompanied by a solid, metallic *bang!*

Pop-pop-pop-pop! The truck's tyres exploded one after the other in staccato fashion, the vehicle subsequently drawn to the ground.

"What the hell?" Alex cried out.

Antoine for his part, continued to groan and whine, clutching at his abused leg, still not entirely with it. The injury was obviously taking its toll on him.

"No!" Hailey squeaked looking in the rear-view mirror. "No, no!"

Despite being offered only a tiny panorama of the scene to their rear, it was enough to chill Benson to her core. Eyes, red and burning, appeared in the reflection; the twin orbs contrasted against a dark and rugged carapace. To her horror, she discovered that the second carnifex had clambered into the pick-up's tray! In that moment, the suggestion of tears played at the edges of Hailey Benson's eyelids; a shallow, constricted breath escaping her parted lips.

Then she screamed.

24.

The truck's rear window exploded inwards! Once more, the cabin's besieged occupants were showered in a torrent of jagged, glass shards. This time however the carnifex's jaws appeared amidst the glistening storm, its massive, yellowed teeth, bared wide and on display. Determined to satiate its bloodlust, the crazed beast jerked to-and-fro, inching towards Hailey and the others. Salivate proceeded to splatter the mangled interior of the truck, dousing the unfortunate passengers inside.

Screaming in horror, Hailey and her companions ducked down, moving just out of reach. Cowering like frightened children, they retreated from the hideous maw as best they could inside the tight confines. All the while, the serpentine creature thrashed viciously from side to side, each snapping movement causing the whole vehicle to rock with it! Fighting to get at Hailey and the others, the monster's entry into the cabin was restricted by the rear window itself, which thankfully acted as a choke-point of sorts.

As Hailey pushed herself away from the rampaging carnifex, she heard Antoine yelp in pain behind her. Twisting in place, she quickly realized she was crushing the game warden against the ruined doorframe to his left.

"Sorry!" she yelped sheepishly.

"What do we do?" Alex bawled frightenedly off to her right, redirecting her attention.

Hailey's eyes quickly surveyed the claustrophobic and chaotic scene, attempting to refocus herself amidst the madness.

"My leg…" Antoine mumbled behind her.

"We've got to get out of here!" Alex cried, shying away from the carnifex's jaws as they swung towards him, gelatinous drool spilling over the uneven contours of its bottom lip.

Hailey didn't reply to either of them. Rather, her eyes continued to dart about the cabin searching for a solution. Alex was right: they needed a way out. But was there one? Was it possible that they were simply trapped with nowhere to go, left to the mercy of this marauding killer?

All the while, the enraged predator snapped its jaws over and over like a rabid dog, desperate to get at them. Off to their right, the other carnifex continued to ram the passenger-side door, the whole truck trembling with each savage foray.

Despite everything that was going on, Doctor Benson continued in her search for a way out, doing her best to block out the chaos and zeroin on something useful. It wasn't long before Hailey's eyes fell upon the rain-laden windscreen. Then she had an idea.

"Out of the way!" Hailey ordered Alex, pushing him off to the side and leaning back against Jackson, before raising her knee and chambering a kick.

Next, she let loose with a hard, Karate-style snap-kick, timing the strike as the carnifex adjusted itself for another thrust. Giving it everything she had, Hailey fired the bottom of her tennis shoe toward the windscreen-

-just as the carnifex jutted forward, going for her leg, its teeth slick and sheening with slaver!

"Ow!" Benson recoiled in pain, her foot bouncing off the windshield.

Whump! the predator's jaws smacked shut, clamping down on nothing but thin air, failing to catch Hailey's leg on its return.

Nice try… the biologist felt her cheeks redden at her feeble attempt to break the window.

"Stupid!" Hailey chastised herself out loud.

She should have known the glass was tougher than she had initially guessed. Still, the marine biologist was desperate, and not surprisingly, Hailey wasn't thinking straight. Quite frankly, the young woman would try anything if it meant there was the slightest possibility of escaping with her life- and those of her friends.

"Here," Antoine croaked somewhat hazily behind her, "let me try my door again."

This time around however, Jackson didn't go for the door handle on the inside. Rather, the game warden reached through the broken remnants of his driver-side window, going for the exterior handle.

Click! The door opened instantly.

Not fully prepared for this eventuality, poor Antoine fell from the cabin, twisting in mid-air so as to avoid planting flat on his face.

"Son of a bitch!" Jackson cried as he landed hard on his back, smashing into the soaked mattress of tarmac below.

Hailey- also caught slightly off-guard- fell from the cabin as well, following almost immediately behind Antoine. Before she could stop herself, Hailey landed on top of the prostrate warden, the pair brusquely brought chest-to-chest. As Benson battered into him, poor Antoine let rip with another pained cry, the air forced from his lungs.

"Are you okay?" Hailey squeaked worriedly, noticing for the first time the gash etched into the side of his head.

"Never better," Antoine coughed groggily, forcing a weak smile for her.

Following close behind them, Alex scampered free of the pick-up, his long legs working overtime. Hovering over the tangled figures of Hailey and Jackson, Alex briskly peeled his friend off the immobilized game warden. Next, the pair began helping Antoine to his feet. One on either side of him, it took the combined efforts of Alex and Hailey to hold Jackson's burly frame aloft. Still, they managed it, difficult as their task was.

In the meantime, the carnifex perched inside the pick-up's tray figured out what was happening. Realizing its intended prey was about to escape, the killer altered its approach. Within seconds of the trio absconding from the truck's cabin, the massive predator set about trying to extricate itself from the back of the pick-up. Unfortunately for the blood-crazed beast, this proved difficult.

The fiend violently jerked its scaled mass backwards. To no avail, it tried dislodging its head and neck from the serrated wound it had opened across the truck's rear window. The mixture of mangled metal and broken glass however worked to trap the predator in place, much to its fury. As such, the monster shrieked and hissed, roiling angrily as it tried to free itself; bits of glass and metal digging painfully into its rough hide, whilst the truck's frame rocked vigorously from side to side like an amusement park ride.

A tangled mess of limbs, Hailey and her two male companions skirted the front of the pick-up, intending to make for SGGC's reception area-

-only to be cut off mid-stride by the other waiting monster!

Peeling around from the truck's right-hand side, the carnifex darted across the group's path, its immense length tensing noticeably at the sight of them. Hissing wildly, the monster flashed its sabre-like fangs, before narrowing its crimson eyes at the trio. Blocking their escape route, it stood stoically between them and the waiting reception area, its webbed array of spines standing erect. Whereas, to their rear, the monster's companion continued in its bid to free itself.

Before either Alex or Benson could stop him, Antoine stepped forward, tearing himself free of his cohorts' combined grasp- much to their surprise. Confronting the armoured horror, the big man bravely placed himself between his friends and the savage beast, somehow finding the strength to stay upright, despite his injured leg, which was still seeping blood. Throwing his arms out, he held them aloft in a defiant display of strength.

"Jackson!" Hailey and Alex yelled in unison, both shocked.

"Stay behind me!" Antoine ordered them, staring down the waiting killer in front of him.

The carnifex watched Antoine's courageous display with a sense of curiosity, pitching its broad, stubby head to one side. Inhaling deeply, the creature's craggy frame expanded before a low hiss escaped from its crater-like nostrils a few moments later.

"Don't move!" Jackson rasped.

Not only did Benson or Alex not make a move, they didn't make a sound either.

Things grew strangely quiet for what could have only been an instant. In fact, the only sound to be heard was the faint pitter-patter of the fading rain, save that is for the intermittent noise of the thrashing beast still tangled amongst the pick-up's abused chassis.

Stunned, Hailey watched the mesmerising scene. Calmly, the carnifex appraised Antoine, sizing him up, trying to gauge how much of a threat the big man was. Briefly, its gaze wandered to Hailey and Alex, its ruby-coloured eyes flicking back and forth between the frightened pair, before returning to the stalwart warden.

"When I say 'go', both of you make a run for it," Antoine Jackson told his friends.

"No, we can't do that!" Hailey exclaimed in a low voice. "We can't just *leave* you here!"

"You have to!" Antoine snapped back. "Otherwise none of us are getting out of this alive!"

"No!" Alex seconded his friend.

"On three," Jackson ignored them both.

"Don't do this, Jackson!" Hailey gritted her teeth. "*Please!*"

"One…" Antoine breathed, his arms still splayed wide.

"Jackson!" Hailey hissed at him, her expression desperate and pleading. "I'm serious! Don't do this!"

"Two…"

Antoine didn't make it to three. Rather, the carnifex beat him to it.

25.

Somewhat awkwardly, the scaled terror propelled itself forward, using its clam-shell-shaped pectoral fins to launch itself head-on at Antoine! In the blink of an eye, the hulking brute left the wet tarmac, cranking its jaws wide as it somehow found the strength to lift its massive length into the air.

Too fatigued to react, Antoine simply stared down the length of the oncoming gullet preparing to swallow him. Indeed, its ribbed, fluid-lined walls seemed to beckon to the warden, the ghastly sight working to turn his stomach.

Crack! Crack! a pair of harsh staccato claps punctuated the night.

As if out of nowhere, two sizzling-hot bullets bored into the predator's right-side mid-flight! One slug buried itself deep into the monster's dark flesh, eliciting a pained shriek from the wounded fiend. Whereas the other projectile shredded a hole in the animal's sail-like length of dorsal spines before then disappearing off into the darkness. Twin gouts of scarlet blood erupted in small, fountain-like geysers; the hot liquid proceeding to cascade over the hardened skin beneath in separate streams.

Screeching in pain, the animal cut its attack short. Reorientating itself, the carnifex crashed back to earth, knocking up a fine, wet mist as it did so. Spinning clumsily on the spot, its huge shifting frame scattered watery droplets helter-skelter, before the monster's serrated caudal fin smashed hard into poor Antoine!

The warden was sent flying through the air. Jackson's journey only ended when his body collided forcefully with the wall of masonry lining the wide roundabout to his rear. At the same time, his two companions lunged in opposite directions, moving just out of harm's way at the last possible second. As for Antoine, after crashing hard into the stone structure, he slumped unconscious onto the grass below.

Robbie Nicholls stared hard down the barrel of his smoking rifle, his blue eyes seeing but not fully comprehending the horrific majesty of the beast before him. Ghostly moonlight bounced off the animal's ridged, wet hide, the rugged shape gleaming with a terrifying beauty.

Wounded and angry, the humongous predator pivoted in the lad's direction, warm blood trickling from its right flank. The venomous look in its wine-coloured eyes sent a chill through him; the usually bulbous orbs turning to the thinnest of slits.

In that instant, Robbie knew deep down he was done for.

Pressed flat against the slippery tract of bitumen, Hailey's auburn hair hung in front of her glossy emerald eyes like curtains. Still, the thin makeshift veil was unable to shield Hailey from the horrors unfolding before her. Indeed, Doctor Benson watched awestruck as the carnifex turned on the FWC warden with an unbridled fury; the beast evidently eager to even the score.

As the creature went for him, Benson found herself wondering just where the young man had come from (not that it really mattered). Her train-of-thought however was quickly derailed as the man's haunting cries came to fill the night air.

***

Robbie quickly tried to crank another round through his rifle, fully aware that the monster was rounding on him. The lad's heart sunk a second later however when the weapon jammed, the bolt stopping short of loading another round.

Turning the weapon over to inspect it, the young warden held the rifle out in front of him. Yet, before he could do anything more, something flashed across Robbie's field of vision and with that the rifle was gone- torn from his grip. He blinked, a little confused as to what had actually happened. Rather unexpectedly, Robbie was overcome by a feeling of dizziness, the world swaying around him. Or was it him who was swaying?

Looking again, Robbie realized not only was the rifle missing, so too were his forearms…

"Aaahhh!" Nicholls screamed into the night, his body suddenly registering the agonizing pain taking hold of him.

Both limbs- from the elbows down- were gone! All that remained were bloodied stumps, the ends of which only just managed to poke out from underneath the shortened sleeves of his tan-coloured shirt. Stringy tendrils of shredded flesh hung limply from the ends of his now shortened arms, the barest suggestion of bone buried somewhere amongst these.

Slowly raising his head, Robbie peeled his glistening blue eyes away from the grisly sight to find something much worse. Only a few feet away, his rifle lay discarded on the damp ground, the instrument slick with a mixture of the beast's viscid saliva and his own blood.

As for the carnifex, the monster watched Robbie with impassive, glowing eyes. Next, the creature swallowed loudly, its broad, leathery gullet expanding and contracting with the sickening action. In that instant, Robbie Nicholls accepted his fate. Indeed, Robbie swore he felt the fight to live leave his body right then and there. The junior warden fell to his knees before the carnifex, offering himself up as blood ran in streams from the abbreviated ends of his mangled limbs.

Take me... he bid the monster to end his suffering.

Robbie Nicholls let loose with one final scream as the carnifex crashed into him, driving its haphazard assortment of teeth hard into his waiting sternum like a bull chasing down a matador.

Hailey lost her voice as she witnessed the carnifex take the mysterious game warden mercilessly to the tarmac. The tan-clad young man virtually disappeared as the monster ravaging him came to all but fill the biologist's already limited field of vision.

Then, all of a sudden, Alex appeared beside her, his arrival completely redirecting the young woman's focus. Whereas Hailey was still prostrate across the ground, Alex had somehow managed to make it to his feet. What's more, the expression the herpetologist wore said he was eager to get moving whilst the large predator was occupied.

"C'mon, we need to get out of here!" he said, leaning down and grabbing at Benson.

Adrenaline pumping through her system, Hailey clumsily joined Alex. Taking his proffered hand, the young woman struggled at first to find her sense of balance. Still, exhausted as she was, Benson made it to her feet. Next, spinning on their heels, the twosome prepared to flee the macabre scene-

-only to be stopped dead in their tracks once more.

Finally wrenching its head free from the broken remains of the pick-up's rear-window, the hulking creature launched itself off the back of the truck, slamming down thunderously onto the tarmac beside it. Indeed, the bitumen beneath the massive predator split as it landed, spiderweb-like cracks spreading away from the animal's monstrous frame.

Inching forward, the carnifex seemed to sneer at the frightened pair, its ugly jaws hanging slightly agape. Hailey found there was a decided lack of empathy in its cold, hard stare. Menacing in its measured ferocity, it resembled a wolf approaching a baby deer.

Petrified, the academics exchanged glances, their eyes locking for the briefest of seconds. Moving in unison, Hailey and Alex back-peddled from the advancing predator, still holding onto one another. A vicious *hiiiiiiss!* to their rear however quickly redirected their attention.

Pivoting on the spot, their soles squelching against the slippery surface beneath them, the biologists were confronted by the other carnifex. Strips of shredded flesh and viscera hung from the gaps in-between its tusk-like teeth, endowing the creature with a most deathly aura.

Hailey felt her stomach drop when she realized they were trapped between the two imposing killers; having allowed themselves to be caught in a pincer movement. This time it was clear they really had nowhere to go. They were simply out of options; left at the mercy of the two imposing beasts flanking them. That being said, Hailey Benson knew this species' strong point most certainly wasn't mercy.

26.

Fierce in its intensity, but nonetheless welcome, the shriek of the incoming EMS sirens tore through the night. The cavalry had finally arrived… and just in time!

Momentarily forgetting about the killers in their midst, Alex and Hailey peered past the outlines of the two pick-ups to the road behind them. Together, they searched the darkness for some sign of the expected red-and-blue lights belonging to the approaching fleet of cop cars, fire-trucks and ambulances.

As for the two scaly predators, they shifted nervously, emitting a series of shrill squeaks and sharp clicks back and forth. Clearly startled by the sound of the incoming vehicles, the ugly behemoths shuffled noisily on the spot, put off by this unexpected development. Just like their human prey, they scanned the darkened scene yonder for the source of the piercing cacophony, their bloodlust abruptly placed in check. Forced as they were by this to re-evaluate the situation, the animals now found themselves unsure of their next move.

For her part, Benson forgot about the sirens, at least for a couple of seconds. Moreover, her feelings of fear and anxiety all but evaporated as they came to be replaced by a sense of curiosity and awe; the scientist in her lured to the surface. Indeed, the biologist's green eyes grew wide when she realized that the creatures were vocalizing- *communicating* with each other, in fact.

"Oh my God…" she breathed, astonished at this.

Before she could contemplate this revelation any further however, the first hints of red and blue began to filter through the gloom, tinging the otherwise darkened, silhouette-laden landscape. In the end, it was this, combined with the wailing sirens, that proved to be the tipping point for the lingering carnifex pair.

Frightened, the beast by the warden's truck turned, its backside- caudal fin and all- buffeting into the mangled vehicle as it proceeded to make its hurried escape. Then, with an almost unnatural speed, the serpentine goliath clambered up the crumbled roundabout, its shimmering, scaly corpus disappearing into the wall of brush perched atop it. Its companion quickly followed suit. A half-step behind its cohort, the second creature peeled around the righthand side of the circular structure, slithering past Alex and Hailey without so much as a backwards glance. Whereas, only moments before, the beast and its companion had been determined to slaughter them both, the two humans were now completely inconsequential to it.

Hailey felt a wave of relief wash over her as the lumbering, spiny profiles merged with the night. Watching their scrambling retreat, Hailey felt confident that they would not return. Twisting her neck slightly, Benson turned to look at Alex standing beside her. She hadn't realized it before, but they were still holding hands, their fingers locked together like grim death, their knuckles turned white. They stood in silence for a second, eyes fixed on one another.

This tender moment proved short-lived, however. A weak, nearly inaudible groan off to Hailey's right interrupted, tearing her gaze away from Alex's smooth, freckled features. It was Antoine. He was still alive!

"Jackson!" Hailey cried in surprise, before wrenching her hand free from Alex's sweaty grip.

Doctor Benson rushed to the downed warden's side. Dropping to a hunched position beside him, the auburn-haired woman leaned in close, the concern evident in her flushed expression.

"Jackson, can you hear me?" Hailey asked, tenderly placing a pale hand to the side of his bruised and bleeding face.

Antoine didn't reply to her. Instantly concerned at his lack of a response, Hailey quickly checked for a pulse before prying Jackson's eyelids open. To her shock, she found only the whites underneath. The only consolation was that he still had a pulse… faint as it was.

"Shit!" Hailey cursed in frustration.

"He needs medical attention," Alex stated bluntly, standing slightly aback from the other two.

"C'mon!" Hailey rose swiftly to her feet, ushering Alex to follow her.

Not wasting any time, she took the lead, stepping out onto the road and moving past the warden's pick-up truck. Although she couldn't see them, Hailey could tell the Emergency Services vehicles were drawing closer; their sirens growing steadily louder with each passing second. Furthermore, the scene before the young woman, although still predominantly an onyx arras, was flecked with azure and crimson hues.

Everything's going to be okay… Doctor Benson told herself.

Slowly, Hailey and Alex edged further down the wending road, continuing in their search for more concrete signs of the Emergency Services vehicles. Distracted as they were, neither Alex nor Hailey noted the mysterious appearance of the wraith-like trio to their rear.

The stealthy profiles detached themselves from the rank of palm trees off to Alex and Hailey's righthand side, their creeping movements both sinuous and sinister. Attired in all black, the threesome silently approached the unsuspecting biologists with measured, predatory steps.

Closing to within only a few metres, the small group fanned out, preparing to rush the distracted scientists.

In the end, Hailey and Alex never knew what hit them.

One figure- the tallest of the three- swiftly produced an extendable baton, the weapon emerging from a baggy sleeve like a tree-snake gliding down a branch. Unfortunately for Alex, he didn't see the individual until it was too late. Indeed, Doctor Scott barely registered the darkened blur of motion at the periphery of his vision, which came only a fraction of a second before a searing pain rode up his right leg, starting at the knee.

"Aaahhh!" Alex cried out, clutching at the injured joint before falling to the ground.

His pained scream startled the unsuspecting Hailey. Spinning on her heel, the frightened young woman found a hooded figure looming ominously over her downed friend. The menacing silhouette, almost at one with the night in its black attire, held a long instrument over its head, preparing to bring it down on Doctor Scott!

"Al-" Hailey made to scream her friend's name, but the cry died in her throat.

Distracted by the sight of her imperilled friend, the two remaining figures swooped in behind Hailey, taking her totally by surprise. Kicking and screaming, Benson found herself locked in a bear-hug, before a noxious-smelling rag was placed over her open mouth. From there, it was all over in a matter of seconds.

A fog-like haze enveloped Hailey as the drug took effect, starting at the edges of her vision. Ultimately, the last thing Doctor Benson saw before she blacked out was the mysterious hooded figure raining down blows on poor Alex.

SATURDAY

27.

When Antoine Jackson finally came to, the frenetic scene awaiting him was nothing short of an assault on his enfeebled senses. Indeed, the organized chaos of the hectic panorama was nigh-on overwhelming in its intensity.

People, almost all of them in uniforms, dashed to-and-fro; several of them animatedly barking instructions at their subordinates- or anyone else who would listen, for that matter. Multi-coloured EMS lights flashed intermittently, coming at Antoine from all directions. As for the vehicles they belonged to, Jackson lost count of the number of police cars, fire-trucks and ambulances on the scene. His heart sunk however when he spotted the quartet of dark-blue coroner's vans also in attendance. It sunk further still when the bleary-eyed warden witnessed a black body-bag being loaded onto a gurney, before then being crammed into the back of one of those bulky, cuboid-shaped vans.

"Damn…" Antoine murmured sadly to himself.

Turning his gaze away from the coroner van, Jackson took in more of the frenzied scene. As far as the warden could tell, it was still night time or possibly even creeping into the early hours of the morning. Whilst a darkness still hung over the area, it was definitely lighter than before.

How long was I out? Jackson wondered. *Minutes? Hours?* He couldn't be sure either way.

"You're awake," said a soft, feminine voice.

"Huh?" Jackson coughed groggily.

Still not totally with it, he forgot about the dismembered voice for a moment. Instead, Antoine focused on something else. His head felt strange. Jackson wasn't sure how to describe the feeling, other than to say the skin around the top of his skull felt tight, constricting even. Placing a hand to his cranium, Antoine discovered it was bandaged. With this, a memory flashed somewhere in the back of his mind. So vivid was the recollection that Antoine swore he heard glass breaking and metal shrieking right then and there. Suddenly, it all came back to him: the carnifex; the truck. Subconsciously, Jackson's hand travelled to his left leg, the limb hidden under a white blanket. Through the thin material he could feel another bandage there as well, wrapped firmly around his thigh.

"Try not to move," a woman's face glided into view, interrupting him. He recognized her voice as the one from only a few moments before.

The woman hovered in front of him for a second. She was young, and pretty too; in her late-twenties or maybe early-thirties, Antoine guessed. Her ebony complexion was almost identical to Antoine's own. Her hair, sheening black, was pulled back in a tight bun. Framed by sharp cheekbones, the female's eyes were an enchanting shade of green. In fact, they reminded Antoine of Hailey's eyes, vibrant as they were.

Hailey... This thought triggered something in Jackson.

Twisting his neck, Antoine searched for some sign of Doctor Benson amidst the madness. It was at this point Jackson realized he was half-sitting, half-lounging in a gurney of his own, and the woman in front of him was a paramedic. Things suddenly became much clearer for the game warden then, the fog in his head dissolving noticeably. Jackson put it down to the rush of adrenaline he experienced at the thought of the absentee Doctor Benson.

"Where's Hailey?" Antoine croaked.

"Who?" the paramedic looked puzzled, her glistening eyes searching his startled features.

"Doctor Benson," Jackson explained pointedly. "Doctor Hailey Benson. She has been helping with our investigation."

The medic looked on vacantly, clearly confused.

"What about Doctor Scott?" Antoine went on. "Alex Scott..." his voice trailed off.

Seeing that he was getting nowhere, Jackson started unbuckling the bulky restraints secured around his legs. Flicking the metal clasps open in quick succession, he freed his thickset limbs before the paramedic had a chance to stop him.

"Wait a minute!" the woman yelped, surprised at his sudden display of mobility and strength.

With a heavy groan, Antoine slid free of the gurney. Using one arm, he steadied himself against the contraption. At the same time, he used his other arm to keep the medic from interfering with his departure. Then letting go of the gurney, he wavered for a second, unsteady on his feet.

"Please, stay seated warden," the paramedic tried to coax Jackson. "You need to be checked out for internal injuries."

"I have to continue with my investigation," Antoine grumbled irritably, stepping away from the gurney and finding his balance.

"This isn't a good idea," the concerned medic trailed after him.

"I have to find her," Jackson murmured in response. "I have to find Hailey."

28.

The sun was only just beginning to crest the horizon when Doctor Benson regained consciousness. For the most part, the world around the young woman remained dark and subdued. Although this was partially on account of the cloud-like veil of fog hanging over the surrounding swamplands. Thick and choking, the steamy blanket blocked out the emerging sun's rays. It wouldn't be long however before the heat from the golden sphere melted through the misty barrier, and with that usher away the last, lingering vestiges of night with it.

Suddenly, memories- none of them good- began flooding back to Hailey. Bombarded by this psychical assault, she flinched and fidgeted reflexively where she lay, almost as if she was caught in the throes of a waking nightmare. Hailey began to panic further still when she came to the startling realization that her wrists were bound tight behind her back. Quickly feeling about with her nimble fingers, the doctor decided they had been zip-tied together by her assailants.

"Relax," cooed a soft and welcome voice.

It was Alex.

Craning her neck, Benson peeled the side of her face away from the cold, metal flooring under her sprawled-out frame. Lifting her head, Hailey found her friend seated on his rump to her left. Like the marine biologist, Doctor Scott's arms were bound behind his back, presumably in the same fashion as Hailey's. Despite their situation, Alex smiled warmly at Benson, glad to see that she was all right (or rather, as good as could be, considering the terrifying circumstances they found themselves in).

Benson noted several cuts and bruises scattered about Alex's face and arms. Hailey's eyes inevitably travelled to Alex's injured leg, however. After all, the limb's abused state was hard to ignore. His right knee, visible just beneath his grey-coloured cargo shorts, was horribly swollen, the skin around the disfigured joint a grotesque mixture of reds, blues and purples. Based on her cursory observation, Benson doubted very much that Alex would be able to walk on it. This would make escaping rather difficult, she decided to herself.

"Oh my God," Hailey gasped with fright. "Your leg! Look at it!"

"*Ssshhh!*" Alex shot her a fierce look. "It's okay, don't worry about it." His voice came out raspy. "Just keep your voice down! They don't know we're awake yet. Stay down and try not to move too much. We don't want to attract their attention."

Taking her companion's words on board, Hailey nervously searched the scene around her with those keen, emerald eyes of hers. It quickly became apparent to the scientist that they were aboard an airboat, albeit one with a considerable lack of seats. Presumably they had been removed, possibly to make room for storage and equipment: the entire midsection of the vessel seemingly hollowed-out.

Beyond the vessel itself, Hailey could make out choking walls of sawgrass lining both flanks. As far as Hailey could tell, they had returned to the Southern Glades. Albeit against their will.

"We have to figure out a way off this thing!" Benson hissed anxiously.

"Agreed." Alex's eyes shifted nervously about the place.

Looking directly ahead, toward what was in fact the rear of the vessel, Hailey picked out three haunting figures- all of them dressed ominously in black. Each member of the group wore hooded sweatshirts- the hoods up of course. Wrapped around the lower halves of their faces were different coloured paisley-patterned bandanas; the combination of these and the hoods working to conceal most of their features. It didn't take a genius to figure out that these were the people who had kidnapped them.

But why? Hailey wondered silently. Ultimately, that was the real question.

One of them, a tall and lanky individual, held a white, hard-plastic bucket, the sides of which were smattered with a collection of haphazard, red smears. Perched on a small seat, another of the black-clad wraiths was situated by the throttle, piloting the stretching craft through the green waters of the slough. The last figure, who appeared to be the shortest of them all, moved with a confidence that bordered on arrogance. It was immediately apparent to Hailey that this person was the one in charge. Indeed, he or she seemed to be doling out instructions to the others, using some kind of instrument (which Benson couldn't quite make out in the dim light) as a tool to point with.

Beyond the menacing threesome, Hailey noted the massive propeller that powered the craft, encased in a circular metal frame, spinning away forcefully. Only then did she truly become aware of the horrid thrumming sound filling her poor ears, horribly accentuated as it was by the harsh sound of the effervescing waves churning underneath the speeding craft.

Benson somehow found the strength to sit upright at this point. Shuffling into position, she rested her shoulders back against the inside of the airboat's chassis, just as Alex had done. Although, she made sure to remain somewhat hunched. This brought the biologists closer together, the pair nuzzling up against each other like teenage sweethearts.

"I bet you wish you hadn't convinced FCU to bring me out here now, huh?" Hailey tried to make light of their dire situation.

"About that..." Alex's voice trailed off.

"What?" Hailey cricked her neck, curiously searching his freckled façade.

"FCU didn't agree to bring you out here," Alex refused to meet her gaze, the man's wavy brown hair framing his full-bodied cheeks. "Turns out you were right. When I approached them with the idea, they told me that they wanted nothing to do with you."

"But..." Benson simply didn't understand. "Then what am I doing here?"

"I took matters into my own hands," Alex finally looked her in the eye.

"*You* paid for it all?" Hailey asked, stunned. "You did that just to get me here?"

"Hailey, someone with your talents needs to be in the field," Alex told her forcefully. "Not couped up in your parents' house away from the world, and the thing you love doing the most." Despite his kind words, Alex's face was ridden with shame. "It is people like you who make a difference in this world."

"Just look at the two of you!" said an unfamiliar, but decidedly female voice. In the end, the shrill, irritating tone worked to cut the scientists' conversation short. "*How cute!*" she went on, her tone derisive to say the least. "Aren't they just adorable?"

Still reeling from the shock of Alex's admission, Hailey turned to look at the voice's source, toward the aft section of the boat. A darkly-clad figure approached them. Short and stocky, the woman wore a black hooded sweatshirt over faded, baggy black jeans. The latter was tucked into Doc Martin boots, which were themselves laced with fluoro-yellow shoestrings. Closing to within a few feet of Hailey and Alex, the as-of-yet unidentified figure slid back her hood to reveal her features.

If Hailey was supposed to be shocked, she wasn't. In fact, the biologist didn't have a fucking clue as to who she was looking at. Indeed, Hailey found a chubby-faced girl with an almost sickly, pallid complexion staring back at her. Someone she didn't recognize- not in the slightest. The unidentified female had a horrible head of dyed, gonorrhoea-green hair, cut short about the back and sides, with the fringe left long.

“Yo! T-Dog!” the woman twisted away from Hailey and Alex for a moment, yelling to the boat’s pilot. “Cut the prop! I can’t hear myself think over here!”

The engine died within a matter of seconds.

Returning her gaze to Hailey, the young woman watched the marine biologist with a fierce intent, her demeanour silent and foreboding. Indeed, her almond-coloured eyes, rimmed with thick eyeliner, trailed over the captive biologist, a sneer playing at the edges of her thin lips. It was then- to her horror- that Hailey realized the instrument which the young woman held was a Bowie knife. By the doctor’s estimation, the blade alone was twelve inches long! All the while, the lass fiddled absentmindedly with the knife in her hands. In fact, she seemed quite at home with it… something that unnerved Hailey greatly.

“We’ve looked high and low for you, Doctor Benson,” she said matter-of-factly. “For almost two years now. And then out of nowhere, you just fall right into our lap! What are the chances, huh?” she smiled wickedly at these last words.

Meanwhile, behind the girl, her lanky cohort moved from bow to bow, slopping a sickly red concoction into the water below. Hailey felt a chill run up her spine at the same time her stomach tightened into a sickening knot, her body reacting instinctively to the sight before her.

Chum… she realized, eyeing the scarlet syrup apprehensively.

Chum was only used for one purpose on the water- to lure predators.

“Who the hell are you people?” Hailey demanded, redirecting her focus back to the young woman in front of her, butterflies proceeding to take flight inside her stomach.

“What?” the female crossed her arms behind her back, sliding the imposing weapon momentarily out of view. “You don’t remember us?”

“What are you talking about?” Hailey grimaced angrily. “Let us go! We’ve done nothing to you! We don’t deserve this!”

“C’mon, Hailey! That’s no way to treat old friends!” the girl smirked, ignoring the marine biologist’s desperate pleas. “We go *way* back.”

With this, a fuzzy memory flashed in a clouded corner of Hailey’s mind: a group of youngsters- five or six of them, she couldn’t be entirely sure of the number- crowded around a protest banner. One face stood out in particular, though: pale and plump and topped with a shock of short-cut, fluoro-pink hair. Despite the drastic difference in hair colour now, Hailey had a pretty good idea it was the same person who was standing in front of her at that very moment.

Those eyes… There was something about them.

Benson remembered feeling uncomfortable about the group's presence on the dock at the time. Yet with bigger fish to fry, she had been more concerned with getting on with the task at hand, and as such forgot about them altogether. Ultimately, this proved to be to her and Ramirez's detriment. Then again, how was she to know they had such deadly intentions?

As the green-haired lass stared vehemently at her, Hailey cast her mind back to a brief discussion she and Deputy Samuels had had on the shores of Lake Minerva. Samuels had even told Hailey the name of the protest group. If she recalled correctly, they were a militant animal rights collective from out of town.

C'mon Hailey, think! said a voice. *What was their name?*

The chubby girl sneered derisively at the biologist as if silently goading her to remember.

Radical something, I think he said...

Hailey desperately tried to conjure up the finer details of the discussion with the young deputy.

That's it! Something finally clicked. *Radical Action for Animal Welfare!*

"RAAW." Hailey uttered the acronym through gritted teeth.

"Looks like we have a winner!" the green-haired girl laughed scathingly.

29.

"Who?" asked Alex, perplexed as to what exactly was unfolding before him.

"Radical Action for Animal Welfare," Hailey explained, not taking her eyes off the scornful girl. "These are the pieces of shit that blew up *the Helicent*."

"Allegedly," the arrogant lass quickly cut in, giving Hailey a smug, malignant smile in the process.

"*The Helicent*?" Alex looked from Hailey to the young woman.

"It was the name of the research vessel Sheriff Ramirez and I used in our attempt to tag the Mako," Benson told him, hoping that it would re-jog his memory.

"*Tag?!*" the girl scoffed at Hailey's use of the word. "Pull the other one, Benson. We all saw the news report. Ramirez made no secret that he intended to kill the Mako."

"I convinced him otherwise," Hailey said calmly, holding her own.

"Bullshit!" the girl snapped, unable to offer up a better retort.

"Listen, you arrogant, pug-faced, little bitch!" Hailey barked furiously, her temper all of a sudden boiling over. "I'm a biologist, not a big game hunter!"

"Don't fuck with me Benson!" the young woman snarled back. "In case you haven't figured it out yet; you aren't long for this world. Now we can make things go quickly for you, or we can take it *slow*. Keep that in mind, before you decide to run your mouth at me again."

"I'm not afraid of you," Hailey replied bluntly, defiantly holding the young woman's icy gaze.

"You fucking should be," the girl smiled wider, a hint of the devil in her hazel eyes. "You're going to pay for your crimes against Mother Earth. Mark my words, bitch."

"Believe whatever you want to believe," Benson turned away from the angry woman. "I didn't become a marine biologist to just needlessly kill animals. That just doesn't make any sense."

"You could have fooled me," said a soft, unassuming voice. This one came from off behind the green-haired woman. Hailey noted it was female as well.

The new voice stopped Doctor Benson in her tracks, if only for a moment. Hailey thought the voice sounded somewhat familiar. Looking past the lime-haired monstrosity, Hailey watched as the third masked figure- the boat's pilot and the one they called 'T-Dog'- made her way to the fore.

"You call yourself a biologist," the faceless individual spat, drawing nearer. "What a joke. At Lake Minerva you slaughtered that shark. Burned it from the inside out with a flare gun, no less!"

"It was kill or be killed," Hailey answered pointedly. "I had no other choice. You people made sure of that. I wouldn't have been in that fucked up situation if it wasn't for you!"

"What about the juvenile carnifex, then?" the masked figure rasped. "I watched you decapitate it- right in front of me! Whose fault was that?"

"It was either the carnifex or those kids," Hailey explained. "I made my choice. I can live with that."

"How. Fucking. Heroic." The fat-faced girl enunciated each word mockingly, re-entering the conversation.

Hailey wasn't really listening to her, however. Rather, the young woman was lost in a fog of sorts by this point. Benson felt what could only be described as a nagging sensation playing at the back of her mind. There was something off about this third figure. Quite simply, she knew too much.

"Wait a minute!" Hailey shook her head. "What did you say?"

"I said-" the full-faced girl started.

"Not you!" Hailey cut her off. "You self-important little dipshit!"

The stocky female's jaw dropped. Yet, before she could recover, Hailey went on, turning her focus solely towards the remaining female in attendance.

"You just said you were there," Benson clarified the airboat pilot's previous statement. "You even used the term 'carnifex'," she went on. "How could you possibly know that name?"

The masked individual didn't answer to begin with. At least verbally, anyway. With a shrug, the pilot casually slid back the dark hood and red bandana covering her face. Hailey's heart skipped a beat when a pair of gleaming, doe eyes and full-bodied lips appeared, set against a smooth, caramel façade.

"Tahlia!" Alex gasped.

30.

"I don't understand…" Alex's voice trailed off.

"It's quite simple really, Doc." Tahlia smiled wickedly at him. "After Lake Minerva and all the heat that situation brought down on us, we- the group, I mean- decided to go our separate ways. At least, for the time being. Demi and Caleb here," Tahlia signalled to her companions, "went to California. As for me, I decided it was time I got a qualification and enrolled at FCU. I'm not totally sure what happened to the other two. Those boys were always kinda flaky, if you ask me."

"It was pure luck that you two fell into our laps, really," Demi joined in, leaning an arm on Tahlia's shoulder, the Bowie knife dangling precariously from between her fingers. "I mean, who in a million years could have guessed that Alex was an old classmate of yours?"

"And to think," Tahlia laughed, "he even went as far as to ask for help from you, of all the people in the world!"

"Must have been fate," Hailey retorted sarcastically.

"I can't believe you would do this, Tahlia." Alex's eyes glistened sadly, looking at his feet. "You betrayed me."

"Life's a bitch, huh?" Tahlia broke away from Demi, dropping down on her haunches in front of Alex.

Leaning in close, the caramel-skinned beauty searched her mentor's face. His solemn expression told her everything: he was a broken man. Worst of all, she revelled in his grief.

"You're kinda cute when you're sad," Miss Mohan grinned.

Reaching out, Tahlia ran a gentle hand down the side of Alex's face.

"Get the *fuck* away from me!" Alex's whole body shook with rage as he uttered these words, leaning out of reach as he retreated from the girl's mocking caress.

All of a sudden, the remaining figure, the tall one Tahlia referred to as Caleb, appeared behind Demi.

"That's the last of the bait," he informed her, pulling back his hood to reveal a face possessed of decidedly pinched features and deceivingly innocent-looking hazel eyes.

Demi didn't respond quickly enough. Instead, a harsh *splaaash!* off the port bow unexpectedly redirected everyone's attention. Even Tahlia rose to her feet, eager to catch a glimpse of the predator- or *predators*- her group had lured.

Hailey twisted towards the source of the commotion. Just beyond the lip of the airboat's frame, she caught a fleeting glimpse of a spiked, hardened carapace, underlined by a tract of pale, silvery-grey scales.

Dramatically, the ugly profile breached the jade surface of the slough sending myriad sparkling droplets to the wind. In the blink of an eye however, the monstrous corpus was gone, disappearing below the frothing waves as it returned to the depths.

"This is gonna be fun!" Demi grinned, her eyes sparkling at the sight of the crimson-tinged waters surrounding the stretching craft.

A second splash drew everyone's eyes to the water once more- this time off to starboard. Hailey Benson's eyes turned to saucers when she witnessed a tall tract of webbed spines cleaving through the emerald waters this time. Fearsome and erect, the vertebral column stood out impressively against the liquid tapestry, producing an unmistakable frothing wake, before gradually receding beneath the agitated surface a few seconds later.

"Caleb, get a hold of him!" the one called Demi ordered, using the knife to point with.

"Wait!" Hailey squealed. "What are you doing?"

Caleb strode determinedly forward, eyes fixed intently on Doctor Scott.

"Stay away from me!" Alex squirmed in fright, trying to stand. His damaged leg failed him however, and he slumped impotently to the ground once more.

"Leave him alone!" Hailey shrieked, getting to her feet.

Attempting to intercede, Hailey cut across Caleb's path, blocking access to Alex. Unfortunately, brave as she was, it didn't work. Unable to defend herself, as a result of her hands locked behind her back, Hailey fell to the floor as an unforgiving backhand smashed into the side of her face! Landing hard on her ass, Benson looked up a second later to find the black-clad figure of Demi looming intimidatingly over her.

"Take a seat, whore!" Demi growled. "I have a feeling you're going to enjoy this. You've got a front-row seat, after all."

Hailey watched dumbstruck, blood pouring out the side of her gaping mouth, as Caleb wrapped his hands around Alex's ankles. Unwilling to give up on her friend, Benson moved to intervene yet again. Another solid strike from Demi stopped Hailey in her tracks however, before Tahlia joined the fray this time as well.

Quick as a cat, the honey-skinned traitor shimmied around behind Doctor Benson, driving a knee into the middle of her back. With that, Tahlia forced the frightened and struggling woman flat against the floor. Next, Tahlia grabbed a handful of the biologist's hair, using this as leverage to yank Benson's head back, the action eliciting a pained scream.

"You're not gonna want to miss this," Tahlia rasped in Hailey's ear, her tone slathered with a bloodthirsty excitement.

By now, Caleb had managed to drag Alex to the airboat's starboard side. Much like Tahlia, he had his prisoner by the hair. The struggling man's head, and especially his neck, were both arched rearwards on an unnatural angle, his Adam's apple poignantly exposed for all to see. Doctor Scott's upper body for that matter was draped over the lip of the boat's chassis, dangling precariously above the undulating green waterline.

Another splash from somewhere out of immediate sight caused Hailey to jump with fright. As if on cue, she felt her heartrate increase and her pulse quicken. Sweat began to seep from her pores, blanketing her skin. Furthermore, Hailey could hear her temples pounding. She hadn't felt a terror like this in years.

"Please!" Hailey begged, tears welling in her eyes. "You don't have to do this!"

Contorted locks of her auburn hair hung at the periphery of Hailey's vision. Still, the terrifying sight before Benson was clear. Fighting back the tears lining her reddened eyelids, Hailey looked on, powerless to act against her friend's tormentors. Demi circled round behind the tangled figures of Caleb and Alex, all the while throwing Hailey an evil, mischievous grin.

"An eye for an eye!" Demi shouted, navigating past her cohort and moving in behind Alex.

"I'm sorry!" Alex screamed at Hailey, his own eyes brimming with tears.

"No!" Hailey screeched, the young woman's heart sliding up into her throat.

Hailey watched helplessly as, yanking back hard, Caleb readjusted Alex for Demi. He manipulated the man's head and neck, straightening the latter so as to allow for better access to their victim.

Next, the green-headed bitch grabbed a tuft of the herpetologist's hair, her eyes on Hailey throughout. Then, ice-cold and utterly remorseless, she took the back of the blade still held in her hand and ran its serrated edge across Alex Scott's waiting throat!

31.

Alex's eyeballs rolled back in his skull, leaving only the whites of them showing. At the same time, blood issued forth in a scarlet torrent from the freshly-opened wound across the man's broad neck; the copper-scented liquid falling to mix with the still, albeit glittering, glassine body of water below.

"Alex..." Hailey whimpered as a flood of tears rolled down her flushed cheeks. "Oh God, *Alex...*" the young woman's voice cracked as she uttered her friend's name, eventually erupting into a shrill shriek of utter despair.

"Oh, Alex!" Demi taunted Benson, giggling as she put her hands to her cheeks in a mock display of concern.

In that moment, Hailey felt the unmistakeable surge of pure, unadulterated hatred filter through her shock-addled body. But ultimately there was nothing she could do about it; no matter how much she may have wanted to cave the sneering girl's head in.

Instead, held captive by the traitor to her rear, Hailey could only watch the murderous duo before her through watering eyes. Still, clouded as her vision was, the doctor was able to make out the callous smiles etched across both Demi and Caleb's foul visages. As for Tahlia, Hailey could only imagine the look on her face at that very moment.

This is all a game to them! Benson realized inwardly. *A fucking game... These people are psychopaths!*

Still in place, Alex's limp profile hung over the side of the boat, seemingly suspended by invisible threads, his opened throat continuing to leak crimson. The man's lifeblood poured freely, mixing with that of the slough. Steadily permeating the green world below, the coppery fluid beckoned to the waiting killers residing beneath the surface...

***

Circling back around, the carnifex pair travelled just beneath the jade surface, their darkened hides barely visible from above the waterline. Propelled by their callused, paddle-like pectoral fins, the animals' tubular lengths pierced the liquescent realm with ease. Approaching from opposing flanks, they honed in on their target, drawn by the distinct, metallic scent.

The female carnifex moved at a slower pace on account of her damaged flank, her movements impaired by the painful, throbbing sensation located just beyond her thick-bodied neck. As for the male, despite the tattered condition of his dorsal webbing and his own damaged flank, he moved at a much faster pace, eager to slake his bloodlust.

Together, they closed on their prey. Silent and methodical, they made for the surface.

Out of nowhere, the water directly in front of Alex's corpse erupted; a frothing, crystalline geyser rising majestically into the air!

"Holy shit!" Demi yelled as both her and Caleb retreated from the bow of the airboat.

Amidst the foaming maelstrom, a massive, splayed maw materialized. Jaws hyperextended, the carnifex's mouthful of rapier teeth loomed large. Coated in a thick fluid, they stood out, glistening in the morning light. A fraction of a second later, the beast's powerful jaws clamped shut- *whump!*- sandwiching Alex's waiting skull between them. In the blink of an eye his handsome face disappeared inside the cavernous orifice. There followed a sickening and very audible *cruuuunch!* as bone and cartilage separated from flesh and muscle! And then the monster was gone. Like some ethereal wraith, the carnifex absconded with its gruesome prize. Peeling away to the side, it retreated swiftly beneath the roiling surface, leaving only a sizzling layer of white foam behind it in its wake.

It wasn't long at all before gravity kicked in and Alex's abused corpse followed close behind the fleeing beast. Knocked off balance, the headless cadaver pitched forward, going overboard and splashing down into the green body of water. Thankfully for her, Hailey was spared the additional savageries exacted upon Alex's carcass, blocked out as they were by the boat's frame.

Doctor Scott's body floated just beyond the bow of the boat, his blood continuing to seep into the water around it. Unlike Hailey, the three RAAW members looked on, watching the horrific scene intently from their respective positions about the stretching vessel.

Several metres out from Scott's ruined remains, a jagged hump breached the surface of the slough. The primeval, armoured hide that emerged was preceded by a stubby, tooth-riddled snout and a pair of imposing, garnet-coloured eyes. The latter of which stood out in stark contrast to the animal's subdued skin. Indeed, the ruby-like orbs endowed the beast with a most menacing aura.

The monster had returned for the remainder of its meal.

"Whoa!" Demi chuckled, leaning forward slightly to get a better view of the predator in her midst. Clearly in her element, the young woman was like a little kid at the zoo. Frankly, it was revolting to watch.

Rushing forwards, the carnifex bore down on Alex's headless corpse, its jaws lifting slightly out of the water as it repositioned itself, preparing to bite down *hard*. Crashing into the waiting hunk of flesh, a fresh effusion of blood stained the water's surface as the monster closed its massive jaws around Alex's waiting torso. In the ensuing frenzy, teeth pierced flesh before grinding against the bone underneath in a gut-churning, visceral display that left little to the imagination for those watching.

"I thought you said there were two of them?" Demi turned to Tahlia, her excitement appearing to dull slightly.

"There it is!" Caleb shouted, pointing overboard and grabbing Demi's attention.

Stealthily, and with next to no commotion, the second monster emerged from the stygian, algae-choked depths. Casual, but nonetheless ferocious, the creature's gnarled snout pierced the liquid arras just shy of Alex's waiting legs. A second later, the newly-arrived carnifex flicked its short head and barrelled neck to the side, its tusk-like incisors smashing down on Doctor Scott's left leg. Tugging hard on the ensnared limb, the second predator made to break itself off a portion.

Its companion had other ideas however.

Still holding onto its quarry's torso, the first beast panicked when it assumed its prize was going to be taken from it, not registering that it was in fact its own mate working against it. What ensued was a tug-of-war. Albeit, a short-lived and decidedly ghoulish tug-of-war. The first carnifex went left, whilst the other went right. The result saw Doctor Scott's cadaver split at the waist, his skin and the flesh beneath tearing like worn denim. The man's innards proceeded to spill from the gaping wound, before the entrails themselves were seemingly absorbed by the swirling, emerald ether, never to be seen again.

"Marvellous…" Demi breathed in astonishment, her golden-brown eyes wide with unashamed enthusiasm.

Beside her, Caleb looked on silently, his smile almost as wide as Demi's. After a few moments, Demi glanced at him, albeit only briefly. Next, she slowly turned her attention towards Tahlia… and lastly, the quivering figure of Doctor Hailey Benson.

Hailey wasn't sure when it was she actually stopped screaming. Time had no real significance for her by this point. Indeed, the doctor felt like she had entered a void of sorts. Stuck on repeat, Alex's horrific execution played over in Benson's mind. Worse still, it resurrected memories of Thomas' death on the waters of Lake Minerva.

In her mind's eye, Hailey could see the Mako lunging from the water to decapitate her former lover, Professor Willard; the horrifying vision overlapped with that of the carnifex's latest exploits. Yet, before she could ponder this any further, events took a sinister, but perhaps not unexpected, turn.

"Bring her over here, *now!*" Demi ordered sternly, pointing in Hailey's direction with her bowie knife.

"*Your turn!*" Tahlia told Doctor Benson gleefully, pulling the mewling biologist roughly to her feet.

32.

Hailey knew she didn't have much time. Unsurprisingly, the adrenaline kicked in right away. She had to act, if she was going to survive this nightmare. In fact, the moment she felt Tahlia trying to nudge her forward, the biologist planted her feet, at the same time lowering her centre of gravity. Hailey wasn't going down without a fight she decided. After all, Doctor Benson was fully-aware of the grisly fate which awaited her.

"Fucking *move*!" Tahlia growled with frustration behind her, struggling to shuffle the defiant biologist forward.

Thinking fast, Hailey quickly snatched a look at the floor of the boat. She noted that (like her) Tahlia was only wearing tennis shoes. A thought flashed through Benson's mind then. Acting quick-smart, Hailey drove her heel down on top of Tahlia's foot, stamping down hard, trying to crush it.

"Aaahhh!" Tahlia cried out, at the same time releasing her grip on Hailey's hair.

Spinning on her heel, Hailey turned to face Tahlia.

"What the fuck?" Benson heard Demi curse at her back.

For the briefest of seconds, Hailey froze, thinking of the other two psychopaths aboard the boat with her. Benson didn't like having her back to them, but she had to deal with Tahlia first.

One thing at a time... she told herself. *Stay focused. Do it for Alex. Fuck that- do it for Ramirez! Do it for Samuels! Do it for all of the people killed here, and at Lake Minerva! These people have to pay for what they've done! For the lives they've destroyed... my life...*

Standing there, Benson watched as Tahlia straightened up, the pain in the girl's foot apparently subsiding. Once her target was fully upright, Hailey didn't waste any more time standing around. Hands still secured painfully behind her back, the marine biologist dashed forward, making sure to keep her centre of gravity as low as possible. At the last possible second, Hailey pivoted on a slight angle, driving her shoulder hard into Tahlia's gut, the impact forcing the wind from the girl's lungs! From here things seemed to unfold in slow-motion.

Tahlia's feet went up in the air as she fell backwards. Attempting to save herself, the screaming girl threw out her arms, trying desperately to latch onto something for support. Unfortunately for Miss Mohan, there just wasn't anything there for her to grab onto, and so Tahlia tumbled into the emerald water below, limbs flailing feverishly about her.

With a resounding *splaaash!* Tahlia crashed into the green slough, foaming waves quickly rising up to envelop her nimble profile. Even so, the honey-skinned girl disappeared for what could have only been a second. When she re-emerged, screaming and drenched, Hailey locked eyes with her. In that moment, the squealing girl's fear was palpable. After all, Tahlia understood- perhaps better than any of the other RAAW activists- the danger residing below the slough's deceivingly calm surface. If Hailey was honest with herself, Tahlia's terror brought the biologist a certain degree of satisfaction. In her opinion, it was poetic justice.

We reap what we sow. Hailey heard her grandfather's voice echoing somewhere in the back of her mind.

It was at this point Hailey noted the presence of a single, dark silhouette shifting just under the surface of the slough, about ten metres out from Tahlia. Like a torpedo, the monster approached from the rear, cutting through the liquid tapestry. Even so, if Hailey read the expression on Tahlia's face correctly, the onyx-haired woman seemed to sense that which was coming for her.

Behind the young woman, an ominous hump appeared, visible just over her shoulder. Shuttling forward, the apex predator closed the distance between them within seconds. Hauntingly, the liquescent canvas that had hitherto worked to both encase and conceal the fearsome apparition peeled away, revealing the approaching killer's more intimate features. Scattering to the wind, sparkling droplets of water fell majestically from its ugly, gnarled corpus; the ravenous, scaled demon rising from the depths to claim its waiting prize.

Without a word, Hailey watched as Tahlia turned to face the horror descending upon her. Spinning in place, the terrified female was greeted by a wide, predatory sneer; the monster's frightening array of fangs coming to fill her entire field of vision.

And then suddenly, things sped up for Doctor Benson, proceeding to unfold in real-time. Or so it seemed.

The monstrous creature pitched to one side, throwing its muscular frame on a forty-five-degree angle as it closed in on Miss Mohan. A split-second later, the sabre-toothed killer battered unforgivingly into Tahlia, its gaping jaws snapping shut like a bear trap, closing around her shoulder and collarbone area! Ultimately Hailey witnessed- in one smooth motion- the carnifex pull the screaming Tahlia beneath the roiling waves and out of sight. In her mind's eye, Hailey imagined the young woman being dragged to a watery hell, the girl's terrified and high-pitched screams muffled only by the liquid realm around her.

Good riddance...

"You killed her!" Hailey heard a male voice shout behind her.

Spinning about-face, Benson was confronted by an incensed Caleb rushing towards her. The young man's pale features were locked in a savage grimace, an extendable baton held high above his head!

Shit! Hailey froze again, if only for a second.

Benson quickly calculated that the lad was within striking distance. Working on pure instinct, Hailey fired a snap-kick into his waiting groin! The black-clad male dropped his baton a split-second after Benson made contact. Stumbling backwards, he clutched at his abused midsection. Thankfully, this sudden reversal in fortunes gave Hailey some breathing room.

But not for long.

Peering past Caleb, Hailey saw the figure of Demi rushing to her comrade's side, knife in hand. She had the look of a woman possessed, her teeth bared like a rabid dog. Hailey did what she could to stop the sense of panic setting in, breathing in slow and deep. She knew she couldn't afford to lose her head.

"You're dead!" Demi barked, pointing the blade at Benson. "*Fucking* dead!"

The green-haired woman made to push past Caleb-

-when out of nowhere the airboat was thrown violently to starboard! Accompanied by the sound of a heavy, thunderous collision, the vessel careened out of control, throwing up waves as it sliced through the emerald sheet of water. All the while, the air was filled with panicked screams and confused shouts.

Thrown off balance, Hailey fell hard on her rump, a sharp pain proceeding to shoot up her back as she landed. Fighting through the agony of it, Hailey snapped her head up to get a better look at the manic scene unfolding around her. Like her, Demi was flat on her ass. As for Caleb, the harsh momentum of the spin sent him flying over the bow of the boat and into the waiting slough! Somersaulting through the air, a plume of spray went up a second later as the young man landed, before he vanished from sight altogether.

"Caleb!" Demi howled, startled by his impromptu departure.

After a few seconds, Hailey could feel the craft beginning to slow. Without its powerplant operating to propel it, the watery carpet beneath the vessel worked to impede its wayward journey. As the shifting world around her began to slow, Benson searched the interior of the craft, her eyes drawn to the port side. The doctor quickly found what she was looking for: an indent in the chassis. Spotting this, she imagined a carnifex lifting out of the water and smashing head-on into the boat.

Reorientating her line of sight after a moment, Doctor Benson found Demi back on her feet and moving straight towards her! A stab of anxiety hit Hailey in the chest right away, followed by another surge of adrenaline. Hailey knew what she had to do.

Rising to her feet, the marine biologist met Demi head-on.

Opposite Hailey, Demi crept forward, a crazed glint in the girl's almond eyes. Inching closer, the blade Demi grasped caught rays of light, shining threateningly.

"You're gonna pay for this!" Demi hissed venomously.

Hailey didn't respond. Instead, she watched her opponent intently, silently weighing up her options. Benson's biggest concern at that point wasn't her adversary's weapon, but rather the fact that her hands were still fixed firmly behind her back.

Stay calm, Hailey thought. *Don't lose control of the situation.*

Despite her attempts to calm herself, Hailey's mind continued to race. What's more, the woman's heart beat furiously in her chest; making her feel somewhat nauseous. Frankly, Hailey was beginning to feel overwhelmed. She wasn't sure how much longer she could keep this up. Her stamina was fading. In fact, it was almost depleted.

Frighteningly, with each second that passed, Demi drew ever closer, knife still held tight. Worse still, lacking a solution, Hailey was no closer to being free of her bonds. By all accounts, the doctor was a sitting duck.

Use your head, Hailey told herself. *You've got to be smart about this.*

By now, Demi was less than six feet away. What's more, to Hailey's total disgust, the girl had a heartless smirk pulled tight across her plump façade.

Use your head, woman.

Three feet and closing…

Use your head…

Before Hailey could fully comprehend it, Demi was right there in front of her, blade at the ready. Then, thrusting with the bowie knife, Demi lunged toward Hailey, letting rip with a guttural war-cry as she did so!

33.

Turning side-on, Hailey shrunk her profile a split-second before Demi hit home with the bowie knife. Indeed, the oversized blade ran parallel to the marine biologist's stomach- missing Hailey by less than an inch!

Stunned by the doctor's cat-like reflexes, Demi froze on the spot; her expression one of utter shock. Whereas Hailey wore a smile like a Cheshire cat's. At this point, the two women were only centimetres apart.

It was then that the biologist made her next move.

Hailey half-stepped toward her enemy, driving her forehead unforgivingly into Demi's pug-like nose. Benson knew she had managed to hit her mark when she heard the bone in her adversary's face crack like a falling tree!

"*Aaahhh!*"

Screaming in agony, Demi retreated clumsily, blood spewing from her face. Reaching for her nose, she dropped the bowie knife involuntarily. Staggering backwards, the wounded girl clutched at her mangled nose, tears streaming down her cheeks.

Meanwhile, forgetting about her injured foe, Hailey zeroed in on the discarded weapon. Dropping down onto her rump, she crouched over the instrument, desperately clawing at it, trying to grab a hold of it with her hands- restricted as they were by her plastic bonds.

Splaaash! A commotion to starboard redirected Hailey's attention momentarily.

Hailey felt the airboat buffet slightly as something collided with it. Although, this collision wasn't anything like the previous one. Instead, if you were to compare the two, it was much softer; like being hit in the face with a pillow, versus say, a boxing glove. Gasping, Doctor Benson's eyes went wide when she saw a skeletal collection of fingers curl around the lip of the airboat's frame. Next, elbows appeared, wrapped in sopping-wet, black fabric. Then, a head and shoulders materialized. Heaving with exertion, Caleb's wan face appeared, soaked and dripping.

"Peek-a-boo!" Caleb's top lip curled as he locked eyes with Hailey, a sheening bead of water rolling down the bridge of his nose.

Benson felt her entire body tighten at the sight of the young man.

How the hell did he manage to evade the carnifexes?

Caleb's savage smile didn't last for long, however. Pausing for a second, Caleb inspected the interior of the craft. His eyes inevitably shifted to Demi's crumpled frame. The girl was on her hands and knees by now, whimpering as blood poured from the middle of her face.

"You fucking bitch!" Caleb cried, shifting his gaze to Hailey. "What did you do to her?"

Sliding forward, Caleb lashed out at Hailey, grabbing at her like a ghoul rising from the grave. Thankfully, he missed as Hailey recoiled at the sight of him. Still, he wasn't about to give up. Making to re-enter the boat, Caleb groaned audibly, cursing through gritted teeth as he lifted himself up. This sudden display of aggression gave Hailey the incentive she needed to hurry up. Working feverishly, the biologist pushed the blade's serrated edge against the plastic zip-tie, sawing back and forth with it.

"Ouch!" Benson yelped as the blade went askew, missing the plastic and digging into one of her hands instead.

Casting a wary glance up ahead, Hailey noted that Demi was in the process of getting back on her feet, albeit rather gingerly. She was a good six feet away, having conceded significant ground as a result of the headbutt. Still, Benson had to hurry. Before long, Caleb would be back in the boat as well. Even if she managed to free her hands, Hailey doubted very much that she could take on the pair of them. Quite simply, Benson had to eliminate one of them from the equation- *by any means necessary.*

With the pain fading in her lacerated hand, Hailey began working the zip-tie against the blade once more. Sweat creased the young woman's forehead, at the same time running down her temples. Hailey could feel her whole body shaking, the tremors working their way to her extremities.

"You're mine now!" Hailey registered Demi's voice, just as the zip-tie burst apart.

Looking up, Benson found Demi looming over her, the girl's chubby face smeared with her own blood. Snatching a sideways glance, Hailey watched Caleb attempt to re-enter the airboat, slipping and sliding as he tried to gain some traction.

Then something strange happened.

As Caleb made to launch himself inside the craft, he jerked backwards, and sharply at that. The young man went rigid, as if an electric shock was passing through his body. For a moment, Hailey thought the lad was convulsing. Although, that being said, rather than a flood of frothing saliva pouring from his thin lips, it was blood. His blood. Dark and red and copious.

Previously bearing down on Hailey, Demi had halted in her tracks at this point, the girl's attention unexpectedly diverted by this development.

In the end, the two young women stared in stunned silence at Caleb. Neither saw the yawning chasm- framed either side by tusk-like teeth- appear directly below him in the water; the gaping maw rising to engulf the waiting man.

Emerging from the depths, the carnifex's jaws wrapped around Caleb's legs, closing shut around his skinny waist. The beast's incisors proceeded to puncture the lad's flesh in a macabre, crimson display. For her part, Hailey shrunk back as she watched Caleb break away from the airboat, carried into the air- propelled no less by the rising monster! Water swirled around Caleb as he ascended, the ensuing storm of displaced droplets mesmerising in its beauty.

Climbing higher into the air, Caleb reached for Demi, shrieking all the while from a combination of sheer agony and unadulterated terror. It was a futile gesture, nonetheless. There was nothing she could do for him. For his part, Caleb could do little more than endure, blood spilling over his lips as he screamed.

Running out of momentum, the carnifex reached its zenith. With that, all one-thousand-plus pounds of the beast came crashing back down into the slough, dragging a shrieking Caleb with it. The resulting torrent of foam and froth hissed furiously as green waves enveloped the fleeing creature and its bleating quarry.

"Caleb!" Demi howled pitifully, watching her lover disappear beneath the roiling surface. "Oh, Caleb…" Demi's voice faded.

"*Oh, Caleb!*" Hailey mocked the grieving girl, rising determinedly to her feet.

Benson sized up her opponent, inching forward, bowie knife in-hand.

"Just you and me now," the biologist gave Demi a wicked smirk.

Across from Benson, Demi spun to look at the marine biologist. The look on the pudgy girl's face was one of shock and defeat, evidently both surprised and demoralized by the reversal of fortunes she and her friends had experienced. Indeed, Demi's eyes widened at the sight of Hailey, armed as she was with the imposing bowie knife. Demi zeroed-in on the sheening blade, her hazel eyes glistening with unmistakable fear.

Hailey stopped momentarily, interrupting her creeping advance. She shifted her line of sight to the weapon gripped in her hand. Benson watched the blade as it captured the morning light. The scientist gave the weapon a moment's contemplation, shifting her gaze from it to her target and back again. Then, stepping forward she launched the bowie knife-

-firing it into the floor of the airboat!

The tip of the blade pierced the metal chassis with a thud, landing between Hailey's tennis shoes, where it stayed, leaning on a slight angle.

Stepping past the discarded weapon, Doctor Benson put herself between it and Demi.

"Let's finish this!" Hailey balled her fists, eyeing her rival intently.

34.

Taking a cue from her opponent, Demi let loose a furious shriek. With a manic look encased in her dark eyes, she raced down the centre of the craft; the vessel's frame trembling underneath her booming steps. The visage of a harpy, she spewed obscenities as her fringe, green and long, flittered wildly in the wind. Then, cocking an arm back, she raced toward the waiting figure of Benson preparing to strike!

Opposite her, Hailey held her ground, refusing to be intimidated by her advancing enemy. Instead, as Demi drew down on her, Hailey half-stepped, moving aftwards. Timing it perfectly, she stepped just out of Demi's striking range. Using her long, lithe arms to her advantage however, Hailey fired out a hard-hitting right cross, driving her balled fist into one of Demi's waiting eye sockets! There was a distinct and resounding *crack!* as flesh and bone smashed together in sickening chorus a moment later.

Overcome with pain, Demi stumbled backwards, her left cheek swelling noticeably as it filled with fluid beneath the injured skin. Grimacing, the young woman eyed Hailey venomously, her jaw clenching in anger, teeth grinding against one another.

"You'll pay for that!" Demi hissed, her dark eyes travelling to the blade just beyond the figure of Hailey.

Benson realized right away what Demi was looking at. Twisting her neck, Hailey couldn't help but smirk when her jade-coloured eyes fell upon the waiting knife; its pointed tip still wedged firmly in the boat's metal chassis.

"Don't even think about it," Hailey told Demi through gritted teeth.

The pair locked eyes for a moment, both of them now silent. Still, no words were needed here to express the enmity each woman shared for the other. Rather, it was written as clear as day on their reddened faces.

"Was it all worth it?" Hailey probed, watching the girl opposite her. "All this death and destruction?"

Demi snorted derisively in response, unable to muster anything more substantial.

"What, no words?" Hailey cocked her head to the side. "Why so shy all of a sudden? You had plenty to say before. Cat got your tongue? Or would carnifex be more appropriate for this type of situation?"

Despite Hailey's attempts to get inside the young woman's head, Demi's gleaming eyes refused to leave the knife. She was locked in on it, her stare intense and unwavering.

"How does it feel to know your friends are dead?" Hailey poked the bear a little further, the woman's balled fists floating by her sweat-laden cheeks.

Demi's mascara-framed eyes instantly left the bowie at these words. Flicking in Benson's direction, the glistening, hazel spheres narrowed to the thinnest of slits.

"It's over," Hailey jibed at her. "You failed. Just give up."

This, it seemed, was the last straw. Demi tensed noticeably at Hailey's harsh, but no less truthful words. Then seemingly both angered and reinvigorated by them, Demi launched herself at her foe once more!

Moving fast, Demi cut left, trying to slip past Benson and get to the bowie knife. Unfortunately for her however, she wasn't fast enough. Hailey cut her off, firing out another hard punch. To Hailey's surprise, Demi slipped the attack- albeit only just- cutting right this time instead. Once again however, Benson was quicker on her feet. Side-stepping, Hailey cut Demi off again, landing a quick one-two combination that forced Demi to retreat back the way she came.

"Fucking bitch!" Demi spat feverishly.

Angered at her ineffectiveness, Demi bellowed with frustration, grabbing at her hair like a toddler lost in a tantrum. Clearly at her wit's end, the young woman's face contorted into a harsh scowl, hatred burning in her eyes. After a few seconds, Demi let go of her hair, taking a few stray strands with her. All the while, the girl's hands remained clenched, eventually coming to rest by her sides, pieces of green hair poking away from them in all directions.

A strange, eerie, almost unnatural calm fell upon the scene then.

Only the distant sound of insects and that of the wind moving through the nearby sawgrass prairies was to be heard. What's more, neither woman had taken their eyes off the other. Cold and calculated, they watched one another attentively.

Then unexpectedly, Demi's lips peeled back, revealing her pearly white teeth. The peculiar smile soon evolved into a high-pitched and irritating laugh, the girl throwing back her head and crowing to the sky above like a lunatic.

What the hell is wrong with this girl? Hailey wondered to herself.

Yet, before she could answer her own question, Demi launched herself at Hailey! Darting forward, the demented girl bull-rushed the marine biologist, taking her off-guard. In the end, she reached Benson in little more than a second. Throwing everything she had into it, Demi spear-tackled the doctor, driving Hailey mercilessly to the deck!

Hailey felt herself leave the ground, forced into the air by her enraged opponent. Still, she only floated for a second before crashing back to earth, slamming hard into the deck of the airboat! Landing with a tremendous thud, Hailey saw stars for a moment, the concussive wave from the impact working through her beleaguered body.

Blinking the dancing balls of light away, Hailey found Demi straddling her. In that instant, the girl gazed down at the biologist with a decidedly demented look in her eye. It was the look of a predator. The look of a killer.

This wasn't good- *not by a long shot*, Benson realized immediately. In the blink of an eye, Hailey had lost her hard-won advantage. She hadn't expected Demi to come at her like that. The girl had proven unpredictable- and this made her dangerous. That being said, Demi's chest was heaving from the exertion of it all. Like Benson, she was close to packing it in. She didn't have the stamina for this kind of ordeal. Hailey could tell by the glint in the girl's eyes that she was looking to end it. And quickly.

All of a sudden, the pudge-faced girl's eyes flashed to the right of Hailey. Startled by this, the doctor followed her opponent's line of sight-

-and found the waiting bowie knife! The weapon was within arm's reach… for both of them.

Reacting quick-smart, Hailey threw out her arm. Lightning-fast, she knocked the weapon out of Demi's reach, skiting it toward the head of the boat. Howling with rage, Demi scampered after it, sliding off Hailey in her bid to get to it.

Subsequently freed by Demi's decision to chase after the knife, Hailey flipped over onto her front. Next, pushing up off the floor, she raced after the scrambling girl, tennis shoes squeaking underneath her as she went. With a guttural bark, Hailey swiped at Demi who was on her hands and knees at this point, still clambering after the bowie knife- which was only a few feet away from her! The doctor's fingers brushed against a swatch of fluoro-green hair, curling into a clenched fist as she took hold of it. Hailey knew she had managed to grab a hold of just the right amount when Demi halted abruptly in her tracks.

With a hellish screech, Demi clawed with her fingernails trying to free herself from Hailey's grasp. Rising to her knees, she thrashed wildly, her back arching involuntarily as Doctor Benson tugged hard on the girl's hair.

"Let go of me!" the girl squealed hysterically, a hot pain tearing through the top of her head.

In any event, Hailey wasn't listening. Instead, she yanked hard on Demi's hair once more, dragging the squirming female away from the knife.

"C'mere!" Hailey growled ferociously.

Collapsing onto her rump, Demi continued to kick and scream as Hailey hauled her along the floor of the airboat. Then with one final heave, Benson pulled the girl back towards the centre of the stretching craft. Next, pivoting on the spot, Hailey slammed her adversary into the side of the boat! There was an audible *thunk!* as the back of Demi's head bounced off the inside of the vessel's chassis. Subsequently dazed by this, the battered girl's eyes flitted about the now hazy scene before her, failing to focus.

"Fucking stay down!" Benson roared at Demi, her tone deep and commanding.

By now, Hailey was nothing more than a darkened silhouette to the badly-beaten Demi, at least at first. Gradually however, the figure of Doctor Benson came into greater focus as Demi's vision sharpened.

"So, you're gonna kill me now, huh?" Demi croaked, sneering away.

"Something like that," Hailey answered flatly.

To be honest, Benson wasn't sure what she was going to do. Certainly, a fury burned deep within her, that much was true. But could she kill, for revenge's sake? In cold blood, no less? A part of her said it was justified. Another part however, wasn't quite so sure. Ultimately, the question that remained to be answered was, did Hailey Benson have it in her? In other words, could she be as ruthless as Demi and the other RAAW activists?

35.

Vision slowly returning to normal, Demi tried her best (despite her injuries) to focus on Hailey. The auburn-haired Amazon was hovering silently in front of her, standing with both fists at the ready, her aura threatening and imposing. With a cold intent evident in her green-coloured eyes, the biologist watched Demi closely. All the while, a deep-seated rage seemed to seep from the scientist's pores.

"Sorry honey," Demi laughed at her, "but you haven't got the guts! Not for this line of work, anyway."

The girl appeared to understand the internal battle being waged deep inside Hailey Benson at that very moment. Indeed, it was written on the woman's troubled face. If Demi read Hailey's expression correctly, there was a hint of indecision residing there. As such, if Demi was going to survive this, she had to play on this apparent weakness- she had to appeal to Hailey Benson's sense of humanity… or what was left of it. After all, she and her friends had done much to strip away at it.

Hailey's jaw clenched along with the rest of her body at Demi's words; that familiar, but no less uncomfortable, rage continuing to build up inside her. It was close to overflowing now. Benson could feel it. Was it enough to push her over the edge, however?

"It just ain't in you," Demi's swollen cheek had doubled in size- so much so she could only see through one eye now. "You're tough, I'll give you that. But you're no killer." She coughed painfully.

She's right… Hailey felt her fists begin to unclench. *Isn't she?*

Gingerly, Demi raised her arms, laying them along the rim of the vessel's chassis to her rear, as if she was lounging on the couch at home just watching a movie. By her estimation, Benson was wavering.

"Killer instinct… some of us have it… some of us don't…" Demi went on, somewhat casually, struggling to breathe in between her words.

Hailey turned her fists over, opening them to look at her palms. The creases in her skin were caked in a mixture of blood and grime. She also noted blue-purple bruises travelling the length of her forearms. Flipping her hands back over, Benson inspected the cuts etched about her knuckles as well.

What have I become? Benson asked herself. *What have they turned me into?*

"Shame about your boyfriend, though," Demi added, the direction of the conversation shifting rather abruptly. "To be honest, he seemed like a nice guy."

In that instant, Alex's boyish face, topped by wavy brown hair, flashed inside Hailey's mind.

"What did you say?" Hailey narrowed her emerald eyes as Alex's visage faded away.

"I said it's a shame…" Demi smiled wickedly, "… that you couldn't do more to save him." The girl winked with her one good eye.

In the end, Demi couldn't help herself… even if it meant losing her life. She was just that type of person: someone who would cut off her nose to spite her face. Ultimately, young and full of hubris, the girl's arrogance sealed her fate.

"Listen, you sick, twisted, little cretin!" Hailey jutted forward, her hands instantly balling into fists once more.

Hunching down in front of Demi, she brought herself nose-to-nose with the belligerent, smug-faced brat. And before she could stop herself, Hailey's left hand unclenched as she smashed it into Demi's windpipe, striking in a horizontal chopping motion!

"Alex!" Hailey screamed. "His name was *Alex*! And his blood is on your hands! Not mine!"

Gagging and spluttering Demi fought to get a breath, the young woman's throat aching horribly. Merciless in her ferocity, Benson didn't let up however. She wrapped her open hand around the girl's throat, applying pressure, slow but nonetheless firm. Demi fought, clawing at Benson, her arms thrashing. But it was no use- she was too weak to properly resist. Their fight had taken its toll on young Demi- she was running on less than fumes at this point.

Watching Demi struggle right there in front of her, Hailey Benson's world went black, before morphing to red as her emotional state reached a fever pitch. Quite simply, the rage burning inside her soul was on the verge of consuming her. What's more, deep down inside, Benson knew as much. Terrifyingly, the young woman wasn't sure she could fight it any longer. With that said, Hailey wasn't even sure she wanted to fight it anymore.

Payback's a bitch… Hailey thought sourly.

Pulling back her right arm, Hailey proceeded to power her fist into Demi's face once more! This time the already swollen skin about the girl's cheek split, blood trickling forth in a small river from the horizontal laceration that was left behind.

"Was it all worth it?" Hailey punched her again, this time about the nose and lips, forcing the girl's head to rock sickeningly. "Answer me, damn it!"

Demi spat up blood, the gruesome liquid spilling over her now bruised and bulging lips.

"Ramirez! Samuels!" she socked her again, thinking of her comrades lost at Lake Minerva. "If it wasn't for you, they'd still be alive!"

Demi's head lolled with yet another punch from the enraged Hailey.

"They were just doing their job!" the biologist cried, lost in a frenzy.

Barely conscious now, Demi's head sagged, her chin coming to rest against her plump chest. Still, Hailey wasn't finished with her. Removing her hand from the girl's throat, Benson grabbed a hold of Demi's fringe, before forcing the young woman's head back. Looking down on her, Hailey watched the veins in Demi's stocky neck bulging as her heart beat furiously.

"You killed them in cold blood," Hailey said in a low voice. "Alex, too!" her voice went up a notch.

"You really did have a soft spot for him, didn't you?" Demi's good eye blinked open and closed slowly. "Wondering what could have been, eh?" that now familiar, arrogant sneer returned to the girl's battered and bloodied façade.

"*Argh!*" Hailey smashed her enemy in the face one more time, throwing everything she had into a savage, hooked punch.

Demi's head snapped to her right, the shock of the impact rippling through her abused cranium. The girl blacked out for a second, and when she came to, Demi found- much to her surprise- Doctor Benson had turned her back on her. Despite her beaten state, it only took Demi a fraction of a second to realize that Hailey was marching back towards the discarded bowie knife!

Within only a few seconds, Benson had reached it. Crouching low, she snatched up the sheening weapon. Next, Hailey turned sharply on her heel, the bowie knife now held menacingly in her hand!

Have I underestimated her? Demi asked herself in that single terrifying moment. *Have I pushed her too far?*

"Maybe you do have it in you, after all." Demi smiled, arms still outstretched behind her, trying to stall the doctor.

It worked.

Hailey halted in her tracks. The woman paused to examine herself, her jade eyes instantly drawn to the weapon gripped in her right hand. Hailey looked somewhat stunned at the fact she was holding the knife, almost as if she didn't truly believe it was actually her holding it.

Demi watched her adversary intently, both curious and afraid… very afraid. In that moment, Hailey Benson was malice incarnate. Her emerald eyes, sharp and glistening, penetrated the fiery veil of hair concealing her pale features. The look in Benson's eyes- that cold, heartless, penetrating stare- told Demi everything she needed to know. The woman's intentions were clear. Indeed, Demi realized then and there that Benson meant to kill her. The marine biologist had finally broken- and it was Demi who had tipped her over the edge.

"See you in hell, Benson!" Demi yelled suddenly.

Groaning with exertion, the green-haired girl pushed off with her feet, planting them hard against the metal decking. Forcing herself up and over the lip of the airboat, she launched back-first into the emerald water below, disappearing from view as she crashed beneath the surface!

Demi let herself sink, the young woman's baggy clothes becoming waterlogged near-instantly. Opening her eyes (or rather *eye*), Demi searched the emerald-tinged world around her. Light from above pierced the liquescent canvas, causing shadows to dance gracefully about her; myriad shapes moving in all directions.

Gradually, Demi sunk deeper, all but swallowed up by the jade environment. She knew that *they* would find her soon enough. In fact, she counted on it. Demi preferred the thought of a carnifex taking her much more than allowing Hailey Benson to have her vengeance. This way Demi would spite her enemy… even in death. Furthermore, at least this way, Demi had some choice as to how she went out.

They who laughs last, laughs the longest, Demi thought macabrely.

Twisting her neck, Demi searched the gloom-laden arras, hoping for some sign of the carnifexes. She wanted to see them one last time before she died. To be honest, the young woman was in awe of them; there was an incredible beauty in their ferociousness.

Demi wasn't sure how much time had passed. Ten or fifteen seconds at most, surely? Even so, the young woman's chest was beginning to hurt, her lungs burning hungrily for oxygen. Demi quickly forgot about her discomfort however as something caught her wandering eye, off to her right.

At first, a single crimson dot appeared; the burning sphere cutting through the darkness. This was followed quickly by a second orb. Looking into the green vacuum, Demi couldn't decide what was more terrifying; the beast's eyes, or what came next. A snout- short and blunted- materialized as if in slow-motion from the murky ether, complete with an assortment of sabre-like teeth. Next came the body proper. Scaly and topped with armour, the serpentine killer closed on her. Demi felt her chest tighten further still as the menacing beast snaked onwards. Its tubular body scythed effortlessly through the green water as its paddle-shaped appendages worked to propel its massive frame.

What's more, its webbed vertebral column stood to attention, helping to guide the goliath on its journey.

It's magnificent... Demi thought.

Rising on an angle, the carnifex climbed through the shimmering water column. Sinuous and leisurely, the monster zeroed in on the outline of the airboat above. As for Demi, it hadn't seemed to have noticed the young woman hanging there in the water, exposed and in the open. Instead, the creature's attention was fixed on the stretching silhouette above.

It doesn't know I'm here...

Suddenly, one of its ruby-coloured eyes flicked in her direction. The organ seemed to widen, as if the monster was surprised to see her drifting there. Demi had spoken too soon it seemed, even if only to herself.

With little more than a flick of its jagged, racket-shaped tailfin, the beast pitched in the water, changing direction instantly. Its body winding vigorously, the monstrous animal coursed straight towards her, a deadly intent in its demonic glower! The creature's speed was amazing; the carnifex managing to close the distance between it and its prey in only a matter of seconds.

In the end, Demi could only stare, in both fear and amazement, as the predator's jaws cranked open, revealing a cavernous, ribbed gullet! Rimmed by talon-like incisors, the yawning orifice raced towards Demi as the killer prepared to engulf her!

Meanwhile, unbeknownst to the young woman, the second carnifex approached from below, moving in silently from her left.

The two beasts hit- almost in unison- one taking Demi by the head and shoulders as the other took out her legs! A turbulent explosion of bubbles generated by the thunderous impact obscured the scene as the three figures became violently intertwined. Carried by their own momentum, the two creatures continued to move in opposite directions, and as such the monstrous fish ultimately fought against one another... the result of which was horrific.

Demi felt a searing pain disperse throughout her body as flesh and tendons were strained to an unnatural degree. Her body was being stretched-

- to breaking point!

Skin split and bones broke, which saw the girl literally wrenched apart by the ravenous beasts. An effusion of blood and innards followed; a scarlet cloud proliferating in the killers' wake like the bombs dropped at Hiroshima and Nagasaki.

When it was all said and done, Demi barely had time to scream. She did have time however to regret her decision. As the gruesome, corrugated, pink-purple gullet bore down on her, the young woman questioned whether it might have been better to die at the hands of Doctor Benson.

36.

Mouth agape, Hailey blinked several times, totally confused by what she had just witnessed. It didn't make any sense (at least to her, that is). The marine biologist's foe had literally thrown herself overboard and into the slough- dropping herself right in amongst the rampaging carnifexes!

Regaining her composure a few moments later, Benson dropped the knife in her hand. Next, she rushed to the bow of the boat. Dropping onto her knees, Hailey peered overboard, her fingers curling around the rim of the vessel's chassis. Staring down into the dark waters, the doctor searched the stygian realm for some sign of Demi. Save for a fleeting collection of abstract shadows lingering a short distance beneath the surface, Benson found nothing concrete. After a few moments however, Hailey became aware of her own reflection staring back at her.

Hailey Benson examined herself against the shifting surface of the slough, using it as a mirror. Her auburn hair was a mess: matted in places and askew in others. The biologist's face wasn't much better either. Hailey noted the small cuts about her cheek where shards of glass had embedded themselves in her skin. What's more, her bottom lip was swollen and bruised, dried blood having collected around the corner of her mouth.

"Jesus kiddo," Hailey muttered away to herself, "you look like shit!"

Indeed, the marine biologist barely recognized herself. This sudden realization seemed to trigger something deep within her then.

Was I really going to do it? Benson asked herself. *Was I going to kill her?*

Movement beneath the waterline unexpectedly took away Hailey's attention before she could answer these questions. Fangs, curved and yellowed, fired towards her, piercing their way through the algae-choked water! Too fatigued to react right away, Hailey froze, awestruck by the sight before her.

Jaws spread wide, the carnifex lunged from the slough, sheening tracts of green water falling from its savage visage! Then, with teeth only inches from her face, Hailey's mind finally kicked over, telling her to get a move on.

With a terrified shriek, Benson threw herself backwards, retreating from the encroaching maw! Kicking with her heels, Hailey slid on her rump, scampering to escape the monster's clutches. Then, as her back slammed against the interior portside, Benson quickly found she had nowhere to go. As such, she watched in horror as the snaking goliath ascended, before it pivoted towards her and the airboat in mid-flight!

Reaching its zenith, the carnifex shifted its weight in the air, turning over before it proceeded to bring itself down hard on the starboard bow! With a horrendous crash, the behemoth smashed its head and neck into the vessel's side. There followed an ear-piercing, metallic screech as the boat's stiff aluminium chassis crumpled under the beast's immense weight!

Seemingly lodged inside the gouge it had created, the carnifex thrashed its stubby head viciously from side-to-side, the rest of its elongated body still in the water. Snapping its maw hungrily, the carnifex's gills- pink and fleshy- flared angrily as it issued forth a gaseous hiss, salivate splattering the vessel's interior. Behind it, the spines lining its craggy hide stood out, tall and imposing. In that moment, the beast was the epitome of terror.

At the same time, Hailey felt the airboat shift to starboard, the craft's portside lifting up out of the water; this sudden development brought about by the added weight of the carnifex! Inevitably, Doctor Benson fell victim to gravity, her limber frame drawn to the thrashing beast's bared jaws! Failing to gain traction as one side of the boat continued to rise into the air and the other dipped below the encroaching waterline, Hailey let loose with a desperate cry, her fear no longer containable.

"*Noooo!*" the doctor screamed, rushing involuntarily towards the waiting creature.

Out the corner of her eye, Benson spotted the bowie knife sliding along the deck of the airboat, the weapon running parallel to her. Throwing herself towards the knife, Hailey altered her trajectory, swinging out to the right. Throwing an arm out, she lunged for the bowie, moaning desperately as she went for it.

Ultimately, Hailey spun a full ninety-degrees before snatching up the knife on the fly. Completing the swinging motion, she also managed to slide out of the monster's reach… or rather, most of her did anyway.

"Aaahhh!" Benson howled.

An agonizing pain, like ice-cold needles piercing her flesh, took hold of the woman's right leg, starting at the ankle! Snatching a glance, Hailey found the carnifex's fearsome, prehistoric-looking maw wrapped firmly around her limb! Hailey's eyes widened when she saw the blood- *her blood*- seeping from the crag-like gaps in its primeval lips.

Gritting her teeth, Hailey fought through the pain, determined to survive her living nightmare. Sitting upright, she flung herself forward, bowie gripped firmly in her right hand. Throwing what little strength she had left into it, Benson brought the blade down on her attacker. With a desperate thrust, Hailey drove the weapon's point hard into one of the carnifex's eyes, burying it deep inside the socket!

The goliath's eyeball disintegrated into a cherry-coloured sludge, its jaws springing open almost instantly. To Benson's relief, this freed her trapped limb. This was followed by a peculiar cry from the injured predator that fluctuated between a horrendous shriek and a guttural roar. Now lost in an agonizing frenzy, the massive fish jerked and bucked, the knife still lodged in its face!

Taking full advantage of this opportunity, Hailey retracted her injured leg, dragging the gushing limb out of harm's way. Moving quickly, she repositioned herself in front of the carnifex. Kneeling precariously before the infuriated animal, Hailey prepared to make her next move.

Meanwhile, water rushed up to meet her, pooling around her folded legs. As she felt the water soaking into the fabric of her jeans, Hailey knew then she didn't have much time left. It wouldn't be long before the airboat sunk. That is of course, if she didn't manage to extricate her unruly companion from it.

Reaching forward, Hailey made for the knife yet again. All the while, the massive predator jerked wildly, reeling from the pain of it all. Gasping with fright, the doctor shrunk from the killer as its broad head unexpectedly pitched forward, the beast's steak-knife-sized fangs brushing fleetingly up against her face and neck!

Then as the carnifex retreated, Hailey made her move.

Darting forward, Hailey swiped a hand in the direction of the waiting bowie knife still lodged in the socket. Fingers wrapping around the handle a second later, Benson retrieved the bloodied instrument with a cat-like quickness. Just as she expected, the giant fish jutted forward in response, jaws parting hungrily as it made for her-

-but Hailey was ready.

"Eat this, you motherfucker!" Hailey raged, her jade eyes gleaming furiously.

Twisting on the spot, she brought the knife around in a sweeping arc, plunging the bowie unforgivingly into the beast's exposed gill! Instantly, the creature shuddered, its pain visibly and undeniable. Hailey on the other hand, wasn't about to give up. She pushed hard, mercilessly driving the blade deeper into the monster's body- forcing the weapon in all the way to the hilt!

Benson looked on as blood erupted from both nostrils like lava spilling from the mouth of a volcano. And with that, the carnifex went limp, its lifeforce slipping from its scaly body. As the monster's massive length relaxed, it crept backwards, edging out into the water and away from the hitherto sinking airboat.

Almost immediately, the vessel's equilibrium altered once more. Hailey felt her stomach lurch as the boat descended, its ass-end slamming down hard into the slough. The craft landed with a harsh *bang!* which was accentuated by an expulsion of foaming waves. And then… nothing. The world fell silent.

Below the darkened waterline, the male carnifex quickly registered the smell of blood- the blood of its own beloved mate. Alarmed by this, the panicked beast rushed to its companion's aid. Coursing through the dim environment, the giant fish issued a series of subsonic clicks and squeaks, trying to communicate with its cohort, hoping for a response. But no reply came.

The male found its counterpart limp and unresponsive. Sinking deeper, the female drifted gradually towards the bottom of the slough. Swooping in from below, the male used its short snout to 'catch' its mate, slowing its descent. Proceeding to nudge it, the distraught creature tried to keep its lifeless companion afloat, but it was no use.

The Matriarch was dead.

37.

The pain in Doctor Benson's ankle remained there, sharp and unrelenting. Noting the blood splattered up her jeans' leg and on the shoe beneath, Hailey set about tearing at the bottom of her singlet top. Finding a nick in the dark material, she used this as leverage to wrench free a section of fabric. Looping this around the seeping wound a couple of times, the young woman tied the makeshift bandage in place, hoping to stem the bleeding until such time she could get proper medical attention.

It'll have to do, she thought.

"Time to get the hell out of here," Hailey muttered wearily to herself.

With that, Benson rose stiffly to her feet. Forced to place the majority of her weight onto her left leg, she could do little more than hobble. Hailey wasn't on her feet for long however when the scene around her started to shift dizzyingly.

Preceded by a hellish *bang!* the tropical panorama around her morphed into a sickening blur of motion. Hailey felt the boat spin beneath her as the craft spiralled out of control, her stomach flip-flopping in response.

Son of a bitch!

Thrown off-balance, Benson fell face-first, her chest slamming into the cold deck of the boat. Throwing her hands out just in time, the young woman thankfully managed to break her fall. Even so, battered as she was, it was the type of landing the doctor could do without.

It must be the other one... Hailey thought instantly of the remaining killer fish, lurking somewhere below her.

Craning her neck, Benson looked towards the stern of the boat. The young woman's eyes immediately locked onto the vessel's massive, fan-like powerplant. In front of this sat the captain's chair- just the thing she was looking for.

Hobbling to her feet once more, Hailey limped towards the waiting seat. With each step, pain shot up the doctor's leg, setting fire to her nerves. Wincing, Benson powered on despite the pain, trying to ignore the angry sensation.

Boom!

The airboat pitched to port as it was assailed from the water once more! The vessel rocked violently beneath her, waves crashing up over the sides; the horrid motion threatening Hailey's fragile sense of balance yet again. This time however, Benson stayed upright- albeit only just.

Heartrate fluttering erratically now, she kept going, eyes fixed firmly on the seat up ahead.

"Where's Jackson when you need him?" the biologist spat sarcastically.

Collapsing into the seat, Hailey set to work on the throttle right away. Powering up the engine a moment later, the giant set of blades managed a single rotation… before then clapping out altogether.

"Shit!" Hailey cursed. "*Why is this never easy?*"

Trying again, Hailey watched the blades spin-

-and thankfully this time they continued to rotate. The propellers whirred to life, the engine roaring along with them. Ultimately an assault on her senses, the combined noise was nigh-on deafening in its intensity, but it was welcome nonetheless. Needless to say, Benson didn't waste any time gunning the engine for all it was worth.

Taking off with a jolt, the airboat proceeded to cut a foaming wake through the jade waterscape surrounding it. Ultimately, the craft wasn't as fast as the marine biologist would have liked, but it was better than not moving at all, she supposed.

Moving deeper into the slough, Hailey scanned the scene before her. Further down the winding channel, about a hundred metres off the port bow, she noticed a hardwood hammock jutting out into the glistening waterway. Beyond this sat a stretch of swampland that seemed like it disappeared into infinity. The smooth incline of the hammock, topped by a densely-knitted nest of trees and other tropical vegetation (in addition to the terrain beyond), was the closest thing to dry land that Benson could see. It certainly wasn't civilization, but it would have to do, Hailey decided.

Realistically, it was her only option.

X marks the spot! the young woman thought excitedly, racing towards it. *Hopefully…*

Making a beeline for the hammock, Benson pushed the airboat to its limits, the motor straining noisily under the pressure of it all. Hailey could tell almost immediately that something was wrong. Going by the sound of clunking parts scraping together inside it, it was obvious that the engine was seriously struggling.

Great! Hailey thought irritably. *Just great!*

The hardwood hammock was about seventy metres away now.

"C'mon, you fucker!" Hailey urged. "Just a little further!"

Fifty metres and closing.

"That's it!" Hailey coaxed the careworn piece of machinery. "You can do it."

Twenty-five metres.

"A little more…" Hailey's voice trailed off.

Ten metres out…

I might just make it! Hailey told herself-

-right as the motor gave out on her.

With less than thirty feet to go, the boat's speed had reduced dramatically. In the end, the vessel did little more than crawl, edging its way towards the hammock, powered purely by its own drastically waning momentum.

"No!" Hailey squealed angrily, banging her fists against the captain's chair. "God damn it!"

The boat, although still creeping forward, had slowed to a snail's pace. Standing up, the seething figure of Benson moved tentatively to the fore of the battered and crippled craft. Peeking ahead, the doctor estimated the distance between the nose of the airboat and the edge of the hardwood hammock to be a little under fifteen feet. Usually, with a good run-up, she would be able to jump that distance. Christ, she could probably spit further.

Unfortunately, Benson didn't fancy her chances all that much; especially considering the current state of her ankle. Walking was difficult enough, never mind trying to make a leap to safety. Still, she *had* to try. After all, what other option did she have?

Hailey edged back in the direction of the captain's seat, contemplating making a run for it. She tenderly placed her right leg forward, putting a little extra weight on it, in order to test it.

"Shit!" she cursed angrily, almost folding over.

The pain was excruciating: like bolts of lightning tearing through the limb!

I don't think I can do this…

In any case, Hailey's concerns were unexpectedly pushed to the back of her mind. Her attention was redirected as- seemingly out of nowhere- a deafening collision sounded to the young woman's rear!

38.

Diving deep, the monster prepared to make another run at the stretching craft floating above. Overcome by a primal fury at the loss of its mate, the male carnifex was determined to have its revenge. Indeed, the fearsome creature would stop at nothing to accomplish this bloody end.

Reaching the swamp bed, the carnifex quickly circled back around, peeling away from the bottom of the slough in one smooth, gliding motion; before it then rushed pell-mell for the surface! Steaming full-speed ahead, the creature rose on a sharp angle, its spiked caudal fin and thick-bodied keel working feverishly to move it through the dim water. Moving at such a swift pace, the carnifex would reach the surface in mere seconds.

Breaching the waterline in an explosion of sparkling liquid, the dark-skinned beast launched itself at the airboat's stern! Smashing into the waiting craft, the massive predator belly-flopped savagely against the metal propeller casing; all one-thousand pounds of it working to crush the rotor assembly and steam-roll it out of its way!

Alerted by the horrendous shriek of folding metal, Hailey spun on her heel, just in time to witness the carnifex collapse the fan assembly! Using all of its weight, the hulking brute forced the circular contraption forward, before the structure inevitably snapped at the hinges securing it to the floor.

Hailey Benson knew then and there that nothing would stand in the predator's way.

At the same time, the force of the collision shunted the airboat forward, pushing it a few feet closer to the shore of the hardwood hammock beyond. Hailey felt a familiar surge of adrenaline hit her system in that single, terrifying instant. Ignoring the pain in her leg as best she could, Benson took off, awkwardly shuffling for the prow.

Meanwhile behind her, the carnifex slithered forth, forcefully extricating itself from the nest of twisted metal it had created. Using its pectoral fins and vestigial pelvic limbs to manoeuvre itself, the serpentine creature rushed after the fleeing woman, its talon-like teeth bared hungrily.

Despite her head start, Doctor Benson was struggling- which gave her cumbersome pursuer the opportunity to catch up. And catch up it did. Close on her heels, the tortuous fiend let loose with a savage *hissss*! Haunting and primordial, the noise was like something out of a nightmare. Even so, Hailey had to remind herself that this was no nightmare… it was very real.

Within a few, short seconds, the carnifex had closed to within only feet of its fleeing prey- entering striking distance. Half-tensing on the fly, the monster prepared to strike out, determined to quench its thirst for blood. Inches from her now, the ruby-eyed beast lunged at Hailey, jaws extended-

-right as the young woman reached the vessel's prow!

Hurriedly stepping up onto the rim of the prow itself, Benson pushed off as best she could, throwing herself into the air and out of the monster's reach… at the last possible second, no less!

Behind her, too slow off the mark, the carnifex's jaws snapped, before barrelling snout-first into the vessel's bowed interior, painfully halting its hurried advance. Next, shaking its aching snout, the carnifex searched about itself, angered by, and a little confused at, its near-miss.

Meanwhile, its quarry had escaped to the water below.

Hailey landed at the periphery of the hammock, splashing down into the green water. But she didn't stop there- she couldn't afford to. Temples pounding and heart racing, Hailey stumbled forwards, sweat rolling down her brow. Moving on her hands and knees, she proceeded to crash through a wall of foliage. Breaching through to the other side a second later, she scrambled up the incline of the hammock, the doctor digging her fingers deep into the moist soil in front of her, ready to make her escape.

Twisting her head, Hailey peered over her shoulder at the airboat behind her, just in time to see the carnifex flop its scaly body overboard; its tubular frame splashing down clumsily into the waiting slough.

Keep moving, kiddo! the biologist told herself.

With that, Hailey Benson left the slough behind, stepping onto dry land proper. Soaked from the waist down, the young woman faltered on regardless of the extra weight added by her now wet apparel. Moving on sore and bleeding limbs, she rushed into the choking sea of vegetation awaiting her, the woman's nimble frame quickly swallowed up by the dense mass of undergrowth.

The carnifex's fearsome, albeit tattered, vertebral column appeared first, the spines and accompanying webbing poking ominously through the jade surface. Gradually, the adjoining armoured flanks breached the waterline as well. Next, came the garnet eyes, bisected by cat-like pupils, and its crooked snout.

Spotting its elusive prey up ahead scampering into the brush, the seething predator dashed forth. Beaching itself, the meandering killer slithered hastily up the incline, hot on the fleeing woman's heels.

Branches and leaves assaulted Hailey's face; the bothersome appendages seemingly rushing at her from every which way. Scratching at her flushed skin they left behind a series of bloodied tracts, but Hailey paid them little mind. As she delved deeper into the tropical abyss, Benson placed her forearms out in front of her, trying to shield herself from the collection of trees whipping about her.

Somewhat disorientated, the world around the panicked woman was a panoply of colours: mostly greens and browns, spotted with the occasional vibrant exception. In any other circumstance, she would have stopped to admire the beauty of it all. But not today.

Behind her, the doctor could hear the rustling of leaves and the snapping of twigs as the monster left the water behind, continuing its deadly chase on dry land. Added to this, was the creature's feverish rasping; noises that chilled Hailey to the core of her very being. Still, in a way, they were a good thing: they kept her going. Fear was a great motivator, at least in her experience.

Breathless by now, the marine biologist navigated the maze of trees and bushes, ducking and weaving as she went, albeit unsure of where exactly she was headed. That being said, Doctor Benson's plan was simple: get as far away from the carnifex as possible.

All of a sudden, Hailey burst out of the suffocating confines of the brush and into a clearing. The area itself was a little smaller than the size of your average tennis court. What's more, it was almost totally devoid of vegetation. Save that is for a lone felled tree trunk situated at the opposite end of it.

Aware she had been stationary for too long, Benson twisted slightly, peeking nervously over her shoulder. The woman's emerald eyes grew wide at the sight of the incoming carnifex; the rampaging beast smashing its way through the green-brown undergrowth. Knocking up a tornado of debris as it closed in, smaller trees fell by the wayside as bits of bark and leaves flew helter-skelter around it.

Hailey took off immediately, the terror written on her face. She had seen enough. Dragging her bloodied leg behind her, the doctor stepped deeper into the hollow. Eyes fixed on the dead tree ahead, she tried to ignore the hideous noises to her rear.

Thankfully, the carnifex was much less agile on land than it was underwater. Still, Benson could feel her stamina waning. What's more, the pain in her leg was growing stronger, making it much harder to ignore, and thus keep moving. It wouldn't be long now before the predator caught up to her. She was quite literally on her last legs.

By now, Hailey had covered half the distance of the clearing. Looking over her shoulder once more, she found the carnifex was in the process of entering the barren hollow. Benson felt her pulse quicken at this.

"Shit!" Hailey cursed, exasperated at her reduced mobility.

Dig deep… said a voice in her head. *Otherwise you won't survive this…*

Sadly, the truth was Hailey Benson wanted to give up. She'd had enough. In all honesty, it felt like she'd been running from predators her whole life. Hailey had forgotten what it was like to be normal; to live a regular life away from all this pain and suffering… and horror.

Still moving, Hailey was lost in her thoughts. As such, Doctor Benson didn't see the smaller tree limb half-buried in the soil at her feet. A sharp pain, starting in her shin, raced up her left leg as she tripped over the gnarled limb. With this, all pretences of balance went out the window. Benson fell forward, arms out in front of her. A split-second later, she felt the wind leave her lungs as she battered chest-first into the humongous, greying tree trunk now in front of her.

Wheezing and gasping for oxygen, the biologist turned herself over. Leaning back against the body of the trunk, she slid down into a seated position, resting her head against the desiccated remains of the tree. Inhaling deep and slow, Hailey tried to regulate the rhythm of her breathing, all the while watching as her stalker approached, slow and determined. Like some massive python, the beast wound its way towards her, its movements sinister and foreboding.

In the end, the carnifex halted mere inches from her face, its long, curved, yellowed teeth slick with saliva. In fact, strands of gelatinous drool fell from the gaps in its teeth, spilling over the legs of her jeans. Hailey noted several chunks of pale flesh lodged at various points about its savage array of dentition. Not surprisingly, the creature's breath was putrid; the horrific stench overpowering, to say the least.

Now at her wit's end, Hailey began to whimper, tears welling in her eyes. It was at this point the monster locked eyes with her. The red spheres burned uncaringly into her own.

"What are you waiting for?" Hailey screamed in its ugly, quasi-reptilian face.

The carnifex responded by blinking slow, seemingly aloof to the torment it was causing its petrified quarry.

"Just do it!" Hailey commanded, tears falling down her cheeks. "Do it, you fucker!"

Tensing at this, the carnifex shrunk back, its body swelling noticeably. Suddenly, the creature rushed forward! Maw arched wide open, the demon hissed in Hailey's face, the subsequent noise like air escaping from a cracked pipe- albeit magnified a thousand-fold!

But it stopped short of killing her, seemingly content to savour the moment.

Hailey's heart thundered against her chest-plate. She was beginning to lose control. Her body was going into shock, she could feel it. The young woman began to hyperventilate as she came to accept that this was it- she was about to die. Trying to calm herself, Hailey Benson closed her eyes, waiting for the end to come.

39.

Out of nowhere, a roar, powerful and guttural, tore through the morning air! Jumping out of her skin, Hailey's eyes instantly snapped open at the sound of the ferocious cry. She knew immediately that it wasn't the carnifex. Indeed, this noise was much different to the rasping hisses and high-pitched shrieks she had become accustomed to. What's more, the angry cry had come from somewhere *behind* her.

This was something else entirely.

What now? Hailey wondered. Although, admittedly the doctor was rather fearful of the answer to this question.

Clearly startled, the scaled predator began to retreat from the shrunken figure of Doctor Benson. Shuffling its huge, armoured frame backwards, the carnifex scanned the scene warily with its distended, red eyes. Whereas only moments before it had been prepared to devour the biologist, its priorities had unexpectedly changed.

Frozen in place, Hailey felt the ground around her start to shake. Craning her neck back against the tree trunk, Benson gazed skyward. An ominous shadow suddenly swept over her, briefly blocking out the glare of the sun. Hailey watched as a shape, dark and shaggy, sailed straight over the top of her, easily clearing the big log!

"Oh my God…" the marine biologist breathed in amazement.

At first, Hailey only knew one thing for certain: whatever this thing was, it was *big*.

The hairy figure landed in front of Benson, albeit with its back to her. On all fours at first, the hulking brute subsequently rose up onto its hind legs. The doctor quickly calculated the figure stood close to seven feet tall. To her surprise, despite its thick coat of dark-coloured fur, Hailey could see that it possessed a serious degree of muscular definition beneath. Sporting a broad, rounded head and distinctly sloped shoulders, the shadowy figure was imposing to say the least. That is, even without having seen its face.

What are you? The puzzled woman watched the figure intently.

All of a sudden, the hairy behemoth pivoted as if in answer to her silent question. Turning side-on, the animal revealed more of its intimidating features to the bemused spectator. Doctor Benson quickly noted the beast's short snout and rounded ears. However, most frightening of all, as far as Benson was concerned, were its claws. Long and sharp, the onyx talons stood out threateningly at the end of its massive, padded paws.

Jesus Christ! Hailey thought silently. *It's a bear!*

It was a Florida black bear.

Examining it closer, Benson noticed one of its ears twitching, a fly buzzing around it. In that instant, Hailey recognized something familiar about the furry giant. The tip of the animal's ear, although healed, was cleaved in two. Hailey instantly thought back to the family of bears which she and the others had encountered before rescuing the Michaels siblings.

"*No way!*" Benson exhaled disbelievingly.

Hailey's jaw sagged open, the young woman stunned by this revelation. For a moment, Hailey pondered the possibility that, like her and her companions, the black bear clan had been hunting the carnifexes.

Could it be the case?

A sudden, reverberating growl redirected Doctor Benson's wandering attention back towards the powerful figure. The bear's top lip curled back, exposing curved incisors, smooth and gleaming. Looming over the carnifex, the black bear watched its adversary intently, poising itself for combat.

On the other hand, the serpent-like carnifex, although clearly hesitant, was by no means backing down. It shuffled slightly, sizing up its brawny, towering opponent. The killer's dorsal webbing, spines and all, stood noticeably erect, save that is for the tattered fore-section shredded the previous night by a warden's well-placed bullet.

This is going to be a bloodbath…

Without warning, the serpentine killer lunged forward, using its pectoral fins to launch itself like a sea lion. Utilizing its keel and lower abdomen, the carnifex was able to balance itself, holding its front-half upright just long enough for it to batter unforgivingly into the black bear! Hailey also noted the fish's vestigial pelvic limbs digging into the ground around it, presumably in an effort to provide itself with a more stable base.

Colliding chest-to-chest, the force of the subsequent impact was evident as it rippled through both animals' massive bodies. Thrashing about like rabid dogs, the two creatures gnashed their jaws wildly, trying to bite down on one another! Strands of spittle flew in all directions as the monsters wrestled, each trying to overpower the other. Needless to say, the savagery of the frenetic scene chilled Hailey to her beleaguered bones.

Planting its feet for good measure, the black bear wrapped its long forelimbs around its scaly adversary, trying desperately to gain some purchase with its big claws. Like sumo wrestlers, both beasts used their own bodyweight as a weapon. Pushing hard up against their opponent, they tried to out-manoeuvre the other. A fine mist, composed of dust particles, blanketed the scene now, kicked up by the duelling animals. All the while, the pair spun, rotating left and right, locked in what could only be described as a violent, primal tango.

Suddenly, the carnifex disengaged, wrenching itself free of the bear's choking embrace, the latter's claws raking free chunks of scaly fish flesh as it did so! All the same, the carnifex paid its injuries no mind. Twisting snake-like on the spot, the serpentine predator turned its back on the bear- but by no means was it about to retreat. A split-second later, the carnifex's caudal fin, rimmed with needle-like spines, splayed itself wide like a Geisha's fan. Then, with a flick of its keel, the enraged beast fired its tail hard into the black bear's chest! The strike was timed perfectly- just as the bear was preparing to charge the carnifex, no less!

Hailey watched in stunned silence as the hairy brute tumbled backwards, knocked clean off its feet. Subsequently, the big bear battered into the ground, its sheening coat undulating with the force of the thunderous impact that followed!

Looking to capitalize, the carnifex shimmied back around, hissing furiously as it prepared to strike at its downed foe once more. Clearly, the monster wasn't taking any prisoners. Benson should have known it would show no mercy.

"No!" Hailey cried, her sympathies firmly with that of the fallen black bear.

After all, had it not been for the shaggy giant's timely arrival, she most likely would be dead, killed by the bloodthirsty carnifex.

Out of the blue, the ground began to rumble once more. This time however, the noise was significantly louder. Once again, the reverberations seemed to originate from somewhere behind Doctor Benson.

"What the hell?" Hailey murmured.

Benson had to duck low this time as two more shapes- big and black, and both covered in fur- bounded over the fallen trunk, each flying past her! The doctor noted the figure in the lead was much larger than the one trailing it, about double the size, in fact. The remaining members of the bear's family had finally come to the party it seemed. And not a moment too soon Hailey wagered, as her green eyes flicked in the direction of the downed beast.

Time's up Goldilocks! Benson thought, glaring at the carnifex.

Meanwhile, the hulking fish had halted its attack, once more forced to re-evaluate its priorities as a result of the other bears' appearance. Cautiously, it watched the other two furry behemoths approach. In the lead was the larger of the two newcomers; the adult bear tentatively creeping forward as it eyed off the serpentine killer.

The cub trailed behind what Doctor Benson assumed to be its mother. As the original bear was slightly larger than its newly-arrived counterpart, she assumed the former was the male. Transitioning to a bipedal stance, the bear cub turned towards Hailey. Inspecting the biologist with its big, black eyes, sharp and inquisitive, the juvenile tilted its head to the side, looking at her as if to say, 'what are *you* doing here?'

A sudden *hiss!* brusquely redirected the baby's attention. The smaller bear turned back towards the waiting carnifex, switching to a quadrupedal stance right away. Following suit, Hailey peered past the furry carnivore, curious as to what was going on. She looked just in time to see the female bear circle towards the carnifex's rear, side-stepping as it tried to outflank the scaly monstrosity. Meanwhile, the downed male rose gingerly to its feet, shaking off its injuries like a wet dog attempting to dry itself.

For its part the carnifex backed up, but not by much, all the while nervously switching its piercing gaze between the two encroaching, adult black bears. Not prepared to give up just yet, it proceeded to rasp vicious warnings at its adversaries, hoping to ward them off.

Quite unexpectedly, movement at the periphery of Benson's vision, just off to her left, caught the biologist's attention. The woman's jade-coloured eyes immediately darted to the cub which was charging straight for the carnifex!

"Jesus, no…" Hailey's words came out as a whisper.

Papa bear saw it first, turning and roaring a disapproving warning at its foolish child. This alerted the mother which let loose with a similar angry bellow of its own. Unfortunately for both parents, the cub wasn't listening and barrelled on ahead.

The combined cries of the adult bears were enough to draw the carnifex's attention to the incoming threat. Fast as lightning, the predator spun on the spot, lashing out with its tail-section yet again. Hitting like a sledgehammer, the carnifex's needle-laden caudal fin and thick-bodied keel smashed brutally into the speeding cub, catching it mid-gallop!

Bringing her hands up to cover her gaping mouth, Benson gasped in shock as the cub was catapulted mercilessly through the air! A split-second later, the baby crash-landed amongst the dusty soil, knocking up a plume of fine debris, before then skidding to a halt only feet from where Hailey lay.

Distraught, the marine biologist rushed to the beaten cub's side. Pressing up against the youngster, Benson scooped up the bear's head, cradling it in her lap. Hailey felt a pang of nerves strike deep in her gut when the woman realized the juvenile wasn't moving.

At the same time, angered at what they had just witnessed, the parents belted out a mournful chorus, before rounding on the carnifex. Without hesitation, they pounced on the scaled demon, fangs bared and murder in their marble-like eyes.

Somewhat lighter than its counterpart, the female was the quicker of the two. Seeking to immobilize what was quickly proving to be the carnifex's most effective weapon, mama bear clamped her jaws tight around the lower-most section of the fish's keel, just before the tail proper. Sinking her teeth in, the female shook her big head and jaws with a savagery only a mother could conjure.

To Hailey's left, papa bear roared as he swiped at the trapped carnifex's head. In the end, the bear wasn't quick enough. The scaly giant managed to duck and weave just in time, avoiding the strike by a few, short inches. Added to this, the carnifex swung back the way it had come, its dagger-laden jaws flexing open before ultimately snapping shut on the bear's waiting forelimb!

Recoiling in pain, the bear gave off a mighty, albeit agonizing, cry. Stepping back, the towering beast pulled hard, trying to free its trapped limb- but it was no use. The fish's jaws were clamped down hard, like a Pitbull with lockjaw.

All the while, Hailey stroked at the bear cub's head, cooing softly, willing the youngster to wake up. The woman watched worriedly as her hand shook with each loving caress.

"C'mon, baby," Benson spoke gently amidst the madness. "You can do it."

To her surprise, over the noise of the raging battle, Hailey thought she could hear the cub mewling away. Hailey knew she was right when she felt the vibrations attached to these noises filtering through the animal's body and into her own.

"That's it," Benson cooed hopefully.

Turning her attention back to the war being waged only a few feet away, the doctor was shocked to find that papa bear's limb remained trapped in the carnifex's jaws. To her horror, blood fell in large drips now too. Crimson and slick, it saturated the ground beneath the panicked bear.

Meanwhile, to her right, mama bear still had the carnifex by the tail, as it were. That was something, Hailey supposed. The bears were still in the fight, it seemed. In fact, Benson almost vomited a moment later when she saw the fish's leaking blood mixing with the female behemoth's foaming spittle.

It was clear to Hailey then that this was a fight to the death!

Suddenly, the carnifex jerked backwards, pulling the male bear with it! Taking the black bear along for the ride, the latter animal collapsed for a second time. Forelimb still locked in its adversary's maw, the furry giant landed awkwardly on its shoulder, crying out in pain as it smashed into the dry earth.

If it keeps going like this, the carnifex is going to win! Hailey realized.

Mama bear seemed to sense this as well. Still, she hadn't given up, not yet anyway.

Desperately burying its teeth deeper, the bear's mate, still holding on firm to the fish's tail-section, responded by jerking its neck sharply to the right. Ultimately, the female's plan worked. The carnifex spasmed noticeably, its body quivering in response.

Perhaps, she hit a nerve? Benson pondered. *Or maybe bit through the muscle?*

Whatever happened, it clearly hurt. Spines flaring, the carnifex instantly let go of the male black bear, rounding on the female with its teeth bared. In that moment, Hailey couldn't help but compare it to a viper trying to envenomate its prey.

Battering into the waiting female, the carnifex closed its mighty jaws around the bear's neck and shoulder. A sickening eruption of blood spilled from the myriad puncture wounds inflicted by the monster's knife-like teeth. At the same time, the female issued a pitiful shriek; the haunting scream a mixture of anger, fear and pain! In the end, the carnifex took the mother bear to the ground as well.

This is it… Hailey thought. *It's all over…*

Still sprawled on the ground, the male black bear looked up in time to see the carnifex assault its mate. The reaction was instantaneous. Overcome with fury, the shaggy goliath rose to its feet. Before Benson knew it, the male had covered the distance between it and the tangled mess that was its shrieking mate and the carnifex- joining them in their orgy of flesh and blood.

Collapsing on top of the killer fish, the black bear wrapped its powerful forelimbs tight around the scaly predator. Hailey winced as several of the carnifex's flexed, blade-like spines pierced the incoming bear's skin, digging in about its right shoulder and chest! Yet- seemingly now impervious to pain- the bear pulled hard on the serpent-like fish. With a guttural roar, it yanked the monster backwards and off of its collapsed mate. The bleeding female however remained sprawled on the ground, unmoving like her cub.

Casting her gaze back to the duelling giants, Doctor Benson's breath caught in her throat a second later. The two beasts stumbled aftwards. Like a pair of drunkards, they continued to struggle with one another. Somehow, the male bear had managed to keep its adversary in a suffocating hug. That being said, it quickly became apparent that the black bear wouldn't be able to hold onto the carnifex forever. Not only was the killer fish too strong, it was much heavier as well.

The black bear had to act quickly. It had to end this fight.

At its wit's end, the bear unleashed a mighty growl, throwing its head skywards and cranking its jaws wide. Next, frustrated at the fish's constant squirming, the black bear stomped down hard on the animal's back, viciously placing its clawed foot about halfway down the fish's snake-like body! There followed a hideous *craaack!* as the carnifex's spine was broken in two!

Hailey Benson didn't know if she should puke or cheer.

Paralysed as a result of the horrendous injury, the monster was seemingly frozen on the spot, albeit propped up against its furry adversary. Benson locked eyes with the predator in that moment. She could see the fear in the fiery orbs looking back at her, clear as day: the same fear experienced by each and every one of its myriad victims.

Although Hailey didn't hate the carnifex and its kind, she certainly didn't feel pity for them either.

Immobilized, the carnifex instantly became much more malleable… and the black bear wasn't about to show its foe any mercy either. With a bellowing cry, the bear fired its right paw- pearl-black claws and all- hard into the fish's exposed gill, burying it deep! Blood flowed in a small river at first, at least whilst the bear's paw remained lodged inside the fish's ribbed gill slits. Then, as the bear retracted its obsidian claws from the wound, the red liquid rushed forth in a gruesome torrent!

Still, the bear wasn't finished.

Grabbing hold of the carnifex's bottom jaw, the black bear used this as an anchor-point to wrench the beast's head to the left, exposing the leathery underside of the fish's broad neck. Wasting no time, the enraged goliath bit down on the carnifex's throat, like Dracula descending on his next victim! Hailey's ears registered a sickening *cruuunch!* as the bear's incisors proceeded to tear through flesh, muscle and cartilage in quick succession. With this, a second effusion of blood followed, the liquid streaming down the carnifex's elongated body.

Satisfied that the carnifex was dead, the bear let go of the serpentine fiend. With that, the humungous beast fell to the ground. The scaled demon flopped lifelessly into the carpet of soil about it, kicking up a choking dust cloud as it landed, never to rise again.

"It's over…" Hailey whispered.

Dropping down onto all-fours with a contented grunt, the bear plodded straight towards its mate, who remained curled on the ground. Reaching the female, the male bear began nudging its companion with its snout, trying to rouse her. Hailey's heart sank when she heard the pained whines that followed. Still, the male persisted, continuing to prod its counterpart with its stubby nose.

Hailey's heart skipped a beat as she took in the moving sight. Slowly, the female began to stir. After a few moments, the mama bear lifted her head, looking up adoringly at her loving and devoted companion. The pair exchanged a few grunts, before finally the female propped herself up, gingerly rising to her feet.

It was at this point, the black bears turned their attention to Doctor Benson.

40.

The two adult black bears approached, moving with slow and determined strides. For her part, Doctor Benson remained frozen on the spot. In the lead was the male, the big, black-brown, shaggy beast limping somewhat, on account of his injured and bloodied forelimb. Eyes narrowed menacingly, the hulking pair stopped only a few short feet from Hailey. Silently, they took their time to appraise the interloper in their midst.

The marine biologist could feel beads of sweat trickling down her forehead, her temples beating out a painful rhythm at the same time. What's more, Hailey could feel herself trembling under the animals' hard-set stares.

Still in the lead, the male lifted its massive frame up onto its hind legs, peering down at the helpless figure of Doctor Benson. Standing fully erect, the bear let its front paws dangle somewhat limply in front of it. As the seconds ticked by, the hairy beast continued to consider Doctor Benson with its big, gleaming, black eyes.

It was several moments before Hailey remembered to take a breath.

Exhaling, Benson felt her pulse quicken when she saw papa bear's top lip curling. Stepping one foot forward, the giant let loose with a thunderous roar- a roar reserved solely for the biologist. Such was the force behind the bellow that the bear's jowls actually shook with it. Hailey's breathing began to falter then, each subsequent exhalation coming out sharp and shallow. In her panicked state, the young woman tried to remember a prayer, but sadly nothing came to mind.

A mewling whine momentarily redirected Hailey's attention. It was the bear cub- the wounded bear cub sitting there with its head propped up in *her* lap.

"Oh shit!" Benson cursed aloud.

The realization hit Hailey like a freight train. More than likely, the bears saw her as just another threat to their offspring. After what they had just gone through it was unlikely that they would be willing to take any chances, even with a human. Whilst they may have killed the carnifex, they certainly weren't the doctor's allies. After all, Hailey just happened to be in the right place at the right time… but not anymore it seemed. A strange twist of fate had brought them to the same place, nothing else.

Ever so slowly, Benson removed her hands from the cub. Inch by inch she lifted them up into the air, putting them out like a trapeze artist in an attempt to demonstrate that she wasn't a threat. Next, Doctor Benson started shuffling backwards on her knees, gently separating herself from the whimpering cub, whose eyelids were only just beginning to crack open.

The male took another step closer, which saw Hailey scuttle back further, upping her pace. Papa bear proceeded to step over the downed infant's prone body. Sweeping in from behind, the mother stooped low, rubbing up against her child. Just as the male had done with her, the female nudged tenderly at the youngster with her snout.

To her surprise, Benson caught a fleeting glimpse of the cub lifting its head-

-before papa bear side-stepped, cutting off her view of the child and its mother. Closing the gap between them before she could react, the black bear belted out another ear-shattering roar! Hailey felt her temples begin to pound painfully once more as her heartrate spiked yet again.

This is it! Benson's body started to shake uncontrollably.

Crack! A lone shot rang out, the noise cutting harshly through the air.

With this, the scene around Hailey became a hectic blur of motion as the bears- all three of them- took off running! Craning her neck, Hailey followed the fleeing clan with her eyes. On all-fours, the family bowled past her, their giant paws beating rhythmically against the hard earth. One after the other, the family disappeared over the collapsed tree trunk to her rear, the animals surprisingly agile for their size. Mother went first, followed by her cub, and lastly papa bear, but not before he gave Benson a final disapproving look. After which, his titanic frame merged with the tropical arras.

Twisting her neck back around, once she was certain the male had fled, Hailey found Antoine Jackson, bandaged and bloodied, at the opposite side of the clearing. Standing on the periphery of the hollow, he held a rifle in one hand, albeit propped up against his pelvis. Watching the biologist with those big, hazel eyes of his he flashed her a cheeky, one-sided grin.

"You owe me, Benson!" he chuckled.

Hailey didn't reply, she just didn't have it in her. So instead, she just laughed, collapsing onto her side and into the dust. She watched from her newfound, and decidedly horizontal, angle as the dark-skinned warden approached. It was only at this point Hailey realized he was flanked either side by deputies. The threesome, each in tan-coloured uniforms, crossed from the opposite end of the clearing, making sure to give the dead carnifex a wide berth… just in case.

Coming to stand over the folded marine biologist, Jackson offered the young woman a hand, smiling as he did so.

"Up you get, Benson," he smiled broadly. "I thought you were tougher than that!"

"Tough enough to kick your ass!" Hailey swung herself up into a sitting position, her matted head of auburn hair falling about her nimble shoulders.

Even battered and bloodied, she looked amazing. Or so Jackson thought. Indeed, the warden had to keep his jaw from jutting.

Meanwhile, taking a moment for herself, Benson smiled warmly at the waiting warden. She had to admit to herself he didn't look too bad either, bandages and all.

"Boy, am I glad to see you," she took his proffered hand.

"Where's Doctor Scott?" Antoine enquired, lifting the woman to her feet.

Hailey felt her eyes start to glisten with tears at this question.

"He didn't make it," Benson told her colleague reluctantly, failing to look him in the eyes.

"Shit," Jackson scowled. "I'm sorry to hear that. Losing a friend can be tough."

He was right, it *was* tough. That being said, Doctor Benson knew quite a bit about loss. Hard as it might be, she would handle it like she always did.

"C'mon," Jackson said, "we should get you out of here."

"I am gonna need a little help," Hailey lifted her wounded ankle for Jackson to see.

"Sure thing," he edged closer, allowing the doctor to wrap a pale arm around his shoulder.

"Y'know who you remind me of?" Benson asked Antoine, leaning in close.

"Tupac?" Jackson smirked.

"No!" Hailey laughed, her green eyes gleaming. "I was gonna say Boris Karloff." The biologist eyed his array of soiled bandages.

"Who?" Jackson stared back quizzically.

"Never mind," Hailey sighed.

He obviously wasn't a fan of the classics, she surmised.

There followed a few seconds of silence as the pair made their way towards the edge of the clearing, gripping each other tight for support.

"So, uh… Benson… I was thinking…" Antoine's voice trailed off.

"Yeah?" Hailey probed unsure of what the game warden intended to ask her.

“Maybe after all this blows over,” Jackson struggled to meet her gaze, “you might want to grab a drink together?”

The pair stopped dead for a moment. Hailey felt herself blushing right away. In fact, she struggled to look the big man in the eye at first. She considered Antoine’s offer for a second before lifting her head to look at him.

“Y’know what?” Benson asked rhetorically. “I think I’d like that.”

Jackson smiled in reply, dimples forming in his cheeks.

“C’mon,” Antoine signalled to the brush beyond with a flick of his head, “we should get to the airboat. I think it’s time we got the hell out of here. Don’t you?”

“Yeah…” the exhaustion was evident in Hailey’s voice.

The pair walked a little further, both of them feeling heavy on their feet.

“How did you know where to find me?” Benson suddenly asked.

“I didn’t,” Antoine replied. “Once I came to, back at SGGC, and I realized you weren’t there, I went back to FCU, but you weren’t there either. I was getting a little worried, to be honest. So, I sent out search parties, myself included- *obviously*. And as fate would have it, we found your wrecked airboat.” Jackson nodded to his two subordinates.

“Lucky me,” Hailey smiled.

“What the hell where you doing out here anyway?” Antoine asked.

“Long story,” Benson sighed. “And not a nice one.”

Reaching the fringe of the clearing, Hailey halted for a moment. Jackson could sense that she needed a minute. He waited dutifully by her side, albeit looking ahead so as not to make her feel uncomfortable.

Meanwhile, Hailey scanned the scene to her rear. Her line of sight travelled first to the figure of the slaughtered carnifex and the pool of blood congealing around it. Its wine-coloured eyes remained open, locked in a haunting, lifeless stare. This naturally sent a chill down Benson’s spine. Feeling uneasy at the sight of this, Hailey shifted her gaze to the desiccated tree trunk at the far end of the clearing.

All of a sudden, the young woman’s heart fluttered. What’s more, Hailey had to stifle a gasp when she spotted a pair of big, black, glistening eyes watching her from amidst the brush beyond. Next, she noted the short snout set at the centre of a broad head, which was itself topped by small rounded ears. The figure was only three feet tall, or thereabouts, she gauged.

For a few short seconds, Hailey Benson watched the black bear cub as it observed her in return. Locking eyes with the fur-covered youngster, she felt her lips curve into a thin smile of appreciation.

And then suddenly it was gone.

Perhaps drawn by a call from one of its parents, the cub turned on its heel and disappeared into the brush, its furry figure melding seamlessly with the tropical, green expanse.

God speed little one, God speed.

With that, Benson signalled to Jackson that she was ready to leave. Still locked together, they left the clearing behind, silently making for the waiting airboat, both of them limping the whole way.

EPILOGUE

SUNDAY...

Drawn to its siblings by their fear-laced secretions, the female moved deeper into the Glades. Fifteen-feet-long and slender, the serpentine predator wound effortlessly through the dark slough. So powerful was her kin's chemical signature, she found it impossible to resist. The carnifex simply had to investigate. Indeed, the liquid environment was virtually saturated with their pheromones, a fact which unnerved the female greatly.

Using the combination of her brethren's lingering chemical-trail and her own memory, the carnifex easily relocated the once-familiar lair: the place of her own birth, no less. Womb-like, the lagoon-style niche was nestled deep in the heart of the Southern Glades, safe and secure away from most predators.

At first, the female had been hesitant to return. As the only surviving progeny from her parents' first brood, the young female had been forced to venture out on her own some years ago. Sadly, on the cusp of sexual maturity, the young female was chased off by her own mother. Considered an emerging sexual rival, the younger female's presence was no longer tolerated by the Matriarch.

Closing to within less than a quarter-mile, the carnifex could sense that something was different about the place she had once considered her home. No, not simply different. Rather, something was *wrong*.

She finally noted the lack of her parents' pheromones: their territorial markers, in particular. This absence was significant... and troubling at the same time. Indeed, there was no trace of them at all she soon found. Hence her siblings' panicked secretions calling for help. She knew then that her progenitors were dead. They would never have abandoned their offspring. At least ones so young, that is.

Things were starting to make sense to the female now.

Entering the lagoon, the carnifex was greeted by its frightened brethren. Swarming towards her, the hundred-strong school- each no longer than an inch- flocked to their much-larger sibling. The tiny fish darted hyperkinetically about their sister, circling her cigar-shaped outline, eager for the protection her monstrous frame offered.

Spreading her mighty jaws wide, the larger carnifex allowed the panicked infants to enter her cavernous maw. The youngsters quickly found sanctuary inside their sister's buccal cavity; a pouch-like flap of skin used by their species- and other fish species the world over- to protect developing fry.

The new matriarch instinctively knew she would have to wait a few years before one of her brothers would be old enough to breed with, and thus produce the next generation of *Machaerodontis carnifex*. Therefore, if her species was to survive, all she could do was wait. Patience was key. As such, she would protect her siblings, and in doing so, protect the future of her species.

This would be the new matriarch's legacy.

THE END

ACKNOWLEDGEMENTS

First and foremost, I would like to thank Gary and all of the staff at Severed Press for making my dream a reality- *FOUR TIMES OVER, NO LESS!*

Secondly, I would like to thank fellow author Dane Hatchell for his kind words, which in fact gave me the confidence to finish this novel. It has been a hell of a journey.

Lastly, over the course of writing this latest novel, I have lost several loved ones. It has been hard and very testing for myself and my wife. So, to my wee man Sarge, my boy Blue, not to mention Miss Lexa, and of course, Nugget, Debbie and I miss you all terribly. You will live in our hearts forever. See you at the Crossroads.

- Chris McInally
  February 2018

SEVEREDPRESS

facebook.com/severedpress

twitter.com/severedpress

CHECK OUT OTHER GREAT DEEP SEA THRILLERS

PREHISTORIC BEASTS AND WHERE TO FIGHT THEM by Hugo Navikov

IN THE DEPTHS, SOMETHING WAITS ...

Acclaimed film director Jake Bentneus pilots a custom submersible to the bottom of Challenger Deep in the Pacific, the deepest point of any ocean of Earth. But something lurks at the hot hydrothermal vents, a creature—a dinosaur—too big to exist.

Gigadon.

It not only exists, but it follows him, hungrily, back to the surface. Later, a barely living Bentneus offers a $1 billion prize to anyone who can find and kill the monster. His best bet is renowned ichthyopaleontologist Sean Muir, who had predicted adapted dinosaurs lived at the bottom of the ocean.

MEGALODON: APEX PREDATOR by S.J. Larsson

English adventurer Sir Jeffery Mallory charters a ship for a top secret expedition to Antarctica. What starts out as a search and capture mission soon turns into a terrifying fight for survival as the crew come face to face with the fiercest ocean predator to have ever existed- Carcharodon Megalodon. Alone and with no hope of rescue the crew will need all their resources if they are to survive not only a 60 foot shark but also the harsh Antarctic conditions. Megalodon: Apex Predator is a deep-sea adventure filled with action, twists and savage prehistoric sharks.

Printed in Great Britain
by Amazon

60279543R00137